# THE WONDERFUL YEAR

# THE
# WONDERFUL YEAR

BY

## WILLIAM J. LOCKE

AUTHOR OF "JAFFERY," "THE FORTUNATE YOUTH,"
"THE BELOVED VAGABOND," ETC.

NEW YORK: JOHN LANE COMPANY
LONDON: JOHN LANE, THE BODLEY HEAD
MCMXVI

Press of
J. J. Little & Ives Company
New York, U. S. A.

# THE WONDERFUL YEAR

# THE WONDERFUL YEAR

## CHAPTER I

THERE is a letter for you, monsieur," said the concierge of the Hôtel du Soleil et de l'Ecosse. He was a shabby concierge sharing in the tarnish of the shabby hotel which (for the information of those fortunate ones who only know of the Ritz, and the Meurice and other such-like palaces) is situated in the unaristocratic neighbourhood of the Halles Centrales.

"As it bears the Paris postmark, it must be the one which monsieur was expecting," said he, detaching it from the clip on the keyboard.

"You are perfectly right," said Martin Overshaw. "I recognise the handwriting."

The young Englishman sat on the worn cane seat in the little vestibule and read his letter. It ran:

DEAR MARTIN,

I've been away. Otherwise I should have answered your note sooner. I'm delighted you're in this God-forsaken city, but what brought you here in August, Heaven only knows. We must meet at once. I can't ask you to my abode, because I've only one room, one chair and a bed, and you would be shocked to sit on the chair while I sat on the bed, or to sit on the bed while I sat on the chair. And I couldn't offer you anything but a cigarette (*caporal, à quatre sous le paquet*) and the fag end of a bottle of grenadine syrup and water. So let us dine together at the place where I take such meals as I can afford. *Au Petit Cornichon,* or as the snob of a proprietor yearns to call it, The "Restaurant Dufour." It's a beast of a hole in the Rue Baret off the Rue Bonaparte; but I don't think either of us could run to the Café de Paris or Paillard's and we'll have it all to ourselves. Meet me there at seven.

Yours sincerely,<br>CORINNA HASTINGS.

Martin Overshaw rose and addressed the concierge.

"Where is the Rue Bonaparte?"

The concierge informed him.

"I am going to dine with a lady at a restaurant called the Petit Cornichon. Do you think I had better wear evening dress?"

The concierge was perplexed. The majority of the British frequenters of the hotel, when they did not dine in gangs at the table d'hôte, went out to dinner in flannels or knickerbockers, and wore cloth caps, and looked upon the language of the country as an incomprehensible joke. But here was a young Englishman of a puzzling type who spoke perfect French with a strange purity of accent, in spite of his abysmal ignorance of Paris, and talked about dressing for dinner.

"I will ask Monsieur Bocardon," said he.

Monsieur Bocardon, the manager, a fat, greasy Provençal, who sat over a ledger in the cramped bureau, leaned back in his chair and threw out his hands.

"Evening dress in a little restaurant of the *quartier. Mais non!* They would look at you through the windows. There would be a crowd. It would be an affair of the police."

Martin Overshaw smiled. "Merci, monsieur," said he. "But as you may have already guessed, I am new to Paris and Paris ways."

"That doesn't matter," replied Monsieur Bocardon graciously. "Paris isn't France. We of the south—I am from Nîmes—care that for Paris——" he snapped his fingers. "Monsieur knows the Midi?"

"It is my first visit to France," said Martin.

*"Mais comment donc?* You speak French like a Frenchman."

"My mother was a Swiss," replied Martin ingenuously. "And I lived all my boyhood in Switzerland—in the Canton de Vaud. French is my mother tongue, and I have been teaching it in England ever since."

"Aha! Monsieur is *professeur?"* Monsieur Bocardon asked politely.

"Yes, *professeur,"* said Martin, conscious for the first time in his life of the absurd dignity of the French title. It appealed to a latent sense of humour and he smiled wryly. Yes. He was a Professor—had been for the last ten years, at Margett's Universal College, Hickney Heath; a professor engaged in cramming large classes of tradesmen's children, both youths and maidens, with such tricksters' command of French grammar and vocabulary as would enable them to obtain high marks in the stereotyped examinations for humble positions in the Public and semi-public services. He had reduced the necessary instruction to an exact science. He had carried hundreds of pupils through their examinations with flying colours; but he had never taught a single human being to speak thirty consecutive coherent words of French or to read and enjoy a French book. When he was very young and foolish he had tried to teach them the French speech as a living, organic mode of communication between human beings, with the result

that his pupils soul-strung for examinations had revolted and the great Cyrus Margett, founder of the
colossal and horrible Strasbourg goose factory known
as Margett's Universal College, threatened to sack
him if he persisted in such damnable and unprofitable
imbecility. So, being poor and unenterprising and
having no reason to care whether a Mr. James Bag-
shawe or a Miss Susan Tulliver profited for more
than the examination moment by his teaching, he
had taught the dry examination-bones of the ·French
language for ten years. And—*"Monsieur est professeur,"* from Monsieur Bocardon!

Then, as he turned away and began to mount the
dingy stairs that led to his bedroom, it struck him
that he was now only a professor *in partibus*. He
was no longer a member of the professorial staff of
Margett's Universal College. The vast, original Margett had retired with fortune, liver and head de-
servedly swollen to county magnateship, leaving, for
pecuniary considerations, the tremendous educational
institution to a young successor, who having adopted
as his watchword the comforting shibboleth, "efficiency," had dismissed all those professors who did
not attain his standard of slickness. Martin Overshaw was not slick. The young apostle of efficiency
had dismissed Martin Overshaw at a month's notice,
after ten years service. It was as though a practised
*gougeur* or hand gorger of geese had been judged
obsolescent and made to give place to one who gorged
them by Hertzian rays. The new Olympian had
flashed a glance, a couple of lightning questions at
Martin and that was the end.

In truth, Martin Overshaw did not emanate efficiency like the eagle-faced men in the illustrated ad-
vertisements who undertake to teach you how to become a millionaire in a fortnight. He was of mild
and modest demeanour; of somewhat shy and self-

depreciatory attitude; a negligible personality in any assemblage of human beings; a man (according to the blasphemous saying) of no account. Of medium height, thin, black-haired, of sallow complexion, he regarded the world unspeculatively out of clear grey eyes, that had grown rather tired. As he brushed his hair before the long strip of wardrobe mirror, it did not occur to him to criticise his reflected image. He made no claims to impeccability of costume. His linen and person were scrupulously clean; his sober suit comparatively new. But his appearance, though he knew it not, suffered from a masculine dowdiness, indefinable, yet obvious. His ill-tied cravat had an inveterate quarrel with his ill-chosen collar and left the collar stud exposed, and innocent of sumptuary crime he allowed his socks to ruck over his ankles. . . . Once he had grown a full black beard, full in the barber's sense, but dejectedly straggling to the commonplace eye· of a landlady's daughter who had goaded him into a tepid flirtation. To please the nymph long since married to a virtuous plumber whom Martin himself had called in to make his bath a going concern, he had divested himself of the offending excrement and contented himself thenceforward with a poor little undistinguished moustache. A very ordinary, unarresting young man was Martin Overshaw. Yet, in his simple, apologetic way—*exempli gratia,* when he smiled with deferential confidence on the shabby concierge and the greasy Monsieur Bocardon—he carried with him an air of good-breeding, a disarming sensitiveness of manner which commanded the respect, contemptuous though it might have sometimes been, of coarser natures. A long, thin, straight nose with delicate nostrils, the only noticeable feature of his face, may have had something to do with this impression of refinement. Much might be written on noses. The Great Master of

Noseology, Lawrence Sterne, did but broach the subject. On account, perhaps, of a long head terminating in a long blunt chin, and a mild patience of expression, he bore at Margett's Universal College the traditional sobriquet of "Cab-horse."

The cab-horse, however, was now turned out to grass—in August Paris. He had been there three days and his head swam with the wonder of it. As he walked along the indicated route to the Petit Cornichon in the airless dark, he felt the thrill of freedom and of romance. Down the Boulevard Sébastopol he went, past the Tour Saint Jacques, through the Place du Châtelet over the Pont au Change and across the Ile de la Cité to the Boulevard Saint Michel, and turned to the right along the Boulevard Saint Germain until he came to the Rue Bonaparte and his destination. It was the sweltering cool of the evening. Paris sat out of doors, at cafés, at gateways in shirt sleeves and loosened bodices, at shop fronts, at dusty tables before humble restaurants. Pedestrians walked languidly in quest of ultimate seats. In the wide thoroughfares the omnibuses went their accustomed route; but motor-cabs whizzed unfrequent for lack of custom—they who could afford to ride in taxi-autos on the *rive gauche* were far away in cooler regions—and the old horses of crawling fiacres hung stagnant heads. Only the stale dregs of Paris remained in the Boul' Mich. Yet it was Fairyland to the emancipated professor *in partibus* who paused here and there to catch the odd phrases of his mother tongue which struck his ears with delicious unfamiliarity. Paris, too, that close, sultry evening, smelled of unutterable things; but to Martin Overshaw it was the aroma of a Wonder City.

He found without difficulty the Café-Restaurant Dufour whose gilded style and title eclipsed the modest sign of the "Petit Cornichon" prudently allowed to remain in porcelain letters on the glass of door and windows. Under the ægis, as it were, of the poor "little gherkin" and independent of the magnificent Dufour establishment, was the announcement displayed: *"Déjeuners 1 fr. 50. Dîners 2 fr. Vin Compris."* The ground floor was a small café, newly decorated with fresco panels of generously unclad ladies dropping roses on goat-legged gentlemen: symptoms of the progressive mind of the ambitious Monsieur Dufour. Only two tables were occupied—by ruddy-faced provincials engaged over coffee and dominoes. To Martin, standing embarrassed, came a pallid waiter.

*"Monsieur désire?"*

*"Le Restaurant."*

*"C'est en haut, monsieur, Au premier."*

He pointed to a meagre staircase on the left-hand side. Martin ascended and found himself alone in a ghostly-tabled room. From a doorway emerged another pallid waiter, who also addressed him with the enquiry: *"Monsieur désire?"*—but the enquiry was modulated with a certain subtle inflection of surprise and curiosity.

"I am expecting a lady," said Martin.

*"Bien, monsieur.* A table for two? *Voici."*

He drew back an inviting chair.

"I should like this one by the window," said Martin. The room being on the entresol, the ceiling was low and the place reeked with reproachful reminders of long-forgotten one-franc-fifty and two-franc meals.

"I am sorry, Monsieur," replied the waiter, "but this table is reserved by a lady who takes here all her repasts. Monsieur can see that it is so by the half-finished bottle of mineral water."

He held up the bottle of Evian in token of his

veracity.  Scrawled in pencil across the label ran the inscription, "Mlle. Hastings."

"Mademoiselle Hastings!" cried Martin.  "Why, that is the lady I am expecting."

The waiter smiled copiously.  Monsieur was a friend of Miss Hastings?  Then it was a different matter.  Mademoiselle said she would be back to-night and that was why her bottle of Evian had been preserved for her.  She was the only one left of the enormous clientele of the restaurant.  It was a restaurant of students.  In the students' season, not a table for the chance comer.  All engaged.  The students paid so much per week or per month for nourishment.  It really was a pension, *enfin,* for board without lodging.  When the students were away from Paris the restaurant was kept open at a loss; not a very great loss, for in Paris one knew how to accommodate oneself to circumstance.  Good provincials and English tourists sometimes wandered in.  One always then indicated the decorations, real masterpieces some of them. . . . Only a day or two ago an American traveller had taken photographs.  If Monsieur would deign to look round . . .

Martin deigned.  Drawings in charcoal and crayon on the distempered walls, caricatures, bold nudes, bars of music, bits of satiric verse, flowing signatures, bore evidence of the passage of many generations of students.

"It amuses them," said the waiter, "and gives the place a character."

He was pointing out the masterpieces when a young voice by the door sang out:

"Hallo, Martin!"

Martin turned and met the welcoming eyes of Corinna Hastings, fair-haired, slender, neatly dressed in blue serge coat and skirt and a cheap little hat to which a long pheasant's feather gave a touch of bravado.

"You're a real Godsend," she declared. "I was thinking of throwing myself into the river, only there would have been no one on the deserted bridge to fish me out again. I am the last creature left in Paris."

"I am more than lucky then to find you, Corinna," said Martin. "For you're the only person in Paris that I know."

"How did you find my address?"

"I went down to Wendlebury——"

"Then you saw them all?" said Corinna, as they took their seats at the window-table. "Father and mother and Bessie and Joan and Ada, etcetera, etcetera down to the new baby. The new baby makes ten of us alive—really he's the fourteenth. I wonder how many more there are going to be?"

"I shouldn't think there would be any more," replied Martin gravely.

Corinna burst out laughing.

"What on earth can you know about it?"

The satirical challenge brought a flush to Martin's sallow cheek. What did he know in fact of the very intimate concerns of the Reverend Thomas Hastings and his wife?

"I'm afraid they find it hard to make both ends meet, as it is," he explained.

"Yet I suppose they all flourish as usual—playing tennis and golf and selling at bazaars and quarrelling over curates?"

"They all seem pretty happy," said Martin, not overpleased at his companion's airy treatment of her family. He, himself, the loneliest of men, had found grateful warmth among the noisy, good-hearted crew of girls. It hurt him to hear them contemptuously spoken of.

"It was the first time you went down since——!"
she paused.

"Since my mother died? Yes. She died early in
May, you know."

"It must be a terrible loss to you," said Corinna
in a softened voice.

He nodded and looked out of window at the houses
opposite. That was why he was in Paris. For the
last ten years, ever since his father's death had hurried him away from Cambridge, after a term or two,
into the wide world of struggle for a living, he had
spent all his days of freedom in the little Kentish
town. And these days were few. There were no
long luxurious vacations at Margett's Universal College, such as there are at ordinary colleges and schools.
The grind went on all the year round, and the staff
had but scanty holidays. Such as they were he passed
them at his mother's tiny villa. His father had given
up the chaplaincy in Switzerland, where he had married and where Martin had been born, to become
Vicar of Wendlebury, and Mr. Hastings was his successor. Mrs. Overshaw, with her phlegmatic temperament, had taken root in Wendlebury and there
Martin had visited her and there he had been received into the intimacy of the Hastings family and
there she had died; and now that the little villa was
empty and Martin had no place outside London to
lay his leisured head, he had satisfied the dream of
his life and come to Paris. But even in this satisfaction there was pain. What was Paris compared
with the kind touch of that vanished hand? He
sighed. He was a simple soul in spite of his thirty
years.

The waiter roused him from his sad reflections
by bringing the soup and a bottle of thin red wine.
Conscious of food and drink and a female companion
of prepossessing exterior, Martin's face brightened.

"It's so jolly of them in Paris to throw in wine like this," said he.

"I only hope you can drink the stuff," remarked Corinna. "We call it *tord-boyau.*"

"It's a rare treat," said Martin. "I can't afford wine in England, and the soup is delicious. Somehow no English landlady ever thinks of making it."

"England is a beast of a place," said Corinna.

"Yet in your letter you called Paris a God-forsaken city."

"So it is in August. The schools are closed. Not a studio is open. Every single student has cleared out and there's nothing in the world to do."

"I've found heaps to do," said Martin.

"The Pantheon and Notre Dame and the Folies Bergère," said Corinna. "There's also the Eiffel Tower. Imagine a three years' art-student finding fun on the Eiffel Tower!"

"Then why haven't you gone home this August as usual?" asked Martin.

Corinna knitted her brows. "That's another story," she replied shortly.

"I beg your pardon. I didn't mean to be impertinent," said Martin.

She laughed. "Don't be silly—you think wallowing in the family trough is the height of bliss. It isn't. I would sooner starve than go back. At any rate I should be myself, a separate entity, an individual. Oh, that being merely a bit of clotted family! How I should hate it!"

"But you would return to Paris in the autumn," said Martin.

Again she frowned and broke her bread impatiently. All that was another story. "But never mind about me. Tell me about yourself, Martin. Perhaps we may fix up something merry to do together. Père

la Chaise or the Tomb of Napoleon. How long are
you staying in Paris?"

"I can only afford a week—I've already had three
days. I must look out for another billet as soon as
possible."

"Another billet?"

Her question reminded him that she was ignorant
of his novel position as professor *in partibus*. He
explained, over the *bœuf flammande*. Corinna putting
the "other story" of her own trouble aside listened
sympathetically. All Paris art-students must learn
to do that; otherwise who would listen sympathetically
to them? And all art-students want a prodigious
amount of sympathy, so uniquely constituted is each
in genius and temperament.

"You can't go back to that dog's life," she said,
after a while. "You must get a post in a good public-
school."

Martin sighed. "Why not in the Kingdom of
Heaven? It's just as possible. Heads of Public
Schools don't engage as masters men who haven't
a degree and have hacked out their youth in low-
class institutions like Margett's. I know only too
well. To have been at Margett's damns me utterly
with the public-schools. I must find another Margett's!"

"Why don't you do something else?" asked the
girl.

"What else in the world can I do? You know very
well what happened to me. My poor old father was
just able to send me to Cambridge because I had a
good scholarship. When he died there was nothing
to supplement the scholarship which wasn't enough
to keep me at the University. I had to go down. My
mother had nothing but my father's life insurance
money—a thousand pounds—and twenty pounds a
year from the Freemasons. When she wrote to her

relations about her distress, what do you think my damned set of Swiss uncles and aunts and cousins sent her? Two hundred francs! Eight pounds! And they're all rolling in money got out of the English. I had to find work at once to support us both. My only equipment was a knowledge of French. I got a post at Margett's through a scholastic agency. I thought it a miracle. When the letter came accepting my application I didn't sleep all night. I remained there till a week or so ago, working twelve hours a day all the year round. I don't say I had classes for twelve hours," he admitted, conscientiously, "but when you see about a couple of hundred pupils a day and they all do written work which needs correcting, you'll find you have as much work in class as out of class. Last night I dreamed I was confronted with a pile of exercise books eight feet high."

"It's a dog's life," Corinna repeated.

"It is," said Martin. *"Mais que veux-tu, ma pauvre Corinne.* I detest it as much as one can detest anything. If even I was a successful teacher—*passe encore*. But I doubt whether I have taught anybody even the *régime du participe passé* save as a mathematical formula. It's heart-rending. It has turned me into a brainless, soulless, heartless, bloodless machine."

For a moment or two the glamour of the Parisian meal faded away. He beheld himself—as he had wofully done in intervals between the raptures of the past few days—an anxious and despairing young man: terribly anxious to obtain another abhorred teachership, yet desperate at the prospect of lifelong, ineffectual drudgery. Corinna, her elbows on the table, poising in her hand a teaspoonful of tepid strawberry ice, regarded him earnestly.

"I wish I were a man," she declared.

"What would you do?"

She swallowed the morsel of ice and dropped her spoon with a clatter.

"I would take life by the throat and choke something big out of it," she cried dramatically.

"Probably an ocean of tears or a Sahara of despair," said a voice from the door.

Both turned sharply. The speaker was a middle-aged man of a presence at once commanding and subservient. He had a shock of greyish hair brushed back from the forehead and terminating above the collar in a fashion suggestive of the late Abbé Liszt. His clean-shaven face was broad and massive; the features large: eyes grey and prominent; the mouth loose and fleshy. Many lines marked it, most noticeable of all a deep, vertical furrow between the brows. He was dressed, somewhat shabbily, in a black frock coat suit and wore the white tie of the French attorney. His voice was curiously musical.

"Good Lord, Fortinbras, how you startled me!" exclaimed Corinna.

"I couldn't help it," said he, coming forward. "When you turn the Petit Cornichon into the stage of the Odéon, what can I do but give you the reply? I came here to find our good friend Widdrington."

"Widdrington went back to England this morning," she announced.

"That's a pity. I had good news for him. I have arranged his little affair. He should be here to profit by it. I love impulsiveness in youth," he said addressing himself to Martin, "when it proceeds from noble ardour; but when it marks the feather-headed irresponsibility of the idiot, I cannot deprecate it too strongly."

Challenged, as it were, for a response, "I cordially agree with you, sir," said Martin.

"You two ought to know one another," said Corinna. "This is my friend, Mr. Overshaw—Martin, let me introduce you to Mr. Daniel Fortinbras, *Marchand de Bonheur.*"

Fortinbras extended a soft white hand and holding Martin's benevolently:

"Which being translated into our rougher speech," said he, "means Dealer in Happiness."

"I wish you would provide me with some," said Martin, laughingly.

"And so do I," said Corinna.

Fortinbras drew a chair to the table and sat down.

"My fee," said he, "is five francs each, paid in advance."

# CHAPTER II

AT this unexpected announcement Martin exchanged a swift glance with Corinna. She smiled, drew a five franc piece from her purse and laid it on the table. Martin, wondering, did the same. The Marchand de Bonheur unbuttoned his frock coat and slipped the coins, with a professional air, into his waistcoat pocket.

"Mr. Overshaw," said he, "you must understand, as our charming friend Corinna Hastings and indeed half the Quartier Latin understand, that for such happiness as it may be my good fortune to provide I do not charge one penny. But having to eke out a precarious livelihood, I make a fixed charge of five francs for every consultation, no matter whether it be for ten minutes or ten hours. And for the matter of that, ten hours is not my limit. I am at your service for an indefinite period of time, provided it be continuous."

"That's very good, indeed, of you," said Martin. "I hope you'll join us," he added, as the waiter approached with three coffee cups.

"No, I thank you. I have already had my after dinner coffee. But if I might take the liberty of ordering something else——?"

"By all means," said Martin hospitably. "What will you have? Cognac? Liqueur? Whisky and soda?"

Fortinbras held up his hand—it was the hand of a comfortable, drowsy prelate—and smiled. "I have not touched alcohol for many years. I find it blunts the delicacy of perception which is essential to a

Marchand de Bonheur in the exercise of his calling. Auguste will give me a *syrop de framboises à l'eau.*"

"*Bien, m'sieu,*" said Auguste.

"On the other hand, I shall smoke with pleasure one of your excellent English cigarettes. Thanks. Allow me."

With something of the grand manner he held a lighted match to Corinna's cigarette and to Martin's. Then he blew it out and lit another for his own.

"A superstition," said he, by way of apology. "It arises out of the Russian funeral ritual in which the three altar candles are lit by the same taper. To apply the same method of illumination to three worldly things like cigars or cigarettes is regarded as an act of impiety and hence as unlucky. For two people to dip their hands together in the same basin, without making the sign of the cross in the water, is unlucky on account of the central incident of the Last Supper, and to spill the salt as you are absent-mindedly doing, Corinna, is a violation of the sacred symbol of sworn friendship."

"That's all very interesting," said Corinna calmly. "But what are Martin Overshaw and I to do to be happy?"

Fortinbras looked from one to the other with benevolent shrewdness and inhaled a long puff of smoke.

"What about our young medical student friend, Camille Fargot?"

Corinna flushed red—as only pale blondes can flush. "What do you know about Camille?" she demanded.

"Everything—and nothing. Come, come. It's my business to keep a paternal eye on you children. Where is he?"

"Who the deuce is Camille?" thought Martin.

"He's at Bordeaux, safe in the arms of his ridiculous mother," replied Corinna tartly.

"Good, good," said Fortinbras. "And you, Mr. Overshaw, where is the lady on whom you have set your affections?"

Martin laughed frankly. "Heaven knows. There isn't one. The *Princesse lointaine,* perhaps, whom I've never seen."

Fortinbras again looked from one to the other. "This complicates matters," said he. "On the other hand, perhaps, it simplifies them. There being nothing common, however, to your respective roads to happiness, each case must be dealt with separately. *Place aux dames*—Corinna will first expose to me the sources of her divine discontent. Proceed, Corinna."

She drummed with her fingers on the table, and little wrinkles lined her young forehead. Martin pushed back his chair.

"Hadn't I better go for a walk until it is my turn to be interviewed?"

Corinna bade him not be silly. Whatever she had to say he was welcome to hear. It would be better if he did hear it; then he might appreciate the lesser misery of his own plight.

"I'm an utter, hopeless failure," she cried with an air of defiance.

"Good," said Fortinbras.

"I can't paint worth a cent."

"Good," said Fortinbras.

"That old beast Delafosse says I'll never learn to draw and I'm colour blind. That's a brutal way of putting it; but it's more or less true. Consequently I can't earn my living by painting pictures. No one would buy them."

"Then they must be very bad indeed," murmured Fortinbras.

"Well, that's it," said Corinna. "I'm done for. An old aunt died and left me a legacy of four hundred pounds. I thought I could best use it by coming to

Paris to study art. I've been at it three years, and I'm as clever as when I began. I have about twenty pounds left. When it's gone I shall have to go home to my smug and chuckling family. There are ten of us. I'm the eldest and the youngest is three months old. Pretty fit I should be after three years of Paris to go back. When I was at home last, if ever I referred to an essential fact of physiological or social existence, my good mother called me immodest and my sisters goggle-eyed and breathless besought me in corners to tell them all about it. When I tell them I know people who haven't gone through the ceremony of marriage they think I'm giving them a peep into some awful hell of iniquity. It's a fearful joy to them. Then mother says I'm corrupting their young and innocent minds and father mentions me at Family prayers. And the way they run after any young man that happens along is sickening. I'm a prudish old maid compared with them. Have you ever seen me running after men?"

"You are a modern Penthesilea," said Fortinbras.

Anyway, Wendlebury—that's my home—would drive me mad. I'll have to go away and fend for myself. Father can't give me an allowance. It's as much as he can do to pay his butcher's bills. Besides, I'm not that sort. What I do, I must do on my own. But I can't do anything to get a living. I can't typewrite, I don't know shorthand. I can scarcely sew a button on a camisole, I'm not quite sure of my multiplication table, I couldn't add up a column of pounds, shillings and pence correctly to save my life, I play the devil with an egg if I put it into a saucepan and if I attempted to bath a baby I should drown it. I'm twenty-four years of age and a helpless, useless failure."

Fortinbras drank some of his raspberry syrup and water and lit another cigarette.

"And you have still twenty pounds in your pocket?"

"Yes," said Corinna, "and I shan't go home until I've spent the last penny. That's why I'm in Paris, drinking its August dregs. I've already bought a third class ticket to London—available for six months —so I can get back any time without coming down on my people."

"That act of pusillanimous prudence," remarked Fortinbras, "seems to me to be a flaw in an otherwise admirable scheme of immediate existence. If the ravens fed an impossibly unhumorous, and probably unprepossessing, disagreeable person like Elijah, surely there are doves who will minister to the sustenance of an attractive and keen-witted young woman like yourself. But that is a mere generalisation. I only wish you," said he, bending forward and paternally and delicately touching her hand, "I only wish you to take heart of grace and not strangle yourself in your exhaustively drawn up category of incompetence."

The man's manner was so sympathetic, his deep voice so persuasive, the smile in his eyes so understanding, the massive, lined face so illuminated by wise tenderness that his words fell like balm on her rebellious spirit before their significance, or want of significance, could be analysed by her intellect. The intensity of attitude and feature with which her confession had been attended relaxed into girlish ease.

She laughed somewhat self-consciously and took a cigarette from the packet offered her by a silent and wondering Martin. She perked up her shapely head and once more the cock-pheasant's plume on her cheap straw hat gave her a pleasant air of braggadocio. Martin noticed for the first time that she had a little mutinous nose and a defiant lift of the chin above a broad white throat. He found it difficult to har-

monise her appearance of confident efficiency with her
lamentable avowal of failure. Those blue eyes somewhat hard beneath the square brow ought to have
commanded success. Those strong nervous hands
were of just the kind to choke the great things out
of life. He could not suddenly divest himself of
preconceived ideas. To the dull, unaspiring drudge,
Corinna Hastings leading the fabulous existence of
the Paris studios had been invested with such mystery as surrounded the goddesses of the Gaiety Theatre and the Headmaster of Eton. . . .

Martin also reflected that in her litany of woe she
had omitted all reference to the medical student now
in the arms of his ridiculous mother. He began to
feel mildly jealous of this Camille Fargot, who assumed the shadow shape of a malignant influence.
Yet she did not appear to be the young woman to
tolerate aggressive folly on the part of a commonplace young man. Fortinbras himself had called her
Penthesilea, Queen of the Amazons. He was puzzled.

"What you say is very comforting and exhilarating,
Fortinbras," remarked Corinna, "but can't you let
me have something practical?"

"All in good time, my dear," replied Fortinbras
serenely. "I have no quack nostrums to hand over at
a minute's notice. Auguste——" he summoned the
waiter and addressed him in fluent French, marred
by a Britannic accent: "Give me another glass of
this obscene though harmless beverage and satisfy
the needs of Monsieur and Mademoiselle, and after
that leave us in peace, and if any one seeks to pene-
trate into this *salle à manger,* say that it is engaged
by a Lodge of Freemasons. Here is remuneration
for your prospective zeal."

With impressive flourish he deposited fifteen centimes in the palm of Auguste, who bowed politely.

"*Merci, m'sieu,*" said he. "*Et monsieur, dame*——?"

He looked enquiringly at Martin and Martin looked enquiringly at Corinna.

"I'm going to blow twenty pounds," she replied. "I'll have a *kummel glacé.*"

"And I'll have the same," said Martin, "though I don't in the least know what it is."

The waiter retired. Corinna leaned across the table.

"You're thirty years of age and you've lived ten years in London and have never seen kummel served with crushed ice and straws?"

"No," replied Martin simply. "What is kummel?"

She regarded him in wonderment. "Have you ever heard of champagne?"

"More often than I've tasted it," said Martin.

"This young man," remarked Corinna, "has seen as much of life as a squirrel in a cage. That may not be very polite, Martin—but you know it's true. Can you dance?"

"No," said Martin.

"Have you ever fired off a gun?"

"I was once in the Cambridge University Rifle Corps," said Martin.

"You used a rifle, not a gun," cried Corinna. "Have you ever shot a bird?"

"No," said Martin.

"Or caught a fish?"

"No," said Martin.

"Can you play cricket, golf, ride——?"

"A bicycle," said Martin.

"That's something, anyhow. What do you use it for?"

"To go backwards and forwards to my work," said Martin.

"What do you do in the way of amusement?"

"Nothing," said Martin, with a sigh.

"My good Fortinbras," said Corinna, "you have your work cut out for you."

The waiter brought the drinks, and after enquiring whether they needed all the electricity, turned out most of the lights.

Martin always remembered the scene: the little low-ceilinged room with its grotesque decorations looming fantastic through the semi-darkness; the noises and warm smells rising from the narrow street; the eyes of the girl opposite raised somewhat mockingly to his, as straw in mouth she bent her head over the iced kummel; the burly figure and benevolent face of their queer companion who for five francs had offered to be the arbiter of his destiny, and leaned forward, elbow on table and chin in hand, serenely expectant to hear the inmost secrets of his life.

He felt tongue-tied and shy and sucking too nervously at his straw choked himself with the strong liqueur. It was one thing to unburden himself to Corinna, another to make coherent statement of his grievance to a stranger.

"I am at your disposal, my dear Overshaw," said the latter, kindly. "From personal observation and from your answers to Corinna's enfilade of questions, I gather that you are not overwhelmed by any cataclysm of disaster, but rather that yours is the more negative tragedy of a starved soul—a poor, starved soul hungering for love and joy and the fruitfulness of the earth and the bounty of spiritual things. Your difficulty now is: How to say to this man, 'Give me bread for my soul.' Am I not right?"

A glimmer of irony in his smiling grey eyes or an inflection of it in his persuasive voice would have destroyed the flattering effect of the little speech. Martin had never taken his soul into account. The diagnosis shed a new light on his state of being. The starvation of his soul was certainly the root of the trouble; an infinitely more dignified matter than mere discontent with one's environment.

"Yes," said he. "You're right. I've had no chance of development. My own fault perhaps. I've not been strong enough to battle against circumstances. Circumstances have imprisoned me, as Corinna says, like a squirrel in a cage, and I've spent my time in going round and round in the profitless wheel."

"And the nature of the wheel?" asked Fortinbras.

"Have you ever heard of Margett's Universal College?"

"I have," said Fortinbras. "It is one of the many mind-wrecking institutions of which our beloved country is so proud."

"I'm glad to hear you say that," cried Martin. "I've been helping to wreck minds there for the last ten years. I've taught French. Not the French language; but examination French. When the son of a greengrocer wants to get a boy-clerkship in the Civil Service, it's essential that he should know that *bal, cal, carnaval, pal, regal, chacal* take an 's' in the plural, in spite of the fact that millions of Frenchmen go through their lives without once uttering the plural words."

"How came you to teach French?"

"My mother tongue—my mother was a Swiss."

"And your father?"

"An English chaplain in Switzerland. You see it was like this——"

And so, started on his course, and helped here and there by a shrewd and sympathetic question, Martin, the ingenuous, told his story, while Corinna, slightly bored, having heard most of it already, occupied herself by drawing a villainous portrait of him on the tablecloth. When he mentioned details unknown to her she paused in her task and raised her eyes. Like her own, his autobiography was a catalogue of incompetence, but it held no record of frustrated ambitions—no record of any ambitious desire whatever. It shewed the tame ass's unreflecting acquiescence in its lot of drudgery. There had been no passionate craving for things of delight. Why cry for the moon? With a salary of a hundred and thirty-five pounds a year out of which he must contribute to the support of his widowed mother, a man can purchase for himself but little splendour of existence, and Martin was not one of those to whom splendour comes unbought. He had lived, semi-content, in a fog splendour-obscuring, for the last ten years. But this evening the fog had lifted. The glamour of Paris, even the Pantheon and the Eiffel Tower sarcastically mentioned by Corinna, had helped to dispel it. So had Corinna's sisterly interest in his dull affairs. And so, more than all, had helped the self-analysis formulated under the compelling power of the philanthropist with shiny coat-sleeves and frayed linen, at once priest, lawyer and physician who had pocketed his five francs fee.

He talked long and earnestly; and the more he talked and the more minutely he revealed the aridity of his young life, the stronger grew within him a hitherto unknown spirit of revolt.

"That's all," he said at last, wiping a streaming brow.

"And very interesting indeed," said Fortinbras.

"Isn't it?" said Corinna. "And he never even kissed"—so complete had been Martin's apologia—"the landlady's daughter who married the plumber." She challenged him with a glance. "I swear you didn't."

With a shy twist of his lips Martin confessed: "Well—I did once."

"Why not twice?" asked Corinna.

"Yes, why not?" asked Fortinbras, seeing Martin hesitate, and his smile was archiepiscopal indulgence. "Why but one taste of ambrosial lips?"

Martin reddened beneath his olive skin. "I hardly like to say—it seems so indelicate——"

"*Allons donc,*" cried Corinna. "We're in Paris, not Wendlebury."

"We must get to the bottom of this, my dear Martin—it's a privilege I demand from my clients to address them by their Christian names—otherwise how can I establish the necessary intimate *rapport* between them and myself? So I repeat, my dear Martin, we must have the reason for the rupture or the dissolution or the termination of what seems to be the only romantic episode in your career. I'm not joking," Fortinbras added gravely, after a pause. "From the psychological point of view, it is important that I should know."

Martin looked appealingly from one to the other—from Fortinbras massively serious to Corinna serenely mocking.

"A weeny unencouraged plumber?" she suggested.

He sat bolt upright and gasped. "Good God, no!" He flushed indignant. "She was a most highly respectable girl. Nothing of that sort. I wish I hadn't mentioned the matter. It's entirely unimportant."

"If that is so," said Corinna, "why didn't you kiss the girl again?"

"Well, if you want to know," replied Martin desperately, "I have a constitutional horror of the smell of onions," and mechanically he sucked through his straw the tepid residue of melted ice in his glass.

Corinna threw herself back in her chair and laughed uncontrollably. It was just the lunatic sort of thing that would happen to poor old Martin. She knew her sex. Instantaneously she pictured in her mind the fluffy, lower middle-class young person who

set her cap at the gentleman with the long Grecian
nose, and she entered into her devasted frame of mind
when he wriggled awkwardly out of further osculatory
invitations. And the good, solid plumber, onion-loving soul, had carried her off, not figuratively but
literally under the nose of Martin.

"Oh, Martin, you're too funny for words!" she
cried.

Fortinbras smiled always benevolently. "If Cleo-
patra's nose had been a centimetre longer—I forget
the exact classical epigram—the history of the world
would have been changed. In a minor degree—for
the destiny of an individual must, of course, be of
less importance than the destiny of mankind—had
it not been for one spring onion, unconsidered fellow
of the robin and the burnished dove and the wanton
lapwing, this young man's fancy would have been fet-
tered in the thoughts of love. One spring onion—and
human destinies are juggled. Martin is still a soul-
starved bachelor, and—and—her name?"

"Gwendoline?"

"And Gwendoline is the buxom mother of five."

"Six," said Martin. "I can't help knowing," he
explained, "since I still lodge with her mother."

Corinna turned her head sideways to scrutinise the
drawing on the tablecloth, and still scrutinising it,
asked:

"And that is your one and only *affaire du cœur?*"

"I'm afraid the only one," replied Martin shame-
facedly. Even so mild a man as he felt the disad-
vantage of not being able to hint to a woman that
he could talk, and he would, of chimes heard at midnight and of broken hearts and other circumstances
hedging round a devil of a fellow. His one kiss
seemed a very bread-and-buttery affair—to say nothing of the mirth-provoking onion. And the ·emotion
attending the approach to it had been of a nature

so tepid that disillusion caused scarcely a pang. It had been better to pose as an out-and-out Sir Galahad, a type comprehensible to women. As the hero of one invertebrate embrace he cut a sorry figure.

"You are still young. The years and the women's lips before you are many," said Fortinbras, laying a comforting touch on Martin's shoulder. "Opportunity makes the lover as it does the thief. And in the bed-sitting-room in Hickney Heath where you have spent your young life where has been the opportunity? It pleases our Paris-hardened young friend to mock; but I see in you the making of a great lover, a Bertrand d'Allamanon, a Chastelard, one who will count the world well lost for a princess's smile——"

Corinna interrupted. "What pernicious nonsense are you talking, Fortinbras? You've got love on the brain to-night. Neither Martin nor I are worrying our heads about it. Love be hanged! We're each of us worried to death over the problem of how to keep body and soul together without going back to prison and you talk all this drivel about love—at least not to me, but to Martin."

"That qualification, my dear Corinna, upsets the logic of your admirable tirade," Fortinbras replied calmly, after drinking the remainder of his syrup and soda water. "I speak of love to Martin because his soul is starved, as I've already declared. I don't speak of it to you, because your soul is suffering from indigestion."

"I'll have another *kummel glacé,*" said Corinna. "It's a stomachic." She reached for the bell-pull behind her chair—she had the corner seat. Auguste appeared. Orders were repeated. "How you can drink all that syrup without being sick I can't understand," she remarked.

"Omnicomprehension is not vouchsafed even to the very young and innocent, my dear," said Fortinbras.

Martin glanced across the table apprehensively. If ever young woman had been set down that young woman was Corinna Hastings. He feared explosion, annihilation of the down-setter. Nothing of the sort happened. Corinna accepted the rebuff with the meekness of a school-girl and sniffed when Fortinbras was not looking. Again Martin was puzzled, unable to divest himself of his old conception of Corinna. She was Corinna, chartered libertine of the land of Rodolfe, Marcel, Schaunard—he had few impressions of the *Quartier Latin* later than Henri Murger—and her utterances no matter how illogical were derived from godlike inspiration. He hung on her lips for some inspired and vehement rejoinder to the rebuke of Fortinbras. When none came he realised that in the seedily dressed and now profusely perspiring *Marchand de Bonheur* she had met an acknowledged master. Who Fortinbras was, whence his origin, what his character and social status, how, save by the precarious methods to which he had alluded, he earned his livelihood, Martin had no idea; but he suddenly conceived an immense respect for Fortinbras. The man hovered over both of them on a higher plane of wisdom. From his kind eyes (to Martin's simple fancy) beamed uncanny power. He assumed the semblance of an odd sort of god indigenous to this Paris wonderworld.

Fortinbras lit another of Martin's Virginian cigarettes—the little tin box lay open on the table—and leaned back in his chair.

"My young friends," said he, "you have each put before me the circumstances which have made you respectively despair of finding happiness both in the immediate and the distant future. Now as Montaigne says—an author whom I would recommend to you for the edification of your happily remote middle-age, having myself found infinite consolation in his sagacity—as Montaigne says: 'Men are tormented by the ideas they have concerning things, and not by the things themselves.' The wise man therefore—the general term, my dear Corinna, includes women—is he who has learned to face things themselves after having dispelled the bogies of his ideas concerning them. It is on this basis that I am about to deliver the judgment for which I have duly received my fee of ten francs."

He moistened his lips with the pink syrup. For the picture you can imagine a grey old lion eating ice-cream.

"You, Corinna," he continued, "belong to the new race of women whose claims on life far exceed their justification. You have as assets youth, a modicum of beauty, a bright intelligence and a stiff little character. But, as you rightly say, you are capable of nothing in the steep range of human effort from painting a picture to washing a baby. Were you not temperamentally puritanical and intellectually obsessed by the modern notion of woman's right to an independent existence, you would find a means of realising the above-mentioned assets, as your sex has done through the centuries. But in spite of amazonian trifling with romantic-visaged and granite-headed medical students, you cling to the irresponsibilities of a celibate career."

"If he asked me, I'd marry a Turk to-morrow," said Corinna.

"Don't interrupt," said Fortinbras. "You disturb the flow of my ideas. I have no doubt that, in your desperate situation, you would promise to marry a Turk; but your essential pusillanimity would make you wriggle out of it at the last moment. You're like 'the poor cat in the adage.'"

"What cat?" asked Corinna.

"The one in Macbeth, Act i, Scene 3, a play by

Shakespeare. 'Letting "I dare not" wait upon "I would," like the poor cat i' the adage.' You require development, my dear Corinna, out of the cat stage. You have had your head choked with ideas about things in this soul-suffocating Paris, and the ideas are tormenting you; but you've never been at grips with things themselves. As for our excellent Martin, he has not even arrived at the stage of the desirous cat."

The smile that lit up his coarse, lined features, and the musical suavity of his voice divested the words of offence. Martin, with a laugh, assented to the proposition.

"He, too, needs development," Fortinbras went on. "Or rather, not so much development as a collection of soul-material from which development may proceed. Your one accomplishment, I understand, is riding a bicycle. Let us take that as the germ from which the tree of happiness may spring. Do you bicycle, Corinna?"

"I can, of course. But I hate it."

"You don't," replied Fortinbras quickly. "You hate your own idea of it. You'll begin your course of happiness by sweeping away all your ideas concerning bicycling and coming to bicycling itself."

"I never heard anything so idiotic," declared Corinna.

"Doubtless," smiled Fortinbras. "You haven't heard everything. Go on your knees and thank God for it. I repeat—or amplify my prescription. Go forth both of you on bicycles into the wide world. They will not be Wheels of Chance, but Wheels of Destiny. Go through the broad land of France filling your souls with sunshine and freedom and your throats with salutary and thirst-provoking dust. Have no care for the morrow and look at the future through the golden haze of eventide."

"There's nothing I should like better," said Martin, with a glance at Corinna, "but I can't afford it. I must get back to London to look out for an engagement."

Fortinbras mopped his brow with an over-fatigued pocket-handkerchief.

"What did you pay me five francs for? For the pleasure of hearing me talk, or for the value of my counsel?"

"I must look at things practically," said Martin.

"But, good God!" cried Fortinbras, with soft uplifted hands, "what is there more practical, more commonplace, less romantic in the world than riding a bicycle? You want to emerge from your Slough of Despond, don't you?"

"Of course," said Martin.

"Then I say—get on a bicycle and ride out of it. Practical to the point of pathos."

Martin objected: "No one will pay me for careering through France on a bicycle. I've got to live, and for the matter of fact, so has Corinna."

"But, my dear young friend, she has twenty pounds. You, on your own showing have forty. Sixty pounds between you. A fortune! You both are tormented by the idea of what will happen when the Pactolus runs dry. Banish that pestilential miasma from your minds. Go on the adventure."

In poetic terms he set forth the delights of that admirable vagabondage. His eloquence sent a thrill through Martin's veins, causing his blood to tingle. Before him new horizons broadened. He felt the necessity of the immediate securing of an engagement grow less insistent. If he got home with twenty pounds in his pocket, even fifteen, at a pinch ten, he could manage to subsist until he found work. And perhaps this blandly authoritative, though seedy angel really saw into the future. The temptation fascinated him. He glanced again at Corinna, who sat demure and silent, her chin propped on her fists, and his heart sank. The proposition was absurd. How could he ride abroad, for an indefinite number of days and nights with a young unmarried woman? Of himself he had no fear. Undesirous cat though he was, sent forth on the journey into the world to learn desire, he could not but remain a gentleman. In his charge she would enjoy a sister's sanctity. But she would never consent. She could not. No matter how profound her belief in his chivalry, her maiden modesty would revolt. Her reputation would be gone. One whisper in Wendlebury of such gipsying and scandal with bared scissor-points would arrest her on the station platform. And while these thoughts agitated his mind, and Corinna kept her eyes always demure and somewhat ironical on Fortinbras, the latter continued to talk.

"I'm not advising you," said he, "to pedal away like little Pilgrims into the Unknown. I propose for you an objective. In the little town of Brantôme in the Dordogne, made illustrious by one of the quaintest of French writers——"

"The Abbé Brantôme of '*La Vie des Dames Galantes*'?" asked Corinna.

Martin gasped. "You don't know that book?"

"By heart," she replied mischievously, in order to shock Martin. As a matter of fact she had but turned over the pages of the immortal work and laid it down, disconcerted both by the archaic French and the full flavour of such an anecdote or two as she could understand.

"In the little town of Brantôme," Fortinbras continued after a pause, "you will find an hotel called the Hôtel des Grottes, kept by an excellent and massive man by the name of Bigourdin, a poet and a philosopher and a mighty maker of *pâté de foie gras*.

A line from me would put you on his lowest tariff,
for he has a descending scale of charges, one for
motorists, another for commercial travellers and a
third for human beings."

"It would be utterly delightful," Martin interrupted,
"if it were possible."

"Why shouldn't it be possible?" asked Corinna
with a calm glance.

"You and I—alone—the proprieties——" he stam-
mered.

Again Corinna burst out laughing. "Is that what's
worrying you? My poor Martin, you're too comic.
What are you afraid of? I promise you I'll respect
maiden modesty. My word of honour."

"It is entirely on your account. But if you don't
mind—" said Martin politely.

"I assure you I don't mind in the least," replied
Corinna with equal politeness. "But supposing," she
turned to Fortinbras, "we do go on this journey, what
should we do when we got to the great Monsieur
Bigourdin?"

"You would sun yourselves in his wisdom," replied
Fortinbras, "and convey my love to my little daughter
Félise."

If Fortinbras had alluded to his possession of a
steam-yacht Corinna could not have been more astonished. To her he was merely the Marchand de
Bonheur, eccentric Bohemian, half charlatan, half
good-fellow, without private life or kindred. She
sat bolt upright.

"You have a daughter?"

"Why not? Am I not a man? Haven't I lived my
life? Haven't I had my share of its joys and sorrows? Why should it surprise you that I have a
daughter?"

Corinna reddened. "You haven't told me about her
before."

"When do I have the occasion, in this world of students, to speak of things precious to me? I tell you now. I am sending you to her—she is twenty—and to my excellent brother-in-law Bigourdin, because I think you are good children, and I should like to give you a bit of my heart for my ten francs."

"Fortinbras," said Corinna, with a quick outstretch of her arm, "I'm a beast. Tell me, what is she like?"

"To me," smiled Fortinbras, "she is like one of the wild flowers from which Alpine honey is made. To other people she is doubtless a well-mannered commonplace young person. You will see her and judge for yourselves."

"How far is it from Paris to Brantôme?" asked Martin.

"Roughly about five hundred kilometres—under three hundred miles. Take your time. You have sixty pounds' worth of sunny hours before you—and there is much to be learned in three hundred miles of France. In a few weeks' time I will join you at Brantôme—journeying by train as befits my soberer age—I go there a certain number of times a year to see Félise. Then, if you will continue to favour me with your patronage, we shall have another consultation."

There was a brief silence. Fortinbras looked from one young face to the other. Then he brought his hands down with a soft thump on the table.

"You hesitate?" he cried indignantly. "You're afraid to take your poor little lives in your hands even for a few weeks?" He pushed back his chair and rose and swept a banning gesture, "I have nothing more to do with you. For profitless advice my conscience allows me to charge nothing." He tore open his frock coat and his fingers diving into his waistcoat pocket brought forth and threw down the two five-franc pieces. "Go your ways," said he.

At this dramatic moment both the young people sprang protesting to their feet.

"What are you talking about? We're going to Brantôme," cried Corinna, gripping the lapels of his coat.

"Of course we are," exclaimed Martin, scared at the prospect of losing the inspired counsellor.

"Then why aren't you more enthusiastic?" asked Fortinbras.

"But we are enthusiastic," Corinna declared.

"We'll start to-morrow," said Martin.

"At six o'clock in the morning," said Corinna.

"At five, if you like," said Martin.

Fortinbras embraced them both in a capacious smile, as he deliberately repocketed the coins.

"That is well, my children. But don't do too many unaccustomed things at once. In the Dordogne you can rise at five—with enjoyment and impunity. In Paris, your meeting at that hour would be fraught with mutual antipathy, and you would not find a shop open where you could hire or buy your bicycles."

"I've got one," said Corinna.

"So have I," said Martin; "but it's in London."

Fortinbras extracted from his person a dim, chainless watch.

"It is now a quarter past one. Time for honest folk to be abed. Meet me here at eleven o'clock to-morrow, booted and spurred, with but a scrip at the back of your bicycles, and I will hand you letters to Félise and the poetic and philosophic Bigourdin, and now," said he, "with your permission, I will ring for Auguste."

Auguste appeared and Martin, waving aside the protests of Corinna, paid the modest bill. In the air-less street Fortinbras bade them an impressive good

night and disappeared in the byways of the sultry
city. Martin accompanied Corinna to the gaunt
neighbouring building wherein her eyrie was situate.
Both were tongue-tied, shy, embarrassed by the prospect of the intimate adventure to which they had
pledged themselves. When the great door, swung
open by the hidden concierge, at Corinna's ring, invited her entrance, they shook hands perfunctorily.

"At a quarter to eleven," said Martin.

"I shall be ready," said Corinna.

# CHAPTER III

THE bicycle journey of two young people through a mere three hundred miles of France is, on the face of it, an Odyssey of no importance. The only interest that could attach itself to such a humdrum affair would centre in the development of tender feelings reciprocated or otherwise in the breasts of both or one of the young people. But when the two of them proceed dustily and unemotionally along the endless, straight, poplar-bordered roads, with the heart of each at the end of the day as untroubled by the other as at the beginning, a detailed account of their wanderings would resolve itself into a commonplace itinerary.

"My children," said Fortinbras, when, after having lunched with them at the Petit Cornichon and given them letters of introduction and his blessing, he had accompanied them to the pavement whence they were preparing to start, "I advise you, until you reach Brantôme to call yourself brother and sister, so that your idyllic companionship shall not be misinterpreted."

"Pooh!"—or some such vocable of scorn—Corinna remarked. "We're not in narrow-minded England."

"In narrow-minded England," Fortinbras replied, "without a wedding ring, and without the confessed brother-and-sisterly relation, inns would close their virtuous doors against you. In France, where a pair of lovers is universally regarded as an object of romantic interest, innkeepers would confuse you with zealous attentions. Thus in either country, though for opposite reasons, you would be bound to encounter impossible embarrassment."

"I don't think there would be any danger of that," laughed Corinna lightly, "unless Martin went mad. But perhaps it would be just as well to play the comedy. I'll stick up my cheek to be kissed every night in the presence of the landlady. *'Bon soir, mon frère.'* —Do you think you can go through the performance, Martin?"

Martin, very uncomfortable, already experiencing at the suggestion of misconstrued relations, the embarrassment foreshadowed by Fortinbras, flushed deeply and took refuge in an examination of his bicycle. The celibate dreamer was shocked by her cool bravado. Since the episode of Gwendoline he had lived remote from the opposite sex; the only woman he had known intimately was his mother and from that knowledge he had formed the profound conviction that women were entirely futile and utterly holy. Corinna kept on knocking this conviction endwise. She made hay, not to say chaos, with his theory of woman. He felt himself on the verge of a fog-filled abysm of knowledge. There she stood, a foot or two away—he scarce dared glance at her— erect, clear-eyed, the least futile person in the world, treating a suggestion the most disconcerting and appalling to maidenhood with the unholiest mockery, and coolly proposing that, in order to give themselves an air of innocence, they should contract the habit of a nightly embrace.

"I'll do anything," said he, "to prevent disagreeableness arising."

Corinna laughed, and, after final farewells, they rode away down the baking little street leaving Fortinbras watching them wistfully until they had disappeared. And he remained a long time following in his thoughts the pair whom he had despatched upon their unsentimental journey. How young they were, how malleable, how agape for hope like young thrushes for worms, how attractive in their respective ways, how careless of sunstroke! If only he could have escaped with them from this sweltering Paris to the cool shadow of the Dordogne rocks and the welcome of a young girl's eyes. What a hopeless mess and muddle was life. He sighed and mopped his forehead, and then a hand touched his arm. He turned and saw the careworn face of Madame Gaussart, the fat wife of a neighbouring print-seller.

"Monsieur Fortinbras, it is only you in this city of misfortune that can give me advice. My husband left me the day before yesterday and has not returned. I am in despair. I have been weeping ever since. I weep now——" she did, copiously regardless of the gaze of the street. "Tell me what to do, my good Monsieur Fortinbras, you whom they call the *Marchand de Bonheur*. See—I have your little honorarium."

She held out the five-franc piece. Fortinbras slipped it into his waistcoat pocket.

"At your service, madame," said he, with a sigh. "Doubtless I shall be able to restore to you a fallacious semblance of conjugal felicity."

"I was sure of it," said the lady already comforted. "If you would deign to enter the shop, Monsieur."

Fortinbras followed her, and for a while lost his envy of Martin and Corinna in patient and ironic consideration of the naughtiness of Monsieur Gaussart.

This first stage out of Paris was the only time when the wanderers braved the midday heat of the golden August. They took counsel together in an earwiggy arbour outside Versailles, where they quenched their thirst with cider. They were in no hurry to reach their destination. A few hours in the early morning—they could start at six—and an hour or two in the cool of the evening would suffice. The remainder of the day would be devoted to repose. . . .

"And churches and cathedrals," added Martin.

"You have a frolicsome idea of a holiday jaunt," said Corinna.

"What else can we do?"

"Eat lotus," said Corinna. "Forget that there ever were such places as Paris or London or Wendlebury."

"I don't think Chartres would remind you of one of them," said Martin. "I've dreamed of Chartres ever since I read *'La Cathédrale'* by Huysmans."

"You're what they call an earnest soul," remarked Corinna. "All the way here I've never stopped wondering why I've come with you on this insane pilgrimage to nowhere."

"I've been wondering the same myself," said Martin.

As he had lain awake most of the night and therefore risen late, the occupations of the morning involving the selection and hire of a bicycle, consultation with the concierge of the Hôtel du Soleil et de l'Ecosse with regard to luggage being forwarded, the changing of his money into French bank-notes and gold, and various small purchases, had left him little time for reflection. It was only when he found himself pedalling perspiringly by the side of this comparatively unknown and startling young woman, who was to be his intimate companion for heaven knew how long, that he began to think. *Qu'allait il faire dans cette galère?* It was comforting to know that Corinna asked herself the same question.

"That old humbug Fortinbras must have put a spell upon us," she continued, without commenting on Martin's lack of gallantry. "He sort of envelops one in such a mist of words uttered in that musical voice of his and he looks so inspired with benevolent wisdom that one loses one's common sense. The old wretch can persuade anybody to do anything. He once inveigled a girl—an art student—into becoming a nun."

Martin's Protestant antagonism was aroused. He expressed himself heatedly. He saw nothing but reprehensibility in the action of Fortinbras. Corinna examined her well-trimmed fingernails.

"It was a question of Saint Clothilde—that I think was the order—or Saint Lazare. Some girls are like that."

"Saint Lazare?"

"Don't you know anything?" she sighed. "What's the good of being decently epigrammatic? Saint Lazare is the final destination of a certain temperament unsupported by good looks or money. It's the woman's prison of Paris."

"Oh!" said Martin.

"How he did it I don't know, but he saved her body and soul. And now she's the happiest creature in the world. I had a letter from her only the other day urging me to go over to Rome and take the vows——"

"I hope you're not thinking of it," said Martin.

"I'm in no danger of Saint Lazare," replied Corinna drily.

There was a long silence. In the leafy arbour screened from the dust and glare of the highway there prevailed a drowsy peace. Only one of the dozen other green blistered wooden tables was occupied— and that by a blue-bloused workman and his wife and baby, all temperately refreshing themselves with harmless liquid, the last from nature's fount itself. The landlord, obese, unshaven and alpaca-jacketed, read the *Petit Journal* at the threshold of the café of which the arboured terrace was but a summer adjunct. A mangy mongrel lying at his feet snapped spasmodically at flies. A couple of tow-headed urchins hung by

the arched entrance, low-class Peris at the gates of a
dilapidated Paradise.

"Who is Fortinbras?" Martin asked.

Corinna shrugged her dainty shoulders.  She did
not know.  Rumour had it—and for rumour she could
not vouchsafe—that he was an English solicitor struck
off the rolls.  With French law at any rate he was
familiar.  He had the Code Napoléon at his finger-
ends.  In spite of the sober black clothes and white
tie of the French attorney which he affected, he certainly possessed no French qualifications which would
have enabled him to set up a regular *cabinet d'avoué*
and earn a professional livelihood.  Nor did he pre-
sume to step within the *avoué's* jealously guarded
sphere.  But his opinion on legal points was so sound,
and his fee so moderate, that many consulted him in
preference to an orthodox practitioner.  That was all
that Corinna knew of him in his legal aspect.  The
rest of his queer practice consisted in advising in all
manner of complications.  He arbitrated in disputes
between man and man, woman and woman, lover and
mistress, husband and wife, parent and child.  He diverted the debtor from the path to bankruptcy.  He
rescued youths and maidens from disastrous nymphs
and fauns.  He hushed up scandal.  Meanwhile his
private life and even his address remained unknown.
Twice a day he went the round of the cafés and restaurants of the *quartier,* so that those in need of his
assistance had but to wait at their respective taverns
in order to see him—for he appeared with the in-
evitability of the sun in its course.

"There are all kinds of parasitical people," said
Corinna, "who try to sponge on students for drinks
and meals and money—but Fortinbras isn't that kind.
Now and again, but not often, he will accept an invitation to lunch or dinner—and then it's always for the
purpose of discussing business.  Whether it's his cun-

ning or his honesty I don't know—but nobody's afraid of him. That's his great asset. You're absolutely certain sure that he won't stick you for anything. Consequently anybody in trouble or difficulty goes to him confident that his five francs consultation fee is the end of the financial side of the matter and that he will concentrate his whole mind and soul on the case. He's an odd devil."

"The most remarkable man I've ever met," said Martin.

"You've not met many," said Corinna.

"I don't know——" replied Martin reflectively. "I once came across a prize-fighter—a remarkable chap —in the bar-parlour of the pub at the corner of our street who was afterwards hanged for murdering his wife, and I once met a member of Parliament, another remarkable man—I forget his name now—and then of course there was Cyrus Margett."

"But none of them is in it with Fortinbras," Corinna smiled with ironic indulgence.

"None," said Martin, "had his peculiar magnetic quality. Not even the member of Parliament. But," he continued after a pause, "is that all that is known of him? He seems to be a very mysterious person."

"I shouldn't mind betting you," said Corinna, "that you and I are the only people in Paris who are aware of his daughter in Brantôme."

"Why should he single us out for such a confidence?" asked Martin. "He said last night that he was giving us a bit of his heart because we were good children—it was quite touching—but why should we be the only ones to have a bit of his heart?"

"Would you like to know?" asked Corinna, meeting his eyes full.

"I should."

"He told me before you turned up at the Petit

Cornichon, this morning, that you interested him as a sort of celestial freak."

"I'm not sure whether to take that as a compliment or not," replied Martin, pausing in the act of rolling a cigarette. "It's tantamount to calling me an infernal ass."

At this show of spirit the girl swiftly changed her tone.

"You may take it from me that Fortinbras doesn't give a bit of his heart to infernal asses. If I had gone to him, on my own, he would never—you heard him—he would never have touched on 'things precious to him.' It's for your sake, not mine."

"But why?"

"Because he's fed up with the likes of me," said Corinna, with sudden bitterness. "There are hundreds and thousands of us."

Martin knitted his brow. "I don't understand."

"Better not try," she said. "Let us pay for the cider and get on."

So they paid and went on and halted at the townlet of Rambouillet, where as Monsieur and Mademoiselle Overshaw, they engaged rooms at the most modest of terms. And to Martin's infinite relief Corinna did not summon him to kiss her cheek in the presence of the landlady, before they retired for the night. He went to bed comforted by the thought that Corinna's bark was worse than her bite.

I have done my best to tell you that this was an unsentimental journey.

So day after day they sped their innocent course, resting by night at tiny places where haughty automobiles halted not. They had but sixty pounds to their joint fortune, and it behoved them not to dissipate it in unwonted luxury. Through Chartres they went, and Corinna quite as eagerly as Martin drank in deep draughts of its Gothic mystery and its splendour of stained glass; through Châteaudun with its grim old castle; through Vendôme with the flaming west front of its cathedral; through Tours in the neighbourhood of which they lingered many days, seeing in familiar intimacy things of which they had but dreamed before—Chinon, Loches, Chenonceaux, Azay-le-Rideau, perhaps the most delicate of all the châteaux of the Loire. And following the counsel of a sage Fortinbras they went but a few kilometres out of their way and visited Richelieu, the fascinating town known only to the wanderer, himself judicious or judiciously advised, that was built by the great Cardinal outside his palace gates for the accommodation of his court; and there it remains now untouched by time, priceless jewel of the art of Louis Treize, with its walls and gates and church and market square and stately central thoroughfare of *hôtels* for the nobles, each having its mansard roof and *porte-cochère* giving entrance to court and garden; and there it remains dozing in prosperity, for around it spread the vineyards which supply brandy to the wide, wide world.

It was here that Martin, sitting with Corinna on a blistered bench beneath a plane tree in the little market-place, said for the first time:

"I don't seem to care whether I ever see England again."

"What about getting another billet?" asked Corinna.

"England and billets are synonymous terms. The further I go the less important does it appear that I should get one. At any rate the more loathsome is the prospect of a return to slavery."

"Don't let us talk of it," she said, fanning herself with her hat. "The mere thought of going back turns the sun grey. Let us imagine we're just going on and on for ever and ever."

"I've been doing so in a general way," he replied.

"I've been living in a sort of intoxication; but now and then I wake up and have a lucid interval. And then I feel that by not sitting on the doorstep of scholastic agents I'm doing something wrong, something almost immoral—and it gives me an unholy thrill of delight."

"When I was a small child," said Corinna, "I used to take the Ten Commandments one by one and secretly break them, just to see what would happen. Some I didn't know how to break—the seventh for instance, which worried me—and others referring to stealing and murder were rather too stiff propositions. But I chipped out with a nail on a tile a little graven image and I bowed down and worshipped it in great excitement; and as father used to tell us that the third commandment included all kinds of swearing, I used to bend over an old well we had in the garden and whisper 'Damn, damn, damn, damn, damn,' until the awful joy of it made my flesh creep. I think, Martin, you can't be more than ten years old."

"Why do you spoil a bit of sympathetic comprehension by that last remark?" he asked.

"Why do you jib at truth?" she retorted.

"Truth?"

"Aren't you like a child revelling in naughtiness— naughtiness just for the sake of being naughty?"

"Perhaps I am," said he. "But why do you mock at me for it?"

"I don't think I'm mocking," she answered more seriously. "When I said you were only ten years old I meant to be rather affectionate. I seem to be ever so old in experience, and you never to have grown up. You're so refreshing after all these people I've been mixed up with—mostly lots younger really than you —who have plumbed the depths of human knowledge and have fished up the dregs and holding them out in their hands say, 'See what it all comes to!' I'm dead sick of them. So to consort, as I've been doing, with an ingenuous mind like yours, is a real pleasure."

Martin rose from his seat and a tortoiseshell cat, the only other denizen of the market-place, startled from intimate ablutions, gazed at him, still poising a forward thrown hind leg.

"My dear Corinna," said he, "I would beg you to believe that I'm not so damned ingenuous as all that!"

For reply Corinna laughed out loud, whereupon the cat fled. She rose too.

"Let us look at the church and cool this heat of controversy."

So they visited the Louis XIII church, and continued their journey. And the idle days passed and nothing happened of any importance. They talked a vast deal and now and then wrangled. After his sturdy declaration at Richelieu, Martin resented her gibes at his ingenuousness. He felt that it was incumbent on him to play the man. At first Corinna had taken command of their tour, ordaining routes and making contracts with innkeepers. These functions he now usurped; the former to advantage, for he discovered that Corinna's splendid misreading of maps had led them devious and unprofitable courses; the latter to the disgusted remonstrance of Corinna, who found the charges preposterously increased.

"I don't care," said Martin. "I don't mind your treating me as a brother, but I'm not going to be treated as your little brother."

In the freedom and adventure of their unremarkable pilgrimage, he had begun to develop, to lose the fear of her ironical tongue, to crave some sort of self-assertion, if not of self-expression. He also discovered in her certain little feminine frailties which flatteringly aroused his masculine sense of superiority. Once they were overtaken by a thunderstorm and in the cowshed to which they had raced for shelter, she sat fear-stricken, holding hands to ears at every clap, while Martin, hands in pockets, stood serene at the doorway interested in the play of the lightning. What was there to be afraid of? Far more dangerous to cross London or Paris streets or to take a railway journey. Her unreasoning terror was woman's weakness, a mere matter of nerves. He would be indulgent; so turning from the door, he put his waterproof cape over her shoulders as she was feeling cold, and the humility with which she accepted his services afforded him considerable gratification. Of course, when the sun came out, she carried her head high and soon found occasion for a gibe; but Martin rode on unheeding. These were situations in which he was master.

Once, also, in order to avoid a drove of steers emerging from a farm-yard gate, she had swerved violently into a ditch and twisted her ankle. As she could neither walk nor ride, he picked her up in his arms.

"I'll take you to the farm house."

"You can't possibly carry me," she protested.

"I'll soon show you," said Martin, and he carried her. And although she was none too light and his muscles strained beneath her weight, he rejoiced in her surprised appreciation of his man's strength.

But half way she railed, white lipped: "I suppose you're quite certain now you're my big brother."

"Perfectly certain," said Martin.

And then he felt her grip around his neck relax and her body weigh dead in his arms and he saw that she had fainted from the pain.

Leaving her in the care of the kind farm people, he went to retrieve the abandoned bicycles and reflected on the occurrence. In the first place he would not have lost his head on encountering a set of harmless steers; secondly, had he accidentally twisted his ankle, Corinna could not have carried him; thirdly he would not have fainted; fourthly, mocking as her last words had been, she had confessed her inferiority; all of which was most comforting to his self-esteem.

Then, some time afterwards, when the farmer put her into a broken-down equipage covered with a vast hood and drawn by a gaunt horse, rustily caparisoned, in order to drive her to the nearest inn some five kilometres distant, Martin superintended the arrangements, leaving Corinna not a word to say. He rode, a mounted constable, by her side, and on arriving at the inn carried her up to her room and talked with much authority.

Then, having passed through Poitiers and Ruffec, they came, three weeks after their start from Paris, to Angoulême, daintiest of cities, perched on its bastioned rocks above the Charente. And here, as it was the penultimate stage of their journey, they sojourned a few days.

They stood on the shady rampart and gazed over the red-roofed houses embowered in greenery at the great plain golden in harvest and drenched in sunshine, and sighed.

"I dread Brantôme," said Corinna. "It marks something definite. Hitherto we have been going along vaguely, in a sort of stupefied dream. At Brantôme we'll have to think."

"I've no doubt it will do us good," said Martin.

"I fail to see it," said Corinna. "We'll just have the same old worry over again."

"I'm not so sure," Martin answered. "In the first place we're not quite the same people as we were three weeks ago——"

"Rubbish," said Corinna.

"I'm not the same person at any rate."

She laughed. "Because you give yourself airs nowadays?"

"Even my giving myself airs," he replied soberly,

"denotes a change. But it's deeper than that—it's difficult to explain. I feel I have a grip on myself I hadn't before,—and also an intensity of delight in things I never had before. The first half hour or so of our rides in the early dewy mornings, our rough *déjeuners* outside the little cafés, the long, drowsy afternoons under the trees, watching the lazy life of the road—the wine wagons and the bullock carts and the sunburnt men and women—and the brown, dusty children with their goats—and the quiet evenings under the stars when we have either sat alone saying nothing or else talked to the *patron* of the *auberge* and listened to his simple philosophy of life. And then to sleep drunk with air and sunshine between the clean coarse sheets—to sleep like a dog until the scurry of the house wakes you at dawn—I don't know," he fetched up lamely. "It has been a thrill, morning, noon and night—and my life before this was remarkably devoid of thrills. Of course," he added after a slight pause, "you have had a good deal to do with it."

"*Je te remercie infiniment, mon frère,*" said Corinna. "That is as much as to say I've not been a too dull companion."

"You've been a delightful companion," he cried boyishly. "I had no idea a girl could be so—so——" He sought for a word with his fingers.

Her eyes smiled on him and lips shewed ever so delicate a curl of irony.

"So what?"

"So companionable," said he.

She laughed again. "What exactly do you mean by that?"

"So sensible," said Martin.

"When a man calls a girl sensible, do you know what he means? He means that she doesn't expect him to fall in love with her. Now you haven't fallen in love with me, have you?"

Martin from his lolling position on the parapet sprang erect. "I should never dream of such a thing!"

She laughed loud and grasped the lapels of his jacket. "Oh, Martin!" she cried, "you're a gem, a rare jewel. You haven't changed one little bit. And for Heaven's sake don't change!"

"If you mean that I haven't turned from a gentleman into a cad, then I haven't changed," said Martin freeing himself, "and I'm glad of it."

She tossed her head and the laughter died from her face. "I don't see how you would be a cad to have fallen in love with a girl who is neither unattractive nor a fool, and has been your sole companion from morning to night for three weeks. Ninety-nine men out of a hundred would have done it."

"I don't believe it," said Martin. "I have a higher estimate of the honour of my fellow-men."

"If that's your opinion of me——" she said, and turning swiftly walked away. Martin overtook her.

"Do you want me to fall in love with you?" he asked.

She halted for a second and stamped her foot. "No. Ten thousand times no. If you did I'd throw vitriol over you."

She marched on. Martin followed in an obfuscated frame of mind. She led the way round the ramparts and out into the narrow, cobble-paved streets of the old town, past dilapidated glories of the Renaissance, where once great nobles had entertained kings and now the proletariat hung laundry to dry over royal salamanders and proud escutcheons, past the Maison de Saint Simon, with its calm and time-mellowed ornament and exquisite oriels, past things over which, but yesterday, but that morning, they had lingered lovingly, into the Place du Mûrier. There she paused, as if seeking her bearings.

"Where are you going?" asked Martin, somewhat breathlessly.

"To some place where I can be alone," she flashed.

"Very well," said he, and raised his cap and left her.

In a few seconds he heard her call.

"Martin!"

He turned. "Yes?"

"I'm anything you like to call me," she said. "It's not your fault. It's my temper. But you've got to learn it's better not to turn women down flat like that, even when they speak in jest."

"I'm very sorry, Corinna," he said, smiling gravely, "but when one jests on such subjects I don't know where I am."

They crossed the square slowly, side by side.

"I suppose neither you nor anybody else could understand," she said. "I was angry with you, but if you had played the fool I should have been angrier still."

"Why?" he asked.

She looked straight ahead with a strained glance and for a minute or two did not reply. At last:

"You remember Fortinbras mentioning the name of Camille Fargot?"

"Oh!" said Martin.

"That's why," said Corinna.

"Is he at Brantôme?" asked Martin, with brow perplexed by the memory of the ridiculous mother.

"No, I wish to God he was."

"Are you engaged?"

"In a sort of a way," said Corinna, gloomily.

"I see," said Martin.

"You don't see a little bit in the world, she retorted with a sudden laugh. "You're utterly mystified."

"I'm not," he declared stoutly. "Why on earth shouldn't you have a love affair?"

"I thought you insinuated that none of your 'fellow men' would look at me twice."

He contracted his brows and regarded her steadily. "I'm beginning to get tired of this argument," said he.

Her eyes drooped first. "Perhaps you really have progressed a bit since we started."

"I was doing my best to tell you, when you switched off onto this idiot circuit."

Suddenly she put out her hand. "Don't let us quarrel, Martin. What has been joy and wonder to you has been merely an anodyne to me. I'm about the most miserable girl in France."

"I wish you had told me something of this before," said Martin, "because I've been feeling myself the happiest man. . . ."

# CHAPTER IV

"THERE is six o'clock striking and those English have not yet arrived."

Thus spake Gaspard-Marie Bigourdin, landlord of the Hôtel des Grottes, a vast man clad in a brown holland suit and a soft straw hat with a gigantic brim. So vast was he that his person overlapped in all directions the Austrian bent-wood rocking-chair in which he was taking the cool of the evening.

"They said they would come in time for dinner, *mon oncle,*" said Félise.

She was a graceful slip of a girl, dark-eyed, refined of feature. Fortinbras with paternal fondness, if you remember, had likened her to the wild flowers from which Alpine honey was made. And indeed, she suggested wild fragrance. Her brown hair was done up on the top of her head and fastened by a comb like that of all the peasant girls of the district; but she wore the blouse and stuff skirt of the well-to-do bourgeoisie.

"Six o'clock is already time for dinner in Brantôme," remarked Monsieur Bigourdin.

"They are accustomed to the hours of London and Paris, where I've heard they dine at eight or nine or any time that pleases them."

"In London and Paris they get up at midday and go to bed at dawn. They are coming here purposely to dis-habilitate themselves from the ways of London and Paris. At least so your father gives me to understand. It is a bad beginning."

"I am longing to see them," said Félise.

61

"Don't you see enough English? Ten years ago an Englishman at Brantôme was a curiosity. All the inhabitants, you among them, *ma petite* Félise, used to run two kilometres to look at him. But now, with the automobile, they are as familiar in the eyes of the good Brantômois as truffles."

By this simile Monsieur Bigourdin did not mean to convey the idea that the twelve hundred inhabitants of Brantôme were all gastronomic voluptuaries. It is true that Brantôme battens on *pâté de foie gras;* but it is the essence of its existence, seeing that Brantôme makes it and sells it and with pigs and dogs hunts the truffles without which *pâté de foie gras* would be a comestible of fat absurdity.

"But no English have been sent before by my father," said Félise.

"That's true," replied Bigourdin, with a capacious smile, showing white strong teeth.

"They are the first people—French or English, I shall have met who know my father."

"That's true also," said Bigourdin. "And they must be droll types like your excellent father himself. *Tiens,* let me see again what he says about them." He searched his pockets, a process involving convulsions of his frame which made the rocking-chair creak. "It must be in my black jacket," said he at last.

"I'll get it," said Félise, and went into the house.

Bigourdin rolled and lit a cigarette and gave himself up to comfortable reflection. The Hôtel des Grottes was built on the slope of a rock and the loggia or verandah on which Bigourdin was taking his ease, hung over a miniature precipice. At the bottom ran the River Dronne encircling most of the old-world town and crossed here and there by flashing little bridges. Away to the northeast loomed the mountains of the Limousin where the river has its source. The tiny place slumbered in the slanting sunshine.

The sight of Brantôme stretched out below him was inseparable from Bigourdin's earliest conception of the universe.  In the Hôtel des Grottes he had been born; there, save for a few years at Lyons whither he had been sent by his mother in order to widen his views on hotel keeping, he had spent all his life, and there he sincerely hoped to die full of honour and good nourishment.  Brantôme contented him.  It belonged to him.  It was so diminutive and compact that he could take the whole of it in at once.  He was familiar with all the little tragedies and comedies that enacted themselves beneath those red-tiled roofs.  Did he walk down the Rue de Périgueux his hand went to his hat as often as that of the President of the Republic on his way to a review at Longchamps.  He was a man of substance and consideration, and he was just forty years of age.  And Félise adored him, and anticipated his commands.

She returned with the letter.  He glanced through it, reading portions aloud:

"I am sending you a young couple whom I have taken to my heart.  They are not relations, they are not married and they are not lovers.  They are Arcadians of the pavement, more innocent than doves, and of a ferocious English morality.  She is a painter without patrons, he a professor without classes.  They are also candidates for happiness performing their novitiate.  Later they will take the vows."

"What does he mean?  What vows?"

"Perhaps they are pious people and are going to enter the convent," Félise suggested.

"I can see your father—anti-clerical that he is—interesting himself in little nuns and monks."

"Yet he and Monsieur le Curé are good friends."

"That is because Monsieur le Curé has much wisdom and no fear.  He would have tried to convert Voltaire himself. . . . Let us continue——"

"As they are poor and doing this out of obedience——"

"*Saprelotte!*" he laughed, "they seem to have taken the three vows already!"

He read on: "——they do not desire the royal suite in your Excelsior Palace. Corinna Hastings has lived under the roofs in Paris, Martin Overshaw over a baker's shop in a vague quarter of London. All the luxury they ask is to be allowed to wash themselves all over in cold water once a day."

"I was sure you had not written to my father about the bathroom," said Félise.

She was right. But the omission was odd. For Bigourdin took inordinate pride in the newly installed bathroom and all the touring clubs of Europe and Editors of Guide Books had heard of it and he had offered it to the admiring inspection of half Brantôme. Monsieur le Maire himself had visited it, and if he had only arrived girt with his tricolour sash, Bigourdin would have jumped in and demanded an inaugural ceremony.

"I must have forgotten," said Bigourdin. "But no matter. They can have plenty of cold water. But if I am to feed them and lodge them and wash them for the derisory price your father stipulates, they must learn that six o'clock is the hour of table d'hôte at the Hôtel des Grottes. It is only people in automobiles who can turn the place upside down, and then they have to pay four francs for their dinner."

He rose mountainously, and, standing, displayed the figure of a vigorous, huge proportioned, upright man. On his face, large and ruddy, a small black moustache struck a startling note. His eyes were brown and kindly, his mouth too small and his chin had a deep cleft, which on a creature of lesser scale would have been a pleasing dimple.

"*Allons dîner,*" said he.

In the patriarchal fashion, now unfortunately becoming obsolete, Monsieur Bigourdin dined with his guests. The *salle-à-manger*—off the loggia—was furnished with the long central table sacred to commercial travellers, and with a few side tables for other visitors. At one of these, in the corner between the service door and the dining-room door, sat Monsieur Bigourdin and his niece. As they entered the room five bagmen, with anticipatory napkins stuck cornerwise in their collars, half rose from their chairs and bowed.

*"Bon soir, messieurs,"* said Bigourdin, and he passed with Félise to his table.

Euphémie, the cook, fat and damp, entered with the soup tureen, followed by a desperate-looking, crop-headed villain bearing plates. The latter, who viewed half a mile off through a telescope might have passed for an orthodox waiter, appeared, at close quarters, to be raimented in grease and grime. He served the soup; first to the five commercial travellers,—and then to Bigourdin and Félise. On Félise's plate he left a great thumb-mark. She looked at it with an expression of disgust.

*"Regarde, mon oncle."*

Bigourdin alluding to him as a sacred animal, asked what she could expect. He was from Bourdeilles, a place of rocks some five miles distant, condemned by Brantôme, chef-lieu du Canton. He summoned him.

"Polydore."

*"Oui, monsieur."*

"You have made a mistake. You are no longer in the hands of the police."

*"Monsieur veut dire——?"*

"I am not the Commissaire who desires to photograph your finger-prints."

"Ah, pardon," said Polydore, and with a soiled napkin he erased the offending stain.

*"Sacré animal!"* repeated Bigourdin, attacking his soup. "I wonder why I keep him."

"I too," said Félise.

"If his grandmother and my grandmother had not been foster-sisters——" said Bigourdin, waving an indignant spoon.

"You would have kept him just because he is ugly," smiled Félise. "You would have found a reason."

"One of these days I'll throw him into the river," Bigourdin declared. "I am patient. I am slow to anger. But when I am roused I am like a lion. Polydore," said he serenely, as the dilapidated menial removed the plates, "if you can't keep your hands clean I'll make you wear gloves."

"People would laugh at me," said Polydore.

"So much the better," said Bigourdin.

The meal was nearly over when the expected guests were announced. Uncle and niece slipped from the dining room into the little vestibule to welcome them. An elderly man in a blouse, name Baptiste, was already busying himself with their luggage—the knapsacks fastened to the back of the bicycles.

"Mademoiselle, Monsieur," said Bigourdin, "it is a great pleasure to me to meet friends of my excellent brother-in-law. Allow me to present Mademoiselle Félise Fortinbras" (he gave the French pronunciation), "my niece. As dinner is not yet over and as you must be hungry, will you give yourselves the trouble to enter the *salle-à-manger.*"

"I should like to have a wash first," said Corinna.

Bigourdin glanced at Félise. They were beginning early.

"There is a bathroom upstairs fitted with every modern luxury."

Corinna laughed. "I only want to tidy up a bit."

"I will show you to your room," said Félise, and conducted her up the staircase beside the bureau.

"And monsieur?"

Martin went over to the little lavabo against the wall beside which hung the usual damp towel.

"This will do quite well," said he.

Bigourdin breathed again. The new arrivals were quite human; and they spoke French perfectly. The men conversed a while until the two girls descended. Bigourdin led his guests into the *salle-à-manger* and installed them at a table by one of the windows looking on the loggia.

"Like this," said he, "you will be cool and also enjoy the view."

"I think," said Corinna, looking up at him, "you have the most delicious little town I have seen in France."

Bigourdin's eyes beamed with gratification. He bowed and went back to his unfinished meal.

"Behold over there," said he to Félise, "a young girl of extraordinary good sense. She is also extremely pretty; a combination which is rare in women."

"Yes, uncle," said Félise demurely.

The five commercial travellers rose, and, bowing as they passed their host, went out in search, after the manner of their kind, of coffee and backgammon at the Café de l'Univers in the Rue de Périgueux. It is only foreigners who linger over coffee, liqueurs and tobacco in the little inns of France. Presently Félise went off to the bureau to make up the day's accounts, and Bigourdin, having smoked a thoughtful cigarette, crossed over to Martin and Corinna. After the good hotel-keeper's enquiry as to their gastronomic satisfaction, he swept his hand through his inch-high standing stubble of black hair, and addressed Martin.

"Monsieur Over—Oversh—forgive me if I cannot pronounce your name——"

"Overshaw," said Martin distinctly.

"Auvershaud — Auverchat — *non—c'est bigrement difficile.*"

"Then call me Monsieur Martin, *à la française.*"

"And me, Mademoiselle Corinne," laughed Corinna.

"*Voilà!*" cried Bigourdin, delighted. "Those are names familiar to every Frenchman." Then his brow clouded. "Well, Monsieur Martin, there is something I would say to you. What profession does my good brother-in-law exercise in Paris?"

Martin and Corinna exchanged glances.

"I scarcely know," said Corinna.

"Nor I," said Martin.

"It is on account of my niece, his daughter, that I ask. You permit me to sit down for a moment?" He drew a chair. "You must understand at once," said he, "that I have nothing against Monsieur Fortinbras. I love him like myself. But, on the other hand, I also love my little niece. She is very simple, very innocent, and does not appreciate the subtleties of the great world. She adores her father."

"I can quite understand that," said Martin, "and I am sure that he adores her."

"Precisely," said Bigourdin. "That is why I would like you to have no doubt as to the profession of my brother-in-law. You have never, by any chance, Mademoiselle Corinne, heard him called '*Le Marchand de Bonheur*'?"

"Never," said Corinna, meeting his eyes.

"Never," echoed Martin.

"Not even when he advised you to come here? It is for Félise that I ask."

"No," said Corinna.

"Certainly not," said Martin.

"But you have heard that he is an *avoué?*"

"An English solicitor practising in Paris. Of course," said Martin.

"A very clever solicitor," said Corinna.

Bigourdin smote his chest with his great hand. "I thank you with all my heart for your understanding. You are the first persons she has met who know her father—it is somewhat embarrassing, what I say— and she, in her innocence, will ask you questions, which he did not foresee——"

"There will be no difficulty in answering them," replied Martin.

"*Encore merci,*" said Bigourdin. "You must know that Félise came to us at five years old, when my poor wife was living—she died ten years ago—I am a widower. She is to me like my own daughter. Although," he added, with a smile and a touch of vanity, "I am not quite so old as that. My sister, her mother, is older than I."

"She is alive then?" asked Corinna.

"Certainly," replied Bigourdin. "Did you not know that? But she has been an invalid for many years. That is why Félise lives here instead of with her parents. I hope, Mademoiselle, you and she will be good friends."

"I am sure we shall," replied Corinna.

A little while later the two wanderers sat over their coffee by the balustrade of the covered loggia and looked out on the velvet night, filled with contentment. They had reached their goal. Here they were to stay until it pleased Fortinbras to come and direct them afresh. Hitherto, their resting-places, mere stages on their journey, had lacked the atmosphere of permanence. The still nights when they had talked together, as now, beneath the stars, had throbbed with a certain fever, the anticipation of the morrow's dawn, the morrow's adventures in strange lands. But now they had come to their destined haven. Here they would remain to-morrow, and the morrow after that, and for morrows indefinite. A phase of their life had ended with curious suddenness.

As the intensity of silence falls on ears accustomed to the whirr of machinery, so did an intensity of peace encompass their souls. And the dim-lit valley itself brought solace. Not here stretched infinite horizons such as those of the plains of La Beauce through which they had passed, horizons whence sprang a whole hemisphere of stars, horizons which embracing nothing set the heart aching for infinite things beyond, horizons in the centre of which they stood specks of despair overwhelmed by immensities. Here the comfortable land had taken them to its bosom. Near enough to be felt, the vague bluish mass of the Limousin mountains sweeping from north to east assured them of the calm protection of eternal forces. Beyond them who need look or crave to look? To the fevered spirit they brought in their mothering shelter all that was needed by man for his happiness: fruitfulness of cornfields, mystery of beech-woods faintly revealed by the rays of a young moon, a quiet town for man's untroubled habitation, guarded by its encircling river, rather guessed than seen and betrayed only here and there by a streak of quivering light. And as the distant glare of great cities—the lights of London reflected in the heavens—in the days of wandering youths seeking their fortunes, compelled them moth-like to the focus, so in its dreamy microcosm did the lights of the little town, a thousand flickering points from the outskirts and a line of long illumination marking the main street athwart the dark mass of roofs and dissipating itself hazily in midair, appeal to the imagination—set it wondering as to the myriad joyous affairs of men.

In low voices they talked of Fortinbras. His spirit seemed to have emerged from the welter of Paris into this pool of the world's tranquillity. In spite of his magnetic force his words had been but words. What they were to meet at Brantôme they knew not. They scarce had thought. What to them had been the landlord of a tiny provincial inn but a good-natured common fellow unworthy of speculation? And what the daughter of the seedy Paris Bohemian, snapper up of unconsidered trifles, but a serving girl of no account, plain and redolent of the scullery? Bigourdin's courteous bearing and delicacy of speech had come upon them as a surprise. So had the refinement of Félise. They had to readjust their conception of Fortinbras. They were amazed, simple souls, to find that he had ties in life so indubitably respectable. And he had a wife, too, a chronic invalid, with whom he lived in the jealous obscurity of Paris. It was pathetic. . . . They had obeyed him hardly knowing why. At the back of their minds he had been but a charlatan of peculiar originality—at the same time a being almost mythical, so remote from them was his life. And now he became startlingly real. They heard his voice soft and persuasive whispering by their side with a touch of gentle mockery.

Then silence fell upon them; their minds drifted apart and they lost themselves in their separate dreams.

At last, Polydore coming to remove the coffee tray and to enquire as to their further wants, broke the spell. When he had gone, Corinna leaned her elbow on the little iron table and asked in her direct fashion:

"What have you been thinking of, Martin?"

He drew his hand across his eyes, and it was a moment or two before he answered.

"When I was in London," said he, "I seem to have lived in a tiny provincial town. Now that I come to a tiny provincial town I have an odd feeling that the deep life of a great city is before me. That's the best I can do by way of explanation. Thoughts like that are a bit formless and elusive, you know."

"What do you think you're going to find here?"

"I don't know. Why not happiness in some form or other?"

"You expect a lot for five francs," she laughed.

"And you?"

"I——?"

"Yes, what have you been thinking of?"

She pointed, and in the gloom he followed the direction of white-bloused arm and white hand.

"Do you see that little house on the quay? The one with the lights and the loggia. You can just get a glimpse of the interior. See? There's a picture and below a woman sitting at a piano. If you listen you can catch the sound. It's Schubert's 'Moment Musical.' Well, I've been wishing I were that woman with her life full of her home and husband and children. Sheltered—protected—love all around her —nothing more to ask of God. It was a beautiful dream."

"You too," said Martin, "feel about this place somewhat as I do."

"I suppose it's the night. It turns one into a sentimental lunatic. Fancy living here for the rest of one's days and concentrating one's soul on human stomachs."

"What do you mean, Corinna?"

"Isn't that what woman's domestic life comes to? She must fill her husband's stomach properly or he'll beat her or run off with somebody else, and she must fill her babies' stomachs properly or they'll get cramps and convulsions and bilious attacks and die. It was a beautiful dream. But the reality would drive me stick, stark, staring mad."

"My ideas of married life," said Martin sagely, "are quite different."

"Of course!" she cried. "You're one of the creatures with the stomach."

"I've never been aware of it," said Martin.

"It strikes me you're too good for this world," said Corinna.

Martin rolled a cigarette from a brown packet of Maryland tobacco—his supply of English 'Woodbines' had long since given out.

"I have my ideals as to love—and so forth," said he.

"And so have I. 'All for Love and the World Well Lost.' That's the title of an old play, isn't it? I can understand it. I would give my soul for it. But it happens once in a blue moon. Meanwhile one has to live. And connubiality and maternity in a little lost hole in Nowhere like this aren't life."

"What the dickens is life?" asked Martin.

But her definition he did not hear, for the vast figure of Bigourdin loomed in the doorway of the *salle-à-manger*.

"I wish you good night," said he.

Martin rose and looked at his watch. "I think it's time to go to bed."

"So do I," yawned Corinna.

## CHAPTER V

THE first thing a cat does on taking up its quarters in a new home is to make itself acquainted with its surroundings. It walks methodically with uplifted tail and quivering nose from vast monument of sideboard to commonplace of chair, from glittering palisade of fender to long lying bastion of couch, creeps by defences of walls noting each comfortable issue, prowls through lanes and squares innumerable formed by intricacies of furniture; and having once gone through the grave business, worries its head no more about topography and points of interests, but settles down to serene enjoyment of such features of the place as have appealed to its æsthetic or grosser instincts. In this respect the average human is nearer a cat than he cares to realise. The first hour on board a strange ship is generally devoted to an exhaustive exploration never repeated during the rest of the voyage, and doubtless a prisoner's first act on being locked into his cell is to creep round the confined space and familiarise himself with his depressing installation.

Obeying this instinct common to cats and men, Martin and Corinna, as soon as they had finished breakfast the next morning, wandered forth and explored Brantôme. They visited the grey remains of the old abbey begun by Charlemagne. But Villon writing in the 15th Century and asking *"Mais où est le preux Charlemaigne?"* might have asked with equal sense of the transitory nature of human things: "Where is the Abbey which the knightly Charlemagne did piously build in Brantôme?" For the Normans came and destroyed it and one eleventh-century tower protecting a Romanesque Gothic church alone tells where the abbey stood. Strolling down to the river level along the dusty, shady road, they came to the terraced hill-side, past which the river once infinitely furious must have torn its way. In the sheer rock were doors of human dwellings, numbered sedately like the houses of a smug row. Above them, at the height of a cottage roof, stretched a grassy plain, from which, corresponding with each homestead, emerged the short stump of a chimney emitting thin smoke from the hearth beneath. Before one of the open doors they halted. Children were playing in the one room which made up the entire habitation. They had the impression of a vague bed in the gloom, a table, a chair or two, cooking utensils by the rude chimney-piece, bunks fitted into the living rock at the sides. The children might have been Peter Pan and Wendy and Michael and John and the rest of the delectable company, and the chimney-stump above them might have been replaced by Michael's silk hat, and on the green sward around it pirates and Red Indians might have fought undetected by the happy denizens below.

Thus announced Corinna with lighter fancy. But Martin, serious exponent of truth, explained that the monks, in the desolate times when their Abbey was rebuilding had hewn out these abodes for cells and had dwelt in them many many years; and to prove it, having conferred, before her descent to breakfast, with the excellent Monsieur Bigourdin, he led her to a neighbouring cave, called in the district, Les Grottes— Hence the name of Bigourdin's hotel—which the good monks, their pious aspiration far exceeding their powers of artistic execution, had adorned with grotesque and primitive carvings in bas-relief, representing the Last Judgment and the Crucifixion.

They paused to admire the Renaissance Fontaine

Médicis, set in startling contrast against the rugged background of rock, with its graceful balustrade and its medallion enclosing the bust of the worthy Pierre de Bourdeille, Abbé de Brantôme, the immortal chronicler of horrific scandals; and they crossed the Pont des Barris, and wandered by the quays where men angled patiently for deriding fish, and women below at the water's edge beat their laundry with lusty arms; and so past the row of dwellings old and new huddled together, a decaying thirteenth-century house with its heavy corbellings and a bit of rounded turret lost in the masonry jostling a perky modern café decked with iron balconies painted green, until they came to the end of the bridge that commands the main entrance to the tiny water-girt town. They plunged into it with childlike curiosity. In the Rue de Périgueux they stood entranced before the shop fronts of that wondrous thoroughfare alive with the traffic of an occasional ox-cart, a rusty one-horse omnibus labelled *"Service de Ville,"* and some prehistoric automobile wheezing by, a clattering impertinence. For there were shops in Brantôme of fair pretension—is it not the *chef lieu du Canton?*—and you could buy *articles de Paris* at most three years old. And there was a Pharmacie Internationale, so called because there you could obtain Pear's soap and Eno's Fruit salt; and a draper's where were exposed for sale frilleries which struck Martin as marvellous, but at which Corinna curved a supercilious lip; and a shop ambitiously blazoned behind whose plate-glass windows could be seen a porcelain bath-tub and other adjuncts of the luxurious bath-room, on one of which, sole occupant of the establishment, a little pig-tailed girl was seated eating from a porringer on her knees; and there were all kinds of other shops including one which sold cabbages and salsifies and charcoal and petrol and picture postcards and rusty iron and vintage eggs and guano and all manner of fantastic dirt. And there was the Librairie de la Dordogne which smiled at you when you asked for devotional pictures or tin-tacks, but gasped when you demanded books. Martin and Corinna, however, demanded them with British insensibility and marched away with an armful of cheap reprints of French classics disinterred from a tomb beneath the counter. But before they went, Martin asked:

"But have you nothing new? Nothing from Paris that has just appeared?"

"*Voici, monsieur,*" replied the elderly proprietress of the Library of the Dordogne, plucking a volume from a speckled shelf at the back of the shop. "*On trouve ça très joli.*" And she handed him *Le Maître de Forges*, by Georges Ohnet.

"But this, madam," said Martin, examining the venerable unsold copy, "was published in 1882."

"I regret, monsieur," said the lady, "we have nothing more recent."

"I'll buy it if it breaks me—as a curiosity," cried Corinna, and she counted out two francs, seventy-five centimes.

"Ninety-five," said the bookseller—she was speckled and dusty and colourless like the back of her library——"

"But in Paris——"

"In Paris it is different, mademoiselle. We are here *en province.*"

Corinna added the extra twopence and went out with Martin, grasping her prize.

This is the deliciousest place in the world," she laughed. "Eighteen eighty-two! Why, that's years before I was born!"

"But what on earth are we going to do for books here?" Martin asked anxiously.

"There is always the railway station," said Corinna.

"And if you kiss the old lady at the bookstall nicely, she will get you anything you want."

"The ways of provincial France," said Martin, "take a good deal of finding out!"

Thus began their first day in Brantôme. It ended peacefully. Another day passed and yet another and many more, and they lived in lotus land. Soon after their arrival came their luggage from Paris, and they were enabled to change the aspect of the road-worn vagabond for that of neat suburban English folk and as such gained the approbation of the small community. They had little else to do but continue to repeat their exploration. In their unadventurous wanderings Félise sometimes accompanied them and shyly spoke her halting English. To Corinna alone she could chatter with quaint ungrammatical fluency; but in Martin's presence she blushed confusedly at every broken sentence. All her young life she had lived in her mother's land and spoken her mother's tongue. She had a vague notion that legally she was English, and she took mighty pride in it, but by training and mental habit she was the little French bourgeoise, through and through. With Martin alone, however, she abandoned all attempts at English, and gradually her shyness disappeared. She gave the first signs of confidence by speaking of her mother in Paris as of a dream woman of wonderful excellencies.

"You see her often, mademoiselle?" Martin asked politely.

"Alas! no, Monsieur Martin." She shook her head sadly and gazed into the distance. They were idling on one of the bridges while Corinna a few feet away made a rapid sketch.

"But your father?"

"Ah, yes. He comes four times a year. It is not that I do not love him. *J'adore papa.* Every one does.

You cannot help it. But it is not the same thing. A
mother——"

"I know, mademoiselle," said Martin. "My mother
died a few months ago."

She looked at him with quick tenderness. "That
must have caused you much pain."

"Yes, mademoiselle," said Martin simply, and he
smiled for the first time into her eyes, realising quite
suddenly that beneath them lay deep wells of sympathy
and understanding. "Perhaps one of these days you
will let me talk to you about her," he added.

She flushed. "Why, yes. Talking relieves the
heart." She used the French word *"soulager"*—that
word of deep-mouthed comfort.

"It does. And your mother, Mademoiselle Félise?"

"She cannot walk," she sighed. "All these years
she has lain on her bed—ever since I left her when I
was quite little. So you see, she cannot come to see
me."

"But you might go to Paris."

"We do not travel much in Brantôme," replied
Félise.

"Then you have not seen her——"

"No. But I remember her. She was so beautiful
and so tender—she had chestnut hair. My father
says she has not changed at all. And she writes to
me every week, Monsieur Martin. And there she lies
day after day, always suffering, but always sweet and
patient and never complaining. She is an angel."
After a little pause, she raised her face to him—
"But here am I talking of my mother, when you asked
me to let you talk of yours."

So Martin then and on many occasions afterwards
spoke to her of one that was dead more intimately
than he could speak to Corinna, who seemed impatient of the expression of simple emotions. Corinna
he would never have allowed to see tears come into

his eyes; but with Félise it did not matter. Her own eyes filled too in sympathy. And this was the beginning of a quiet understanding between them. Perhaps it might have been the beginning of something deeper on Martin's side had not Bigourdin taken an early opportunity of expounding certain matrimonial schemes of his own with regard to Félise. It had all been arranged, said he, many years ago. His good neighbour, Monsieur Viriot, *marchand de vins en gros* —oh, a man everything there was of the most solid, had an only son; and he, Bigourdin, had an only niece for whom he had set apart a substantial dowry. A hundred thousand francs. There were not many girls in Brantôme who could hide as much as that in their bridal veils. It was the most natural thing in the world that Lucien should marry Félise—nay, more, an ordinance of the *bon Dieu*. Lucien had been absent some time doing his military service. That would soon be over. He would enter his father's business. The formal demand in marriage would be made and they would celebrate the *fiançailles* before the end of the year.

"Does Mademoiselle Félise care for Lucien?" asked Martin.

Bigourdin shrugged his mountainous shoulders.

"He does not displease her. What more do we want? She is a good little girl, and knows that she can entrust her happiness to my hands. And Lucien is a capital fellow. They will be very happy."

Thus he warned a sensitive Martin off philandering paths, and, with his French adroitness, separated youth and maiden as much as possible. And this was not difficult. You see Félise acted as manageress in the Hôtel des Grottes, and her activities were innumerable. There was the kitchen to be ruled, an eye to be kept on the handle of the basket—if it danced too much, according to the French phrase, the cook was exceeding her commission of a sou in the franc; there were the bedrooms and clean dry linen to be seen to, and the doings of Polydore, the unclean, and of Baptiste, the haphazard, to be watched; there were daily bills to be made out, accounts to be balanced, impatient bagmen to be cajoled or rebuked; orders for *pâté de foie gras* and truffles to be despatched—the Hôtel des Grottes had a famous manufactory of these delights and during autumn and winter supported a hive of workers and the shelves in the cool store-house were filled with appetising jars; and then the laundry and the mending and the polishing of the famous bathroom—*ma foi,* there was enough to keep one small manageress busy. Like a *bon hôtelier,* Bigourdin himself supervised all these important matters, ordering and controlling, as an administrator, but Félise was the executive. And like an obedient and happy little executive Félise did not notice a subtle increase in her duties. Nor did Martin, honest soul, in whose eyes a betrothed maiden was as sacred as a married woman, remark any change in facilities of intercourse. For him she flashed, a gracious figure, across the half real tapestry of his present life. A kindly word, a smiling glance, on passing, sufficed for the maintenance of his pleasant understanding with Félise. For feminine companionship of a stimulating kind, there was always Corinna. For masculine society he had Bigourdin and his cronies of the Café de l'Univers, to whom he was introduced in his professorial dignity.

It was there, at the café table, in the midst of the notables of the little town, that he learned many things either undreamed of or uncared for during his narrow life at Margett's Universal College. It startled him to find himself in the company of men passionately patriotic. Hitherto, as an Englishman living remote from Continental thought, he had taken patriotism for granted; his interest in politics had been mild and parochial; he had adopted a vague conservative outlook due, most likely, to antipathy to his democratic Swiss relatives, who sent eight pounds to the relief of his impoverished mother, and to a nervous shrinking from democracy in general as represented by his pupils. But in this backwater of the world he encountered a political spirit intensely alive. Vital principles formed the subject of easy, yet stern discussion. Beneath the calm of peaceful commerce and agriculture he felt the pulse of France throbbing in fierce determination to maintain her national existence. Every man had been a soldier; some of the elders had fought in 1870, and those who had grown up sons were the fathers of soldiers. Martin realised that whereas in England, in time of peace, the private soldier was tolerated as a picturesque, good-natured, harum-scarum sort of fellow, the *picu-piou* in France was an object of universal affection. The army was woven into the whole web of French life; it permeated the whole of French thought; it coloured the whole of French sentiment. It was not a machine of blood and iron, as in Germany, but the soul sacrifice of a nation. *"Vive la France!"* meant *"Vive l'armée!"* And that mere expression *"Vive la France!"*—how often had he heard it during his short sojourn in the country. He cudgelled his brains to remember when he had heard a corresponding cry in England. It seemed to him that there was none. There was no need for one. England would live as long as the sea girded her shores and Britannia ruled the waves. We need not trouble our English heads any further. But in France conditions are different. From the Vosges to the Bay of Biscay, from Calais to the Mediterranean, every stroke on a Krupp anvil reverberated through France.

"*Ça vient*—when no one knows," said the comfortable citizens, "but it is coming sooner **or** later, and then we shed the last drop of our blood. We are prepared. We have learned our lesson. There will never be another Sedan."

They said it soberly, like men whose eyes were set on an implacable foe. And Martin knew that through the length and breadth of the land comfortable citizens held the same sober and stern discourse. Every inch of French soil was dear to these men, and to guard it they would shed the last drop of their blood.

Corinna informed of these conversations said lightly:

"You haven't lived among them as long as I have. It's just their Gallic way of talking."

But Martin knew better. His horizons were expanding. He began, too, to conceive a curious love for a country so earnest, whose speech was the first that he had spoken. He had a vague impression that he was learning to live a corporate, instead of an individual life. When he tried to interpret these feelings to Corinna she cried out upon him:

"To hear you talk one would think you hadn't any English blood. Isn't England good enough for you?"

"It's because I'm beginning to understand France that I'm beginning to understand England," he replied in his grave way.

"Like practising on the maid before you dare make love to the mistress."

"Very possibly," said he, digging the blunt end of his fork into the coarse salt—they were at lunch. "To put it another way—if you learn Latin you learn the structure of all languages."

"What a regular schoolmaster's simile," she remarked, scornfully.

He flushed. "I'm no longer a schoolmaster," said he.

"Since when?"

"Since I came here."

"Do you mean to say you're not going back to it?"

He paused before replying to the sudden question which accident had occasioned. To himself he had put it many times of late, but hitherto had evaded a definite answer. Now, with a thrill, he looked at her.

"Never," said he.

She laid down her knife and fork and stared at him. Was he, after all, taking this fool journey seriously? To her it had been a reckless adventure, a stolen trip into lotus-land, with the knowledge of an inevitable return to common earth eating into her heart. Even now she dreaded to ask how much of her twenty pounds had been spent. But she knew that the day of doom was approaching. She could not live without money. Neither could he.

"What do you propose to do for a living?"

"God knows," said he. "I don't. Anyhow, the squirrel has escaped from his cage, and he's not going back to it."

"What's he going to do? Sit on a tree and eat nuts? Oh, my dear Martin!"

"There are worse fates," he replied, answering her laughter with a smile. "At any rate, he has God's free universe all around him."

"That's all very well; but analogies are futile. You aren't a squirrel and you can't live on acorns and east wind. You must live on bread and beef. How are you going to get them?"

"I'll get them somehow," said he. "I'm waiting for Fortinbras."

To this determination had he come after three weeks residence in Brantôme. The poor-spirited drudge had drunk of the waters of life and was a drudge no more. He had passed into another world. Far remote, as down the clouded vista of long memory, he saw the bare, hopeless class room and the pale, pinched faces of the students. All that belonged to a vague past. It had no concern with the present or the future. How

he had arrived at this state of being he could not tell.
The change had been wrought little by little, day by
day.   The ten years of his servitude had been blocked
out.   He had the thrilling sense of starting life afresh
at thirty, as he had started it, a boy of twenty.   There
was so much more in the open world than he had
dreamed of.   If the worst came to the worst he could
go forth into it, knapsack on shoulders and seek his
fortune; and every step he took would carry him further from Margett's Universal College.

"When is that fraud of a *marchand de bonheur* coming?" Corinna cried impatiently.

She put the question to Bigourdin the next time
she met him alone—which was after the meal, on the
*terrasse*.   He could not tell.   Perhaps to-night, to-morrow, the week after next.   Fortinbras came and went
like the wind, without warning.   Did Mademoiselle
Corinne desire his arrival so much?

"I should like to see him here before I go."

"Before you go?   You are leaving us, Mademoiselle?"

She laughed at his look of dismay.   "I can't stay
idling here for ever."

"But you have been here no time at all," said he.
"Just a little bird that comes and perches on this balustrade, looks this side and that side out of its bright
eyes and then flies away."

"*Oui, c'est comme ça,*" said Corinna.

"*Voilà!*"   He sighed and turned to throw his broad-
brimmed hat on a neighbouring table.   "That's the
worst of our infamous trade of hotel keeping.   You
meet sincere and candid souls whose friendship you
crave, but before you have time to win it, away they
go like the little bird, for ever and ever out of your
life."

"But you have won my friendship, Monsieur Bigourdin," said Corinna, with rising colour.

"You are very gracious, Mademoiselle Corinne. But why take it from me as soon as it is given?"

"I don't," she retorted. "I shall always remember you and your kindi ess."

"*Aïe, aïe!* You know our saying: *Tout passe, tout casse, tout lasse.* It is the way of the world, the way of humanity. We say that we will remember—but other things come to dim memory, to blunt sentiment —*enfin,* we forget, not because we want to, but because we must."

"If we must," laughed Corinna, "you'll forget our friendship too. So we'll be quits."

"Never, mademoiselle," he cried illogically. "Your friendship will always be precious to me. You came into this dull house with your youth, your freshness, your wit and your charm—different from the ordinary hotel guest you have joined my little intimate family life—Félise, for example adores you—were it not for her mother, you would be her ideal. And I——"

"And you, Monsieur Bigourdin?"

Her voice had the flat sound of a wooden mallet striking a peg. The huge man bowed with considerable dignity.

"I shall miss terribly all that you have brought into this house, Mademoiselle."

Corinna relaxed into a mocking smile.

"Fortinbras warned us that you were a poet, Monsieur Bigourdin."

"Every honest man whose eyes can see the beautiful things of life must be a poet of a kind. It is not necessary to scribble verses."

"But do you? Do you write verse?"

"*Jamais de la vie,*" he declared stoutly. "An *hôtelier* like me count syllables on his fingers? *Ah, non!* I can make excellent pâté de foie gras—no one better in Périgord—but I should make execrable verses. *Ah, voyons donc!*"

He laughed lustily and Corinna laughed too; and Martin, appearing on the verandah, asked and learned the reason of their mirth. After a word or two their host left them fanning himself with his great hat.

"What on earth brought you here?" said Corinna. "I was having the flirtation of my life."

# CHAPTER VI

A WEEK passed and Fortinbras did not come. Corinna wrote to him. He replied:

"Have patience, cultivate Martin's sense of humour and make Félise give you lessons in domestic economy. The cook might instruct you in the various processes whereby eggs are rendered edible and you might also learn how to launder clothes without disaster to flesh or linen. I am afraid you are wasting your time. Remember you're not like Martin who needs this rest to get his soul into proper condition. I will come whither my heart draws me—for I yearn to see my little Félise—as soon as I am allowed to do so by my manifold avocations and responsibilities."

Corinna, in a fury, handed the letter to Martin and asked him what he thought of it. He replied that, in his opinion, Fortinbras gave excellent advice. Corinna declared Fortinbras to be an overbearing and sarcastic pig and rated Martin for standing by and seeing her insulted.

"You gave him five francs for putting you on the road to happiness," he replied. "He has done his best, and seems to keep on doing it—without extra charge. I think you ought to be grateful. His suggestions are full of sense."

"Confound his suggestions," cried Corinna.

"I think our friend Bigourdin would be pleased if you followed them."

"I don't see what our friend Bigourdin has to do with it."

"He would give you all the help he could. A Frenchman likes a woman to know how to do things."

"I won't wash clothes," said Corinna defiantly.

"You might rise superior to a brand of soap," retorted Martin.

She turned her back on him and went her way. His gross sense of humour required no cultivation. It was a poisonous weed. And what did he mean by dragging in Bigourdin? She would never speak to Martin again, after his disgraceful innuendo. It took the flavour from the sympathetic relations that had been set up between her host and herself during the past week. A twinge of conscience exacerbated her anger against Martin. She certainly had encouraged Bigourdin to fuller professions of friendship than is usual between landlord and guest. The fresh flowers he had laid by her plate at every meal she wore in her dress. Only the night before she had ever so delicately hinted that Martin was capable of visiting the Café de l'Univers without a bear-leader, and the huge and poetical man had sat with her in the moonlight and in terms of picturesque philosophy had exposed to her the barren loneliness of his soul. She had enjoyed the evening prodigiously, and was looking forward to other evenings equally exhilarating. Now Martin had spoiled it all. She called Martin names that would have shocked Mrs. Hastings and caused her father to mention her specially during family prayers.

Then she defended herself proudly. Who was there to talk to in that Nowhere of a place? The conversation of Félise stimulated as much as that of a ten-year-old child. Martin she had sucked dry as a bone during their seven weeks companionship. He of course could hob-nob with men at the café. He also had picked up a curious assortment of acquaintance, male and female in the town, and had acquired a knack of conversing with them. A day or two ago she had come upon him in one of the rock dwellings discussing politics with a desperate villain who worked in the freestone quarries, while the frowsy mistress of the house lavished on him smiles and the horrible grey wine of the country which he drank out of a bowl. She, Corinna, had no café; nor could she find anything in common with desperadoes of quarrymen and their frowsy wives; to enter their houses savoured of district visiting, a philanthropic practice which she abhorred with all the abhorrence of a parson's rebellious daughter. Where was she to look for satisfying human intercourse? She knew enough of the French middle-class manners and customs to be aware that she might live in Brantôme a thousand years before one lady would call on her—a mere question of social code as to which she had no cause for resentment. But she craved the stimulus, the give-and-take of talk, such as had been her daily food in Paris for the last three years. Huge, not at all commonplace, but somewhat of an enigma, Bigourdin lumbered on to her horizon. His first-hand knowledge of men and things was confined to Brantôme and Lyons. But with that knowledge he had pierced deep and wide. He had read little but astonishingly. He had a grasp of European, even of English internal affairs that disconcerted Corinna, who airily set out to expound to him the elements of world politics. Two phases of French poetry formed an essential factor of his intellectual life—the Fifteenth Century Amorists, and the later romanticists. He could quote Victor Hugo, Alfred de Musset, Théodore de Banville by the mile. When stirred he had in his voice disquieting tones. He recited the *"Chanson de Fortunio"* and the *"Chanson de Barberine"* in the moonlight, and Corinna caught her breath and felt a shiver down her spine. It was a new sensation for Corinna to feel shivers down her spine at the sound of a man's voice.

> *Mais j'aime trop pour que je die*
> *Qui j'ose aimer,*

*Et je veux mourir pour ma mie*
*Sans la nommer.*

She went to bed with the words singing in her ears
like music.

Altogether it was much more comforting to talk
to Bigourdin than to take lessons in household management from Félise.

At last the day came when she plucked up courage
and demanded of Martin an account of his stewardship.
He tried to evade the task by flourishing in her face
a bundle of notes. They had heaps, said he, to go on
with. But Corinna pressed her enquiry with feminine
insistence. Had he kept any memoranda of expendi-
ture? Of course methodical Martin had done so.
Where was it? Reluctantly he drew a soiled note book
from his pocket and side by side at a little table on
the verandah, her fair hair brushing his dark cheek,
they added up the figures and apportioned and di-
vided and eventually struck the balance. Corinna was
one franc seventy-five centimes in Martin's debt. She
had not one penny in the world. She had one franc
seventy-five centimes less than nothing. She rose
white-lipped.

"You ought to have told me."

"Why?" asked Martin. "There's plenty of money
in the common stock."

"There never was any such thing as a common
stock."

"I thought there was," said Martin. "I thought
we had arranged it with Fortinbras. Anyhow, there's
one now."

"There isn't," she cried indignantly. "Do you suppose I'm going to live on your money? What kind of
a girl do you take me for?"

"An unconventional one," said Martin.

"But not dishonourable. To assert my freedom and

live by myself in Paris and run about France alone with you may be unconventional. But for a girl to accept support from a man when—when she gives him nothing in return—is a different thing altogether."

They argued for some time, and at the end of the argument neither was convinced. She upbraided. Martin ought to have struck a daily balance. He continued to put forward the plea of the common stock to which she had apparently given her tacit agreement.

"Well, well," said Martin at last, "there's no dishonour in a loan. You can give me an I. O. U. That's a legal document."

"But how do you suppose I am ever going to pay you?"

"That, my dear Corinna," said he, "is a matter which doesn't interest me in the least."

She turned on him furiously. "Do you know what you are? Would you like me to tell you? You're the most utterly selfish man in the wide, wide world."

She flung away through the empty *salle-à-manger,* and left Martin questioning the eternal hills of the Limousin. "I offer," said he, in effect, "to share my last penny, in all honour and comradeship, with a young person of the opposite sex whom I have always treated with the utmost delicacy, who is absolutely nothing to me, who would scoff at the idea of marrying me and whom I would no more think of marrying than a Fifth of November box of fireworks, who has heaped on me all sorts of contumelious epithets—I offer, I repeat, to divide my last crust with her, and she calls me selfish. Eternal hills, resolve the problem." But the hills enfolded themselves majestically in their autumn purple and deigned no answer to the little questionings of man.

Unsuccessful he strolled through the dining-room and vestibule and at the hotel entrance came upon the

ramshackle hotel omnibus and the grey, raw-boned
omnibus horse standing unattended and forlorn. To
pass the time the latter shivered occasionally in order
to jingle the bells on his collar and scatter the majenta
fly-whisk hung between his eyes. Martin went up and
patted his soft muzzle and put to him the riddle. But
the old horse, who naturally thought that these over-
tures heralded a supply of bodily sustenance, and, in
good faith, had essayed an expectant nibble, at last
jerked his head indignantly and refused to concern
himself with such insane speculation. Martin
was struck by the indifferent attitude of hills and
horses towards the queer vagaries of the human female.

Then from the doorway sallied forth a flushed
Corinna booted and spurred for adventure. I need not
tell you that a woman's boots and spurs are on her
head and not on her feet. Corinna wore the little hat
with the defiant pheasant feather which she had not
put on since her last night in Paris. A spot of red
burned angrily on each cheek. Martin accustomed to
ask: "Where are you going?" was on the point of
putting the mechanical question when he was checked
by one of her hard glances. Obviously she would have
nothing to do with him. She passed him by and
walked down the hill at a brisk pace. Martin watched
her retreating figure until a turn in the road hid it from
his view and then retiring into the house, went up to
his room and buried himself in Montaigne, to which
genial author, it may be remembered, he had been
recommended by Fortinbras.

They did not meet till dinner, when she greeted him,
all smiles. She apologised for wayward temper and
graciously offered, should she need money, to accept a
small loan for a short period. What her errand had
been when she set forth in her defiant hat she did not
inform him. He shrewdly surmised she had gone to

the *Postes et Télégraphes* in the town; but he was within a million miles of guessing that she had despatched a telegram to Bordeaux.

The meal begun under these fair auspices was enlivened by a final act of depravity on the part of the deboshed waiter, Polydore. He had of late given more than usual dissatisfaction, to the point of being replaced by the chambermaid and Félise when fashionable motordom halted at the Hôtel des Grottes. Once Martin himself, beholding through the *terrasse* doorway Félise struggling around a large party of belated and hungry Americans, came to her assistance and lent an amused hand. The guests taking him for a deputy landlord, explained their needs in bad French. Félise thanked him in blushing confusion, while Bigourdin, as he had done a hundred times before, gave a week's notice to Polydore, who, acting scullion, was breaking plates and dishes with drunken persistency. And now the truth is out as regards Polydore. With the sins of sloth, ignorance, and uncleanliness he combined the sin of drunkenness. Polydore was nearly always fuddled. Yet because of the ties of blood, the foster-sisterdom of respective grandmothers, Bigourdin had submitted to his inefficiency. Once more he revoked the edict of dismissal. Once more Polydore kept sober for a few days. Then once more he backslided. And he backslided irretrievably this night at dinner.

All went fairly well at first. It was a slack night. Only three *commis-voyageurs* sat at the long table, and thus there were only seven persons on whom to attend. It is true that his eye was somewhat glazed and his hand somewhat unsteady; but under the awful searchlight of Bigourdin's glance, he nerved himself to his task. Soup and fish had been served satisfactorily; then came a long, long wait. Presently Polydore reeled in. As he passed by Bigourdin's table he

held up the finger of a dirty hand bound with a drip-
ping bloody rag.

"*Pardon, je me suis coupé le doigt,*" he announced
thickly and made a bee-line to Corinna, with the os-
tensible purpose of removing her plate.  But just as he
reached her, the extra dram that he must have taken
to fortify himself against the shock of his wound, took
full effect.  He staggered, and in order to save himself clutched wildly at Corinna, leaving on her bare
neck his disgusting sanguine imprint.  She uttered a
sharp cry and simultaneously Bigourdin uttered a
roar and, rushing across the room, in a second had
picked up the unhappy varlet in his giant arms.

"*Ah, cochon!*"—he called him the most dreadful
names, shaking him as Alice shook the Red Queen.
"*En voilà la fin!*  I will teach you to dare to spread
your infamous blood.  I will break your bones.  I
will crush your skull, so that you'll never set foot
here again.  *Ah! triple cochon!*"

A flaming picture of gigantic wrath, he swept with
him to the door, whence he hurled him bodily forth.
There was a dull thud.  And that, as far as the three
commercial travellers (standing agape with their napkins at their throats), Corinna, Martin, Félise and
Bigourdin were concerned, was the end of Polydore.
Bigourdin, with an agility surprising in so huge a
man, was in an instant by Corinna's side with finger
bowl full of water and a clean napkin.

"Mademoiselle, that such a bestial personage should
have dared to soil your purity with his uncleanness
makes me mad, makes me capable of assassinating
him.  Permit me to remove his abominable contamina-
tion."

"Let me do it, *mon oncle,*" said Félise, who had run
across.

But Bigourdin waved her aside, and with reverent
touch, as though she were a goddess, he cleansed Cor-

inna. She underwent the operation in her cool way
and when it was over smiled her thanks at Bigourdin.
"Mademoiselle Corinna," he cried, "what can I
say to you? What can I do for you? How can I
repair such an outrage as you have suffered in my
house? You only have to command and everything
I have is yours. Command—insist—ordain." He
spread his arms wide, an agony of appeal in his eyes.

Martin, who had started to his feet, in order to save
Corinna from the grip of the intoxicated Polydore,
but had been anticipated by the impetuous rush of
Bigourdin, gazed for a moment or two at his host and
then gasped, as his vision pierced into the huge man's
soul. This perfervid declaration was not the good
innkeeper's apology for a waiter's disgusting behaviour. It was the blazing indignation of a real man at
the desecration inflicted by another on the body of
the woman he loved. A shiver of comprehension of
things he had never comprehended before swept
through Martin from head to foot. He knew with
absolute knowledge that should she rise and, with a
nod of her head, invite Bigourdin to follow her to
the verandah, she could be mistress absolute of Bigourdin's destiny. He held his breath, for the first
time in his dull life conscious of the meaning of love
of women, conscious of eternal drama. He looked at
Corinna smiling with ironic curl of lip up at the impassioned man. And he had an almost physical feeling within him as though his heart sank like a stone.
But a week ago she had declared, with a vulgarity of
which he had not thought her capable, that she had
had the flirtation of her life with Bigourdin. She
must have known then, she must know now that the
man was in soul-strung earnest. What was her attitude to the major things of Life? His brain worked
swiftly. If, in her middle-class English snobbery, she
despised the French innkeeper, why did she admit him

to her social plane on which alone flirtation—he had a sensitive gentleman's horror of the word—was possible? If she accepted him as a social equal, recognising in him, as he, Martin, recognised, all that was vital in modern France—if she accepted him, woman accepting man, why that infernal smile on her pretty face? I must give you to understand that Martin knew nothing whatever about women. His ignorance placed him in this dilemma. He watched Corinna's lips eager to hear what words would issue from them.

She said coolly: "So long as this really is the end of Polydore, honour is satisfied."

Bigourdin stiffened under her gaze, and collecting himself, bowed formally.

"As to that, Mademoiselle," said he, "I give you my absolute assurance." He turned to the commercial travellers. "Messieurs, I ask your pardon. You will not have to wait any longer. *Viens, Félise.*"

And landlord and niece took Polydore's place for the rest of the meal.

"Bigourdin's a splendid fellow," said Martin.

Elbow on table she held a morsel of bread to her lips. "He waits so well, doesn't he?" she said.

He shrugged his shoulders. What was the use of arguing with a being with totally different standards and conception of values? Some little wisdom he was beginning to acquire. He spent the evening at the Café de Périgueux with Bigourdin, who, with an unwonted cloud on his brow, abused the Government in *atrabiliar* terms.

The next morning Corinna, attired in her daintiest, wandered off to sketch lonely and demure. At *déjeuner* she made a pretence of eating and entertained Martin with uninteresting and (to him) unintelligible criticism of Parisian actors. Bigourdin passed a moment or two of professional commonplace at the table and retired. An inexperienced young woman of the town, with the chambermaid's assistance, replaced the villain of last night's tragedy. Corinna continued her hectic conversation and took little account of Martin's casual remarks. A mind even less subtle than her companion's would have assigned some nervous disturbance as a reason for such feverish behaviour. But of what nature the disturbance? Vaguely he associated it with the Sundayfied raiment. Could it be that she intended, without drum or trumpet, to fly from Brantôme?

"By the way, Martin," she said suddenly, when the last wizened grape had been eaten, "have you ever taken those snapshots of the Château at Bourdeilles?"

"I'm afraid I haven't," said he.

"You promised to get them for me."

"I'll go over with my camera one of these days," said Martin.

"That means *aux Kalendes Grecques*. Why not this beautiful afternoon?"

"If you'll come with me."

"I've rather a headache—or I would," said Corinna. "As it is, I think I'll have to lie down. But you go. It would do you good."

"Aha!" thought Martin astutely, "she wants to get rid of me, so that she can escape by the afternoon train to Paris." Aloud he said, "I'll go to-morrow."

"Why not to-day?"

"I don't feel like it," said he.

Not for the first time she struck an obstinate seam in Martin. He turned a deaf ear both to her cajolings and her reproaches. To some degree he felt himself responsible for Corinna, as a man must do who acts as escort or what you will to an attractive and penniless young woman. If she had decided to rush home to England, it was certainly his duty to make commodious arrangements for her journey.

"I'm going to loaf about to-day," he announced.

"Like the selfish pig you always are," said Corinna.

*"Comme tu veux,"* said Martin cheerfully.

"Can't you see I want you to go away for the afternoon?" said Corinna angrily.

"Any idiot could see that," replied Martin.

"Then why don't you?"

"I want to keep an eye on you."

She flushed scarlet and rose from the table. "All right. Spy as much as you like. It doesn't matter to me."

Once more she left him with a dramatic whirl of skirts. The procedure having become monotonous impressed Martin less than on previous occasions. He even smiled at the conscious smile of sagacity. There was something up, he reflected, with Corinna, or he would eat his hat. She contemplated some idiotic action. Of that there could be no doubt. It behoved him, as the only protector she had in the world, to mount guard. He mounted guard, therefore, over cigarette and coffee in the vestibule of the hotel, and for some time held entertaining converse with Bigourdin on the decadence of Germanic culture, and while Martin was expounding the futile vulgarity of the spectacle of Sumurum which, on one of his rare visits to places of amusement, he had witnessed in London, the word of Corinna's enigma was suddenly and dustily flashed upon him.

From a dusty two-seater car that drew up noisily at the door, sprang a dusty youth with a reddish face and a little black moustache.

"Is Mademoiselle Hastings in the hotel?" he asked.

"Yes, monsieur," said Bigourdin.

"Will you kindly let her know that I am here—Monsieur Camille Fargot?"

"Monsieur Fargot," repeated Bigourdin.

"Mademoiselle Hastings expects me," said the young man.

*"Bien, monsieur,"* said Bigourdin. He retired, his duty as a good innkeeper compelling him.

Martin, comfortable in his cane chair, lit another cigarette and with dispassionate criticism inspected Monsieur Camille Fargot, who stood in the doorway, his back to the vestibule, frowning resentfully on the little car.

This then was the word of Corinna's enigma. To summon him by telegraph had been the object of her sortie in the hat with the pheasant's plume. To welcome him had been the reason of her festive garb. In order to hold unembarrassed converse she had tried to send Martin away to photograph Bourdeilles. This then was the famous student in medicine who was supposed to have won Corinna's heart. Martin who had of late added mightily to his collection of remarkable men thought him as commonplace a young student as he had encountered since the far off days of Margett's Universal College. He seemed an indeterminate, fretful person, the kind of male over whom Corinna in her domineering way would gallop and re-gallop until she had trampled the breath out of him. Being a kindly soul, he began to feel sorry for Camille Fargot. He was tempted to go up to the young fellow, lay a hand on his shoulder and say: "If you want to lead a happy married life, my dear chap, drive straight back to Bordeaux and marry somebody else." By doing so, he would indubitably contribute to the greatest happiness of the greatest number of human beings and would rank among the philanthropists of his generation. But Martin still retained much of his timidity and he also had a comradely feeling towards Corinna. If she regarded this dusty and undistinguished young gentleman as the rock of her salvation, who was he, powerless himself to indicate any other rock of any kind, to offer objection?

So realising the absurdity of standing on guard

against so insignificant a danger as Monsieur Camille Fargot, student in medicine, and not desiring to disconcert Corinna by his presence should she descend to the vestibule to meet her lover, he courteously begged pardon of the frowning young man who blocked the doorway, and, passing by him, walked meditatively down the road.

# CHAPTER VII

WHEN Martin returned to the hotel a couple of hours later, he found that Monsieur Camille Fargot had departed, and that Corinna had entrenched herself in her room. On the wane of the afternoon she sent word to any whom it might concern that, not being hungry, she would not come down for dinner. To Félise, anxious concerning her health, she denied access. Offers of comforting nourishment on a tray made on the outer side of the closed door she curtly declined. Mystery enveloped the visit of Camille Fargot.

Martin learned from a perturbed Bigourdin that she had descended immediately after he had left the vestibule and had led Fargot at once into the *Salon de Lecture,* a moth-eaten and fusty cubby-hole in which commercial travellers who found morbid pleasure in the early stages of asphyxiation sometimes wrote their letters. There they had remained for some time, at the end of which Monsieur Fargot—*"il avait l'air hébété,"* according to Baptiste, a witness of his exit— had issued forth alone and jumped into his car and sped away, presumably to Bordeaux. After a moment or two Mademoiselle Corinne, in her turn, had emerged from the *Salon de Lecture* and looking very haughty with her pretty head in the air—(again Baptiste)— had mounted to her apartment.

Those were the bare facts. Bigourdin narrated them simply, in order to account for Corinna's non-appearance at dinner. With admirable taste he forbore to question Martin as to the relations between the lady and her visitor. Nor did Martin enlighten him. An

art-student in Paris like Corinna must necessarily have
a host of friends. What more natural than that one,
finding himself in her neighbourhood, should make a
passing call. Such was the tacit convention between
Martin and Bigourdin. But the breast of each har-
boured the conviction that the visit had not been a
success of cordiality. Bigourdin exhibited brighter
spirits that night at the Café de l'Univers. He played
his game of backgammon with Monsieur le Maire and
beat him exultantly. Around him the coterie cursed
the Germans for forcing the three years' service on
France. He paused, arm uplifted in the act of throwing the dice.

"Never mind. They seek it—they will get it. *Vous
l'avez voulu, Georges Dandin.* The *bon Dieu* is on
our side, just as He is on mine in this battle here.
*Vlan!*"

The dice rattled out of the box and they showed
the number that declared him the winner. A great
shout arose. The honest burgesses cried miracle.
*Voyons,* it was a sign from heaven to France. *"In
hoc signo vinces!"* cried a professor at the *Ecole Normale,* and the sober company had another round of
bocks to celebrate the augury.

Martin and Bigourdin walked home through the
narrow, silent streets and over the bridges. There was
a high wind sharpened by a breath of autumn which
ruffled the dim surface of the water; and overhead a
rack of cloud scudded athwart the stars. A light or
two far up the gloomy scaur shewed the Hôtel
des Grottes. Bigourdin waved his hand in the dark-
ness.

"It is beautiful, all this."

Martin assented and buttoned up his overcoat.

"It is beautiful to me," said Bigourdin, "because it
is my own country. I was born and bred here and my
forefathers before me. It is part of me like my legs

and my arms. I don't say that I am beautiful myself," he added, with a laugh, his French wit seeing whither logic would lead him. "But you understand."

"Yes," said Martin. "I can understand in a way. But I have no little corner of a country that I can call my own. I'm not the son of any soil."

"Périgord is very fruitful and motherly. She will adopt you," laughed Bigourdin.

"But I am English of the English," replied Martin. "Périgord would only adopt a Frenchman."

"I have heard it said and I believe it to be true," said Bigourdin, "that every English artist has two countries, his own and France. And it is the artist who expresses the national feeling and not the university professors and philosophers; and all true men have in them something of the artistic, something which responds to the artistic appeal—I don't know if I make myself clear, Monsieur Martin—but you must confess that all the outside inspiration you get in England in your art and your literature is Latin. I say 'outside,' for naturally you draw from your own noble wells; but for nearly a generation the *fin esprit anglais,* in all its delicacy and all its subtlety and all its humanity is in every way sympathetic with the *fin esprit français.* Is not that true?"

"Now I come to think of it," said Martin, "I suppose it is. I represent the more or less educated middle-class Englishman, and, so far as I am aware of any influence on my life, everything outside of England that has moved me has been French. As far as I know, Germany has not produced one great work of art or literature during the last forty years."

"*Voilà!*" cried Bigourdin, "how could a pig of a country like that produce works of art? I haven't been to Berlin. But I have seen photographs of the Allée des Victoires. *Mon cher,* it is terrible. It is sculpture hewn out by orders of the drill sergeant's cane. *Ah, cochon de pays!* But you others, you English—at last, after our hundred years of peace, you realise how bound you are to France. You realise—all the noble souls among you—that your language is half Latin, that for a thousand years, even before the Norman conquest, all your culture, all the sympathies of your poetry and your art are Roman—and Greek—*enfin* are Latin. Your wonderful cathedrals—Gothic —do you get them from Teutonic barbarism? No. You get them from the Comacine masters—the little band of Latin spiritualists on the shores of Lake Como. I am an ignorant man, Monsieur Martin, but I have read a little and I have much time to think and —*voilà*—those are my conclusions. In the great war that will come——"

"It can't come in our time," said Martin.

"No? It will come in our time. And sooner than you expect. But when it does come, all that is noble and spiritual in England will be passionately French in its sympathies. *Tiens, mon ami*—" he planted himself at the corner of the dark uphill road that led to the hotel, and brought his great hands down on Martin's shoulders. "You do not yet understand. You are a wonderful race, you English. But if you were pure Frisians, like the German, you would not be where you are. Nor would you be if you were pure Latins. What has made you invincible is the interfusion since a thousand years of all that is best in Frisian and Latin. You emerged English after Chaucer—Saxon bone and Latin spirit. That is why, my friend, you hate all that is German. That is why you love now all that is French. And that is why we, *nous autres Français,* feel at last that England understands us and is with us."

Having thus analysed the psychology of the Entente Cordiale in terms which proceeding from the lips of a small English innkeeper would have astounded Mar-

tin, Bigourdin released him and together they mounted
homewards.

"I was forgetting," said he, as he bade Martin good-
night. "All of what I said was to prove that if you
were in need of a foster-mother, Périgord will take
you to her bosom."

"I'll think of it," smiled Martin.

He thought of it for five minutes after he had gone
to bed and then fell fast asleep.

Early in the morning he was awakened by a great
thundering at his door. Convinced of catastrophe,
he leaped to his feet and opened. On the threshold the
urbane figure of Fortinbras confronted him.

"You?" cried Martin.

"Even I. Having embraced Félise, breakfasted,
washed and viewed Brantôme proceeding to its daily
labours, I thought it high time to arouse you from your
unlarklike slumbers."

Saying this he passed Martin and drew aside the
curtains so that the morning light flooded the room.
He was still attired in his sober black with the *avoué's*
white tie which bore the traces of an all-night journey. Then he sat down on the bed, while Martin, in
pyjamas and bare-foot, took up an irresolute position
on the cold boards.

"I generally get up a bit later," said Martin with an
air of apology.

"So I gather from my excellent brother-in-law.
Well," said Fortinbras, "how are you faring in Arca-
dia?"

"Capitally," replied Martin. "I've never felt so
fit in my life. But I'm jolly glad you've come."

"You want another consultation? I am ready to give
you one. The usual fee, of course. Oh, not now!"
As Martin turned to the dressing table where lay a
small heap of money, he raised a soft, arresting hand.
"The hour is too early for business even in France.

I have no doubt Corinna is equally anxious to consult me. How is she?"

"Much the same as usual," said Martin.

"By which you would imply that she belongs to the present stubborn and stiff-necked generation of young Englishwomen. I hope you haven't suffered unduly."

"I? Oh, Lord, no!" Martin replied, with a laugh. "Corinna goes her way and I go mine. Occasionally when there's only one way to go—well, it isn't hers."

"You've put your foot down."

"At any rate Corinna hasn't put her foot down on me. I think," said Martin, rubbing his thinly clad sides meditatively, "my journey with Corinna has not been without profit to myself. I've made a discovery."

He paused.

"My dear young friend," said Fortinbras, "let me hear it."

"I've found out that I needn't be trampled on unless I like."

Fortinbras passed his hand over his broad forehead and his silver mane and regarded the young man acutely. Whatever possibilities he might have seen of a romantic attachment between the pair of derelicts no longer existed. Martin had taken cool measure of Corinna and was not the least in love with her. The Dealer in Happiness smiled in his benevolent way.

"Although in your present ruffled and unshorn state you're not looking your best, you're a different man from my client of two months ago."

"Thanks to your advice," said Martin, "my three weeks' journey put me into gorgeous health and here I've been living in clover."

"And the environment does not seem to be unfavourable to moral and intellectual development."

"That's Bigourdin and his friends," cried Martin. "He is a splendid fellow, a liberal education."

"He's an apostle of sanity," replied Fortinbras with an approving nod. "Meanwhile sanity would not recommend your standing about in this chilly air with nothing on. I will converse with you while you dress."

"I'll have my tub at once," said Martin.

He disappeared into the famous bath-room and after a few moments returned and made his toilet while he gossiped with Fortinbras of the things he had learned at the Café de l'Univers.

"It's a funny thing," said he, "but I can't make Corinna see it."

"She's Parisianised," replied Fortinbras. "In Paris we see things in false perspective. All the little finnicky people of the hour, artists, writers, politicians are so close to us that they loom up like mountains. You learn more of France in a week at Brantôme than in a year at Paris, because here there's nothing to confuse your sense of values. Happy young man to live in Brantôme!"

He sighed and, seeing that Martin was ready, rose and accompanied him downstairs. Félise, fresh and dainty, with heightened colour and gladness in her eyes due to the arrival of the adored father, poured out Martin's coffee. They were old-fashioned in the Hôtel des Grottes, and drank coffee out of generous bowls without handles, beside which, on the plate, rested great spoons for such sops of bread as might be thrown therein.

"It is as you like it?" she asked in her pretty, clipped English.

"It's always the best coffee I have ever drunk," smiled Martin. He looked up at Fortinbras lounging in the wooden chair usually occupied by Corinna. "Do you know, Mr. Fortinbras, that Mademoiselle Félise has so spoilt me with food and drink that I shall never be able to face an English lodging-house meal again?"

Fortinbras passed his arm round his daughter's waist and drew her to him affectionately.

"She would spoil me too, if she had the chance. It is astonishing what capability there is in this little body."

Félise, yielding to the caress, touched her father's hair. "It's like *mamman,* when she was young, *n'est-ce pas?*" She spoke in French which came more readily.

"Yes," said Fortinbras, in a deep voice. "Just like your mother."

"I try to resemble her. *Tu sais,* every time I feel I am lazy or missing my duties, I think of *mamman,* and I say, 'No, I will not be unworthy of her.' And so that gives me courage."

"I've heard so much of Mrs. Fortinbras," said Martin, "that I seem to know her intimately."

A smile of great tenderness and sadness crept into Fortinbras's eyes as he turned them on his daughter.

"It is good that you still think and speak so much of her. Ideals keep the soul winged for flight. If it flies away into the empyrean and comes to grief like Icarus and his later fellow pioneers in aviation, at least it has done something."

He released her and she sped away on her duties. Presently she returned with a scared face.

"Monsieur Martin, what has happened? Here is Corinna going to leave us this morning."

"Corinna going? Does she know I'm here?" asked Fortinbras in wonderment.

"I don't know. I haven't seen her. I did not dream that she was up—she generally rises so late. But she has told Baptiste to take down her boxes for the omnibus to catch the early train for Paris. *Mon Dieu,* what has happened to drive her away?"

"Perhaps the visit yesterday of Monsieur Camille Fargot," said Martin.

"Eh?" said Fortinbras sharply. Then turning to

Félise. "Go, my dear, and lay my humble homage at the feet of Mademoiselle Corinna and say that as I have travelled for nearly a day and a night in order to see her, I crave her courtesy so far as to defer her departure until I can have speech with her. You can also tell Baptiste that I'll break his neck if he touches those boxes. The omnibus might also anticipate its usual hour of starting."

Félise departed. Fortinbras lit a cigarette, and holding it betwen his fingers, frowned at it.

"Camille Fargot? What was that spawn of nothingness doing here?"

"I fancy she sent for him," said Martin. "I suppose I had better tell you all about it. I haven't as yet —because it was none of my business."

"Proceed," said Fortinbras, and Martin told him of the famous balance-striking and of Corinna's subsequent behaviour, including last night's retirement into solitude after her mysterious interview with the spawn of nothingness.

"Good," said Fortinbras, when Martin had finished. "Very good. And what had my excellent brother-in-law to say to it?"

"Your excellent brother-in-law," replied Martin, with a smile, "seems to be a very delicate-minded gentleman."

Fortinbras did not press the subject. Waiting for Corinna, they talked of casual things. Martin, now a creature of health and appetite, devoured innumerable rolls and absorbed many bowls of coffee, to the outspoken admiration of Fortinbras. But still Corinna did not come. Then Martin filled a pipe of caporal and, smoking it with gusto, told Fortinbras more of what he had learned at the Café de l'Univers. He expressed his wonder at the people's lack of enthusiasm for their political leaders.

"The adventurer politician is the curse of this country," said Fortinbras. "He insinuates himself into every government. He is out for plunder and his hand is at the throat of patriotic ministers, and he strangles France, while into his pockets through devious channels filters a fine stream of German gold."

"I can't believe it," cried Martin.

"Oh! He isn't a traitor in the sense of being suborned by a foreign Power. He is far too subtle. But he knows what policy will affect the world's exchanges to his profit; and that policy he advocates."

"A gangrene in the body politic," said Martin.

Fortinbras nodded assent. "It will only be the sword of war that will cut it out."

On this, in marched Corinna dressed for travel, with a little embroidered bag slung over her arm. She crossed the room, her head up, her chin in the air, defiant as usual, and shook hands with Fortinbras.

"I've come as you asked," she said. "But let us be quick with the talking, as I've got to catch a train."

"Sit down," said Fortinbras, setting a chair for her.

She obeyed and there the three of them were sitting once more round a table in an empty dining room. But this time it was a cloudy morning in early November, in the heart of France, the distant mountains across the town half-veiled in mist, and a fine rain falling. Gusts of raw air came in through the open terrace window at the end of the room.

"So, my dear Corinna," said Fortinbras, "you have not waited for the second consultation which was part of our programme."

"That's your fault, not mine," said Corinna. "I expected you weeks ago."

"Doubtless. But your expectation was no reason for my coming weeks ago. My undertaking, however, was a reason for your continuing to expect me and being certain that sooner or later I should come."

"All right," said Corinna. "This is mere talk. What do you want with me?"

"To ask you, my dear Corinna," replied Fortinbras, in his persuasive tones, "why you have disregarded my advice?"

"And what was your advice?"

"To do nothing headstrong, violent and lunatic until we met again."

"You should have come sooner. I find I am living now on Martin's charity and the time has come to put all this rubbish aside and go home to my people with my tail between my legs. It's vastly pleasant, I assure you."

"Oh, young woman of little faith!—Why did you not put your trust in me, instead of in callow medical students with ridiculous mothers?"

Corinna flushed crimson and her eyes hardened in anger. "I suppose every gossiping tongue in this horrid little hotel has been wagging. That's why I'm going off now, so that they can wag in my absence."

"But my dear Penthesilea," said Fortinbras soothingly, "why get so angry? Every living soul in this horrid hotel is on your side. They would give their eyes and ears to help you and sympathise with you and shew you that they love you."

"I don't want their sympathy," said Corinna stubbornly.

"Or any human expression of affection or regret? You want just to pay your bill like any young woman in an automobile who has put up for the night and go your way?"

"No. I don't. But I've been damnably treated and I want to get away back to England."

"Who has treated you damnably here?" asked Fortinbras.

"Don't be idiotic," cried Corinna. "Everybody here has been simply angelic to me—even Martin."

"On the whole I think I've behaved fairly decently since we started out together," Martin observed.

"At any rate you act according to the instincts of a gentleman," she admitted.

Fortinbras leaned back in his chair and drew a breath of relief.

"I'm glad to perceive that this hurried departure is not an elopement."

"Elopement!" she echoed. "Do you think I'd——"

Fortinbras checked her with his uplifted hand. "Sh! Would you like me to tell you in a few words everything that has happened?" He bent his intellectual brow upon her and held her with his patient, tired eyes. "Being at the end of your resources, not desiring to share in the vagabond's pool with Martin, and losing faith in my professional pledge, you bethink you of the young popinjay with whom, in your independent English innocence, but to the scandal of his French relatives, you have flaunted it in the restaurants and theatres of Paris. *Il vous a conté fleurette.* He has made his little love to you. All honour and no blame to him. At his age"—he bowed—"I would have done the same. You correspond on the sentimental plane. But in all his correspondence you will find not one declaration in form."

Corinna mechanically peeled off her gloves. Fortinbras drew a whiff of his cigarette. He continued:—

"You think of him as a possible husband : I am frank —it is my profession to be so. But your heart,"—he pointed dramatically to her bosom—"has never had a flutter. You don't deny it. Good. In your extremity, as you think, you send him an urgent telegram, such as no man of human feeling could disregard. He borrows his cousin's husband's motor-car and obeys your summons. You interview him in yonder little fly-blown, suffocating salon. You put your case before him—with no matter what feminine delicacy. He perceives that he is confronted with a claim for a demand in marriage. He draws back. He cannot by means of any quirk or quibble of French law marry you without his parent's consent. This they would never give, having their own well-matured and irrefragable plans. Marriage is as impossible as immediate canonization. 'But,' says he, 'we are both young. We love each other, we shall both be in the *quartier* for time indefinite'—time is never definite, thank God, to youth—'Why should we not set up housekeeping together? I have enough for both—and let the future take care of itself.'"

Corinna rose and looked at him haggardly and clutched him by the shoulder.

"How, in the name of God, do you know that? Who told you? Who overheard that little beast propose that I should go and live with him as his mistress?"

Fortinbras patted the white-knuckled hand and smiled, as he looked up into her tense face. "Do you suppose, my dear child, that I have been the father confessor of half the *Rive Gauche* for twenty years without knowing something of the ways of the *Rive Gauche?* without knowing something, not exactly of international, but say of multi-national codes of social observance, morality, honour, and so forth, and how they clash, correspond and interact? I know the two international forces—yours and Camille Fargot's, converging on the matrimonial point—and with simple certanity I tell you the resultant. It's like a schoolboy's exercise in mathematics."

She freed herself and sat down again dejectedly. Everything had happened as Fortinbras declared. His only omission, to repair which she had not given him time, was the scene of flaming indignation incident to Camille Fargot's dismissal. And his psychology was correct. The young man's charming love-making had flattered her, had indeed awakened foolish hopes; but

she had never cared a button for him.  Now she loathed
him with a devastating hate.  She thrummed with her
fingers on the table.

"What is there left for me to do?"

"Ah, now," said Fortinbras genially, "we're talking
sense.  Now we come to our famous second professional consultation."

"Go ahead then," said Corinna.

"I mentioned the word 'professional,' " Fortinbras
remarked.

Martin laughed and put a ten-franc piece into the
soft open palm.

"I'll pay for both," said he.

"It's like having your fortune told at a fair," said
Corinna.  "But hurry up!" she glanced at her watch.
"As it is, I shan't have time to pay my bill.  Will you
see after it?" she drew from her bag one of the bor-
rowed notes and threw it across to Martin.  "Well, I
am all attention.  I can give you three minutes."

But just then a familiar sound of scrunching wheels
came through the open doors of the vestibule and
dining-room.  She started.

"That's the omnibus going."

"The omnibus gone," said Fortinbras.

"I'll miss my train."

"You will," said Fortinbras.

"My luggage has gone with it."

"It has not," said Fortinbras.  "I gave instructions
that it should not be brought down."

Corinna gasped.  "Of all the cool impertinence——!"  She looked at her watch again.  "And
the beastly thing has started long before its time!"

"At my request," said Fortinbras.  "And now, as
there is no possibility of your getting away from
Brantôme for several hours, perhaps you might, with
profit, abandon your attitude of indignation and listen
to the voice of reason."

"By the way," said Martin, "have you had your *petit déjeuner?*"

"No," said Corinna sullenly.

"Good God!" cried Fortinbras, holding up his hands, "and they let women run about loose!"

# CHAPTER VIII

CORINNA fortified by urgently summoned nourishment lit a cigarette and sarcastically announced her readiness to listen to the oracle. The oracle bowed with his customary benevolence and spoke for a considerable time in florid though unambiguous terms. To say that Corinna was surprised by the proposal which he set before her would inadequately express her indignant stupefaction. She sat angry, with reddened cheek-bones and tightly screwed lips, perfectly silent, letting the wretched man complete his amazing pronouncement before she should annihilate him. He was still pronouncing, however, when Bigourdin appeared at the door. Fortinbras broke off in the middle of a sentence and called him into the room.

"My good Gaspard," said he, in French, for Bigourdin knew little English, "I am suggesting to mademoiselle a scheme for her perfect happiness of which I have reason to know you will approve. Sit down and join our conclave."

"I approve of everything in advance," said the huge man, with a smile.

"Then I suppose you're aware of this delicious scheme?" she asked.

"Not at all," said he; "but I have boundless confidence in my brother-in-law."

"His idea is that I should enter your employment as a kind of forewoman in your *fabrique*."

"But that is famous!" exclaimed Bigourdin, with a sparkle in his eyes. "It could only enter into that wise head yonder. The trade is getting beyond Félise and

myself.   Sooner or later I must get some one, a woman, to take charge of the manufacturing department.
I have told Daniel my difficulties and he comes now
with this magnificent solution.   *Car c'est vraiment
magnifique.*"   He beamed all over his honest face.

"You would have to learn the business from the
beginning," said Fortinbras quickly.   "That would be
easy, as you would have willing instructors, and as
you are not deficient in ordinary intelligence.   You
would rise every day in self-esteem and dignity and
at last find yourself of use in the social organism."

"You propose then," said Corinna, restraining the
annihilatory outburst owing to Bigourdin's presence
and shaking with suppressed wrath, "you propose then
that I should spend the life that God has given me in
making *pâté de foie gras.*"

"Better that than spend it in making bad pictures or
a fool of yourself."

"I've given up painting," Corinna replied, "and every woman makes a fool of herself.   Hence the per-
petuation of the human species."

"In your case, my dear Corinna," said Fortinbras,
"that would be commendable folly."

"You are insulting," she cried, her cheeks aflame.

"*Tiens, tiens!*" said Bigourdin, laying his great hand
on his brother-in-law's arm.

But Fortinbras stroked back his white mane and
regarded them both with leonine serenity.

"To meet a cynical gibe with a retort implying that
marriage and motherhood are woman's commendable
lot cannot be regarded as an insult."

Corinna scoffed: "How do you manage to do it?"

"Do what?"

"Talk like that."

"By means of an education not entirely rudimen-
tary," replied Fortinbras in his blandest tone.   "In the
meanwhile you haven't replied to my suggestion.

Once you said you would like to take life by the throat and choke something big out of it. You still want to do it—but you can't. You know you can't, my dear Corinna. Even the people that can perform this garrotting feat squeeze precious little happiness out of it. Happiness comes to mortals through the most subtle channels. I suggest it might come to you through the liver of an overfed goose."

At Corinna's outburst, Bigourdin's sunny face had clouded over. "Mademoiselle Corinna," said he earnestly, "if you would deign to accept such a position, which after all has in it nothing dishonourable, I assure you from my heart that you would be treated with all esteem and loyalty."

The man's perfect courtesy disarmed her. Of course she was still indignant with Fortinbras. That she, Corinna Hastings, last type of emancipated English womanhood, bent on the expression of a highly important self, should calmly be counselled to bury herself in a stuffy little French town and become a sort of housekeeper in a shabby little French hotel. The suggestion was preposterous, an outrage to the highly-important self, reckoning it a thing of no account. Why not turn her into a chambermaid or a goose-herd at once? The contemptuous assumption fired her wrath. She was furious with Fortinbras. But Bigourdin, who treated the subject from the point of view of one who asked a favour, deserved a civil answer.

"Monsieur Bigourdin," she said with a becoming air of dignity tempered by a pitying smile, "I know that you are everything that is kind, and I thank you most sincerely for your offer, but for private reasons it is one that I cannot accept. You must forgive me if I return to England, where my duty calls me."

"Your duty—to whom?" asked Fortinbras.

She petrified him with a glance. "To myself," she replied.

"In that case there's nothing more to be said," remarked Bigourdin dismally.

"There's everything to be said," declared Fortinbras. "But it's not worth while saying it."

Corinna rose and gathered up her gloves. "I'm glad you realise the fact."

Bigourdin rose too and detained her for a second. "If you would do me the honour of accepting our hospitality for just a day or two"—delicately he included Félise as hostess—"perhaps you might be induced to reconsider your decision."

But she was not be moved—even by Martin who, having smoked the pipe of discreet silence during the discussion, begged her to postpone her departure.

"Anyhow, wait," said he, "until our good counsellor tells us what he proposes to do for me. As we started in together, it's only fair."

"Yes," said Corinna. "Let us hear. What *ordonnance de bonheur* have you for Martin?"

"Are you very anxious to know?" asked Fortinbras.

"Naturally," said Martin, and he added hastily in English, being somewhat shy of revealing himself to Bigourdin: "Corinna can tell you that I've been loyal to you all through. I've had a sort of blind confidence in you. I've chucked everything. But I'm nearly at the end of the financial tether, and something must happen."

"*Sans doute,*" said Fortinbras. So as to bring Bigourdin into range again, he continued in French. "To tell you what is going to happen is one of the reasons why I am here."

"Well, tell us," said Corinna, "I can't stand here all day."

"Won't you sit down, mademoiselle?" said Bigourdin.

Corinna took her vacated chair.

"Aren't you ever going to begin?"

"I had prepared," replied Fortinbras benevolently, "an exhaustive analysis of our young friend's financial, moral and spiritual state of being. But, as you appear to be impatient, I will forego the pleasure of imparting to you this salutary instruction. So perhaps it is better that I should come to the point at once. He is practically penniless. He has abandoned all ideas of returning to his soul-stifling profession. But he must, in the commonplace way of mortals, earn his living. His soul has had a complete rest for three months. It is time now that it should be stimulated to effort that shall result in consequences more glorious than the poor human phenomenon that is, I can predict. My prescription of happiness, as you, Corinna, have so admirably put it, is that Martin shall take the place of the unclean Polydore, who, I understand, has recently been ejected with ignominy from this establishment."

His small audience gasped in three separate and particular fashions.

"*Mon vieux, c'est idiot!*" cried Bigourdin.

"What a career," cried Corinna, with a laugh.

"I never thought of that," said Martin, thumping the table.

Fortinbras rubbed his soft hands together. "I don't deal in the obvious."

"*Mon vieux,* you are laughing at us," said Bigourdin. "Monsieur Martin, a gentleman, a scholar, a professor——!"

"A speck of human dust in search of a soul," said Fortinbras.

"Which he's going to find among dirty plates and dishes," scoffed Corinna.

"In the eyes of the Distributing Department of the Soul Office of Olympus, where every little clerk is a Deuce of a High God, the clatter of plates and dishes is as important as the clash of armies."

Corinna looked at Bigourdin. "He's raving mad," she said.

Fortinbras rose unruffled and laid a hand on Martin's shoulder. "My excellent friend and disciple," said he, "let us leave the company of these obscurantists, and seek enlightenment in the fresh air of heaven."

Whereupon he led the young man to the terrace and walked up and down discoursing with philosophical plausibility while his white hair caught by the gusty breeze streamed behind like a shaggy meteor.

Bigourdin, who had remained standing, sat down again and said apologetically:

"My brother-in-law is an oddity."

"I believe you," assented Corinna.

There was a short silence. Corinna felt that the time had come for a dignified retirement. But whither repair at this unconscionably early hour? The hotel resembled now a railway station at which she was doomed to wait interminably, and one spot seemed as good as another. So she did not move.

"You have decided then to leave us, Mademoiselle Corinna?" said Bigourdin at last.

"I must."

"Is there no means by which I could persuade you to stay? I desire enormously that you should stay."

Her glance met his and lowered. The tone of his voice thrilled her absurdly. She had at once an impulse to laugh and a queer triumphant little flutter of the heart.

"To make *pâté de foie gras?* You must have unwarrantable faith in me."

"Perhaps, in the end," said he soberly, "it might amuse you to make *pâté de foie gras.* Who knows? All things are possible." He paused for a moment, then bent forward, elbow on table and chin in hand. "This is but a litle hotel in a little town, but in it one might find tranquillity and happiness—*enfin*, the significance of things,—of human things. For I believe that where human beings live and love and suffer and strive, there is an eternal significance beneath the commonplace, and if we grasp it, it leads us to the root of life, which is happiness. Don't you think so, mademoiselle?"

"I suppose you're right," she admitted dubiously, never having taken the trouble to look at existence from the subjective standpoint. Her attitude was instinctively objective.

"I thank you, mademoiselle," said he. "I said that because I want to put something before you. And it is not very easy. I repeat—this is but a little hotel in a little town. I too am but a man of the people, Mademoiselle; but this hotel—my father added to it and transformed it, but it is the same property—this hotel has been handed down from father to son for a hundred years. My great-grandfather, a simple peasant, rose to be *Général de Brigade* in the *Grand Armée* of Napoléon. After Waterloo, he would accept no favour from the Bourbons, and retired to Brantôme, the home of his race, and with his little economies he bought the Hôtel des Grottes, at which he had worked years before as a little *va-nu-pieds*, turnspit, holder of horses—*que sais-je, moi?* Those were days, mademoiselle, of many revolutions of fortune."

"And all that means——?" asked Corinna, impressed, in spite of English prejudice, by the simple yet not inglorious ancestry of the huge innkeeper.

"It means, mademoiselle," said Bigourdin, "that I wish to present myself to you as an honest man. But as I am of no credit, myself, I would like to expose to you the honour of my family. My great grandfather, as I have said, was *Général de Brigade* in the *Grande Armée*. My grandfather, *simple soldat,* fought side by side with the English in the Crimea. My father, Sergeant of Artillery, lost a leg and an arm in the War of 1870. My younger brother was killed in Morocco. For me, I have done my *service militaire*. *Ou fait ce qu'on peut.* It is chance that I am forty years of age and live in obscurity. But my name is known and respected, in all Périgord, mademoiselle——"

"And again—all that means?"

"That if a *petit hôtelier* like me ventures to lay a proposition at the feet of a *jeune fille de famille* like yourself—the *petit hôtelier* wishes to assure her of the perfect *honorabilité* of his family. In short, Mademoiselle Corinne, I love you very sincerely. I can make no phrases, for when I say I love you, it comes from the innermost depths of my being. I am a simple man," he continued very earnestly, and with an air of hope, as Corinna flashed out no repulse, but sat sphinx-like, looking away from him across the room, "a very simple man; but my heart is loyal. Such as I am, Mademoiselle Corinne—and you have had an opportunity of judging—I have the honour to ask you if you will be my wife."

Corinne knew enough of France to realise that all this was amazing. The average Frenchman, whom Bigourdin represented, is passionate but not romantic. If he sets his heart on a woman, be she the angel-eyed spouse of another respectable citizen or the tawdry and naughty little figurante in a provincial company, he does his honest (or dishonest) best to get her. *C'est l'amour,* and there's an end to it. But he envisages marriage from a totally different angle. Far be it from me to say that he does not entertain very sincere and tender sentiments towards the young lady he proposes to marry. But he only proposes to marry a young lady who can put a certain capital into the business partnership which is an essential feature of marriage. If he is attracted towards a damsel of pleasing ways but

devoid of capital, he either behaves like the appalling
Monsieur Camille Fargot, or puts his common sense,
like a non-conducting material, between them, and in
all simplicity, doesn't fall in love with her.  But here
was a manifestation of freakishness.  Here was Bigourdin, man of substance, who could have gone to
any one of twenty families of substance in Périgord
and chosen from it an impeccable and well-dowered
bride—here he was snapping his fingers at French
bourgeois tradition—than which there is nothing more
sacrosanct—putting his common sense into his cap and
throwing it over the windmills, and acting in a manner
which King Cophetua himself, had he been a Frenchman, would have condemned as either unconventional
or insane.

Corinna's English upper middle-class pride had revolted at the suggestion that she should become an em-
ployee in a little bourgeois inn; but her knowledge of
French provincial life painfully quickened by her experience of yesterday assured her that she was the re-
cipient of the greatest honour that lies in the power of
a French citizen to offer.  An English innkeeper daring to propose marriage she would have scorched with
blazing indignation, and the bewildered wretch would
have gone away wondering how he had mistaken for
an angel such a Catherine-wheel of a woman.  But
against Bigourdin, son of other traditions so secure in
his integrity, so delicate in his approach, so intensely
sincere in his appeal, she could find within her not
a spark of anger.  All conditions were different.  The
plane of their relations was different.  She would never
have confessed to a flirtation with an English innkeeper.  Besides, she had a really friendly feeling for
Bigourdin, something of admiration.  He was so big,
so simple, so genuine, so intelligent.  In spite of Martin's complaint that she could not realise the spirit of
modern France, her shrewd observation had missed

little of the moral and spiritual phenomena of Brantôme. She was well aware that Bigourdin, *petit ho-
têlier* that he was, stood for many noble ideals outside
her own narrow horizon. She respected him; she also
derived feminine pleasure from his small mouth and
the colour of his eyes. But the possibility of marrying
him had never entered her head. She had not the remotest intention of marrying him now. The proposal
was grotesque. As soon as she got clear of the place
she would throw back her head and roar with laughter
at it; a gleeful little devil was already dancing at the
back of her brain. For the moment, however, she did
not laugh: on the contrary a queer thrill again ran
through her body, and she felt a difficulty in looking
him in the face. After having thrown herself at a
man's head yesterday only to be spurned, her outraged
spirit found solace in having to-day another man sup-
pliant at her feet. Of his sincerity there could be no
possible question. This big, good man loved her. For
all her independent ways and rackety student experiences, no man before had come to her with the loyalty
of deep love in his eyes, no man had asked her to be
his wife. Absurd as it all was, she felt its flattering
deliciousness in every fibre of her being.

"*Eh bien,* Mademoiselle Corinne, what do you answer?" asked Bigourdin, after a breathless silence during which, with head bent forward over the table, she
had been nervously fiddling with her gloves.

"You are very kind, Monsieur Bigourdin. I never
thought you felt like that towards me," she said falter-
ingly, like any well-brought-up school-girl. "You
should have told me."

"To have expressed my feelings before, Mademoiselle, would have been to take advantage of your position under my roof."

Suddenly there came an unprecedented welling of
tears in her eyes, and a lump in her throat. She sprang

to her feet and with rare impulsiveness thrust out her hand.

"Monsieur Bigourdin, you are the best man I have ever met. I am your friend, your very great friend. But I can't marry you. It is impossible."

He rose too, holding her and put the eternal question.

"But why?"

"You deserve a wife who loves you. I don't love you. I never could love you"—and then from the infinite spaces of loneliness there spread about her soul a frozen desolation, and she stood as one blasted by Polar wind—"I shall never love a man all my life long. I am not made like that."

And she seemed to shrivel in his grasp and, flitting between the snow-clad tables like a wraith, was gone.

"*Bigre!*" said Bigourdin, sitting down again.

Soon afterwards, Fortinbras and Martin, coming in from the terrace, found him sprawling over the table a monumental mass of dejection. But, full of their own conceits, they did not divine his misery. Fortinbras smote him friendly wise on his broad back and aroused him from lethargy.

"It is all arranged, *mon vieux* Gaspard," he cried heartily. "I have been pouring into awakening ears all the divine distillations of my philosophy. I have initiated him into mysteries. He is a neophyte of whom I am proud."

Bigourdin, in no mood for allusive hyperbole, shook himself like a great dog.

"What kind of imbecility are you talking?"

"The late Polydore——" Fortinbras began.

"Ah! Finish with it, I beg you," interrupted Bigourdin, with an unusual air of impatience.

"It isn't a joke, I assure you," said Martin. "I have come to the end of my resources. I must work. You

will, sooner or later have to fill the place of Polydore.
Give me the wages of Polydore and I am ready to fill
it.  I could not be more incapable, and perhaps I am
a little more intelligent."

"It is serious?"

."As serious as can be."

Bigourdin passed his hand over his face.  "I went
to sleep last night in a commonplace world, I wake up
this morning to a fantastic universe in which I seem
to be a leaf, like those outside"—he threw a dramatic
arm—"driven by the wind.  I don't know whether I
am on my head or my heels.  Arrange things as seems
best to you."

"You accept me then as waiter in the Hôtel des
Grottes?"

"*Mon cher,*" said Bigourdin, "in the state of upheaval in which I find myself I accept everything."

The upheaval or rather overthrow—for he used the
word "*bouleversement*"—of the big man was evident.
He sat the dejected picture of defeat.  No man in the
throes of sea-sickness ever cared less what happened
to him.  Fortinbras looked at him shrewdly and his
thick lips formed themselves into a noiseless whistle.
Then he exchanged a glance with Martin, who suddenly conjectured the reason of Bigourdin's depression.

"She ought to be spanked," said he in English.

Fortinbras beamed on him.  "You do owe something
to me, don't you?"

"A lot," said Martin.

Félise, her face full of affairs of high importance
ran into the *salle-à-manger*.

"*Mon Oncle,* le Père Didier sends word that he has
decided not to kill his calf till next week.  What shall
we do?"

"We'll eat asparagus," Bigourdin replied and lumbered out into the November drizzle.

Three pairs of wondering eyes sought among themselves a solution of this enigmatic utterance.

*"Mais qu'est-ce que cela veut dire?"* cried Félise, with pretty mouth agape.

"It means, my child," said Fortinbras, "that your uncle, with a philosopher's survey of the destiny of the brute creation, refuses to be moved either to ecstatic happiness or to ignoble anger by the information that the life of the obscure progeny of a bull and a cow has been spared for seven days. For myself I am glad. So is our tender-hearted Martin. So are you. The calf has before him a crowded week of frisky life. Send word to Père Didier that we are delighted to hear of his decision and ask him to crown the calf with flowers and send him along to-day for afternoon tea."

He smiled and waved a dismissing hand. Félise, laughing, kissed him on the forehead and tripped away, having little time to spare for pleasantry.

The two men smoked in silence for some time. At last Fortinbras, throwing the butt end of his cigarette into Corinna's coffee-bowl, rose, stretched himself and yawned heartily.

"Having now accomplished my benevolent purpose," said he, "I shall retire and take some well-earned repose. In the meanwhile, Monsieur Polydore Martin, you had better enter upon your new duties."

So Martin, after he had procured a tray and an apron from the pantry, took off his coat, turned up his shirt-sleeves and set to work to clear away the breakfast things.

# CHAPTER IX

BEHOLD Martin, the professor, transformed into the perfect waiter—perfect, at least, in zeal, manner and habiliment. His dress suit, of ancient cut but practically unworn, gave the *salle-à-manger* an air of startling refinement and prosperity. At first Bigourdin, embarrassed by the shifting of the relative position, had deprecated this outer symbol of servitude. A man could wait in a lounge suit just as well as in a tail-coat—a proposition which Fortinbras vehemently controverted. He read his perplexed brother-in-law a lecture on the psychology of clothes. They had a spiritual significance, bringing subjective and objective into harmony. A judge could not devote his whole essence to the administration of justice if he were conscious of being invested in the glittering guise of a harlequin. If Martin wore the tweeds of the tourist he would feel inharmonious with his true waiter-self, and therefore could not wait with the perfect waiter's spiritual deftness. Besides, he had not counselled his disciple to wait as an amateur. The way of the amateur was perdition. No, when Martin threw his napkin under his left arm, he should flick a bit of his heart into its folds, like a true professional.

"Arrange it as you like," said the weary Bigourdin.

Fortinbras arranged and Martin became outwardly the perfect waiter. Of the craft itself he had much to learn, chiefly under the guidance of Bigourdin and sometimes under the shy instruction of Félise. Its many calls on intelligence and bodily skill surprised him. To balance a piled-up tray on one bent-back hand required the art of a juggler. He practised for days with a trayful of bricks before he trusted himself with plates and dishes. By means of this exercise his arm became muscular. He discovered that the long, grave step of the professor—especially when he bore a load of eatables—did not make for the perfect waiter's celerity. He acquired the gentle arts of salad making and folding napkins into fantastic shapes. Never handy with his fingers, and, like most temperate young men in London lodgings, unaccustomed to the corkscrew, he found the clean prestidigitation of cork-drawing a difficult accomplishment. But he triumphed eventually in this as in all other branches of his new industry. And he liked it. It amused and interested him. It was work of which he could see the result. The tables set before the meal bore testimony to his handicraft. Never had plate been so polished, cutlery so lustrous, glass so transparent in the hundred years history of the Hôtel des Grottes. And when the guests assembled it was a delight to serve them according to organised scheme and disarm criticism by demonstration of his efficiency. He rose early and went to bed late, tired as a draught-dog and slept the happy sleep of the contented human.

Bigourdin praised him, but shrugged his shoulders. "What you are doing it for, *mon ami,* I can't imagine."

"For the good of my soul," laughed Martin, "and in order to attain happiness."

"Our good friends the English are a wonderful race," said Bigourdin, "and I admire them enormously, but there's not one of them who isn't a little bit mad."

To the coterie of the Café de l'Univers, however, he gave a different explanation altogether of Professor Martin's descent in the social scale. The Professor, said he, had abandoned the *professoriat* for the more lucrative paths of commerce and had decided to open a hotel in England, where every one knew the hotels were villainous and provided nothing for their clients but overdone bacon and eggs and raw beef-steaks. The Professor, more enlightened than his compatriots, was apprenticing himself to the business in the orthodox Continental fashion. As the substantial Gaspard Bigourdin himself, son of the late equally substantially, although one-armed and one-legged Armédée Bigourdin, had, to the common knowledge of Brantôme, served as scullion, waiter, *sous-chef de cuisine, sous-maître d'hôtel,* and bookkeeper at various hotels in Lyons, in order to become the *bon hôtelier* that he was, his announcement caused no sensation whatever. The professor of the *Ecole Normale* bewailed his own chill academic lot and proclaimed Monsieur Martin an exceedingly lucky fellow.

"But, *mon cher patron,* it isn't true what you have said at the Café de l'Univers," protested Martin, when Bigourdin told him of the explanation.

Bigourdin waved his great arm. "How am I to know it isn't true? How am I to get into the English minds of you and my *farceur* of a brother-in-law so as to discover why you arrive as an honoured guest at my hotel and then in the wink of an eye become the waiter of the establishment? What am I to say to our friends? They wouldn't care a hang (*ils se ficheraient pas mal*) for your soul. If you are to continue to mix with them on terms of equality they must have an explanation, *nom de Dieu,* which they can understand."

"I never dreamed," said Martin, "of entering the circle at the Café again."

"*Mais, j'y ai pensé, moi, animal!*" cried Bigourdin. "Because you have the fantasy of becoming my waiter, are you any less the same human being I had the pleasure of introducing to my friends?"

And then, perhaps for the first time, Martin appreciated his employer's fine kindness and essential loy-

alty.  It would have been quite easy for the innkeeper
to dismiss his waiter from the consideration of the
hierarchy of Brantôme as a mad Englishman, an adventurer, not a professor at all, but a broken-down
teacher of languages giving private lessons—an
odd-job instructor who finds no respect in highly cen-
tralised, bureaucratic France; but the easy way was
not the way of Gaspard Bigourdin.  So Martin, driven
by *force majeure,* lent himself to the pious fraud and,
when the evening's work was done, divested himself
of his sable panoply of waiterdom and once more took
his place in the reserved cosy corner of the Café de
l'Univers.

The agreeable acidity in his life which he missed
when Corinna, graciously dignified, had steamed off
by the night train, he soon discovered in the pursuit
of his new avocation.  Euphémie, the cook, whose sur-
reptitious habits of uncleanliness carefully hidden from
Félise, but unavoidably patent to an agonised Martin,
supplied as much sourness as his system required.  She
would not take him seriously and declared her antipathy to *un monsieur* in her kitchen.  To bring about
an *entente cordiale* was for Martin an education in
diplomacy.  The irritability of a bilious commercial
traveller, poisoned by infected nourishment at his last
house of entertainment—the reason invariably given
for digestive misadventure—so that his stomach was
dislocated, often vented itself on the waiter serving an
irreproachable repast at the Hôtel des Grottes.  The
professional swallowing of outraged feelings also gave
a sub-acid flavour to existence.  Motorists on the
other hand, struck by his spruceness and polite demeanour, administered pleasant tonic in the form of
praise.  They also bestowed handsome tips.

These caused him some misgiving.  A gentleman
could be a waiter or anything you pleased, so long as
it was honest, and remain a gentleman: but could he

take tips? Or rather, having taken tips, was it consonant with his gentility to retain them? Would it
not be nobler to hand them over to Baptiste or
Euphémie? Bigourdin, appealed to, decided that it
would be magnificent but would inevitably disorganise
these excellent domestics. Martin suggested the *Assistance Publique* or the church poor-box.

"I thought," said Bigourdin, "you became a waiter
in order to earn your living?"

"That is so," replied Martin.

"Then," said Bigourdin, "earn it like a waiter.
Suppose I were the manager of a Grand Hotel and
gave you nothing at all—as it is your salary is not that
of a prince—how would you live? You are a serv-
ant of the public. The public pays you for your services. Why should you be too proud to accept payment?"

"But a tip's a tip," Martin objected.

"It is good money," said Bigourdin. "Keep your
fine five-franc pieces in your pocket and *elles feront des
petits,* and in course of time you will build with them
an hotel on the Côte d'Azur."

In a letter to Corinna, Martin mentioned the disquieting problem. Chafing in her crowded vicarage
home she offered little comfort. She made the sweeping statement that whether he kept his tips or not, the
whole business was revolting. He wrote to Fortinbras. The Dealer in Happiness replied on a postcard: "Will you never learn that a sense of humour
is the beginning and end of philosophy?"

After which, Martin, having schooled himself to the
acceptance of *pourboires,* learned to pocket them with
a professional air and ended by regarding them as
part of the scheme of the universe. As the heavens
rained water on the thirsty fields, so did clients shower
silver coins on hungry waiters. How far, as yet, it
was good for his soul he could not determine. At any

rate, in his mild, unambitious way, he attained the lower rungs of happiness. I do not wish it to be understood that if he had entered as a stranger, say, the employment of the excellent proprietor of the excellent Hôtel de Commerce at Périgueux, he would have found the same contentment of body and spirit. The alleviations of the Hôtel des Grottes would have been missing. His employer, while acknowledging his efficiency still regarded him as an eccentric professor, and apart from business relations treated him as friend and comrade. The notables of the town accepted him as an equal. To the cave-dwellers and others of the proletariat with whom he had formed casual acquaintance, he was still "Monsieur Martin," greeted with the same shade of courteous deference as before, although the whole population of Brantôme knew of his social metamorphosis. Wherever he went, in his walks abroad, he met the genial smile and raised hat. He contrasted it all with the dour unwelcome of the North London streets. There he had always felt lost, a drab human item of no account. Here he had an identity, pleasantly proclaimed. So would a sensitive long-sentence Convict, B 2278, coming into the world of remembering men, rejoice that he was no longer a number, but that intensely individual entity Bill Smith, recognised as a lover of steak-and-kidney pudding. As a matter of fact, he seldom heard his surname. The refusal of Bigourdin's organs of speech to grapple with the Saxon "Overshaw" has already been remarked upon. From the very first Bigourdin decreed that he should be "Monsieur Martin"—Martin pronounced French fashion—and as "Monsieur Martin" he introduced him to the Café de l'Univers, and "Monsieur Martin" he was to all Brantôme. But of what importance is a surname, when you are intimately known by your Christian name to all of your acquaintance? Who in the world save his mother and the

Hastings family had for dreary ages past called him "Martin"? Now he was "Martin"—or "Monsieur Martin"—a designation which agreeably combined familiarity with respect—to all who mattered in Périgord. It must be remembered that it was an article of faith among the good Brantômois that, in Périgord, only Brantôme mattered.

"You people are far too good to me," he remarked one day to Bigourdin. "It is a large-hearted country."

"Did I not say, my friend," replied Bigourdin, "that Périgord would take you to her bosom?"

And then there was Félise, who in her capacity of task-mistress called him peremptorily "Martin"; but out of official hours nearly always prefixed the "Monsieur." She created an atmosphere of grace around the plates and dishes, her encouraging word sang for long afterwards in his ears. With a tact only to be found in democratic France she combined the authority of the superior with the intellectual inferior's respect. Apparently she concerned herself little about his change of profession. Her father, the all-wise and all-perfect, had ordained it; her uncle, wise and perfect, had acquiesced; Martin, peculiarly wise and almost perfect, had accepted it with enthusiasm. Who was she to question the doings of inscrutable men?

They met perforce more often than during his guesthood, and, their common interests being multiplied, their relations became more familiar. They had reached now the period of the year's stress, that of the great *foie gras* making when fatted geese were slain and the masses of swollen liver were extracted and the huge baskets of black warty truffles were brought in from the beech forests where they had been hunted for by pigs and dogs. Martin, like every one else in the household, devoted all his spare moments to helping in the steaming kitchen supervised by a special chef, and in the long, clean-smelling work-room where rows of white-aproned girls prepared and packed the delectable compound. Here Bigourdin presided in brow-knit majesty and Félise bustled a smiling second in command.

"It is well to learn everything," she said to Martin. "Who knows when you may be glad to have been taught how to make *pâté de foie gras?*"

So Martin, though such a course was not contemplated in his agreement with the Hôtel des Grottes, received much instruction from her in the delicate craft, which was very pleasant indeed. And the girls looked on at the lessons after the way of their kind and exchanged glances one with another, and every one, save perhaps Bigourdin, who had not yet recovered his serenity overclouded by Corinna's rejection of his suit, was exceedingly contented.

And then, lo and behold, into this terrestrial paradise strayed the wandering feet of Lucien Viriot.

Not that Lucien was unexpected. His father, Monsieur Viriot, *marchand de vins en gros,* and one of the famous circle at the Café de l'Univers, had for the past month or two nightly proclaimed the approaching release of the young man from military service. Martin had heard him. Bigourdin on their walks home together had dilated on the heaven-decreed union of the two young people and the loneliness of his lot. Where would he find, at least, such a *ménagère* as Félise?

"It's a pity Corinna hadn't any sense," said Martin on one of these occasions.

Bigourdin heaved a mighty sigh. "Ah, *mon vieux!*" said he by way of answer. The sigh and the "Ah, *mon vieux!*" were eloquent of shattered ideals.

"There is always Madame Thuillier who used to help me when Félise was little," he continued after a while, meditatively. "She has experience, but she is as ugly as a monkey, the poor woman!"

Whereupon he sighed again, leaving Martin in doubt as to the exact position he intended the ill-favoured lady to occupy in his household.

Anyhow, Martin was forewarned of the ex-war-rior's advent. So was Félise. "But I cannot leave you, *mon oncle*," she cried in dismay. "What would become of you? Who would mend your linen? What would become of the hotel? What would become of the fabrique?"

"Bah!" said he, snapping his fingers at such insignificant considerations. "There is always the *brave* Madame Thuillier."

"But I thought you detested her—as much as you can detest anybody."

"You are mistaken, *mon enfant*," replied Bigourdin. "I have a great regard for her. She has striking qualities. She is a woman of ripe age and much common sense."

Which shows how double-tongued men may be.

"*C'est une vieille pimbêche!*" cried Félise.

"*Tais-toi*," said Bigourdin severely. For a "*vieille pimbêche*" means, at the very least, a horrid old tabby with her claws out.

"I won't be silent," laughed Félise rebelliously. "*C'est une vieille pimbêche,* and I'm not going to leave you to her. I don't want to leave you. I don't want to marry."

"That is what all little girls say," replied Bigourdin. "But when you see Lucien return, *joli garçon,* holding his head in the air like a brave little soldier of France, and looking at you out of his honest eyes, you will no longer tell me, '*Je ne veux pas me marier, mon oncle.*'"

She laughed at his outrageous mimicry of a modest little girl's accent.

"It's true all the same," she retorted. "I don't want

to marry anybody, and Lucien after having seen all the pretty girls of Paris won't want to marry me."

"If he doesn't——!" cried Bigourdin threateningly. "If he dares——!"

"Well, what then?" asked Félise.

"I'll have a serious conversation with his father," declared Bigourdin.

Thus both Martin and Félise, as I have said, were forewarned. Yet neither took much notice of the warning. Martin had been aware, all along, of the destiny decreed for her by the omnipotent Triumvirate consisting of her uncle, the bon Dieu and Monsieur Viriot, and, regarding her as being sealed to another, had walked with Martin-like circumspection (subject, in days not long since past, for Corinna's raillery) along the borderline of the forbidden land of tenderness. But this judicious and conscientious skirting had its charm. I would have you again realise that the eternal feminine had entered his life only in the guise: first, of the kissed damsel who married the onion-loving plumber; secondly, of Corinna, by whose "Bo!" he had been vastly terrified until he had taken successfully to saying "Bo!" himself, a process destructive of romantic regard; and thirdly, of Félise, a creature—he always remembered Fortinbras's prejudiced description —"like one of the wild flowers from which Alpine honey is made," and compact of notable, gentle and adorable qualities. Naturally, of the three, he preferred Félise. Félise, for her part, like the well brought up damsel of the French bourgeoisie, never allowed her eyelids to register the flutterings of the heart which the mild young Englishman's society set in action. She scarcely admitted the flutterings to herself. Possibly, if he had been smitten with a fine frenzy of love-making, she would have been shocked. But as he shewed respectful gratification at being allowed to consort with her and gratitude for her little bits of sympathetic understanding, and as she found she could talk with him more spontaneously than with any other young man she had ever met, she sought rather than avoided the many daily opportunities for pleasant intercourse. And there was not the least harm in it; and the bogey of a Lucien (whom she had liked well enough, years ago in a childish way) was still hundreds of miles from Brantôme. In fact they entered upon as pretty a Daphnis and Chloe idyll as ever was enacted by a pair of innocents.

Then, one fine day, as I have stated, in swaggered Lucien Viriot, ex-cuirassier, and spoiled the whole thing.

His actual hour of swaggering into Martin's ken was unexpected—by Martin, at any rate. He was playing backgammon with the Professor of the *Ecole Normale* in the midst of elders discussing high matters of local politics, when all of a sudden an uproar arose among these grave and reverend seniors, clapping of hands and rattling on tables, and Martin, looking up from his throw of the dice, perceived the stout, square-headed, close-cropped Monsieur Viriot, *marchand de vins en gros,* his eyes sparkling and his cheeks flushed above his white moustache and imperial, advancing from the café door, accompanied by his square-headed, close-cropped, sturdy, smiling, swaggeringly-sheepish, youthful replica. And when they reached the group, the young man bowed punctiliously before grasping each outstretched hand; and every one called him *"mon brave,"* to which he replied *"bien aimable";* and Monsieur Viriot presented him formally—*"mon fils qui vient de terminer son service militaire"*—to Monsieur Beuzot, *Professor à l'Ecole Normale,* a newcomer to Brantôme, and to Monsieur Martin, *ancien professeur anglais.* Whereupon Monsieur Lucien Viriot declared himself enchanted at meeting the two learned gentlemen, and the two learned gentlemen re-

ciprocated the emotion of enchantment. Then amid
scuffling of chairs and eager help of waiters, room was
made for Monsieur Viriot and Monsieur Lucien; and
the proprietor of the café, Monsieur Cazensac, swarthy,
portly and heavy-jowled, a Gascon from Agen, who,
if the truth were known took the good, easy folk of
Périgord under his protection, came up from behind
the high bottle-armamented counter, where Madame
Cazensac, fat and fair, prodigally beamed on the
chance of a ray reaching the hero of the moment—
which happened indeed before Cazensac could get in a
word, and brought Lucien to his feet in a splendid
spread of homage to the lady—Monsieur Cazensac, I
say, came up and grasped Lucien by the hand and
welcomed him back to the home of his fathers. He
turned to Monsieur Viriot.

"Monsieur orders——?"

*"Du vin de champagne."*

Happy land of provincial France where you order
champagne as you order brandy and soda and are contented when you get it. There is no worry about brand
or vintage or whether the wine is *brut* or *extra-sec*.
You just tell the good landlord to bring you champagne
and he produces the sweet, sticky, frothy, genuine
stuff, and if you are a Frenchman, you are perfectly
delighted. It is champagne, the wine of feasts, the
wine of ceremony, the wine of ladies, the wine of
toasts—*Je lève mon verre*. If the uplifted glass is not
beaded with bubbles winking at the brim, what
virtue is there in the uplifting? It is all a symbolical
matter of sparkle. . . . So, at the Café de l'Univers,
Monsieur Cazensac disappeared portentously, and a
few moments later re-appeared ever so much more portentously, followed by two waiters, one bringing the
foot-high sacred glasses, the other the uncorked bottles labelled for all who wished to know what they
were drinking: "Grand Champagne d'Ay," with the

vine-proprietor's name inconspicuously printed in the right-hand bottom corner. All, including Monsieur Cazensac, clinked foaming glasses with Lucien, and, after they had sipped in his honour, they sipped again to the cries of *"Vive l'Armée"* and *"Vive la France,"* whereupon they all settled down comfortably again to the enjoyment of replenished goblets of the effervescing syrup.

Martin looked with some envy at the young man who sat flushed with his ovation and twisted his black moustache to the true cuirassier's angle, yet bore himself modestly among his elders. Willing and gay of heart he had given the years of his youth to the service of his country; when the great struggle should come —and all agreed it was near—he would be one of the first to be summoned to defend her liberty, and willing and gay of heart he would ride to his death. And now, in the meanwhile, he had returned to the little square hole in France that had been ordained for him (little square peg) before he was born, and was to be reserved for him as long as his life should last. And Martin looked again at the chosen child of destiny, and this time with admiration, for he knew him to be a man; a man of the solid French stock that makes France unshakable, of the stock that in peace may be miserly of its pence, but in war is lavish of its blood. "I am not that young fellow's equal," thought Martin humbly; and he felt glad that he had not betrayed Bigourdin's trust with regard to Félise. What kind of a wretch would he have been to set himself up as a rival to Lucien Viriot? Bigourdin had been right in proclaiming the marriage as arranged by the bon Dieu. He loved Félise—who knowing her did not? But he loved her in brotherly fashion and could reconcile it to his heart to bestow her on one so worthy. And all this without taking into account the sentiments of Félise. Her heart, in military phrase, was a *ville ouverte.* Lucien had but to march in and take it.

After a while Lucien, having looked about the café, rose and went from table to table where sat those citizens who, by reason of lowlier social status or personal idiosyncrasies, had not been admitted into the Inner Coterie of Notables, and greeted old acquaintances. Monsieur Viriot then caught Martin's eye and lifted his glass again.

"*A votre santé,* Monsieur Martin."

Martin bowed. "*A la vôtre, monsieur!*"

"I hope that you and my son will be good friends. It is important that the youth of our two countries, so friendly, so intimately bound, should learn to know and appreciate each other; especially when one of them, like yourself, has the power of translating England into terms of France."

And with the courteous simplicity of a grey, square-headed, close-cropped *marchand de vins en gros,* he lifted his glass again.

"*A l'Entente Cordiale.*"

When Lucien returned to the circle, his father reintroduced him to Martin.

"In fact," he concluded, "here is an Englishman who not only speaks French like you and me, but eats truffles and talks the idiom of the quarrymen and is qualifying himself to be a good Périgordin."

It was charmingly said. The company hummed approval.

"*C'est bien vrai,*" said Bigourdin.

Lucien again bowed. He would do himself the honour of presenting himself at monsieur's hotel. Monsieur was doubtless staying at the Hôtel des Grottes.

"Monsieur Bigourdin has taken me as a waiter into his service," replied Martin.

"*Ah! Tant mieux!*" exclaimed Lucien, as if the

announcement were the most ordinary one in the world, and shook hands with him heartily.

"Like that, as my father says, one becomes a good Périgordin."

So Martin went home and contentedly to bed. Again a little corner of the earth that he might call his own was offered him in this new land so courteous to, yet so sensitively aloof from the casual Englishman, but on the other hand, so generous and hospitable to the Englishman into whom the spirit of France had entered. Was there here, thought he, the little round hole which he, little round peg, after thirty years of square-holed discomfort, had been pre-ordained to fill? The thought soothed him.

He woke up in the night, worried by some confused dream. In his head stuck the Latin tag: *Ubi bene ibi patria.* He kicked indignantly against the aphorism. It was the infamous philosophy of the Epicurean opportunist. If he had been comfortable in Germany would he regard Germany as his fatherland? A million times no. When you wake up at four o'clock in the morning to a soul-stirring proposition, you think in terms of millions. He was English of the English. His Swiss motherdom was but an accident of begetting. He was of his father's race. Switzerland did not exist in his being as a national influence. English, narrowly, stupidly, proudly, he was and English he would remain to the end of time. To denaturalise himself and become a Frenchman—still less a mere Périgordin—was abhorrent. But to remain an Englishman, and as an Englishman—an obscure and menial Englishman—to be given the freedom of a province of old France was an honour of which any man breathing the breath of life might be justly proud. I can, thought he, in the intense, lunatic clarity of four o'clock in the morning, show France what England stands for. I have a chance of one in a million. I am an Englishman given a home in the France that I am learning to love and to understand, I am a hyphen between the two nations.

Having settled that, he turned over, tucked the bed-clothes well round his shoulders and went soundly to sleep again.

# CHAPTER X

A FEW evenings afterwards Bigourdin gave a
dinner of cereomny to the Viriots—and a dinner of ceremony in provincial France is a very
ceremonious and elaborate affair. All day long there
had been anxious preparations. Félise abandoning
the *fabrique,* toiled assiduously with Euphémie, while
Bigourdin, expert chef like all good hotel-keepers, con-
trolled everything with his master touch. The crazily
ceremonious hour of seven-thirty was fixed upon; not
only on account of its ceremoniousness, but because
by that time the commercial travellers would have finished their meal and melted away. The long middle
table was replaced by a round table prodigally adorned
with flowers and four broad tricolour ribbons, each
like the sash of Monsieur le Maire, radiating from
under a central silver épergne laden with fruit of
which a pineapple was the crown. A bewildering number of glasses of different shapes stood at each place,
to be filled each kind in its separate order with the
wine ordained for each separate course. Martin re-
hearsed the wine service over and over again with a
solemn Bigourdin. As a lieutenant he had the *plongeur* (or washer-up of glass and crockery) from the
Café de l'Univers, an earnest neophyte tense with the
excitement of practising a higher branch of his profession.

Hosts and guests were ceremoniously attired; Bigourdin and the elder Viriot suffocated in tightly
buttoned frock-coats of venerable and painful fit;
Lucien, more dashing, wore a morning coat (last
cry of Bond Street) acquired recently from the "High

Life" emporium in Paris; all three men retained yellow dogskin gloves until they sat down to table. Madame Viriot, stout and placid, appeared in her black silk dress and an old lace collar and her very best hat with her very best black ostrich feather secured by the old rose-diamond buckle, famous throughout the valley of the Dordogne, which had belonged to her great-great-grandmother; and, lastly, Félise wore a high-necked simple frock of dazzling whiteness which might have shewn up her delicate dark colouring had not her cheeks been inordinately pale.

Bigourdin had Madame Viriot on his right, Monsieur Viriot on his left, and Félise sat between Monsieur Viriot and Lucien. Every one was most ceremoniously polite. It was *"mon cher* Viriot," and *"mon cher* Bigourdin," and the formal *"vous,"* instead of the *"mon vieux"* and the *"tu"* of the café and of ordinary life; also, *"chère madame,"* and "Monsieur Lucien" and *"ma nièce."* And although from childhood Félise and Lucien had called each other by their Christian names, it was now "monsieur" and "mademoiselle" between them. You see, marriage is in France a deuce of a ceremony which begins months before anybody dreams of setting the wedding bells a-ringing. This dinner of ceremony was the first scene of the first act of the elaborate drama which would end on the curtain being run down to the aforesaid wedding-bells. Really, when one goes into the question, and considers all the barbed wire entanglements that French law and custom interpose between two young people who desire to become man and wife, one not only wonders how any human pair can go through the ordeal and ever marry at all, but is profoundly convinced that France is the most moral country on the face of the globe. As a matter of fact, it is.

It was a long meal of many courses. Martin, aided

by the *plongeur,* acquitted himself heroically.  Manners professional and individual, and also the strain of service prevented him from attending to the conversation.  But what he could not avoid overhearing did not impress him with its brilliance.  It was a self-conscious little company.  It threw about statistics as to the state of the truffle crop; it listened to Lucien's modest anecdotes of his military career; it decided that Parisians were greatly to be pitied in that fate compelled them to live in Paris instead of Brantôme.  Even the flush of good cheer failed to inspire it with heartiness.  For this perhaps the scared unresponsiveness of one of the chief personages was responsible.

"Are you fond of dogs, mademoiselle?" asked Lucien, valiant in small talk.

*"Oui, monsieur,"* replied Félise.

"Have you any now, mademoiselle?"

*"Non, monsieur,"* replied Félise.

"The beautiful poodle that was so clever is dead, I believe," remarked Madame Viriot in support of her son.

*"Oui, madame,"* replied Félise.

However alluring to the young Frenchman about to marry may be timid innocence with downcast eyes, yet, when it is to such a degree monosyllabic, conversation does not sparkle.  Martin, accustomed to her tongue wagging charmingly, wondered at her silence.  What more attractive companion could she desire than the *beau sabreur* by her side?  And she ate next to nothing.  When she was about to decline a *bécasse au fumet,* as to the success of which Euphémie's heart was beating like a sledge-hammer, he whispered in her ear,

"Just a little bit.  Do."

And as she helped herself, he saw the colour mount to her neck.  He felt quite pleased at having prevailed on her to take nourishment.

What happened after the meal in the private salon, where Félise, according to sacred rite, served coffee and liqueurs, Martin did not know. He was too busy with Euphémie and the chambermaid and Baptiste and the *plongeur* in cleaning up after the banquet. Besides, as the waiter of the establishment, what should he have been doing in that ceremonious gathering?

When the work was finished and a concluding orgy on broken meats and half emptied bottles had been temperately concluded, and Euphémie for the hundredth time had been informed of the exact appreciation which each particular dish had received from Monsieur and Madame Viriot—"young people, you see," she explained, "have their own affairs and they see everything rose-coloured, and you could give them boiled horse-liver and they wouldn't know the difference between that and *ris-de-veau à l'Impériale;* it doesn't matter what you put into the stomachs of children; but with old, serious folks, it is very important. I made the stomach of Monsieur Viriot the central idea of my dinner—I have known the stomach of Monsieur Viriot for twenty years—also that of Madame, for old ladies, *voyez-vous,* know more than you think"—and when the weary and zealous servants had gone their separate ways, Martin locked up, and, escaping from the generous atmosphere of the kitchen, entered the dimly lit vestibule with the idea of smoking a quiet cigarette before going to bed. There he found Bigourdin, sprawling his great bulk over the cane-seated couch.

"Did things go all right?" he asked.

"Wonderfully. Everybody dined well. They can go to the *ban* and *arrière-ban* of their friends and relations and say that there is not such a *cuisine* in Périgord as at the Hôtel des Grottes. And the service was excellent. Not the smallest hitch. I congratulate you and thank you, *mon ami.* But *ouf!*"—he took a great breath of relief—"I am glad it is over. I was not built for the formalities of society. *Ça vous fatigue!*"

"It's also fatiguing from the waiter's point of view," laughed Martin.

"But it is all necessary when one has a young girl to marry. The father and mother of the young man expect it. It is very complicated. Soon there will be the formal demand in marriage. They will wear gloves—*c'est idiot*—but what would you have? It is the custom. And then there will be a dinner of ceremony at the Viriots'. He has some Chambertin in his cellar, my old friend Viriot—ah, *mon petit* Martin!"—he blew a kiss to the purple goddess beloved of Bacchus and by him melted into each cobwebbed bottle—"It is the only thing that reconciles me to it. Truth to say, one dines abominably at the Viriots. If he does not produce some of that Chambertin, I withdraw the dowry of Félise."

"It's all arranged then?" Martin asked.

"All what?"

"The marriage."

"Without doubt."

"Then Monsieur Lucien has been accepted by Mademoiselle Félise? I mean, he has proposed to her, as we English say?"

"*Mais non!*" cried Bigourdin, with a shocked air. "Lucien is a correctly brought up young man and would not offend the proprieties in that matter. It is not the affair of Lucien and Félise, it is the affair of the two families, the parents; and for Félise I am *in loco parentis*. Propose to Félise! What are you talking about?"

"It all interests me so much," replied Martin. "In England we manage differently. When a man wants to marry a girl, he asks her, and when they have fixed up everything between themselves, they go and announce the fact to their families."

To which Bigourdin made the amazing answer:
*"C'est le phlègme britannique!"*
British phlegm! When a man takes his own un-
phlegmatic way with a maid! Martin could find no
adequate retort. He was knocked into a cocked hat.
He threw away his cigarette and, being very tired,
half stifled a yawn. Bigourdin responded mightily
and rose to his feet.
*"Allons dodo,"* said he. "All this has been terribly
fatiguing."

So fatiguing had it all been that Félise, for the first
time since the chicken-pox and measles of childhood,
remained in her bed the next day. Euphémie, her
personal attendant, found her in the morning a wan
ghost with a splitting headache, and forbade her to
rise. She filled her up with *tilleul,* the decoction of
lime-leaves which in French households is the panacea
for all ills, and, good and comfortable gossip, ex-
tolled, in Gallic hyperbole, the dazzling qualities of
Monsieur Lucien. At last, fever-eyed and desperate,
Félise sat up in bed and pointed to the door.
*"Ma bonne Euphémie, laisse-moi tranquille! Va-
t'en! Fich'-moi la paix!"*
Euphémie gaped in bewilderment. It was as though
a dove had screamed:
"Leave me alone! Go away! Go to Blazes!"
*"Ah, la! la! ma pauvre petite!"* Euphémie knew
not what she was saying, but she went. She went to
Bigourdin and told him that mademoiselle was in
delirium, she had brain-fever, and if he wanted to save
her reason, he must send at once for the doctor. The
doctor came, diagnosed a chill on the vaguest of symptoms, and ordered *soupe à l'huile.* This invalid fare
is a thin vegetable soup with a layer of salad oil floating on the top with the object of making the liquid
slip gratefully down the gullet: the French gullet, be

it understood. Félise, in spite of her lifelong French training, had so much of England lingering in her œsophagus, that it abhorred *soupe à l'huile*. The good doctor's advice failed. She fasted in bed all day, declaring that, headache apart, she was perfectly well, and the following morning, a wraith of herself, arose and went about her ordinary avocations.

"But what is the matter with her?" asked Bigourdin of Martin. "Nothing could have disagreed with her at that abominable dinner, because she didn't eat anything."

As Martin could throw no light on the sudden malady of Félise, Bigourdin lit a cigarette and inhaled a huge puff.

"It needs a woman, *voyez-vous*, to look after a young girl. Men are no good. There are a heap of secrets——" With his arms he indicated Mount Blanc piled on Mount Everest. "I shall be glad when she is well and duly married. Perhaps the approaching betrothal affects her. Women have nerves like that. She is anxious to know the result of the negotiations. At the present moment the Viriots are free to make or make not their demand. It would be good to reassure her a little. What do you think?"

Martin gave utterance to the profound apophthegm: "There is nothing so upsetting as uncertainty."

"That is my idea!" cried Bigourdin. "Pardon me for consulting you on these details so intimate and a little sacred. But you have a clear intelligence and a loyal heart."

So it came to pass that, after *déjeuner*, Bigourdin took Félise into their own primly and plushily furnished salon, and, like an amiable bull in a boudoir, proceeded to smash up the whole of her universe.

"There is no doubt," he proclaimed, "Monsieur and Madame Viriot have dreamed of it for ten years. I give you a dowry—there is no merit in it, because I love you like my own daughter—but I give you a dowry such as there are not many in Périgord. Lucien loves you. He is *bon garçon*. It has never entered his head to think of another woman for his wife. It is all arranged. In two or three days—you must allow for the *convenances*—Monsieur Viriot and Lucien will call on me. So, my dear little angel, do not be afraid."

Félise had listened to this, white-faced and hollow-eyed. "But I don't want to marry Lucien, *mon oncle!*"

"*Comment?* You don't want to marry Lucien?"

"No, *mon oncle.*"

"But——" He swept the air with a protesting gesture.

"I have already told you so," said Félise.

"But, *ma chère petite,* that wasn't serious. It was because you had some stupid and beautiful idea of not deserting me. That is all imbecile. Young people must marry, *sacrebleu!* so that the race is perpetuated, and fathers and mothers and uncles don't count."

"But what has that to do with it, *mon oncle?*" protested Félise. "I find Lucien very charming; but I don't love him. If I loved him, I would marry him. But as I don't love him, I can't marry him."

"But marry him and you will love him," cried Bigourdin, as millions of French fathers and uncles have cried for the last three or four hundred years. "It is very simple. What more do you want than a gallant fellow like Lucien?"

Then, of course, she broke down, and began to cry. Bigourdin, unused to feminine tears, tried to clutch his hair. If it had been longer than half an inch of upstanding bristle, he would have torn it.

"You don't understand, *mon oncle,*" she sobbed, with bowed head. "It is only my mother who can advise me. I must see my mother."

Bigourdin put his arm round the girl's slender

shoulders. "Your mother, my poor Félise, sees nobody."

She raised her head and flashed out: "She sees my father. She lives with him in the same house. Why shouldn't she see me?"

"*Tiens, tiens,* my little Félise," said Bigourdin soothingly. "There is no need for you to consult your mother. Both your father and your mother have a long while ago decided that you should marry Lucien. Do you think I would take a step of which they did not approve?"

"A long while ago is not to-day," sobbed Félise. "I want to talk to my mother."

Bigourdin walked across the salon, with his back to her, and snapped his fingers in peculiar agitation, and muttered below his breath: "*Nom de Dieu, de nom de Dieu, de nom de Dieu!*" Kindest-hearted of mortals though he was, he resented the bottom being knocked out of his scheme of social existence. For years he had looked forward to this alliance with the Viriots. Personally he had nothing to gain: on the contrary, he stood to lose the services of Félise and a hundred thousand francs. But he had set his heart on it, and so had the Viriots. To go to them and say, "My niece refuses to marry your son," would be a slash of the whip across their faces. His failure to bring up a young girl in the proper sentiments would be a disgrace to him in the eyes of the community. He felt hurt, too, because he no longer sufficed her; she wanted her mother; and it was out of the question that she should go to her mother. No wonder he swore to himself softly.

"But, *mon Dieu,*" said he, turning round. "What have you against Lucien?"

Whereupon they went over all the argument again. She did not love Lucien. She didn't want to marry Lucien. She would not marry a man she did not love.

"Then you will die an old maid," said Bigourdin. "An old maid, *figure-toi!* It would be terrible!"

Félise sniffed at such terrors. Bigourdin, in desperation, asked what he was to tell the Viriots. "The truth," said Félise. But what was the truth?

"Tell me, my little Félise," said he, gently, "there is, by chance, no one else?"

Then Félise waxed indignant and routed the unhappy man. She gave him to understand that she was a *jeune fille bien élevée* and was not in the habit of behaving like a kitchenmaid. It was cruel and insulting to accuse her of clandestine love-affairs. And Bigourdin, bound by his honourable conventions, knew that she was justified in her resentment. Again he plucked at his bristles, scared by the spectacle of outraged maidenhood. The tender-eyed dove had become a flashing little eagle. A wilier man than he might have suspected the over-protesting damsel. Womanlike, she pressed her advantage.

"*Mon oncle,* I love you with all my heart, but you are a man and you don't understand."

"That is absolutely true," said he.

"So you see there is only one person I can explain it to, and that is my mother."

Thus she completed the vicious little circle. And again the helpless Bigourdin walked across the salon and turned his back on her and muttered the incantation which brings relief to distracted man. But this time she went up to him and put an arm round his great body and laid her face against his sleeve.

"*Tu sais, je suis bien malheureuse.*"

It was a knife stuck in the honest fellow's heart. He caught her to him and in his turn protested vehemently. He would not allow her to be unhappy. He would cut off his head rather than allow her to be unhappy. He would do anything—his French caution forbade an

offer to send the Viriots packing—anything in reason
to bring the colour back to her white cheeks.

Suddenly he had an inspiration which glowed all
over his broad face and caused him to hold her out at
arms' length and laugh joyously.

"You can't see your mother—but there is your good
Aunt Clothilde. She will be a second mother to you.
A woman so pious and so sympathetic. You will be
able to tell her all your troubles. She has married
a regiment of daughters. What she doesn't know
of young girls isn't worth knowing. You are tired,
you are ill. You need a change, a little holiday. Go
and spend a month with her, and when you come
back we'll see what can be done with regard to Lucien.
I'll write to her now."

And without waiting to hear her demure *"Bien, mon
oncle,"* he escaped to the *bureau* where he should find
the writing materials which did not profane the sacred
primness of the salon, and plunged into correspondence. Félise, left alone, pondered for a moment or
two, with faint wrinkling of her smooth forehead, and
then, sketching a gesture of fatalistic resignation, went
off to the kitchen, where a great special boiling of goose
livers was in progress. On the way she met Martin
carrying a load of porcelain pots. But she passed
him by coldly; and for the rest of the day she scarcely
threw at him a couple of words.

Meanwhile Bigourdin beamed over the letter to his
elder sister Clothilde, a comfortable and almost opulent widow who lived at Chartres. They had not met
for a dozen years, it is true, and she had only once
seen Félise; but the sense of the family is very strong
in France, especially where marriage alliances are concerned, and he had no doubt that she would telegraph,
as requested, and authorise him to entrust Félise to
her keeping. Verily it had been an inspiration. It
was a solution of difficulties. The Viriots had given

signs of an almost indecent hurry, which naturally had scared Félise. A month was a long time. Clothilde was a woman of experience, tact and good sense. She would know how to bring Félise to a reasonable state of mind. If she did not succeed—well—he was not the man to force his little Félise into a distasteful marriage. In any case he had a month's respite.

Having stated his case at length, he went out into the town to post such an important letter at the central *Postes et Télégraphes,* and on the way back, looked in at the shop of the very respectable Madame Chauvet, who, with her two elderly daughters, sold crucifixes and rosaries and books of devotion and candles and all that would supply the devout needs of the religious population. And after a prolonged and courtly conversation, he induced Madame Chauvet, in consideration of their old friendship, her expenses and an honorarium of twenty francs, to undertake the safe convoy of Félise from Brantôme to the house of Madame Robineau, her Aunt Clothilde, at Chartres.

## CHAPTER XI

MADAME ROBINEAU was tall, angular, thin-lipped and devout, and so far as she indulged in social intercourse, loved to mingle with other angular, thin-lipped and devout ladies who belonged to the same lay sisterhood. She dressed in unrelieved black and always wore on her bosom a bronze cross of threatening magnitude. She prayed in the Cathedral at inconvenient hours, and fasted as rigorously as her Confessor, Monsieur l'Abbé Duloup, himself. Monsieur l'Abbé regarded her as one of the most pious women in Chartres. No doubt she was.

But Félise, although a good Catholic in her very simple way, and anxious to win favour by observance of the rules of the solitary household, was wicked enough to wish that her aunt were not quite so pious. In religious matters a wide latitudinarianism prevailed at the Hôtel des Grottes. There, with a serene conscience, one could eat meat on Fridays and crack a mild joke at the expense of the good Saint Peter. But neither forbidden flesh nor jocularity on any subject, let alone on a saint's minor foibles, mitigated the austerities of the perky, wind-swept little house at Chartres. No wonder, thought Félise, Aunt Clothilde had married off a regiment of daughters—four to be exact; it had been an easy matter; she herself would have married any caricature of a man rather than spend her life in an atmosphere so rarefied and so depressing. She pitied her cousins, although, according to her Aunt Clothilde's pragmatical account, they were all doing splendidly and had innumerable babies. By the end of the first week of her visit, she consolidated an

intense dislike to Chartres and everything in it, especially the Cathedral.  Now, it may be thought that
any one who can shake the fist of disapprobation at
the Cathedral of Chartres, is beyond the pale of human
sympathy.  But when you are dragged relentlessly
thither in the icy dark of every winter morning, and
the bitter gloom of every winter evening, to say nothing of sporadic attendances during the daytime, you
may be pardoned if your æsthetic perceptions are ob-
scured by the sense of outrage inflicted on your personal comfort.  To many generations of men the
Cathedral has been a symbol of glories, revelations and
eternities.  In such slanting shafts of light, mystically
hued, the Grail might have been made manifest, the
Sacred Dove might have glided down to the Head of
the Holy One. . . .  But what need to tell of its spiritual wonders and of its mystery, the heart of which
it is given to every suffering man to pluck out according to his own soul's needs?  It was a little tragedy
that to poor Félise the Cathedral symbolised nothing
but an overwhelming tyranny.  She hated every stone
of it, as much as she hated every shiny plank and every
polished chair in her aunt's frigid salon.  Even the
streets of Chartres repelled her by their bleakness.
They lacked the smiling homeliness of Brantôme;
and the whole place was flatter than the Sahara.  She
sighed for the rocks and hills of Périgord.

She also ate the unaccustomed bread of idleness.
Had her aunt permitted, she would delightedly have
helped with the house-work.  But Madame Robineau,
widow of a dealer in grain who, before his death, had
retired on a comfortable fortune, lived, according to
her lights, at her ease, her wants being scrupulously
administered to by a cook and a maid.  There was no
place in the domestic machine for Félise.  Her aunt
passed long chilly hours over ecclesiastical embroidery,
sitting bolt upright in her chair with a *chaufferette*

beneath her feet. Félise, unaccustomed needlewoman, passed longer and chillier hours (having no *chaufferette*) either playing with a grey ascetic cat or reading aloud *La Croix,* the only newspaper allowed to cross the threshold of the house. Now and again, Madame Robineau would drop her thin hands into her lap and regard her disapprovingly. One day she said, interrupting the reading,

"My poor child, how your education has been neglected. You scarcely know how to hold a needle, you can't read aloud without making faults, and you are ignorant of the elements of our holy religion."

"My Aunt," Félise replied, "I know how to manage an hotel."

"That would be of little use to your husband."

Félise winced at the unhappy word.

"I am never going to marry, *ma tante,*" she said.

"You surely do not expect to be admitted into a convent?"

"Heaven forbid!" cried Félise.

"Heaven would forbid," said Madame Robineau severely, "seeing that you have not the vocation. But the *jeune fille bien élevée*"—in the mouth of her Aunt Clothilde the familiar phrase assumed a detestable significance, implying, to Félise's mind, a pallid young creature from whom all blood and laughter had been driven by undesirable virtues—"the *jeune fille bien élevée* has only two careers offered to her—the convent or marriage. For you, my dear child, it is marriage."

"Well," said Félise, with a smile, preparing to resume the article in the newspaper over which she had stumbled, "perhaps the beautiful prince will come along one of these days."

But Madame Robineau rebuked her for vain imaginings.

"It is true, what I said, that your education has been neglected. A young girl's duty is not to look for princes, but to accept the husband chosen by the wisdom of her family."

"*Ma tante,*" said Félise demurely, after a pause during which her aunt took up her work again. "If you would teach me how to embroider, perhaps I might learn to be useful in my future home."

From this and many other conversations, Félise began to be aware of the subtle strategy of Bigourdin. On the plea of providing her with pro-maternal consolation, he had delivered her into the hands of the enemy. This became abundantly clear as the days went on. Aunt Clothilde, incited thereto by her uncle, was opening a deadly campaign in favour of Lucien Viriot. Now, the cathedral, though paralysing, could be borne for a season, and so could the blight that pervaded the house; but the campaign was intolerable. If she could have resented the action of one so beloved as Bigourdin, she would have resented his sending her to her Aunt Clothilde. Under the chaperonage of the respectable Madame Chauvet she had fallen into a pretty trap. She had found none of the promised sympathy. Aunt Clothilde, although receiving her with the affectionate hospitality due to a sister's child, had from the first interview frozen the genial current of her little soul. The great bronze cross in itself repelled her. If it had been a nice, gentle little cross, rising and falling on a motherly bosom, it would have worked its all-human, adorable influence. But this was a harsh, aggressive, come-and-be-crucified sort of cross, with no suggestion of pity or understanding. The sallow, austere face above it might have easily been twisted into such a cross. It conveyed no invitation to the sufferer to pour out her troubles. Uncle Bigourdin was wrong again. Rather would Félise have poured out her troubles into the portentous ear of the Suisse at the Cathedral.

Her aunt and herself met nowhere on common

ground. They were for ever at variance. Madame Robineau spoke disparagingly of the English, because they were Protestants and therefore heretics.

"But I am English, and I am not a heretic," cried Félise.

"You are not English," replied her aunt, "because you have a French mother and have been brought up in France. And as for not being a heretic, I am not so sure. Monsieur l'Abbé Duloup thinks you must have been brought up among Freemasons."

"*Ah non, par exemple!*" exclaimed Félise indignantly. For, in the eyes of the Church, French Freemasons are dreadful folk, capable of anything sacrilegious, from denying the miracle of Saint Januarius to slitting the Pope's weasand. So—"*Ah! non par exemple!*" cried Félise.

Freemasons, indeed! Her Uncle Gaspard, it is true, did not attend church regularly—but yes, he did attend regularly—he went once a year, every Easter Sunday, and he was the best of friends with Monsieur le Curé of their Paroisse. And as for herself, Monsieur le Curé, who looked like a venerable saint in the holy pictures, had always a smile and a *ma chère enfant* for her whenever they met. She was on excellent terms with Monsieur le Curé; he would no more have dreamed of associating her with Freemasons than of accusing her of being in league with devils.

He was a good, common-sensical old curé, like thousands of the secular clergy in France, and knew how to leave well alone. Questioned by the ecclesiastically environed Abbé Duloup as to the spiritual state of Félise, he would indubitably have answered with serene conviction:—

"If a soul so pure and so candid, which I have watched from childhood, is not acceptable to the *bon Dieu,* then I know no more about the *bon Dieu* than I know about the Emperor of Patagonia."

But Félise, disliking the Abbé Duloup and many of his works, felt a delicacy in dragging her own curé into the argument and contented herself with protesting against the charge of heresy. As a matter of fact, she proclaimed her Uncle Gaspard was not a Freemason. He held in abhorrence all secret political societies as being subversive of the State. No one should attack her Uncle Gaspard, although he had betrayed her so shabbily.

In vain she sought some link with her aunt. Even Mimi, the lean old cat, did not form a bond of union. As a vagrant kitten it had been welcomed years ago by the late good-natured Robineau, and the widow tolerated its continued presence with Christian resignation. Félise took the unloved beast to her heart. From Aunt Clothilde's caustic remarks she gathered that her four cousins, of whose exemplary acceptance of husbands she had heard so much, had eyed Mimi with the coldness of their mother. She began to thank Providence that she did not resemble her cousins, which was reprehensible; and now and then manifested a lack of interest in their impeccable doings, which was more reprehensible still, and thus stirred up against her the maternal instincts of Madame Robineau.

Relations grew strained. Aunt Clothilde spoke to her with sharp impatience. From her recalcitrance in the matter of Lucien she deduced every fault conceivable. For the first time in her life Félise dwelt in an atmosphere where love was not. She longed for home. She longed especially for her father and his wise tenderness. Because she longed so greatly she could not write to him as a father should be written to; and the many-paged letters into which, at night, she put all her aching little heart, in the morning she blushed at the thought of sending. In spite of his lapse from grace she could not be so disloyal to the beloved Uncle Gaspard. Nor could she distress her suffering angel mother by her incoherent account of things. If only she could see her!

At last, one dreary afternoon, Madame Robineau opened an attack in force.

"Put down that cat. I have to talk to you."

Félise obeyed and Aunt Clothilde talked. The more she talked, the more stubborn front did Félise oppose. Madame Robineau lost her temper. Her thin lips twitched.

"I order you," she said, "to marry Lucien Viriot."

"I am sorry to say anything to vex you, *ma tante*," replied Félise valiantly; "but you have not the power."

"And I suppose your uncle has not the power to command you?"

"In matters like that, no, *ma tante*," said Félise.

Aunt Clothilde rose from her straight-backed chair and shook a long, threatening finger. The nail at the end was also long and not very clean. Félise often wondered whether her aunt abhorred a nail-brush by way of mortification.

"When one considers all the benefits my brother has heaped on your head," she cried in a rasping voice, "you are nothing else than a little monster of ingratitude!"

Félise flared up. She did not lack spirit.

"It is false," she cried. "I adore my Uncle Gaspard. I would give him my life. I am not ungrateful. It is worse than false."

"It is true," retorted Madame Robineau. "Otherwise you would not refuse him the desire of his heart. Without him you would have not a rag to your back, or a shoe to your foot, and no more religion than a heathen. It is to him you owe everything—everything. Without him you would be in the gutter where he fished you from."

She ended on a shrill note. Félise, very pale, faced her passionately, with a new light in her mild eyes.

"What do you mean? The gutter? My father——?"

"Bah! Your father! Your vagabond, ne'er-do-weel scamp of a father! He's a scandal to the family, your father. He should never have been born."

The girl reeled. It was a foul bludgeon blow. Madame Robineau, with quick realisation of folly, checked further utterance and allowed Félise, white, quivering and vanquished, but carrying her little head fiercely in the air, to retire from the scene with all the honours of war.

Madame Robineau was sorry. She had lost both temper and dignity. Her next confession would be an unpleasant matter. Possibly, however, the Abbé Duloup would understand and guess the provocation. She shrugged her lean shoulders. It was good sometimes for hoity-toity damsels to learn humility. So she sat down again, pursing her lips, and continued her embroidered stole until it was the hour of vespers. Contrary to custom, she did not summon Félise to accompany her to the Cathedral. An hour or two of solitude, she thought, not unkindly, would bring her to a more reasonable frame of mind. She went out alone.

When she returned she found that Félise had left the house.

It was a very scared young person that presented herself at the *guichet* at the railway station and asked for a second class ticket to Paris. She had never travelled alone in her life before. Even on her rare visits to the metropolis of Périgueux, in whose vast emporium of fashion she clothed herself, she was attended by Euphémie or the chambermaid. She felt lost, a tiny, helpless creature, in the great, high station in which an engine letting off steam produced a bewildering uproar. How much she paid for her ticket, thrifty and practised housekeeper that she was, she did not know. She clutched the change from a hundred franc note which, a present from her uncle before leaving Brantôme, she had preserved intact, and scuttled like a little brown rabbit to the door of the *salle d'attente.*

"*Le train de Paris? A quatre heures cinquante,*" said the official at the door, as though this palpitating adventure were the commonplace of every minute.

"And that will be?" she gasped.

He cocked an eye at the clock. "In half an hour."

A train was on the point of starting. There was a scuttle for seats. She felt sure it was the Paris train. From it emanated the magic influence of the great city whither she was bound. A questioned porter informed her it was going in the opposite direction. The Paris express left at four-fifty. The train steamed out. It seemed to Félise as though she had lost a friend. She looked round helplessly, and seeing a fat peasant woman sitting on a bench, surrounded by bundles and children, she ran to her side for protection. It is the unknown that frightens. In the Hôtel des Grottes she commanded men with the serenity of a Queen Elizabeth, and as for commercial travellers and other male visitors, she took no more account of them than of the geese that she plucked. And the terrifying Aunt Clothilde had terrified in vain. But here, in this cold, glass-roofed, steel-strutted, screeching, ghostly inferno of a place, with men prowling about like roaring lions seeking probably whom they might devour, conditions were terrifyingly unfamiliar.

Yet she did not care. Under the blasphemous roof of her Aunt Clothilde she could not have remained. For, in verity, blasphemy had been spoken. Her father was loved and honoured by all the world; by her mother, by Uncle Gaspard, by Corinna, by Martin. And she herself—did she not know her father? Was there ever a man like him? The insulting words rang

through her brain. She would have confronted terrors
a millionfold more grisly than these in order to escape
from the blasphemer, whom she could never forgive
—no, not for all the curés and abbés in Christendom.
An intense little soul was that of Félise Fortinbras.
It swept her irresistibly out of the unhallowed villa,
with a handbag containing a nightgown, a toothbrush
and a faded little photograph of her father and mother
standing side by side in wedding garb, on the way to
the dread, fascinating whirlpool of Paris, where dwelt
the worshipped gods of her idolatry. And, as she sat
in the comforting lee of the fat and unafraid peasant
woman and her bundles and her children, she took herself to task for cowardice.

The journey, under two hours, was but a trifle.
Had it been to Brantôme, an all-night affair, she might
have had reason for quailing. But to Paris it was
practically but a step. . . . The Abbé Duloup spoke
of going to Paris as her uncle spoke of going to
Périgueux. Yet her heart thudded violently during
the interminable half hour. And there was the grim
possibility of the appearance of a pursuing Aunt Clothilde. She kept a fearful eye upon the doorway of
the *salle d'attente*.

At last the train rushed in, and there was clangour
of luggage trucks and clamour of raucous voices an-
nouncing the train for Paris; and a flow of waiting
people, among whom was her neighbour with her
varied impedimenta, swept across the lines and scaled
the heights of the carriages. By luck, in front of
Félise loomed a compartment showing second class
on the door panel and *"Dames seules"* on the window.
She clambered in and sank into a seat. Who her
lonely lady fellow-travellers were she could not afterwards remember; for she kept her eyes closed, absorbed in the adventure that still lay before her. Yet
it was comforting to feel that as long as the train went

on she was safe in this feminine sanctuary, free from
depredations of marauding males.

Paris. One of the ladies, seeing that she was about
to remain in the carriage, jerked the information over
a descending shoulder. Félise followed and stood for
a moment more confused than ever in the blue glare
and ant-hill hurry of the Gare de Montparnasse. A
whole town seemed to have emerged from the train
and to stream like a rout of refugees flying from disaster, men, women and children, laden with luggage,
towards the barrier. Carried along, she arrived there
at length, gave up her ticket, and, issuing from the
station, found herself in a narrow street, at the end
of which, still following the throng, she came to a
thundering thoroughfare. Never, in all her imaginings
of Paris, had she pictured such a soul-stunning phantasmagoria of flashing light and flashing movement.
There were millions of faces passing her by on the
pavement, in the illuminated interiors of omnibuses,
in the dimmed recesses of taxi-autos, on waggons, on
carts, on bicycles; millions in gaily lit cafés; before her
dazzled eyes millions seemed to be reflected even in
the quivering, lucent air. She stood at the corner of
the Place de Rennes and the Boulevard de Montparnasse paralysed with fear, clutching her handbag tight
to her side. In that perilous street thousands of thieves
must jostle her. She could not move a step, overwhelmed by the immensity of Paris. A good-natured
sergent de ville, possibly the father of pretty daughters, noticed her agonised distress. It was not his
business to perform unsolicited deeds of knight er-
rantry; but having nothing else to do for the moment,
he caught her eye and beamed paternal encouragement.
Now a sergent de ville is a *sergent de ville* (recognis-
able by his uniform) all France over. Félise held
Père Chavrol, who exercised that function at Brantôme, in high esteem. This policeman had a fat, dark,

grinning, scrubbily-moustached face which resembled
that of Père Chavrol.  She took her courage and her
handbag in both hands.

"Monsieur," she said, "can you direct me to the
Rue Maugrabine?"

He couldn't.  He did not know that street.  In what
*quartier* was it?  Félise was ignorant.

*"C'est là où demeure mon père,"* she added.  *"C'est
Monsieur Fortinbras.  Tout le monde le connaît à
Paris."*

But alas! the sergent de ville had never heard of the
illustrious Fortinbras: which was strange, seeing that
all Brantôme knew him, although he did not live
there.

"What then shall I do, Monsieur," asked Félise, "to
get to my father?"

The sergent de ville pushed his képi to the back of
his head and cogitated.  Then, with uplifted hand, he
halted a crawling fiacre.  Rue de Maugrabine?  Of
course the glazed-hatted, muffled-up driver knew it.
Somewhere between the Rue de la Roquette and the
Avenue de la République.  The sergent de ville smiled
vaingloriously.  It was only *ces vieux collignons,* old
drivers of fiacres, that knew their Paris, he explained.
The chauffeur of a taxi-auto would have been ignorant
of the whereabouts of the Arc de Triomphe.  He advised her to engage the omniscient cabman.  The Rue
Maugrabine was infinitely distant, on the other side
of the river.  Félise suggested that a cab would cost
enormously.  In Brantôme legends were still current
of scandalous exactions levied by Paris cabmen on provincials.  The driver twisted his head affably and
hoarsely murmured that it would not cost a fortune.
Perhaps two francs, two francs fifty, with a little
*pourboire.*  He did not know.  The amount would be
registered.  The sergent de ville pointed out the taximeter.

"Be not afraid, Mademoiselle. Enter. What number?"

"Number 29."

He opened the door of the stuffy little brougham. Félise held out her hand as she would have held it out to Père Chavrol, and thanked him as though he had preserved her from legions of dragons. The last she saw of him as she drove off was in the act of majestically sweeping back a group of idlers who had halted to witness the touching farewell.

The old cab jolted and swerved through blazing vistas of unimagined thoroughfares; over bridges spanning mysterious stretches of dark waters and connecting looming masses of gigantic buildings; and through more streets garish with light and apparent revelry. Realisation of its glory came with a little sob of joy. She was in Paris, the Wonderland of Paris transcending all her dreams. Brantôme and Chartres seemed afar off. She had the sensation of a butterfly escaping from the chrysalis. She had been a butterfly for ages. What unremembered kind of state had been her grub condition? Thrills of excitement swept her little body. She was throbbingly happy. And at the end of the magic journey she would meet her father, marvel among men, and her mother, the strange, sweet, mystical being, the enchanted princess of her childish visions, the warm, spiritual, all understanding, all embracing woman of her maiden longings.

The streets grew narrower, less important. They were passing through the poor neighbourhood east of the Place de la Bastille. Fairyland suffered a sinister touch. Slight fears again assailed her. Some of the streets appeared dark and suspect. Evil-looking folk haunted the pavements. She wondered, with a catch of the breath, whither she was being driven. At last the cab swung into a street, darker, more suspect, more ill-odoured than any, and stopped before a large open doorway. She peered through the window. Above the door she could just discern the white figures "29" on the blue plaque. Her rosy dreams melted into night, her heart sank. She alighted.

"This is really 29 Rue Maugrabine?"

"*Bien sûr, mademoiselle.*"

She had forgotten to look at the taximeter, but taking three francs from her purse, she asked the driver if that was enough. He thanked her with raised hat for munificence, and, whipping up his old horse, drove off.

Félise entered a smelly little paved courtyard and gazed about her helplessly. She had imagined such another decent little house as her aunt's, at which a ring at the front door would ensure immediate admittance. In this extraordinary dank well she felt more lost than ever. Paris was a bewildering mystery. A child emerged from some dark cavern.

"Can you tell me where Monsieur Fortinbras lives?"

The child advised her to ask the concierge, and pointed to the iron bell-pull. Félise rang. The frowsy concierge gave the directions.

"*Au quatrième au coin, à gauche.*"

Félise entered the corner cavern and came on an evil-smelling stone staircase, lit here and there by naked gas-jets which blackened the walls at intervals. The cold gathered round her heart. On the second landing some noisy, ill-dressed men clattered past her and caused her to shrink back with fear. She mounted the interminable stairs. Here and there an open door revealed a squalid interior. The rosy dream became a nightmare. She had made some horrible blunder. It was impossible that her father should live here. But the concierge had confirmed the address. On the fourth floor she paused; then, as directed, turned down a small, ill-lit passage to the left. On a door facing her at the end, she noticed the gleam of a card. She approached. It bore the printed legend,

"DANIEL FORTINBRAS,
*Ancien Avoué de Londres,*
*Agent de Famille, &c, &c."*

And written in pencil was the direction: *"Sonnez, S. V. P."*

The sight reassured and comforted her. Behind this thin barrier dwelt those dearest to her on earth, the dimly remembered saintly mother, the wise and tender father. She forgot the squalor of the environment. It was merely a feature of Paris mighty and inscrutable, so different from Brantôme. She felt a little throb of pride in her daring, in her achievement. Without guidance—ungenerously she took no account of the sergent de ville, the cabman and the concierge —she had travelled from Chartres to this inmost heart of Paris. She had accomplished her stupendous adventure. . . . The card invited her to ring. Above it hung a bit of wood attached in the middle to a length of twine. She pulled and an answering clang was heard from within the apartment. Her whole being vibrated.

After a moment's waiting, the door was flung open by a coarse, red-faced, slatternly woman standing in a poverty-stricken little vestibule. She looked at the girl with curiously glazed eyes and slightly swayed as she put up a hand to dishevelled hair.

*"Vous désirez?"*

"Monsieur Fortinbras," gasped Félise, scared by the abominable apparition.

"Monsieur Fortinbras?" She mimicked the girl's clear accent.

*"Oui, madame,"* replied Félise.

Whereupon the woman withered her with a sudden volley of drunken abuse. She knew how Fortinbras occupied himself all day long. She did not complain.

But when the *gonzesses* of the *rive gauche* had the in-
decency to come to his house, she would very soon put
them across her knee and teach them manners.    This
is but a paraphrase of what fell upon Félise's terror-
stricken ears.   It fell like an avalanche; but it did not
last long, for suddenly came a voice well known but
pitched in an unfamiliar key of anger:
   *"Qu'est-ce qu'il y a?"*
And Fortinbras appeared.
As he caught sight of his daughter's white face, he
clapped his hands to his head and reeled back, horror
in his eyes.   Then:
   *"Tais-toi!"* he thundered, and seizing the woman
masterfully by the arms, he pushed her into some inner
room, leaving Félise shaking on the threshold.   In a
moment or two he reappeared, caught overcoat and
old silk hat from a peg, and motioning Félise back,
marched out of his home and slammed the door behind
him.   Father and daughter were now in the neutral
ground at the end of the dim, malodorous passage.
   "What in the name of God are you doing here,
Félise?"
   "I came to see my mother."
The fleshy, benign face of the man fell into the sags
of old age.   His lower lip hung loose.   His mild blue
eyes, lamping out from beneath noble brows, stared
agony.
   "Your mother?"
   "Yes.   Where is she?"
He drew a deep breath.   "Your mother—well—she
is in a nursing home, dear.   No one, not even I, can see
her."   He took her by the arm and hurried her to the
staircase.   "Come, come, dear, we must get away from
this.   You understand.   I did not tell you your mother
was so ill, for fear of making you unhappy."
   "But that dreadful woman, father?" she cried.   And
the Alpine flower from which honey is made looked

like a poor little frost-bitten lily of the valley. She faced him on the landing.

"That woman—that——" he waved an arm. "That," said he, quoting bitterly, "is a woman of no importance."

"Ah!" cried Félise.

With some of the elemental grossnesses of life she was acquainted. You cannot manage a hotel in France which is a free, non-Puritanical country, and remain in imbecile ignorance. She was shocked to the depths of her being.

"Come," said Fortinbras with outstretched hand. But she shrank from him. "Come!" he commanded. "There's no time to lose. We must get out of this."

"Where are we going?" she asked.

"To the Gare de Montparnasse. You must return at once to Chartres."

"I will never enter the house of Aunt Clothilde again," said Félise.

"But what has happened? My God! what has happened?" he asked, as they hurried down the stairs.

Breathlessly, brokenly, she told him. In the courtyard he paused, put his hand to his head.

"But what can I do with you? My God! what can I do with you in this dreadful city?"

"Isn't there a hotel in Paris?" she asked, coldly.

He laughed in a mirthless way. "There are many. There are the Ritz and the Meurice and the Elysée Palace. Yes—there are hotels enough!"

"I have plenty of money," she said.

"No, no, my child," said he. "Not an hotel. I should go mad. I have an idea. Come."

They had just reached the evil pavement of the Rue Maugrabine, when Cécile Fortinbras, sister of the excellent Gaspard Bigourdin and the pious Clothilde Robineau, and mother of Félise, recovered from the stupor to which the unprecedented fury of her husband had reduced her, and reeled drunkenly to the flat door.

*"Je vais arracher les yeux à cette putain-là!"*

She started to tear the hussy's eyes out; but by the time she had accomplished the difficult descent and had expounded her grievances to an unsympathetic concierge, a motor omnibus was conveying father and daughter silent and anguished to the other side of the River Seine.

# CHAPTER XII

THE huge door on the Boulevard Saint Germain swung open at Fortinbras's ring and admitted them to a warm, marble-floored vestibule adorned with rugs, palms and a cast or two of statuary. Facing them, in its cage of handsome wrought iron-work, stood the lift. All indicated a life so far apart from that of the Rue Maugrabine that Félise, in spite of the despair and disillusion that benumbed her soul, uttered an exclamation of surprise.

"Who lives here?"

"Lucilla Merriton, an American girl. Pray God she is in," replied Fortinbras, opening the lift gate. "We can but see."

He pressed the second-floor button and the lift shot up. On the landing were the same tokens of luxury. A neat maid answered the door. Mademoiselle Merriton was at home, but she had just begun dinner. Fortinbras drew a card from a shabby pocketbook.

"Tell Mademoiselle that the matter is urgent."

The maid retired, leaving them in a small lobby beyond which was a hall lit by cunningly subdued lights, and containing (to Félise's unsophisticated vision) a museum of costly and beautiful objects. Strange skins of beasts lay on the polished floor, old Spanish chests in glowing crimson girt with steel, queer chairs with straight, tall backs, such as she had seen in the sacristies of old churches in the Dordogne, and richly carved tables were ranged against the walls, and above them hung paintings of old masters, such as she was wont to call "holy pictures," in gilt frames. From the soft mystery of a corner gleamed a marble copy of the Venus de' Medici, which, from Félise's point of view, was not holy at all. Yet the sense of beauty and comfort pervading the place, appealed to her senses. She stood on the threshold looking round wonderingly, when a door opened, and, in a sudden shaft of light, appeared a tall, slim figure which advanced with outstretched hand. Félise shrank behind her father.

"Why, Fortinbras, what good wind has brought you?" The lady spoke in a rich and somewhat lazy contralto. "Excuse that celestial idiot of a Céleste for leaving you standing here in the cold. Come right in."

She led the way into the hall, and then became aware of Félise and flashed a glance of enquiry.

"This is my little daughter, Lucilla."

"Why? Not Félise?" she gave her both hands in a graceful gesture. "I'm so glad to see you. I've heard all about you from Corinna Hastings. I put her up for the night on her way back to London, you know. Now why"—still holding Félise's hands—"have you kept her from us all this time, Fortinbras? I don't like you at all."

"Paris," said Fortinbras, "isn't good for little girls who live in the heart of France."

"But surely the heart of France is Paris!" cried Lucilla Merriton.

"Paris, my dear Lucilla," replied Fortinbras gravely, "may be the liver, the spleen, the pancreas—whatever giblets you please of France; but it is not its heart."

Lucilla laughed; and when she laughed she had a way of throwing up her head which accentuated the graceful setting of her neck. Her thick brown hair brushed back, ever so little suggestive of the Pompadour, from her straight forehead, aided the unconscious charm of the habit.

"We won't argue the point. You've brought Félise here because you want me to look after her. How did

I guess? My dear man, I've lived twenty-seven years in this ingenuous universe. How babes unborn don't spot its transparent simplicity I never could imagine. You haven't dined."

"I have," said Fortinbras, "but Félise hasn't."

"You shall dine again. It's the first time you have condescended to visit me, and I exact the penalty."

She went to the open door whence she had issued.

"Céleste!"—the maid appeared—"Monsieur and Mademoiselle are dining with me and Mademoiselle is staying the night. See she has all she wants. *Allez vite.* Go, my dear, with Céleste, and be quick, for dinner's getting cold."

And when Félise, subdued by her charming masterfulness, had retired in the wake of the maid, Miss Merriton turned on Fortinbras.

"Now, what's the trouble?"

In a few words he told her what was meet for a stranger to know.

"So she ran away and came to you for protection and you can't put her up? Is that right?"

"The perch of an old vulture like myself," said he, "is no fit place for my daughter."

Lucilla nodded. "That's all right. But, say—you don't approve of this mediæval sort of marriage business, do you?"

"I retain my English views. I shall explain them to my brother-in-law and forbid the alliance. Besides, the excellent Bigourdin is the last man in the world to force her into a distasteful marriage. Reassure her on that point. She can go back to Brantôme with a quiet mind."

"Will you remain in Paris with a mind equally serene?" Lucilla asked, her deep grey eyes examining his face, which he had vainly endeavoured to compose into its habitual aspect of detached benevolence. He met her glance.

"The derelict," said he, "is a thing of no account. But it is better that it should not lie in the course of the young and living ship."

Lucilla put her hands behind her back and sat on the corner of an old Venetian table. And she still looked at him, profoundly interested. Here was a Fortinbras she had never met before, a broken man, far removed from the shrewd and unctuous *marchand de bonheur* of the Latin Quarter with his rolling periods and opportunist philosophy.

"There's something behind all this," she remarked. "If I'm to be any good, I ought to know."

He recovered a little and smiled. "Your perspicacity does credit to your country," said he. "Also to your sex. There is much behind it. An unbridgeable gulf of human sorrow. Remember that, should my little girl be led away—which I very much doubt— to talk to you of most unhappy things. She only came to the edge of the gulf half an hour ago. The marriage matter is but a thistledown of care."

"I more or less see," said Lucilla. "The vulture's perch overhangs the gulf. Right. Now what do you want me to do?"

"Just keep her until I can find a way to send her back to Brantôme."

Lucilla raised a hand, and reflected for a few seconds. Then she said: "I'll run her down there myself in the car."

"That is most kind of you," replied Fortinbras, "but Brantôme is not Versailles. It is nearly three hundred miles away."

"Well? What of that? I suppose I can commandeer enough gasoline in France to take me three hundred miles. Besides, I am due the end of next week, anyway, to stay with some friends at Cap Martin, before going to Egypt. I'll start a day or two earlier and drop Félise on my way. Will that suit you?"

"But, again, Brantôme is not on your direct route to Monte Carlo," he objected.

She slid to her feet and laughed. "Do you want me to be a young mother to your little girl, or don't you?"

"I do," said he.

"Then don't conjure up lions in the path. See here," she touched his sleeve. "You were a good friend to me once when I had that poor little fool Effie James on my hands—I shouldn't have pulled her through without you—and you wouldn't accept more than your ridiculous fee—and now I've got a chance of shewing you how much I appreciate what you did. I don't know what the trouble is, and now I don't want to know. But you're my friend, and so is your daughter."

Fortinbras smiled sadly. "It is you that are the *marchand de bonheur*. You remove an awful load from my mind." He took his old silk hat from the console where he had deposited it, and held out his hand. "The old vulture won't stop to dinner. He must be flying. Give my love, my devoted love to Félise."

And with an abruptness which she could not reconcile with his usual suave formality of manner, he turned swiftly and walked through the lobby and disappeared. His leave-taking almost resembled the flight he spoke of.

The wealthy, comely, even-balanced American girl looked blankly at the flat door and wondered, conscious of tragedy. What was the gulf of which he spoke? She knew little about the man. . . . Two years before a girl from Cheyenne, Wyoming, who had brought her letters of introduction, came to terrible grief. There was blackmail at her throat. Somebody suggested Fortinbras as counsellor. She, Lucilla, consulted him. He succeeded in sending a damsel foolish, reprehensible and frightened, but intact in reputation and pocket, back to her friends in Cheyenne. His fees for so doing amounted to twenty francs. For two years therefore, she had passed the time of day friendliwise with Fortinbras whenever she met him; but until her fellow-student, Corinna Hastings, sought her hospitality on the way back to England, and told her of Brantôme and Félise, she had regarded him merely as one of the strange, sweet monsters, devoid of domestic attributes, even of a private life, that Paris, city of portents and prodigies, had a monopoly in producing. . . . And now she had come upon just a flabby, elderly man, piteously anxious to avert some sordid misery from his own flesh and blood. She sighed, turned and saw Félise in charge of Céleste.

"Come, you must be famished." She put her arm round the girl's waist and led her into the dining-room. "Your father couldn't stay. But he told me to give you his love and to regard myself as a sort of young mother to you."

Félise murmured a shy acknowledgement. She was too much dazed for coherent thoughts or speech. The discovery of the conditions in which her father lived, and the sudden withering of her faith in him, had almost immediately been followed by her transference into this warm wonder-house of luxury owned and ruled by this queenly young woman, so exquisite in her simple marvel of a dress. The soft lights, the pictures, the elusive reflections from polished wood, the gleam of heavy silver and cut glass, the bowl of orchids on the table, the delicate napery—she had never dreamed of such though she held herself to be a judge of table-linen—the hundred adjuncts of a wealthy woman's dining room, all filled her with a sense of the unreal, and at the same time raised her poor fallen father in her estimation by investing him with the character of a magician. Dainty food was placed before her, but she could scarcely eat.  Lucilla, to put her more at her ease, talked of Corinna and of Brantôme which she was dying to visit and of the quaint Englishman, she had forgotten his name, who had become a waiter.  How was he getting on?

"Monsieur Martin?  Very well, thank you."

She put down the glass of wine which she was about to raise to her lips.  For nearly an hour she had not thought of Martin.  She felt sundered from him by many seas and continents.  Since seeing him through what scorching adventures had she not passed?  She had changed.  The world had changed.  Nothing would ever be the same again.  Tears came into her eyes.  Lucilla, observing them, smiled.

"You like Monsieur Martin?"

"Everybody likes him; he is so gentle," said Félise.

"But is that what women look for in a man?" asked Lucilla.  "Doesn't she want some one strong to lean on?  Something to appeal to the imagination?  Something more *panache*?"

Félise thought of Lucien Viriot and his cavalry plume and shivered.  No.  She did not want *panache*. Martin's quiet, simple ways, she knew not why, were worth all the clanking of all the sabres in the world put together.

"That depends on temperament, mademoiselle," said Félise, in French.

Lucilla laughingly exclaimed: "You dear little mouse.  I suppose a tom-cat frightens you to death."

But Félise was only listening with her outer ears.  "I am very fond of cats," she replied simply.

Whereupon Lucilla laughed again with quick understanding.

"I have a half-grown Persian kitten," she said, "rather a beauty.  Céleste, *apportez-moi le shah de Perse*.  That's my little joke."

"*C'est un calembour*," said Félise, with a smile.

"Of course it is. It's real smart of you to see it. I call him Padishah."

Céleste brought a grey woolly mass of felinity from a basket in a dim corner and handed it to Félise. The beast purred and stretched contentedly in her arms.

"Oh, what a dear!" she cried. "What a fluffy little dear! For the last week or two," she found herself saying, "my only friend has been a cat."

"What kind of a cat?" asked Lucilla.

"Oh, not one like this. It was a thin old tabby." And under the influence of the soft baby thing on her bosom and the kind eyes of her young hostess, the shyness melted from her, and she told of Mimi, and Aunt Clothilde, and the abhorred cathedral and the terrors of her flight to Paris.

She had come, more or less, to an end, when Céleste brought in a Pekinese spaniel, and set him down on the hearth-rug to a plate of minced raw beef, which he proceeded to devour with lightning gluttony. Having licked the polished plate from hearth-rug to clattering parquet and licked it underneath in the hope of a grain of nourishment having melted through, he arched his tail above his back and composing his miniature leonine features, regarded his mistress with his soul in his eyes, as who should say: "Now, having tasted, when shall I truly dine?" But Lucilla sent him to his chair, where he assumed an attitude of polite surprise; and she explained to Félise, captivated by his doggy winsomeness, that she called him "Gaby," which was short for Heliogabalus, the voluptuary; which allusion Félise, not being familiar with The Decline and Fall of the Roman Empire, did not understand. But, when Lucilla, breaking through rules of discipline, caught up the tawny little aristocrat and apostrophized him as "the noseless blunder," Félise laughed heartily, thinking it very funny, and, holding the kitten in her

left arm, took him from Lucilla with her right, and
covered the tiny hedonist with caresses.

When the meal was over, Lucilla took her, still
embracing kitten and dog, into the studio—the wealthy
feminine amateur's studio—a room with polished floors
and costly rugs and divans and tapestries and an easel
or two and a great wood fire blazing up an imitation
Renaissance chimneypiece.    And Lucilla talked not
only as though she had known Félise all her life, but as
though Félise was the most fascinating little girl she
had ever met . And it was all more Wonderland for
Félise.    And so it continued during the short evening;
for Lucilla, seeing that she was tired, ordered the re-
moval to their respective padded baskets of dog and
cat, both of which Félise had retained in her embrace,
and sent her to bed early; and it continued during the
process of undressing amid the beautiful trifles wherewith she performed her toilette; and after she had
put on the filmy, gossamer garment adorned with embroidered miracles that Céleste had laid out for her;
and after she had sunk asleep in the fragrant linen of
the warm nest.    But in the middle of the night she
awoke and saw the face of the dreadful woman in the
Rue Maugrabine and heard the voice of her Aunt
Clothilde speaking blasphemy against her father, and
then she upbraided herself for being led away by the
enchantment of the Wonder-house, and breaking
down, sobbed for her lost illusions until the dawn.

In the meanwhile a heart-broken man sat in a sordid
room toiling dully at the task of translating French
commercial papers into English, by which means he
added a little to his precarious income, while on the
other side of the partition his wife slept drunkenly.
That had been his domestic life, good God! he reflected, for more years than he cared to number.    But
up to then Félise had been kept in ignorance.    Now the
veil had been lifted.    She had, indeed, retained the

mother of her dreams, but at what a cost to him! Would it not have been better to tell her the truth? He stared at the typewritten words until they were hidden by a mist of tears. He had lost all that made life sweet for him—the love of Félise.

He bowed his head in his hands. Judgment had at last descended on him for the sins of his youth; for he had erred grievously. All the misery he had endured since then had been but a preparation for the blow that had now fallen. It would be easy to go to her to-morrow and say: "I deceived you last night. The woman you saw was your mother." But he knew he would never be able to say it. He must pay the great penalty.

He paid it the next day when he called humbly to see her. She received him dutifully and gave him her cheek to kiss, but he felt her shrink from him and read the anguished condemnation in her eyes. He saw, too, for he was quick at such things, how her glance took in, for the first time in her life, his worn black clothes, his frayed linen, his genteel shabbiness, a grotesque contrast to the air of wealth in which she found herself. And he knew that she had no mean thoughts but was pierced to the heart by the discovery; for she turned her head aside and bit her lip, so that he should not guess.

"I should like to tell you what I have done," said he, after some desultory and embarrassed talk about Lucilla. "I have telegraphed to Chartres and Brantôme to say that you are safe and sound, and I have written to your Uncle Gaspard about Lucien Viriot. You will never hear of the matter again, unless your Aunt Clothilde goes to Brantôme, which I very much doubt."

"Thank you, father," said Félise, and the commonplace words sounded cold in her ears. She was delivered, she knew, from the nightmare of the past few weeks; but she found little joy in her freedom. Then she asked:

"Have you told Uncle Gaspard why I ran away from Aunt Clothilde?"

"Enough, dear, for him to understand. He will ask you no questions, so you needn't tell him anything."

"Won't that be ungrateful? I have treated him ungratefully enough already."

Fortinbras stretched out his hand to lay it caressingly on her head, as he had done all her life, but, remembering, withdrew it, with a sigh.

"Your uncle is the best and truest man I have ever met," said he. "And he loves you dearly and you love him—and with love ingratitude can't exist. Tell him whatever you find in your heart. But there is one thing you need never tell him—what you saw in the Rue Maugrabine last night. I have done so already. In this way there will be nothing secret between you."

She sat with tense young face, looking at her hands. Again she saw the squalid virago. She would see her till her dying day. To no one on earth could she speak of her.

Fortinbras rose, kissed her on the forehead and went forth to his day's work of dealing out happiness to a clamouring world.

# CHAPTER XIII

LUCILLA MERRITON had much money, a kind heart and a pretty little talent in painting. The last secured her admittance to the circle of art-students round about the Rue Bonaparte, the second made her popular among them and the money enabled her to obey any reasonable dictate of the kind heart aforesaid. When those who were her intimates, mainly hard-working and none too opulent English girls, took her to task for her luxurious way of living, and pointed out that it was not in keeping with the Spartan, makeshift traditions of the Latin Quarter, and that it differentiated her too much from her fellows, she replied, with the frankness of her country, first, that she saw no sense in pretending to be other than she was, second, that in the atmosphere of luxury to which she had been born, she was herself, for whatever that self was worth; and thirdly, that any masquerading as a liver of the simple life would choke all the agreeable qualities out of her. When, looking round her amateur studio, they objected that she did not take her art seriously, she cordially agreed.

"I take what you call my art," she would say, "just as it suits me. I can command too many things in the world for me to sacrifice them to the mediocre result I can get out of a paint-brush and a bit of canvas. I shall never need paint for money, and if I did I'm sure I shouldn't earn any. But I love painting for its own sake, and I have enough talent to make it worth while to have good instruction in technique, so that my

pictures shall more or less satisfy myself and not
set my friends' teeth on edge. And that's why I'm
here."

She was a wealthy vagabond of independent fortune inherited from her mother long since deceased,
with no living ties save her father, a railway director
in America, now married to a young wife, a school-
mate of her own, whom, since her childhood, she had
peculiarly abhorred. But in the world, which lay
wide open to her, *videlicet* the civilised nations of the
two hemispheres, she had innumerable friends. No
human will pretended to control her actions. She
was as free to live in Rosario as in Buda-Pesth; in
Nairobi as in Nijni Novgorod. For the last two or
three years she had elected to establish her headquarters in Paris and study painting. But why the latter
process should involve a hard bed in a shabby room
and dreadful meals at the Petit Cornichon, she could
never understand. Occasionally, on days of stress at
the *atélier,* she did lunch at the Petit Cornichon. It
was convenient, and, as she was young and thirsty for
real draughts of life, the chatter and hubbub of in-
sensate ambitions afforded her both interest and amusement; but she found the food execrable and the universal custom of cleaning knife, fork, spoon and plate
before using them exceedingly disgusting. Yet, being
a lady born and bred, she performed the objectionable
rite in the most gracious way in the world; and when
it came to comradeship, then her democratic traditions
asserted themselves. Her student friends ranged the
social gamut. If the wearer were a living spirit, she
regarded broken boots and threadbare garments merely as an immaterial accident of fortune, like a broken
nose or an amputated limb. The flat on the Boulevard
St. Germain was the haven of many a hungry girl and
boy. And they found their way thither (as far as
Lucilla was concerned) not because they were hungry,

but because that which lay deep in their souls had won her accurate recognition.

By way of digression, an essential difference in point of view between English and Americans may here be noted. If an Englishman has reason to admire a tinker and make friends with him, he will leave his own respectable sphere and enter that of the tinker, and, in some humble haunt of tinkerdom, where he can remain incognito, will commune with his crony over pots of abominable and digestion-racking ale. The instinct of the American, in sworn brotherhood with a tinker, is, on the other hand, to lift the tinker to his own habitation of delight. He will desire to take him into a saloon which he himself frequents, fill him up with champagne and provide him with the best, biggest and strongest cigar that money can buy. In both cases appear the special defects of national qualities. The Englishman goes to the tinker's boozing ken (thereby, incidentally, putting the tinker at his ease) because he would be ashamed of being seen by any of his own clan in a tinker's company. The American does not care a hang for being seen with the tinker; he wants to give his friend a good time; but, incidentally, he has no intuitive regard for the tinker's feelings, predilections and timidities.

From which disquisition it may be understood how Lucilla played Lady Bountiful without the slightest consciousness of doing so. She played it so well, with regard to Félise, as to make that young woman in the course of a day or two her slave and worshipper. She shewed her the sights of Paris, Versailles, the Galeries de Lafayette, the Tomb of Napoleon, Poiret's, the Salon d'Hiver, the Panthéon and Cartier's in the Rue de la Paix. With the aid of pins and scissors and Céleste, she also attired her in an evening frock and under the nominal protection of an agreeable young compatriot from the Embassy took her to dine

at the Café de Paris and then to the Théâtre du Gym-
nase. A great, soft-cushioned, smooth, noiseless car
carried them luxuriously through the infinite streets;
and when they were at home it seemed to await them
night and day by the kerb of the Boulevard Saint
Germain. Lucilla set the head of the little country
mouse awhirl with sensations. Félise revered her as
a goddess, and whispered in awe the Christian name
which she was commanded to use.

A breathless damsel, with a jumble of conflicting
scraps of terror and delight instead of a mind, her
arms full of an adored Persian kitten and an adoring
Pekinese spaniel, after a couple of days' flashing course
through France, was brought in the gathering dusk,
with a triumphant sweep up the hill, to the familiar
front door of the Hôtel des Grottes. Baptiste, green-
aproned, gaped as he saw her, and, scuttling indoors,
shouted at the top of his voice:

*"Monsieur, monsieur, c'est mademoiselle!"*

In an instant, Bigourdin lumbered out at full speed.
He almost lifted her from the car, scattering outraged kitten and offended dog, hid her in his vast
embrace and hugged her and kissed her and held her
out at arm's length and laughed and hugged her
again. There was no doubt of the prodigal's welcome.
She laughed and sobbed and hugged the great man
in return. And then he recovered himself and became
the *bon hôtelier* and assisted Lucilla to alight, while
Félise greeted a smiling Martin and suffered the embrace of Euphémie, panting from the kitchen.

"If mademoiselle will give herself the trouble of
following me——" said Bigourdin, and led the way
up the stairs, followed by Lucilla and Céleste, guardian
of the jewel case. He threw open the door of the
*chambre d'honneur,* a double-windowed room, above
the terrace, overlooking the town and the distant

mountains of the Limousin, and shewed her with pride
a tiny salon adjoining, the only private sitting-room
in the hotel, crossed the corridor and flung to view
the famous bathroom, disclosed next door a room for
the maid, and swept her back to the bed-room, where
a pine-cone fire was blazing fragrantly.

"*Voilà, mademoiselle,*" said he. "*Tout à votre dis-
position.*"

"I think it is absolutely charming," cried Lucilla.
She looked round. "Oh! what lovely things you
have!"

Bigourdin beamed and made a little bow. He took
inordinate pride in his *chambre d'honneur* in which
he had stored the gems of the Empire furniture acquired by his great-grandfather, the luckless Général
de Brigade. The instantaneous appreciation of a casual glance enchanted him.

"I hope, mademoiselle," said he, in his courteous
way, "you will do Félise and myself the honour of
being our guest as long as you deign to stay at Brantôme."

Lucilla met his bright eyes. "That's delightful of
you," she laughed. "But I'm not one solitary person,
I'm a caravan. There's me and the maid and the
chauffeur and the car and the dog and the cat."

"The hotel is very little, mademoiselle," replied Bigourdin, "but our hearts are big enough to entertain them."

Nothing more, or, at least, nothing more by way
of protest, was to be said. Lucilla put out her hand
in her free, generous gesture.

"Monsieur Bigourdin, I accept with pleasure your
delightful hospitality."

"*Je vous remercie infiniment, mademoiselle,*" said
Bigourdin.

He went downstairs in a flutter of excitement. Not
for four generations, so far as he was aware, had

such an event occurred in the Hôtel des Grottes. Members of the family, of course, had stayed there without charge. Once, towards the end of the Second Empire, a Minister of the Interior had occupied the *chambre d'honneur,* and had gone away without paying his bill; but that remained a bad black debt in the books of the hotel. Never had a stranger been an honoured guest. He had offered the position, it is true, to Corinna; but then he was in love with Corinna, which makes all the difference. The French are not instinctively hospitable; when they are seized, however, by the impulse of hospitality, all that they have is yours, down to the last crust in the larder; but they are fully conscious of their own generosity, they feel the tremendousness of the spiritual wave. So Bigourdin, kindest-hearted of men, lumbered downstairs aglow with a sense of altruistic adventure. In the vestibule he met Félise who had lingered there in order to obtain from Martin a *compte rendu* of the household and the neighbourhood. Things had gone none too well—Monsieur Peyrian, one of their regular commercial travellers, having discovered a black-beetle in his bread, had gone to the Hôtel du Cygne. The baker had indignantly repudiated the black-beetle, his own black-beetles being apparently of an entirely different species. Another baker had been appointed, whose only defect was his inability to bake bread. The *brave* Madame Thuillier, who had been called in to superintend the factory, had quarrelled, after two days, with everybody, and had gone off in dudgeon because she did not eat at the *patron's* table. Then they had lost two of their best hands, one a young married woman who was reluctantly compelled to add to the population of France, and the other a girl who was discharged for laying false information against the very respectable and much married Baptiste, saying that he had pinched her. The old Mère Maquoise, *marchande de quatre saisons,* who was reputed to have known Général Bigourdin, was dead, and one of the hotel omnibus horses had come down on its knees.

Félise, forgetful of the Maison de Blanc and Nôtre Dame, wrung her hands. She had descended from fairyland into life's dear and important realities.

"It's desolating, what you tell me," she cried.

"And all because you went away and left us," said Martin.

"She is not going to leave us again!" cried Bigourdin, swooping down on her and carrying her off.

In the prim little salon he hugged her again and said gripping her hands:

"It appears you have greatly suffered, my poor little Félise. But why didn't you tell me from the first that you were unhappy with your Aunt Clothilde? I did not know she had turned into such a *vieille pimbèche.* She has written. And I have answered. Ah! I tell you, I have answered! You need never again have any fear of your Aunt Clothilde. I hope I am a Christian. But I hope too that I shall always differ from her in my ideas of Christianity. *Mais tout ça est fini— bel et bien fini.* We have to talk of ourselves. I have been a miserable man since you have been away, *ma petite* Félise. I tell you that in all frankness. Everything has been at sixes and sevens. I can't do without my little *ménagère.* And you shall never marry anybody, even the President of the Republic, unless you want to. *Foi de Bigourdin! Voilà!"*

Félise cried a little. *"Tu es trop bon pour moi, mon oncle."*

*"Allons donc!* I seem to have been an old bear. Yet, in truth, I am harmless as a sheep. But have confidence in me, and in my very dear friend, your father—there are many things you cannot understand—and things will arrange themselves quite happily. You love me just a little bit, don't you?"

She flung her arms round the huge man's neck. *"Je t'adore, mon petit oncle,"* she cried.

Ten minutes afterwards, with bunch of keys slung at her waist, she was busy restoring to order the chaos of the interregnum. Terrible things had happened during the absence of the feminine eye. Even Martin shared the universal reprimand. For Félise, manageress of hotel, and Félise, storm-tossed little human soul, were two entirely different entities.

"My dear Martin, how could you and my uncle pass these napkins from that infamous old thief of a laundress. They are black!"

And ruthlessly she flicked a napkin folded mitre-wise from the centre table before the eyes of the folder and revealed its dingy turpitude.

"It is well that I am back," she declared.

"It is indeed, Mademoiselle Félise," said Martin.

She gave him a swift little glance out of the tail of her eye, before she sped away, and the corners of her lips drooped as though in disappointment. Then perhaps reflecting that she had been addressing the waiter and not the man, her face cleared. At all events he had taken her rating in good part.

Dinner had already begun and the hungry commercials, napkins at neck, were finishing their soup lustily, when Lucilla entered the dining room. The open Medici collar to a grey velvet dress shewed the graceful setting of her neck and harmonised with the brown hair brushed up from the forehead. She advanced smiling and stately, giving the impression of the perfect product of a new civilisation. Martin, who had but seen her for a few seconds in the dusk confusedly clad in furs, stood spell-bound, a pile of used soupplates in his hands. Never had so radiant an apparition swum before his gaze. Bigourdin, dining as usual with Félise, rose immediately and conducted his guest to the little table by the terrace where once Martin and Corinna had sat. It was specially adorned with tawny chrysanthemums.

"I fell dreaming before the fire in the midst of your wonderful, old-world things, and had to hurry into my clothes, and so I'm late," she apologised.

"If only you found all you needed, mademoiselle——" said Bigourdin anxiously. "It is the provinces and not Paris."

She assured him that Félise had seen to every conceivable want and he left her to her meal. Martin delivered his soup-plates into the arms of the chambermaid and hovered over Lucilla with the menu card.

"Will mademoiselle take the dinner?" he asked in French.

She regarded him calmly and humorously and nodded. He became aware that her eyes were of a deep, deep grey, full of light. He found it difficult not to keep on looking at them. Breaking away, however, he fetched her soup and went off to attend to the others. At every pause by her table he noted some new and incomparable attribute. When bending over the platter from which she helped herself, he saw that her hands were beautifully shaped, plump, with long thin fingers and with delicate markings of veins beneath the white skin. An upward glance caught more blue veins on the temples. Another time he was struck by the supple grace of her movements. There were infinite gleams in her splendid hair. The faintest suggestion of perfume arose from her garments. She declined the vegetable course and, declining, looked up at him and smiled. He thought he had never seen a brow so noble, a nose so exquisitely cut, lips so kind and mocking. Her face was that of a Romney duchess into which the thought and spiritual freedom of the twentieth century had entered. As he sped about the service, thrusting dishes beneath bearded or blue, ill-shaven chins, her face floated before his eyes; every now and then he stole a distant glance at it, and longed for the happy though transient moment when he should come close to it again.

While he was clearing her table for dessert she said:

"Why do you speak French to me, when you know I'm an American?"

"It is the custom of the house when a guest speaks such excellent French as mademoiselle."

"That's very kind of you," she said in English; "but it seems rather ridiculous for an American and an Englishman to converse in a foreign language."

"How do you know I am English, mademoiselle?" he asked, his heart a-flutter at the unexpected interchange of words.

She laughed. "I have eyes. Besides, I know all about you—first from our friend Corinna Hastings, and lately from my little hostess over the way."

He flushed, charmed by the deep music of her voice and delighted at being recognised by her not only as an individual (for she radiated an attraction which had caused him to hate the conventional impersonality of waiterdom) but as a member more or less of her own social class. He paused, plate of crumbs in one hand and napkin in the other.

"Do you know Corinna Hastings?"

"Evidently. How else could she have told me of your romantic doings?" she replied laughingly, and Martin flushed deeper, conscious of an idiot question.

He set the apples and little white grapes before her. "I ought to have asked you," said he, "how Miss Hastings came to talk to you about me?"

"She came on the train from Brantôme and rang my bell in Paris. She kept me up talking till four o'clock in the morning—not of you all the time. Don't imagine it.  You were just interestingly incidental."

"*Garçon,*" cried a voice from the centre table.

"*Bien, m'sieur.*"

Martin tucked his napkin under his arm and turned away, followed by Lucilla's humorous glance.

"*L'addition.*"

"*Bien, m'sieur.*"

He became the perfect waiter again, and brought the bill to the commercial traveller who had merely come in for dinner.  The latter paid in even money, rose noisily—he was a stout, important, red-faced man—and, fumbling in several pockets rendered difficult of access by adiposity and good cheer, at last produced four coppers which he deposited with a base, metallic chink in Martin's palm.

"*Merci, m'sieur.  Bon soir, m'sieur,*" said the perfect waiter.  But he would have given much to be able to dispose of the horrible coins otherwise than by thrusting them in his trouser pocket, to be able, for instance, to hurl them at the triple sausage neck of the departing donor; for he knew the starry, humorous eyes of the divinity were fixed on him.  He felt hot and clammy and did not dare look round.  And the hideous thought flashed through his mind:  "Will she offer me a tip when she leaves?"

He busied himself furiously with his service, and, in a few moments, was relieved to see her ceremoniously conducted by Bigourdin and Félise from the *salle-à-manger*.  On the threshold Bigourdin paused and called him.

"You will serve coffee and liqueurs in the *petit salon,* and if you go to the Café de l'Univers, you will kindly make my excuses to our friends."

To enter the primly and plushily furnished salon, bearing the tray, and to set out the cups and glasses and bottles was an ordeal which he went through with the automatic rigidity of a highly trained London footman, looking neither to right nor left.   He had a vague impression of a queenly figure reclining comfortably in an arm chair, haloed by a little cloud of cigarette smoke.   He retired, finished his work in the pantry, swallowed a little food, changed his things and went out.

Instinct led him along the quays and through the narrow, old-world streets to the patch of yellow light before the Café de l'Univers.   But there he halted, suddenly disinclined to enter.   Something new and amazing had come into his life—he could not yet tell what—discordant with the commonplace of the familiar company.   He looked through the space left between the edge of the blind and the jamb of the window and saw Beuzot, the professor at the Ecole Normale, playing backgammon with Monsieur Callot, the postmaster; and a couple of places away from them was visible the square-headed old Monsieur Viriot, smiting his left palm with his right fist.   The excellent old man always did that when he inveighed against the government.   To-night Martin cared little about the Government of the French Republic; still less for backgammon.   He had a nostalgia for unknown things and an absurd impulse to walk abroad to find them beneath the moon and stars.   Obeying the impulse, he retraced his steps along the quays and struck the main-road past the habitations of the rock dwellers. He walked for a couple of miles between rocks casting jagged shadows and a calm, misty plain without finding anything, until, following a laborious, zig-zag course, a dissolute quarryman of his acquaintance in incapable charge of a girl child of five, lurched into him and laid the clutch of a drowning mariner upon his shoulder.

"Monsieur Martin," said he.   "It is the good God who has sent you."

"Boucabeille," said Martin—for that was the name

of the miscreant—"you ought to be ashamed of yourself."

"You need not tell me, Monsieur Martin," replied Boucabeille.

As the child was crying bitterly and the father was self-reproachful—he had taken the *mioche* to see her aunt, and coming back had met some friends who had enticed him into the Café of the Mère Diridieu, where they had given him some poisoned, leg-dislocating alcohol—Martin took the child in his arms, and trudged back to the rock-dwellings where the drunkard lived. On the way Boucabeille, relieved of paternal responsibility, the tired child now snuggling sleepily and comfortably against Martin's neck, grew confidential and confessed, with sly enjoyment, that he had already well watered his throttle before he started. The man, he declared, with the luminousness of an apostle, who did not get drunk occasionally was an imbecile denying himself the pleasures of the Other Life. Martin recognised in Boucabeille a transcendentalist, no matter how muddle-headed. The sober clod did not know adventures. He did not know happiness. The path of the drunkard, Boucabeille explained, was strewn with joy.

The anxious wife who met them at the door called Martin a saint from heaven and her husband a stream of unmentionable things. He staggered under the outburst and laid his hand again on Martin's shoulder.

"Monsieur Martin, I have committed a fault. I take you to witness"—his wife paused in her invective to hear the penitent—"if I was more drunk I wouldn't pay attention to anything she says. I have committed a fault. I haven't got drunk enough."

"*Sale cochon!*" cried the lady, and Martin left them, meditating on the philosophy of drunkenness. *Quo me rapis Bacche, plenum tui?* To what godlike adventure? But the magic word was *plenum*—right full to the lips. No half-and-half measures for Bacchus. Apparently Boucabeille had failed in his adventure and had missed happiness by a gill. Browning's lines about the little more and the little less came into his head, and he laughed. Both the poet and the muddle-headed quarryman were right. Adventures not brought through to the end must be dismal fiasco. . . . His mind wandered a little. His shoulder was ever such a trifle stiff from carrying the child; but he missed the warmth of her grateful little body, and the trusting clasp of her tiny arms. It had been an insignificant adventure, an adventure, so to speak, in miniature; but it had been complete, rounded off, perfect. The proof lay in the glow of satisfaction at the thing accomplished. Materially, there was nothing to complain about. But from a philosophic standpoint the satisfaction was not absolute. For the absolute is finality, and there is no finality in mundane things. From a thing so finite as human joy eternal law decreed the evolution of the germs of fresh desires. There had been a strange sweetness in the clasp of those tiny arms. How much sweeter to a man would be the clasp, if the arms were his own flesh and blood? Martin was shocked by the suspicion that things were not going right with him as a human being.

The pleasant mass of the Hôtel des Grottes looming dimly white against its black background came into view. The lights in an uncurtained and unshuttered window, above the terrace, were visible. A figure passed rapidly across the room and sent drunkards and adventures and curly-headed five-year-olds packing from his mind. But he averted his eyes and walked on and came to the Pont de Dronne, and then halted to light a cigarette. The frosty silence of sharp moonlight hung over the town. The silver shimmer reflected from reaches of water and from slated roofs invested it with unspeakable beauty and peace. A lit-

tle cold caressing wind came from the distant mountains, seen in soft outline.  Near black shelves of rock
and dark mysteries of forest and masses of houses
beyond the bridge-end closed other horizons.  He remembered his first impression of Brantôme, when he
had sat with Corinna on the terrace, a mothering shelter from all fierce and cruel things.

"And yet," thought he, as he puffed his cigarette
smoke in the clear air, "beyond this little spot lies a
world of unceasing endeavour and throbbing pulses
and women of disturbing beauty.  Such a woman on
her meteoric passage from one sphere of glory to another has flashed before my eyes to-night.  Why am
I here pursuing an avocation, which, though honest,
is none the less greasy and obscure?"

Unable to solve the enigma, he sighed and threw his
cigarette, which had gone out during his meditation,
into the river.  A patter of quick footsteps at the approach of the bridge caused him to turn his head, and
he saw emerge from the gloom into the moonlight a
tall, fur-clad figure advancing towards him.  She gave
him a swift look of recognition.

"Monsieur Martin——"

He raised his cap.  "Good evening, Miss Merriton."

She halted.  "My good host and hostess are gone
to bed.  I couldn't sit by my window and sentimental-
ise through the glass; so I came out."

"It's a fine night," said Martin.

"It is.  But not one to hang about on a windy
bridge.  Come for a little walk, if you have time, and
protect me against the dangers of Brantôme."

Go for a walk with her?  Defend her from dangers?  Verily he would go through the universe with
her!  His heart thumped.  It was in his whirling
brain to cry: "Come and ride with me throughout
the world and the more dragons I can meet and slay

in your service, the more worthy shall I be to kiss the hem of your sacred grey velvet dinner-gown." But from his fundamental, sober, commonsense he replied:

"The only dangers of Brantôme at this time of night are prudish eyes and scandalous tongues."

She drew a little breath. "Thank you," she said. "That's frank and sensible. I'm always forgetting that France isn't New York, or Paris for the matter of that, where one can do as one likes. I don't know Provincial France a little bit, but I suppose, for red-hot gossip, it isn't far behind a pretty little New England village. Still, can't we get out of range, somehow, of the eyes? That road over there"—she waved a hand in the direction of the silent high-road, which Martin had lately travelled—"doesn't seem to be encumbered with the scandal-mongers of Brantôme."

He laughed. "Will you try it?"

She nodded assent.

They set forth briskly. The glimpse into her nature delighted him. She appreciated at once the motive of his warning, but was serenely determined to have her own way.

"We were just beginning an interesting little talk when you were called off," she remarked.

Martin felt himself grow red, remembering the tightly pocketed bagman who took the stage while he searched for eleemosynary sous.

"My profession has its drawbacks," said he.

"So has every profession. I've got a friend in America—I have met him two or three times—who is conductor on the Twentieth Century Express between New York and Chicago. He's by way of being an astronomer, and the great drawback of his profession is that he has no time to sit on top of a mountain and look at stars. The drawback of yours is that you can't carry on pleasant conversations whenever you like.

But the profession's all right, unless you're ashamed of it."

"But why should I be ashamed of it?" asked Martin.

"I don't know. Why should you? My father, who was the son of a New England parson——"

"My father was a parson," said Martin.

"Was he? Well, that's good. We both come of a God-fearing stock, which is something in these days. Anyway, my father, in order to get through college, waited on the men in Hall at Harvard, and was a summer waiter at a hotel in the Adirondacks. Of course there are some Americans who would like it to be thought that their ancestors brought over the family estates with them in the *Mayflower*. But we're not like that. Say," she said, after a few steps through the sweet keenness of the moonlit night. "Have you heard lately from Corinna?"

He had not. In her last letter to him she had announced her departure from the constricting family circle of Wendlebury. She was going to London.

"Where she would have a chance of self-development," said Lucilla, with a laugh.

"How did you know that?" Martin asked in simple surprise, for those had been almost Corinna's own words.

"What else would she go to London for?"

"I don't know," said Martin. "She did not tell me."

They did not discuss Corinna further. But Martin felt that his companion had formulated his own diagnosis of Corinna's abiding defect: her suspicion that the cosmic scheme centred round the evolution of Corinna Hastings. In a very subtle way the divinity had established implied understandings between them. They were of much the same parentage. In her own family the napkin had played no ignoble part. They were at one in their little confidential estimate of their common friend. And when she threw back her adorable head and drew a deep breath and said: "It's just lovely here," he felt deliciously near her. Deliciously and dangerously. A little later, as they came upon the rock dwellings, she laid a fleeting, but thrilling touch on his arm.

"What in the world are those houses?"

He told her. He described the lives of the inhabitants. He described, on the way back, for the rocks marked the limit of their stroll, his adventure with Boucabeille. Ordinarily shy, and if not tongue-tied, at least unimaginative in speech, he now found vivid words and picturesque images, his soul set upon repaying her, in some manner for her gracious comradeship. Her smiles, her interest, her quick sympathy, the occasional brush of her furs against his body, as she leaned to listen, intoxicated him. He spoke of France, the land of his adoption, and the spiritual France that no series of hazardous governments could impair, with rhapsodical enthusiasm. She declared, in her rich, deep voice, as though carried away by him:

"I love to hear you say such things. It is splendid to get to the soul of a people."

Her tone implied admiration of achievement. He laughed rather foolishly, in besotted happiness. They had reached the steep road leading to the Hôtel des Grottes. She threw a hand to the moonlit bridge, where they had met.

"Were you thinking of all that when I dragged you off?"

He laughed again. "No," he confessed. "I was wondering what on earth I was doing there."

"I think," said she softly, "you have just given me the *mot de l'enigme.*"

In the vestibule they came across Bigourdin, cigarette in mouth, sprawling as might have been expected,

on the cane-bottomed couch. He was always the last
to retire, a fact which the blissful Martin had forgotten. Lucilla sailed up, radiant in her furs, the flush
of exercise on her cheeks visible even under the dim
electric light. Bigourdin raised his ponderous bulk.

"I found Monsieur Martin outside," she said, "and
I commandeered him as an escort round the neighbourhood. He couldn't refuse. I hope I haven't done
wrong."

"Martin knows more about Brantôme," replied Bigourdin courteously, "than most of the Brantômois
themselves."

Céleste appeared from the gloom of the stairs. Lucilla, after an idle word or two, retired. Bigourdin
closed and bolted the front door. To do that he would
trust nobody, not even Martin. Having completed the
operation, he advanced slowly towards his employé.

"Did you go to the café to-night?"

"No," replied Martin. "I was walking with mademoiselle, who, as she may have told you, is a friend
of Mademoiselle Corinna."

"Yes, yes, she told me that," said Bigourdin. "There
is no need of explanations, *mon ami*. But I am
glad you did not go to the café. I ought to have
warned you. We must be very discreet towards
the Viriots. There is no longer any marriage.
Félise doesn't want it. Her father has formally forbidden it. I have no desire to make anybody unhappy.
But there it is. *Foutu, le mariage*. And I haven't said
anything as yet to the Viriots. And, again, I can't
say anything to Monsieur Viriot, until he says something to me. *Voilà la situation. C'est d'une delicatesse
extraordinaire.*"

He passed his hand over his head and tried to grip
the half-inch stubble.

"I tell you this, *mon cher* Martin, because you know
the intimate affairs of the family. So"—he shook an

impressive finger—"act towards the Viriots, father and son, as if you knew nothing, nothing at all. *Laissez-moi faire.*"

Martin pledged the discretion of the statues in the old Alhambra tale. What did the extraordinary delicacy of the situation between Bigourdin and the Viriots matter to him? When he reached his room, he laughed aloud, oblivious of Bigourdin, the Viriots and poor little Félise who (though he knew it not) lay achingly awake.

At last a woman, a splendid wonder of a woman, a woman with the resplendent dignity of the King's daughter of the fairy tales, with the bewilderment of beauty of face and of form and of voice like the cooing of a dove, with the delicate warm sympathy of sheer woman, had come into his life.

The usually methodical Martin threw his shirt and trousers across the room and walked about like a lunatic in his under things, until a sneeze brought him to the consciousness of wintry cold.

The only satisfying sanction of romance is its charm of intimate commonplace.

# CHAPTER XIV

THEY had further talk together the next afternoon. A lost remnant of golden autumn freakishly returned to warm the December air. The end of the terrace caught a flood of sunshine wherein Lucilla, wrapped in furs and rugs and seated in one of the bent-wood rocking-chairs brought out from winter quarters for the occasion, had established herself with a book. The little dog's head appeared from under the rug, his strange Mongolian eyes staring unsympathetically at a draughty world. Martin sauntered out to breathe the beauty of the hour, which was that of his freedom. He explained the fact when she informed him that Félise and Bigourdin had both left her a few minutes before in order to return to their duties. Martin being free, she commanded him to stay and entertain her.

"If I were a good American," she said, "I should be racing about in the car doing the sights of the neighbourhood; but to sit lazily in the sun is too great a temptation. Besides," she added, "I have explored the town this morning. I went round with Monsieur Bigourdin."

"He is very proud of Brantôme," said Martin.

She dismissed Brantôme. "I have lost my heart to him. He is so big and comfortable and honest, and he talks history like a poetical professor with the manners of an Embassy attaché. He's unique among landlords."

"I love Bigourdin," said Martin, "but the type is not uncommon in these old inns of France—especially those which have belonged to the same family for generations. There is the proprietor of the Hôtel du Commerce at Périgueux, for instance, who makes *pâté de foie gras,* just like Bigourdin, and is a well-known authority on the prehistoric antiquities of the Dordogne. He once went to London, for a day; and what do you think was his object? To inspect the collection of flint instruments at the Guildhall Museum. He told me so himself."

"That's all very interesting," said Lucilla, "but I'm sure he's nothing like Bigourdin. He can't be. And his hotel can't be like this. It's the queerest hotel I've ever struck. It's run by such unimaginable people. I think I've lost my heart to all of you. There's Bigourdin, there's Félise, the dearest and most delicate little soul in the world, the daughter of a remarkable mystery of a man, there are Baptiste and Euphémie and Marie, the chambermaid, who seem to exude desire to fold me to their bosoms whenever I meet them, and there is yourself, an English University man, an exceedingly competent waiter and a perfectly agreeable companion."

The divinity crowned with a little sealskin motoring toque which left unhidden the fascination of her upbrushed hair, cooed on deliciously. The knees of Martin, leaning against the parapet, became as water. He had a crazy desire to kneel at her feet on the concrete floor of the terrace. Then he noticed that between her feet and the cold concrete floor there was no protecting footstool. He fetched one from the dining room and had the felicity of placing it for her and readjusting the rugs.

"I suppose you're not going to be a waiter here all your life," she said.

He signified that the hypothesis was correct.

"What are you going to do?"

It was in his awakened imagination to say:

"Follow you to the ends of the earth," but common sense replied that he did not know. He had made no plans. She suggested that he might travel about the wide world. He breathed an inward sigh. Why not the starry firmament? Why not, rainbow-winged and golden spear in hand, swoop, a bright Archangel, from planet to planet?

"You ought to see Egypt," she said, "and feel what a speck of time you are when the centuries look down on you. It's wholesome. I'm going early in the New Year. I go there and try to paint the desert; and then I sit down and cry—which is wholesome too—for me."

Before Martin's inner vision floated a blurred picture of camels and pyramids and sand and oleographic sunsets. He said, infatuated: "I would give my soul to go to Egypt."

"Egypt is well worth a soul," she laughed.

Words and reply were driven from his head by the sight of a great splotch of grease on the leg of his trousers. A dress suit worn daily for two or three months in pursuit of a waiter's avocation, does not look its best in stark sunlight. Self-conscious, he crossed his legs, as he leaned againt the parapet, in order to hide the splotch. Then he noticed that one of the studs of his shirt had escaped from the frayed and blackened buttonhole. Again he felt her humorous eyes upon him. For a few moments he dared not meet them. When he did look up he found them fixed caressingly on the Pekinese spaniel, which had slipped upon its back in the hope of a rubbed stomach, and was waving feathery paws in pursuit of her finger. A moment's reflection brought heart of grace. Greasy suit and untidy stud-hole must have been obvious to her from his first appearance on the terrace —indeed they must have been obvious while he had waited on her at déjeuner. Her invitation to converse was proof that she disregarded outer trappings, that she recognised the man beneath the soup-stained raiment. He uncrossed his legs and stood upright. Then he remembered her remark.

"The question is," said he, "whether my soul would fetch enough to provide me with a ticket to Egypt."

She smiled lazily. The sunlight being full on her face, he noticed that her eyelashes were brown. Wondrous discovery!

"Anyhow," she replied, "where there's a soul, there's a way."

She took a cigarette from a gold case that lay on the little iron table beside her. Martin sprang forward with a match. She thanked him graciously.

"It isn't money that does the real things," she said, after a few meditative puffs. "To hear an American say so must sound strange to your English ears. You believe, I know, that Americans make money an Almighty God that can work any miracles over man and natural forces that you please. But it isn't so. The miracles, such as they are, that America has performed, have been due to the naked human soul. Money has come as an accident or an accretion and has helped things along. We have a saying which you may have heard: 'Money talks.' That's just it. It talks. But the soul has had to act first. Money had nothing to do with American Independence. It was the soul of George Washington. It wasn't money that invented the phonograph. It was the soul of the train newsboy Edison. It wasn't money that brought into being the original Cornelius Vanderbilt. It was the soul of the old ferryman that divined the power of steam both on sea and land a hundred years ago, and accidentally or incidentally or logically or what you please, founded the Vanderbilt fortune. I could go on for ever with instances from my own country—instances that every school-child knows. In the eyes of the world the Almighty Dollar may seem to rule America

—but every thinking American knows in his heart of
hearts that the Almighty Dollar is but an accidental
symbol of the Almighty soul of man. And it's the
soul that we're proud of and that keeps the nation
together. All this more or less was at the back of
my mind when I said where there's a soul there's a
way."

As this little speech progressed her face lost its expression of serene and humorous contentment with the
world, and grew eager and her eyes shone and her
voice quickened. He regarded her as some fainéant
Homeric warrior might have regarded the goddess
who had descended cloud-haste from Olympus to ex-
hort him to noble deeds. The exhortation fluttered
both pride and pulses. He saw in her a woman capable of great things and she had appealed to him as a
man also capable.

"You have pointed me out the way to Egypt," he
said.

"I'm glad," said Lucilla. "Look me up when you
get there," she added with a smile. "It seems a big
place, but it isn't. Cairo, Luxor, Assouan—and at any
rate the Semiramis Hotel at Cairo."

And then she began to talk of that wonderful land,
of the mystery of the desert, the inscrutable gods of
granite and Karnac brooding over the ghost of Thebes.
She spoke from wide knowledge and sympathy. An
allusion here and there indicated how true a touch she
had on far divergent aspects of life. Apart from her
radiant adorableness which held him captive, she possessed a mind which stimulated his own so long lain
sluggish. He had not met before the highly educated
woman of the world. Instinctively he contrasted her
with Corinna, who in the first days of their pilgrimage had dazzled him with her attainments. She had
a quick intelligence, but in any matter of knowledge
was soon out of her depth; yet she exhibited singular

adroitness in regaining the shallows where she found
safety in abiding. Lucilla, on the other hand, swam
serenely out into deep blue water. From every point
of view she was a goddess of bewildering attributes.

After a while she shivered slightly. The sun had
disappeared behind a corner of the hotel. Greyness
overspread the terrace. The glory of the short winter
afternoon had departed. She rose, Heliogabalus, also
shivering, under her arm. Martin held the rugs.

"I wonder," said she, "whether you could possibly
send up some tea to my quaint little salon. Perhaps
you might induce Félise to join me."

That was all the talk he had with her. In the evening the arrival of an English motor party kept him
busy, both during dinner and afterwards; for not only
did they desire coffee and liqueurs served in the vestibule, but they gave indications to his experienced judgment of requiring relays of whiskies and sodas until
bedtime. Again he did not visit the Café de l'Univers.

The next morning she started for the Riviera. She
was proceeding thither via Toulouse, Carcassonne,
Narbonne and the coast. To Martin's astonishment
Félise was accompanying her, on a visit for ten days
or a fortnight to the South. It appeared that the
matter had been arranged late the previous evening.
Lucilla had made the proposal, swept away difficulty
after difficulty with her air of a smiling, but irresistible providence and left Bigourdin and Félise not a
leg save sheer churlishness to stand on. Clothes?
She had ten times the amount she needed. The perils
of the lonely and tedious return train journey? Never
could Félise accomplish it. Bigourdin turned up an
*Indicateur des Chemins de Fer*. There were changes,
there were waits. Communications were arranged,
with diabolical·cunning, not to correspond. Perhaps
it was to confound the Germans in case of invasion.
As far as he could make out it would take seventy-

four hours, forty-three minutes to get from Monte Carlo to Brantôme. It was far simpler to go from Paris to Moscow, which as every one knew was the end of the world. Félise would starve. Félise would perish of cold. Félise would get the wrong train and find herself at Copenhagen or Amsterdam or Naples, where she wouldn't be able to speak the language. Lucilla laughed. There was such a thing as L'Agence Cook which moulded the *Indicateur des Chemins de Fer* to its will. She would engage a man from Cook's before whose brass-buttoned coat and a gold-lettered cap band the Indicateur would fall to pieces, to transfer Félise personally, by easy stages, from house to house. Félise had pleaded her uncle's need. Lucilla, in the most charming way imaginable, had deprecated as impossible any such colossal selfishness on the part of Monsieur Bigourdin. Overawed by the Olympian he had peremptorily ordered Félise to retire and pack her trunk. Then, obeying the dictates of his sound sense he had asked Lucilla what object she had in her magnificent invitation. His little girl, said he, would acquire a taste for celestial things which never afterwards would she be in a position to gratify. To which, Lucilla:

"How do you know she won't be able to gratify them? A girl of her beauty, charm and character, together with a little knowledge of the world of men, women and things, is in a position to command whatever she chooses. She has the beauty, charm and character and I want to add the little knowledge. I want to see a lovely human flower expand"—she had a graceful trick of restrained gesture which impressed Bigourdin. "I want to give a bruised little girl whom I've taken to my heart a good time. For myself, it's some sort of way of finding a sanction for my otherwise useless existence."

And Bigourdin clutching at his bristles had plucked

forth no adequately inspired reply.  The will of the New World had triumphed over that of the Old.

All the staff of the hotel witnessed the departure.

"Monsieur Martin," said Félise in French, about to step into the great car, a medley, to her mind, of fur rugs and dark golden dogs and grey cats and maids and chauffeurs and innumerable articles of luggage, "I have scarcely had two words with you.  I no longer know where I have my head.  But look after my uncle and see that the laundress does not return the table-linen black."

"*Bien,* Mademoiselle Félise," said Martin.

Lucilla, pink and white and leopard-coated, shook hands with Bigourdin, thanked him for his hospitality and reassured him as to the perfect safety of Félise.  She stepped into the car.  Martin arranged the rugs and closed the door.  She held out her hand to him.

"We meet in Egypt," she said in a low voice.  As the car drove off, she turned round and blew a gracious kiss to the little group.

"*Voilà une petite sorcière d'Américaine,*" said Bigourdin.  "Pif! Paf! and away goes Félise on her broomstick."

Martin stood shocked at hearing his Divinity maligned as a witch.

"Here am I," continued Bigourdin, "between pretty sheets.  I have no longer a housekeeper, seeing that Madame Thuillier rendered herself unbearable.  However"—he shrugged his shoulders resignedly—"we must get on by ourselves as best we can.  The trip will be good for the health of Félise.  It will also improve her mind.  She will stay in many hotels and observe their organisation."

From the moment that Martin returned to his duties he felt unusual lack of zeal in their performance.  Deprived of the Celestial Presence the Hôtel des Grottes

seemed to be stricken with a blight. The rooms had
grown smaller and barer, the furniture more common,
and the terrace stretched outside a bleak concrete
wilderness. Often he stood on the bridge and repeated the question of the memorable evening. What
was he doing there when the wide world was illuminated by a radiant woman? Suddenly Bigourdin,
Félise, the circle of the Café de l'Univers became alien
in speech and point of view. He upbraided himself
for base ingratitude. He realised, more from casual
talk with Bigourdin, than from sense of something
wanting, the truth of Félise's last remark. In the
usual intimate order of things she would have related
her experiences of Chartres and Paris in which he
would have manifested a more than brotherly interest.
During her previous absence he had thought much of
Félise and had anticipated her return with a throb of
the heart. The dismissal of Lucien Viriot, much as he
admired the gallant ex-cuirassier, pleased him mightily. He had shared Bigourdin's excitement over the
escape from Chartres, over Fortinbras's prohibition of
the marriage, over her return in motoring state. When
she had freed herself from Bigourdin's embrace, and
turned to greet him, the clasp of her two little hands
and the sight of her eager little face had thrilled
him. He had told her, as though she belonged to him,
of the things he knew she was dying to hear. . . .
And then the figure of the American girl with her
stately witchery had walked through the door of the
*salle-à-manger* into his life.

The days went on dully, shortening and darkening
as they neared Christmas. Félise wrote letters to her
uncle, artlessly filled with the magic of the South.
Two letters from Lucilla Merriton decreed extension
of her guest's visit. Bigourdin began to lose his genial
view of existence. He talked gloomily of France's
unreadiness for war. There were thieves and traitors

in the Cabinet. Whole Army Corps were notoriously deficient in equipment and transport. It was enough, he declared, to make a patriotic Frenchman commit protesting suicide in the lobby of the Chamber of Deputies. And what news had Martin received of Mademoiselle Corinna? Martin knew little save that she was engaged in some mysterious work in London.

"But what is she doing?" cried Bigourdin, at last.

"I haven't the remotest idea," replied Martin.

"*Dites donc, mon ami,*" said Bigourdin, the gloom of anxiety deepening on his brow. "You do not think, by any chance"—he hesitated before breathing the terrible surmise—"you do not think she has made herself a suffragette?"

"How can I tell?" replied Martin. "With Corinna all things are possible."

"Except to take command of the Hôtel des Grottes," said Bigourdin, and he sighed vastly.

One evening he said: "My good friend Martin, I am feeling upset. Instead of going to the Café de l'Univers, let us have a glass of the *vieille fine du Brigadier* in the *petit salon* where I have ordered Marie to make a good fire."

The old Liqueur Brandy of the Brigadier was literally, from the market standpoint, worth its weight in gold. In the seventies Bigourdin's father, during the course of reparations, had discovered, in a blocked and forgotten cellar, three almost evaporated casks bearing the inscription just decipherable beneath the mildew in Brigadier General Bigourdin's old war-dog handwriting: "Cognac. 1812." His grandson, who had lost a leg and an arm in 1870, knew what was due to the brandy of the *Grande Armée*. Instead of filling up the casks with newer brandy and selling the result at extravagant prices, he reverently bottled the remaining contents of the three casks and on each bottle stuck a printed label setting forth the great history of the brandy, and stored the lot in a dry bin which he charged his son to venerate as one of the sacred depositaries of France in the family of Bigourdin.

Now in any first-class restaurant in Paris, Monte Carlo, Aix-les-Bains, you can get Napoleon Brandy. The bottle sealed with the still mind-stirring initial "N" on the neck, is uncorked solemnly before you by the silver-chained functionary. It is majestic liquid. But not a drop of the distillation of the Napoleonic grape is there. The casks once containing it have been filled and refilled for a hundred years. For brandy unlike port does not mature in bottle. The best 1812 brandy bottled that year would be to-day the same as it was then. But if it has remained for over sixty years in cask, you shall have a precious fluid such as it is given to few kings or even emperors to taste. I doubt whether there are a hundred gallons of it in the wide, wide world.

The proposal to open a bottle of the Old Brandy of the Brigadier portended a state of affairs so momentous that Martin gaped at the back of Bigourdin on his way to the cellar. On the occasion of what high solemnity the last had been uncorked, Martin did not know: certainly not on the occasion of the dinner of ceremony to the Viriots, in spite of the fact that the father of the prospective bridegroom was *marchand de vins en gros* and was expected by Bigourdin to produce at the return dinner some of his famous Chambertin.

"Come," said Bigourdin, cobwebbed bottle in hand, and Martin followed him into the prim little salon. From a cupboard whose glass doors were veiled with green-pleated silk, he produced two mighty quart goblets which he set down on a small table, and into each poured about a sherry-glass of the precious brandy.

"Like this," he explained, "we do not lose the perfume."

Martin sipped; it was soft like wine and the delicate flavour lingered deliciously on tongue and palate.

"I like to think," said Bigourdin, "that it contains the soul of the *Grande Armée.*"

They sat in stiff arm chairs covered in stamped velvet, one on each side of the wood fire.

"My friend," said Bigourdin, lighting a cigarette, "I am not as contented with the world as perhaps I ought to be. I had an interview with Monsieur Viriot to-day which distressed me a great deal. The two families have been friends and the Viriots have supplied us with wine on an honourable understanding for generations. But the understanding was purely mercantile and did not involve the sacrifice of a virgin. *Le Père* Viriot seems to think that it did. I exposed to him the disinclination of Félise, and the impossibility of obtaining that which is necessary, according to the law, the consent of her parents. He threw the parents to the four winds of heaven. He conducted himself like a man bereft of reason. Always beware of the obstinacy of a flat-headed man."

"What was the result of the interview?" asked Martin.

"We quarrelled for good and all. We quitted each other as enemies. He sent round his clerk this afternoon with his account, and I paid it in cash down to the last centime. And now I shall have to go to the Maison Prunier of Périgueux, who are incapable of any honourable understanding and will try to supply me with abominable beverages which will poison and destroy my clientèle."

Recklessly he finished his brandy and poured himself out another portion. Then he passed the bottle to Martin.

*"Sers-toi,"* said he, using for the first time the familiar second person singular. Martin was startled, but said nothing. Then he remembered that Bigourdin, contrary to his usual abstemious habits, had been supplied at dinner with a cradled quart of old Corton which awakens generosity of sentiment towards their fellows in the hearts of men.

*"Mon brave,"* he remarked, after a pause, "my heart is full of problems which I cannot resolve and I have no one to turn to but yourself."

"I appreciate your saying so very much," replied Martin; "but why not consult our wise and experienced friend Fortinbras?"

*"Voilà,"* cried Bigourdin, waving a great hand. "It is he who sets me the greatest problem of all. Why do you think I have let Félise go away with that pretty whirlwind of an American?" Martin stiffened, not knowing whether this was a disparagement of Lucilla; but Bigourdin, heedless, continued: "It is because she is very unhappy, and it is out of human power to give her consolation. You are a gentleman and a man of honour. I will repose in you a sacred confidence. But that which I am going to tell you, you will swear never to reveal to a living soul."

Martin gave his word. Bigourdin, without touching on long-past sorrows, described the visit of Félise to the Rue Maugrabine.

"It was my sister," said he, "for years sunk in the degradation of drunkenness—so rare among Frenchwomen—it is madness, *que veux-tu?* Often she has gone away to be cured, with no effect. I have urged my brother-in-law to put her away permanently in a *maison de santé;* but he has not been willing. It was he, he maintains, who in far-off, unhappy days, when, *pauvre garçon,* he lifted his elbow too often himself, gave her the taste for alcohol. For that reason he treats her with consideration and even tenderness. *C'est beau.* And he himself, you must have remarked, has not drunk anything but water for many years."

"Of course," said Martin, and his mind went back to his first meeting with Fortinbras in the lonely Petit Cornichon, when the latter imbibed such prodigious quantities of raspberry syrup and water. It seemed very long ago. Bigourdin went on talking.

"And so," said he, at last, "you see the unhappy situation which Fortinbras, like a true Don Quixote, has arranged between himself and Félise. She retains the sacred ideal of her mother, but holds in horror, very naturally, the father whom she has always adored. It is a bleeding wound in her innocent little soul. What can I do?"

Martin was deeply moved by the pitifulness of the tale. Poor little Félise, how much she must have suffered.

"Would it not be better," said he, "to sacrifice a phantom mother—for that's what it comes to—for the sake of a living father?"

Bigourdin agreed, but Fortinbras expressly forbade such a disclosure. In this he sympathised with Fortinbras, although the mother was his own flesh and blood. Truly he had not been lucky in sisters—one a *bigote* and the other an *alcoolique*. He expressed sombre views as to the family of which he was the sole male survivor. Seeing that his wife had given him no children, and that he had not the heart to marry one of the damsels of the neighbourhood, he bewailed the end of the good old name of Bigourdin. But perhaps it were best. For who could tell, if he begat a couple of children, whether one would not be afflicted with alcoholic, and the other with religious mania? To beget brave children for France, a man, *nom de Dieu!* must put forth all the splendour and audacity of his soul. How could he do so, when the only woman who could conjure up within him the said splendour and audacity would have nothing to do with him? To fall in love with a woman was a droll affair. But if you loved her, you loved her, however little she responded. It was a species of malady which must be supported with courageous resignation. He sighed and poured out a third glass of the brandy of the Brigadier. Martin did likewise, thinking of the woman whose white fingers held the working of the splendour and audacity of the soul of Martin Overshaw. He felt drawn into brotherly sympathy with Bigourdin; but, for the life of him, he could not see how anybody could be dependent for soul provisions of splendour and audacity upon Corinna Hastings. The humbly aspiring fellow moved him to patronising pity.

Martin strove to comfort him with specious words of hope. But Bigourdin's mental condition was that of a man to whom wallowing in despair alone brings consolation. He had been suffering from a gathering avalanche of misfortunes. First had come his rejection, followed by the unsatisfied longing of the devout lover. It cannot be denied, however, that he had borne himself gallantly. Then the fading of his dream of the Viriot alliance had filled him with dismay. Félise's adventure in the Rue Maugrabine and its resulting situation had caused him sleepless nights. Lucilla Merriton had taken him up between her fingers and twiddled him round, thereby depriving him of volition, and having put him down in a state of bewilderment, had carried off Félise. And to-day, last accretion that set the avalanche rolling, his old friend Viriot had called him a breaker of honourable understandings and had sent a clerk with his bill. The avalanche swept him into the Slough of Despond, wherein he lay solacing himself with hopeless imaginings and the old brandy of the Brigadier. But human instinct made him beckon to Martin, call him *"tu"* and bid him to keep an eye on the quagmire and stretch out a helping hand. He also had in view a subtle and daring scheme.

*"Mon brave ami,"* said he, "when I die"—his broad face assumed an expression of infinite woe and he spoke as though he were seventy—"what will become of the Hôtel des Grottes? Félise will benefit principally, *bien entendu,* by my will; but she will marry one of these days and will follow her husband, who probably will not want to concern himself with hotel keeping." He glanced shrewdly at Martin, who regarded him with unmoved placidity. "To think that the hotel will be sold and all its honourable traditions changed would break my heart. I should not like to die without any solution of continuity."

"But, my dear Bigourdin," said Martin, "what are you thinking of? You're a young man. You're not stricken with a fatal malady. You're not going to die. You have twenty, thirty, perhaps forty years before you in the course of which all kinds of things may happen."

Bigourdin leant forward and stretched out his great arm across the fireplace until his fingers touched Martin's knee.

"Do you know what is going to happen? War is going to happen. Next year—the year after—five years hence—*que sais-je, moi?*—but it has to come. All these pacifists and anti-militarists are either imbeciles or traitors—those that are not dreaming madhouse dreams of the millennium are filling their pockets —of the latter there are some in high places. There is going to be war, I tell you, and many people are going to die. And when the bugle sounds I put on my old uniform and march to the cannon's mouth like my fathers before me. And why shouldn't I die, like my brother in Morocco? Tell me that?"

In spite of his intimacy with the sturdy thought of provincial France, Martin could not realise how the vague imminence of war could affect so closely the personal life of an individual Frenchman.

"No matter," said Bigourdin, after a short discussion. "I have to die some day. It was not to argue about the probable date of my decease that I have asked you to honour me with this special conversation. I have expressed to you quite frankly the motives which actuate me at the present moment. I have done so in order that you may understand why I desire to make you a business proposition."

"A business proposition?" echoed Martin.

"*Oui, mon ami.*"

He replenished Martin's enormous beaker and his own and gave the toast.

"*A l'Entente Cordiale*—between our nations and between our two selves."

Lest the uninitiated may regard this sitting as a dram drinking orgy, it must be borne in mind that in such brandy as that of the Brigadier, strength has melted into the gracious mellowness of old age. The fiery spirit that the *cantinière* or the *vivandière* of 1812 served out of her little waist-slung barrel to the warriors of the *Grande Armée,* was now but a fragrant memory of battles long ago.

"A business proposition," repeated Bigourdin, and forthwith began to develop it. It was the very simplest business proposition in the world. Why should not Martin invest all or part of his little heritage in the century-old and indubitably flourishing business of the Hôtel des Grottes, and become a partner with Bigourdin? Lawyers would arrange the business details. In this way, whether Bigourdin met with a gory death within the next two or three years or a peaceful one a quarter of a century hence, he would be reassured that there would be no solution of con-

tinuity in the honourable tradition of the Hôtel des
Grottes.

It was then that Martin fully understood the solemnity of the occasion—the *petit salon* with fire specially lit, the Brigadier brandy, the preparatory revelation of the soul-state of Bigourdin. The unexpected-
ness of the suggestion, however, dazed him. He said
politely:

"My dear friend, your proposal that I should asso-
ciate myself with you in this business is a personal
compliment, which I shall never cease to appreciate.
But——"

"But what?"

"I must think over it."

"Naturally," said Bigourdin. "One would be a lin-
net or a butterfly instead of a man if one took a step
like that without thinking. But at least the idea is
not disagreeable to you."

"Of course not," replied Martin. "The only question is how should I get the money?"

"Your little heritage, *parbleu.*"

"But that is in Consols—*rentes anglaises,* and I
only get my dividends twice a year."

"You could sell out to-morrow or the next day and
get the whole in bank notes or golden sovereigns."

"I suppose I could," said Martin. Not till then had
he realised the simple fact that if he chose he could
walk about with a sack of a thousand sovereigns over
his shoulder. He had taken it in an unspeculative
way for granted that the capital remained locked up
behind impassable doors in the Bank of England. Instinct, however, restrained him from confessing to
Bigourdin such innocence in business affairs.

"If I did not think it would be as safe here as in
the hands of the British Government, I would not
make the suggestion."

Martin started upright in his chair.

"My dear friend, I know that," he cried ingenuously, horrified lest he should be thought to suspect Bigourdin's good faith.

"And you would no longer wear that costume." Bigourdin smiled and waved a hand towards the dress-suit.

"Which is beginning to show signs of wear," said Martin.

He glanced down and caught sight of the offending splotch of grease. The quick association of ideas caused a vision of Lucilla to pass before his eyes. He heard her rich, deep voice: "We meet in Egypt." But how the deuce could they meet in Egypt or in any other Lucilla-lit spot on the earth if he started inn-keeping with Bigourdin, and tied himself down for life to Brantôme? A chill ran down his spine.

"*Eh, bien?*" said Bigourdin, recalling him to the *petit salon*.

Martin had an inspiration of despair. "I should like," said he, "to talk the matter over with Fortinbras."

"It is what I should advise," said Bigourdin heartily. "You can go to Paris whenever you like. And now *n'en parlons plus*. I feel much happier than at the beginning of the evening. It is the brandy of the brave old Brigadier. Let us empty the bottle and drink to the repose of his soul. He would ask nothing better."

# CHAPTER XV

THE days went on, and nothing more was said of the proposal, it being understood that, as soon as Félise had wrought order out of chaos for a second time, Martin should consult with Fortinbras, his bankers, his solicitors and other eminent advisers. They resumed their evening visits to the Café de l'Univers, where Bigourdin and Monsieur Viriot sat as far apart as was consonant with membership of the circle. On meeting they saluted each other with elaborate politeness and addressed each other as "Monsieur" when occasion required interchange of speech. Every one knew what had happened, and, as every one was determined that the strained relations between them should not interfere with his own personal comfort, nobody cared.. The same games were played, the same arguments developed. A favourite theme was the probable action of the Socialists on the outbreak of war. Some held, Monsieur Viriot among them, that they would refuse to take up arms and would spread counsels of ignominy among the people. The Professor at the Ecole Normale, allowed to express latitudinarian views on account of his philosophic position, was of opinion that the only safeguard against a European war lay in the solidarity of the International Socialist Brotherhood.

"The Prussian drill-sergeant," said the Mayor, "will soon see that there is no solidarity as far as Germany is concerned."

"We have no drill-sergeants. The *sous-officier* is under the officer who is under the general who is bought by the men we are so besotted as to put into

power to play into the hands of the enemy.   Our Socialists will cleave to their infamous principles." Thus
declared Monsieur Viriot, who was a reactionary re-
publican and regarded Socialism and Radicalism and
Anti-clericalism as punishments inflicted by an outraged Heaven on a stiff-necked generation.   "The Socialist will betray us," he cried.

"Monsieur," replied Bigourdin loftily, "you are
wrong to accuse the loyalty of your compatriots.   I
am not a socialist.   I, as every one knows, hold their
mischievous ideas in detestation.   But I have faith in
the human soul.   There's not a Socialist, not an An-
archist, not even an Apache, who, when the German
cannon sounds in his ears, will not rush to shed his
blood in the defence of the sacred soil of France."

"Bravo!" cried one.

"*C'est bien dit!*" cried another.

"After all, the soil is in the blood," said a third.

Monsieur Cazensac, the landlord, who stood listening, said with a certain Gascon mordancy:

"Scratch even a Minister and you will find a Frenchman."

And so the discussion—and who shall say it was
a profitless one?—went on evening after evening, as
it had gone on, in some sort of fashion conditioned
by circumstances for over forty years.

On Christmas Eve came Félise, convoyed as far as
Périgueux, where Bigourdin met her train, by the
promised man from Cook's.   It was a changed little
Félise, flushed with health and armoured in sophistica-
tion that greeted Martin.   Her first preoccupation was
no longer the disasters that might have occurred under
helpless male rule during her absence.

"I've had the time of my life," she asserted with a
curious lazy accent.   "It would take weeks to tell you.
Monte Carlo is too heavenly for words.   Lucilla committed perjury and swore I was over twenty-one and

got me into the rooms and into the Sports Club, and what do you think? I won a thousand francs," she tapped her bosom. "I have it here in good French money."

Martin stared. The face was the face of Félise, but the voice was the voice of Lucilla. The English too of Félise was no longer her pretty halting speech, but fluent, as though, by her frequentation of English-speaking folk, all the old vocabulary of childhood had returned, together with sundry accretions. She rattled off a succinct account of the loveliness of the Azure Coast, with its flowers and seas and sunshine, the motor drives she had taken, the lunches, dinners and suppers she had eaten, the people she had met. Lucilla seemed to have friends everywhere, mainly English and American. They had seldom been alone. Félise had lived all the time in a social whirl.

"You will find Brantôme very dull now, Félise," said Martin.

She laughed. "If you think my head's turned, you're mistaken. It's a little head more solid than that." Then, growing serious—"What I have seen and heard yonder, in a different sort of world, will enable me to form a truer judgment of things in Brantôme."

Bigourdin came near the truth when he remarked later with a smile and a sigh:

"Here is our little girl transformed, in a twinkling, into a woman. She has acquired the art of hiding her troubles and of mocking at her tears. She will tell me henceforward only what it pleases her that I should know."

Félise took up her duties cheerfully, performing them with the same thoroughness as before, but with a certain new and sedate authority. Her pretty assumption of dignified command had given place to calm assertion. Euphémie and Baptiste accustomed to girlish rebukes and rejoinders grumbled at the new phase. When Félise cut short the hitherto wonted argument by a: *"Ma bonne Euphémie,* the way it is to be done is the way I want it done," and marched off like a duchess unperturbed, Euphémie shook her head and wondered whether she were still in the same situation. In her attitude towards Martin, she became more formal as a mistress and more superficial as friend. She had caught the trick of easy talk, which might have disconcerted him had the world been the same as it was before the advent of Lucilla. But the world had changed. He lived in Brantôme an automatic existence, his body there, his spirit far away. His mind dwelt little on any possible deepening or hardening in the character of Félise. So her altered attitude, though he could not help noticing it, caused him no disturbance. He thought casually: "Compared with the men she has met in the great world, I am but a person of mediocre interest."

The New Year came in, heralded by snow and ice all over Europe. Beneath the steel-blue sky Brantôme looked pinched with cold. The hotel was almost empty, and Martin found it hard to occupy long hours of chilly idleness otherwise than by dreaming of Lucilla and palms and sunshine. Lucilla of course was always under the palms and the palms were in the sunshine; and he was talking to Lucilla, alone with her in the immensities of the desert. When he had dreamed long enough he shivered, for the Hôtel des Grottes still depended for warmth on wood fires and there was no central heating and the bath in the famous bathroom received hot water through a gas geyser. And then he wondered whether the time had not come for him to make his momentous journey to Paris.

"I've had a letter from Miss Merriton," said Félise one day, "she asks for news of you and sends you her kind regards."

Martin, who, in shirt-sleeves and apron, was laying tables in the *salle-à-manger,* flushed at his goddess's message.

"It's very good of her to remember me."

"Oh, she remembers you right enough," said Félise.

That meant that his goddess must have spoken of him, not only once but on various occasions. She had carried him so far in her thoughts as to be interested in his doings. Did her words imply a veiled query as to his journey into Egypt? A lover reads an infinity of significance in his mistress's most casual utterance, but blandly fails to interpret the obvious tone in which the woman with whom he is not in love makes an acid remark.

"Where is Miss Merriton now?" he asked.

She informed him coldly—not at all with the air of the wild flowers from which Alpine honey is made— that Lucilla was sailing next week for Alexandria. "And," said she, "as I am a sort of messenger, what reply shall I make?"

Martin, who had developed a lover's cunning, answered: "Give her my respectful greetings and say that I am very well." No form of words could be less compromising.

That same evening, on their cold way back from the Café de l'Universe, Bigourdin said, using as he had done since the night of the intimate conversation the *"tu"* of familiarity:

"Now that Félise has returned, and all goes on wheels and business is slack, don't you think it is a good opportunity for you to go to Paris for your holiday and your consultations?"

"I will go the day after to-morrow," replied Martin.

"Have you told Félise of your proposed journey?"

"Not yet," said Martin.

*"C'est bien.* When you tell her, say it is for the

sake of a change, your health, your little affairs, what you will. It is better that she should not know of our scheme until it is all arranged."

"I think that would be wiser," said Martin.

"In the event of your accepting my proposition," said Bigourdin, after a pause, "have you ever thought of the possibility of becoming a naturalised Frenchman? Like that, perhaps, business might roll more smoothly. We have already spoken, you and I, of your becoming a good Périgordin."

Martin, hands in pockets and shoulders hunched so as to obtain ear-shelter beneath the upturned collar of his great coat, was silent for a few moments. Then—

"Nationality is a strange thing," said he. "The more I live in France, the more proud I am of being an Englishman."

Bigourdin sprang a pace apart, wounded to the quick. *"Mais non par exemple!* You of all men," and it was the *"vous"* of formality, "ought not to say that."

*"Mais que tu es bête!* You misunderstand me. You don't let me proceed," cried Martin, halting before him in the semi-darkness of the quay. "In France I have learned the meaning of the word patriotism. I have been surrounded here with the love of country, and I have reflected. This impulse is so strong in all French hearts, ought it not to be as strong in the heart of an Englishman? France has taught me the finest of lessons. I am as loyal a Frenchman as any of our friends at the Café de l'Univers, but—" adapting a vague reminiscence of the lyric to Lucasta—"I should not love France so much, if I did not love England more."

*"Mon brave ami!"* cried Bigourdin, holding out both hands, in a Frenchman's instinctive response to a noble sentiment adequately expressed, "Pardon me. Let us say no more about it. The true Englishman

who loves France is a better friend to us than the Englishman who has lost his love for England."

Martin went to bed in a somewhat tortured frame of mind. He was very simple, very honest, very conscientious. It was true that the flame of French patriotism had kindled the fire of English patriotism within him. It was true that he had learned to love this sober, intense, kindly land of France. It was true that here was a generous bosom of France willing to enfold him, an alien, like one of her own sons. But it was equally true that in his ears rang a clarion call sounded not by mother England, not by foster-mother France, but by *une petite sorcière Américaine,* a fair witch neither of England nor of France, but from beyond the estranging seas. And the day after tomorrow he was journeying to Paris to take the advice of Fortinbras, *Marchand de Bonheur.* What would the dealer in happiness decide? To wait until some turn of Fortune's wheel should change his career and set him free to wander forth across the world, or to invest his all in an inglorious though comfortable future? Either way there would be heart-racking.

But Bigourdin, as he secured the Hôtel des Grottes with locks and bolts, whistled *"Malbrouck s'en va-t-en guerre,"* a sign of his being pleased with existence. He had no doubt of Fortinbras's decision. Fortinbras had practically given it in a letter he had received that afternoon. For he had told Fortinbras his proposal, which was based on the certainty of a marriage between Félise and Martin, as soon as the latter should find himself in a position that would warrant a declaration up to now impossible to a man of delicate honour. "They think I am an old mole," he had written, "but for certain things I have the eyes of a hawk. Why did Félise suddenly refuse Lucien Viriot? Why has Martin during her last absence been in a state of depression lamentable to behold? And now that Félise has returned, changed from a young girl into that thing of mystery, a woman, why are their relations once so fraternal marked by an exquisite politeness? And why must Martin travel painful hours in a train in order to consult the father of Félise? Tell me all that! When it comes to real diplomacy, *mon vieux* Daniel, trust the solid head of Gaspard Bigourdin."

Which excerpt affords a glimpse into the workings of a subtle yet ingenuous mind. He hummed *"Malbrouck s'en va-t-en guerre"* as he went upstairs. The little American witch never crossed his thoughts, nor did a possible application of the line *"Ne sais quand reviendra."*

The High Gods hold this world in an uncertain balance; and, whenever they decree to turn things topsy-turvy, they have only to flick it the myriadth part of a millimetre. The very next day they gave it such a flick, and it was Bigourdin and not Martin who went to Paris.

*"Ma petite* Félise," said Bigourdin the next day, "I have received this morning from Paris a telegram despatched last night summoning me thither on urgent business. I may be away three or four days, during which I have arranged for the excellent Madame Chauvet who devoted such maternal care to you on the journey to Chartres to stay here *pour les convenances."*

The subtle diplomatist smiled; so that when she questioned him as to the nature of this urgent business and he replied that it was a worrying matter of lawyers and stockbrokers, she accepted the explanation. But to Martin—

*"Mon pauvre ami,"* said he, with woe-begone face, "it is the mother of Félise. She is dying. A syncope. We must not let Félise know or she would insist

on accompanying me, which would be impossible."

Martin took a detached view of the situation.

"Why?" he asked. "She is a woman now and able to accept her share in the tragedy of life with courage and with reason. Why not let her go and learn the truth?"

Bigourdin waved a gesture of despair. "I detest like you this deception. Lying is as foreign to my character as to yours. But *que veux-tu?* In the tragedy of my brother-in-law there is something at once infinitely piteous and sublime. In a matter like this the commands of a father are sacred. Ah, my poor Cécile!" said he, passing a great hand swiftly across his eyes. "Twenty years ago, what a pretty girl she was! Of a character somewhat difficult and bizarre. But I loved her more than my sister Clothilde, who had all the virtues of the *petite rosaire.*" He fetched a deep sigh. "One is bound to believe in the eternal wisdom of the All-Powerful. There is nothing between that and the lunatic caprice of an almighty mad goat. That is why I hold to Christianity and embark on this terrible journey with fortitude and resignation."

He held out his packet of *Bastos* to Martin. They lit cigarettes. To give this confidential information he had drawn Martin into the murky little *bureau* whose window looked upon the sad grey vestibule.

"I am sorry," he said, "that your holiday has to be postponed. But it will only be for a few days. In the meantime I leave Félise in the loyal care of yourself and the good Madame Chauvet."

Bigourdin went to Paris and deposited his valise at a little hotel in a little street off the Boulevard Sébastopol, where generations of Bigourdins had stayed, perhaps even the famous Brigadier General himself; where the proposed entertainment of an Englishman

would have caused the host as much consternation as
that of a giraffe; where the beds were spotless, the
*cuisine* irreproachable and other arrangements of a
beloved and venerable antiquity. Here the good Périgordin found a home from his home in Périgord.
The last thing a solid and virtuous citizen of central
France desires to do in Paris is to Parisianise himself.
The solid and virtuous inhabitants of Périgord went
to the Hôtel de la Dordogne which flourishes now and
feeds its customers as succulently as it did a hundred
years ago.

Having deposited his valise at this historic hostelry,
Bigourdin proceeded to the Rue Maugrabine. He had
never been there before, and his heart sank, as the
heart of Félise had sunk, when he mounted the grimy,
icy stairs and sought the home of Fortinbras. His
sister Clothilde, severe in awful mourning, admitted
him, encaged him in a ghostly embrace and conducted
him into the poverty-stricken living room where Fortinbras, in rusty black and dingy white tie, stood waiting to receive him.

"Unfortunately, my dear Gaspard," said Fortinbras, "you are not in time."

He opened the flimsy door set in the paper-covered
match-board partition. Bigourdin entered the bedroom and there, with blinds drawn and candles burning at head and feet lay all that remained of Cécile
Fortinbras. He returned soon afterwards drying his
eyes, for memories of childhood had brought tears.
He wrung Fortinbras by the hand.

"Here, *mon vieux* Daniel, is the very sad end of a
life that was somewhat tragic; but you can console
yourself with the thought of your long devotion and
tenderness."

Clothilde Robineau tossed her head and sniffed:

"I don't see around me much evidence of those two
qualities."

"Your reproaches, Clothilde," said Fortinbras, "are as just as Gaspard's consolation is generous."

"I am glad you acknowledge, at last, that it was you who dragged my unfortunate sister down to this misery."

Fortinbras made no reply. Lives like his one must understand and pardon as Bigourdin had done. Nothing that he could say could mitigate the animosity of Clothilde which he had originally incurred by marrying her sister. She would be moved by no pleading that it was his wife's extravagance and intemperance that had urged him to the mad tampering with other people's money (money honestly repaid, but all the same diverted wrongly for a time) which had caused him to be struck off the roll of solicitors and to leave England a disgraced man. She would have retorted that had he not been addicted to *boissons alcooliques*, a term which in France always means fiery spirits, and had he not led the life of the theatre and the restaurant, Cécile would have been sober and thrifty like herself and Gaspard. And Fortinbras would have beat his breast saying "Mea culpa." He might have pleaded the after years of ceaseless struggle. But to what end? As soon as his wife was laid beneath the ground, Clothilde would gather together her skirts and pass for ever out of his life. Bigourdin knew of his remorse, his home of unending horror, his efforts ever frustrated, the weight at his feet that not only prevented him from rising, but dragged him gradually down, down, down.

But even Bigourdin, who had not been to Paris for ten years, had not appreciated till now the depths of poverty into which Fortinbras and his sister had sunk. His last visit to them had been painful. A drunken, dishevelled hostess, especially when she is your own sister, does not make for charm. But they lived in a reputable apartment at Auteuil, and there was a good

carpet on the floor of the salon and chairs and tables
such as are found in Christian dwellings, and on the
mantelpiece stood the ormolu clock, and on the walls
hung the pictures which had once adorned their home
in London. How had they come down to this? He
shivered, cold and ill at ease.

"As you must be hungry after your long journey,
Gaspard," said Madame Robineau, "I should advise
you to go out to a restaurant. The cuisine of the
*femme de journée* I do not recommend. For me, I
must keep watch, and it being Friday I fast as usual."

Fortinbras made no pretence at hospitality. Had
he been able to set forth a banquet, he felt that every
morsel would have been turned into stone by the
basilisk eyes of Clothilde. Both men rose simultaneously, glad to be free. They went out, took an
omnibus haphazard and eventually entered a restaurant in the neighbourhood of the Tour Saint-Jacques.

"*Mon vieux* Daniel," said Bigourdin, as soon as
they were seated. "Tell me frankly, for I don't understand. How comes it that you are in these dreadful straits?"

Fortinbras smiled sadly.

"One earns little by translating from French into
English and still less by dispensing happiness to
youth."

"But——" Bigourdin hesitated. "But you have
had other resources—not much certainly, but still
something."

"What do you mean?" asked Fortinbras. "You
know that in five years Cécile scattered her own dowry
to the winds and left me at the edge of a whirlpool of
debt. All of my own I could scrape together and bor-
row I threw in to save myself from prison. She had
no heritage from her father. On what else can we
have lived save on my precarious earnings?"

Bigourdin, both elbows on the table, plucked at his

upstanding bristles and gazed intently at Fortinbras.

"Ever since the great misfortune, when you returned to France, Cécile has had her own income."

"You are dreaming, Gaspard. From what source could she obtain an income?"

"From me, *parbleu!*" cried Bigourdin. "I always thought my father's will was unjust. Cécile should have had her share. When I thought she needed assistance, I arranged with my lawyer, Maître Dupuy, 33 Rue des Augustins, Paris, to allow her five thousand francs a year in monthly instalments, and I know—*sacre bleu!*—that it has been paid."

Fortinbras also put his elbows on the table, and the two men looked close into each other's faces.

"I know absolutely nothing about it. Cécile has not had one penny that I have not given to her."

"It is horrible to speak like this," said Bigourdin. "But one cannot drink to excess without spending much money. Where did she get it?"

"There are alcohols unknown to the Hôtel des Grottes, which it takes little money to buy. To get that little she has pawned the sheets off the bed."

"*Nom de Dieu!*" said Bigourdin.

It was a miserable meal, ending almost in silence. When it was over they called at the cabinet of Maître Dupuy. They found everything in order. Every month for years past Madame Fortinbras had received the sum of four hundred and sixteen francs, sixty-five centimes. She had come personally for the money. Maître Dupuy remembered his first interview with Madame. She had expressly forbidden him to send the money to the house lest it should fall into the hands of her husband. He infinitely regretted to make such a statement in the presence of Monsieur, but those were the facts.

"All this is evidence in favour of what I told you," said Fortinbras.

"I never doubted you!" cried Bigourdin, "and this is proof. But what can she have done with all that money?"

It was a mystery. They went back to the Rue Maugrabine. On the way Fortinbras asked:

"Why have you never told me what you were doing?"

"I took it for granted that you knew, and that, *par délicatesse*, the subject was not to be mentioned between us."

"And Clothilde?"

But Bigourdin was one of those who kept the left hand in ignorance of the generous actions of the right. He threw out his great arms, to the disturbance of pedestrian traffic.

"Tell Clothilde? What do you take me for?"

A day or two of continuous strain and hopelessness, and then under the auspices of the *Pompes Funèbres* and the clergy of the parish, the poor body of Cécile Fortinbras was laid to rest. Not till then did any one send word to Félise. Even Madame Robineau agreed that it was best she should not know. As she had left Chartres, self-willed and ungovernable, so, on the receipt of the news of her mother's death, might she leave Brantôme. Her appearance amid these squalid happenings would be *inconvenable*.

"I have no reason to love Félise," she added. "But she is a young girl of our family, and it is not correct that she should see such things."

When the train carrying Madame Robineau back to Chartres steamed out of the Gare Montparnasse, both men drew a breath of relief.

"*Mon ami*," said Bigourdin. "The Bible taught the Church the beautiful history of Jesus Christ. The Church told a Bishop. The Bishop told a priest. The priest told the wife of the sub-prefect. The wife of the sub-prefect told the wife of the mayor. The wife of the mayor told the elderly, unmarried sister of the corn-chandler, and the unmarried sister of the corn-chandler told Clothilde. And that's all she (Clothilde) knows about Christianity. Still," he added, in his judicious way, "she is a woman of remarkable virtue. She has a strong sense of duty. Without a particle of love animating her heart, she has just spent three days and nights without sleep, food or fresh air. It's fine, all the same."

"I am not ungrateful," said Fortinbras.

They entered a café for the sake of shelter from the bitter January wind, and they talked, as they had done lately, of many intimate things; of the past, of Martin, of the immediate future. Fortinbras would not accompany Bigourdin to Brantôme. His presence would only add poignancy to the grief of Félise. It was more impossible now than ever to undeceive her, as one could not speak ill of the dead. No; he would remain in Paris, where he had much to do. First he must move from the Rue Maugrabine. The place would be haunted. Besides, what did one old vagabond want with two rooms and a kitchen? He would sell his few belongings, and take a furnished room somewhere among the chimney-pots. . . . Bigourdin lifted his *petit verre* of Armagnac, and forgetting all about it, put it down again.

"What I am going to tell you," said he, "may seem cynical, but it is only common sense. Do not leave the Rue Maugrabine without having searched every corner, every box, every garment, every piece of furniture."

"Search?—what for?"

"The little economies of Cécile," said Bigourdin.

Fortinbras put up a protesting hand. Instinct revolted. "Impossible!" he declared.

Bigourdin persisted. "Although you have lived long in the country and been married to a French-

woman, you do not know, like myself who have it in
my veins, of what the peasant blood of France is
capable where money is concerned. It is impossible
on your own showing, that Cécile should have spent
five thousand francs a year. You have seen for yourself that she received the money. What has she done
with it?" He leaned across the table and with great
forefinger tapped the shoulder of Fortinbras. "She
has hoarded it. It is there in the Rue Maugrabine."

Fortinbras shook his leonine head. "It was absurd.
In the olden days, when she had money, had she not
scattered it recklessly?" Bigourdin agreed.

"But then," said he, "you struck misfortune, poverty. Did you not observe a change in her habits, and
in her character? Of course, we have often spoken
of it. It was the outer trappings of the bourgeois that
had disappeared and the *paysanne* asserted herself.
For many years my father supported my mother's
mother, a peasant from La Beauce who gave out that
she was penniless. When she died they accidentally
found the mattress of her bed stuffed with a little fortune. The blood of Grandmère Tidier ran in the veins
of Cécile. And Cécile like all the family knew of the
fortune of Grandmère Tidier."

All that in Fortinbras was half-forgotten, buried
beneath the rubbish heap of years, again protested: his
gently nurtured childhood, his smooth English home,
his impeccable Anglo-Indian father, Major-General
Fortinbras, who had all the servants in morning and
evening for family prayers and read the lessons in
the little village church on Sundays, his school-days—
Winchester, with its noble traditions—all, as we English understand it, that goes to the making of an honourable gentleman. If Pactolus, dammed by his wife,
poured through the kitchen taps, he would not turn
them.

"It is I then that will do it," said Bigourdin. "I am

not Anti-Semite in any way; but to present a Jew
dealer, who is already very well off, with many thousands of francs is the act of an imbecile."

He tossed off his glass of Armagnac, beckoned the
waiter, threw down the coins for payment and rose.

"*Allons!*" said he.

Fortinbras, exhausted in mind and soul, followed
him. An auto-taxi took them to the Rue Maugrabine.
The desolate and haggard *femme de journée* was restoring the house of death to some sort of aimless
order. Bigourdin put a ten-franc piece into her hand.

"That is for you. Come back in two hours' time."

The woman went. The two men were left alone in
the wretched little room, whose poverty stared from
its cracked and faded wall paper, from its bare floor,
from the greasy plush couch with one maimed leg stuck
in an old salmon tin.

Fortinbras threw himself with familiar recklessness
on the latter article of furniture and covered his eyes
with his hand.

"A quarter of a century is a long time, my dear
Gaspard," said he. "A quarter of a century's daily
and nightly intimate associations with another human
being leaves a deep imprint in one's soul. I have been
very unhappy, it is true. But I have never been so
unhappy and so hopeless as I am now. Let me be for
a little. My head is stupefied."

"*Mon pauvre vieux,*" said Bigourdin, very gently.
He glanced around and seeing a blanket, which Clothilde had used during her vigil, neatly folded by the
*femme de Journée* and laid upon a wooden chair, he
threw it over the recumbent Fortinbras. "*Mon pauvre
vieux,* you are exhausted. Stay there and go to sleep."

The very weary man closed his eyes. Two hours
later, the *femme de journée* appeared. Bigourdin,
with his finger to his lips, pointed to the sleeper and
told her to come in the morning. It was then six

o'clock in the afternoon. Bigourdin wrapped in whatever coverings he could find, dozed in a ricketty armchair for many hours, until Fortinbras awoke with a start.

"I must have fallen asleep," he said. "I'm very sorry. What is the time?"

Bigourdin pulled out his watch.

"Midnight," said he.

Fortinbras rose, passed both hands over his white flowing hair.

"I too, like Clothilde, haven't slept for two or three nights. Sleep came upon me all of a sudden, let me see——" he touched his broad forehead—"you brought me back here for some purpose."

"I did," said Bigourdin. "Come and see."

He took the lamp from the table and led his brother-in-law into the bedroom.

"I told you so," said he, pointing to the bed.

The upper ticking had been ripped clean away. And there, in the horsehair, on the side where Cécile had slept, were five or six odd little nests. And each nest was stuffed tight with banknotes and gold.

"It's all yours," said Fortinbras.

Bigourdin, swinging arms like a windmill, swept imbeciles like Fortinbras to the thirty-two points of the compass.

"It is the property of Cécile. I have nothing to do with it. I am a man of honour, not a scoundrel. It belonged to Cécile. It now belongs to you."

They argued for a long time until sheer hunger sent them forth. And over supper in a little restaurant of the quarter, they argued, until at last Bigourdin, very wearied, retired to the Hôtel de la Dordogne, and Fortinbras returned to the Rue Maugrabine, to find himself the unwilling possessor of about two thousand pounds.

## CHAPTER XVI

THE interest which Félise manifested in Madame Chauvet's conversation surprised that simple-minded lady. Madame Chauvet fully realised her responsibilities. She performed her dragonly duties with the conscientiousness of a French mother who had (and was likely to have to the end of the chapter) marriageable daughters. But commerce is commerce, and the young girl engaged in commercial management in her own house has, in France, owing to the scope required by her activities, far more freedom than her school contemporary who leads a purely domestic life: a fact recognised by the excellent Madame Chauvet as duly established in the social scheme. She was ready to allow Félise all the necessary latitude. Félise claimed scarcely any. She kept the good Madame Chauvet perpetually pinned to her skirts. She had not a confidential word to say to Martin.

Now Madame Chauvet liked Martin, as did every one in Brantôme. He was courteous, he was modest, he was sympathetic. Whatever he did was marked by an air of good-breeding which the French are very quick to notice. Whether he handed her the stewed veal or listened to the latest phase of her chronic phlebitis, Madame Chauvet always felt herself in the presence of what she termed, *une âme d'élite*—a picked and chosen soul; he was also as gentle as a sheep. Why, therefore, Félise, in her daily intercourse with Martin, should insist on her waving the banner of the proprieties over their heads, was more than the good lady could understand. Félise was more royalist than the King, more timid than a nunnery, more white-wax

and rose-leaves than her favourite author, Monsieur
Réné Bazin, had ever dared to portray as human. If
Martin had been six foot of thews and muscles, with
conquering moustaches, and bold and alluring eyes, she
would not have hesitated to protect Félise with her
Frenchwoman's little plump body and unshakable courage. But why all this precaution against the mild,
grey-eyed, sallow-faced Martin, *doux comme un mou-
ton*? And why this display of daughterly affection
suddenly awakened after fifteen years' tepid acquaintance? Even Martin, unconscious of offence, wondered at such prim behaviour. The fact remained,
however, that she scarcely spoke to him during the
greater part of Bigourdin's absence.

But when the news came that her mother was dead
and laid to rest, and she had recovered from the first
overwhelming shock, she dropped all outer trappings
of manner and became once more the old Félise. Madame Chauvet, knowing nothing of the dream-mother,
offered her unintelligent consolation. She turned instinctively to Martin, in whom she had confided. Martin was moved by her grief and did his best to sympathise; but he wished whole-heartedly that Bigourdin
had not told him the embarrassing truth. Here was
the poor girl weeping her eyes out over a dead angel
whom he knew to be nothing of the kind. He upbraided himself for a sacrilegious hypocrite when he
suggested that they would meet in Heaven. She withdrew, however, apparently consoled.

A few hours later, she came to him again—in the
vestibule. She had dried her eyes and she wore the
air of one who has accepted sorrow and bravely faced
an unalterable situation. She showed also a puzzled
little knitting of the brows.

"Tell me truly, Martin," she said. "Did my uncle,
before he left, give you the real reason of his going
to Paris?"

Challenged, Martin could not lie. "Yes. Your mother was very ill. But he commanded me not to tell you, in order to save you suffering. He didn't know. She might recover, in which case all would have been well."

"So you, too, were dragged into this strange plot, to keep me away from my mother."

"I've never heard of one, Félise," answered Martin, this time with conscience-smiting mendacity, "and my part has been quite innocent."

"There has been a plot of some kind," said Félise, breaking into the more familiar French. "My uncle, my father, my Aunt Clothilde have been in it. And now you—under my uncle's orders. There has been a mystery about my mother which I have never been able to understand—like the mystery of the Trinity or the Holy Sacraments. And to-day I understand still less. I have not seen my mother since I was five years old. She has not written to me for many years, although I have written regularly. Did she get my letters? These are questions I have been asking myself the last few hours. Why did my father not allow me to see her in the hospital in Paris? Why did my Aunt Clothilde always turn the mention of her name aside and would tell me nothing about her? And now, when she died, why did they not telegraph for me to go to Paris, so as to look for one last time on her face? They knew all that was in my heart. What have they all been hiding from me?"

"My poor Félise," said Martin, "how can I tell?"

And how could he, seeing that he was bound in honour to keep her in ignorance?

"Sometimes I think she may have had some dreadful disease that ravaged her dear features, and they wished to spare me the knowledge. But my father has always drawn me the picture of her lying beautiful as she always was upon the bed she could not leave."

"Whatever it was," said Martin, "you may be sure that those who love you acted for the best."

"That is all very well for a child; but not for a grown woman. And it is not as though I have not shown myself capable of serious responsibilities. It is heartrending," she added after a little pause, "to look into the eyes of those one loves and see in them something hidden."

Sitting there sideways on the couch by Martin's side, her girlish figure bent forward and her hands nervously clasped on her knee, the oval of her pretty face lengthened despondently, her dark eyes fixed upon him in reproachful appeal, she looked at once so pathetic and so winning that for the moment he forgot the glory of Lucilla and longed to comfort her. He laid his hand on her white knuckles.

"I would give anything," said he——

She loosened her clasp, thus eluding his touch, and moved a little aside. Madame Chauvet appeared from the kitchen passage, bearing a steaming cup.

"*Ma pauvre petite,*" she said, "I have brought you a cup of camomile tea. Drink it. It calms the nerves."

Martin rose and the good lady took his seat and discoursed picturesquely upon her mother's last illness, death and funeral, until Félise, notwithstanding the calming properties of the camomile tea, burst into tears and fled to her room.

"Poor little girl," said Madame Chauvet, sympathetically. "I cried just like that. I remember it as if it were yesterday."

The next day Bigourdin returned. He walked about expanding his chest with great draughts of air like the good provincial who had suffocated in the capital. He railed at the atmosphere, the fever, the cold-heartedness of Paris.

"One is much better here," said he. "And we have

made much further progress in civilisation. Even the Hôtel de la Dordogne has not yet a bath-room."

He was closeted long with Félise, and afterwards came to Martin, great wrinkles of perturbation marking his forehead.

"She has been asking me questions which it has taken all my tact and diplomacy to answer. *Mon Dieu, que j'ai menti!* But I have convinced her that all we have done with regard to her mother has been right. I will tell you what I have said."

"You had better not," replied Martin, anxious to have no more embarrassing confidences; "the less I know, the simpler it is for me to plead ignorance when Félise questions me—not to say the more truthful."

"You are right," said Bigourdin. *"Magna est veritas et prœvalebit."* And as Martin, not catching the phrase as pronounced in continental fashion, looked puzzled, he repeated it. "It's Latin," he added. "Why should I not quote it? I have received a good education."

Now about this time a gracious imp of meddlesomeness alighted on Lucilla's shoulder and whispered into her ear. She arose from a sea of delicate raiment and tissue paper whose transference by Céleste into ugly trunks she and Heliogabalus were idly superintending, and, sitting down at the writing-desk of her hotel bedroom, scribbled a short letter. If she had blown the imp away, as she might easily have done, for such imps are irresponsible dragon-fly kind of creatures, Martin might possibly have foregone his consultation with Fortinbras and remained at Brantôme. Félise having once restored him to the position he occupied in her confidence, allowed him to remain there. In his thoughts she assumed a new significance. He realised, in his blundering masculine way, that she was many-sided, complex, mysterious; at one turn, simple and caressive as a child, at another passionate in her affections, at yet another calm and self-reliant; altogether that she had a strangely sweet and strong personality. For the first time, the alliance so subtly planned by Bigourdin, entered his head. If Bigourdin thought him worthy to be his partner and carry on the historic traditions of the Hôtel des Grottes, surely he would look with approval on his carrying them on in conjunction with the most beloved member of his family. And Félise? There his inexperience came to a stone wall. He was modest. He did not in the least assume as a possibility that she might have already given him her heart. But he reflected that, after all, in the way of nature, maidens did marry unattractive and undeserving men; that except for an unaccountable phase of coldness, she had always bestowed on him a friendly regard which, if courteously fostered, might develop into an affection warranting on her part a marriage with so unattractive and undeserving a man as himself. And Bigourdin, great, splendid-hearted fellow, claimed him, and this warm Périgord, this land of plenty and fat things, claimed him. Here lay his destiny. Why not blot out, with the blackest curtain of will, the refulgent figure that was making his life a torture and a dream?

And then came the imp-inspired letter.

Dear Mr. Overshaw,

I am starting for Egypt to-morrow. I hope you will redeem your promise.

With kind regards,

Yours sincerely,

Lucilla Merriton.

Paralysed then were the promptings towards sluggish plentitude and tepid matrimonial comfort. Love summoned him to fantastic adventure. For a while he lost mental balance. He decided to put himself in the hands of Fortinbras. He would abide loyally by his decision. Under his auspices he had already made one successful bid for happiness. By dismissing Margett's Universal College to the limbo of irretrievable things, according to the Dealer's instructions, had he not tasted during the past five months hundreds of the once forbidden delights of life? Was he the same man who in apologetic trepidation had written to Corinna in August? His blind faith in Fortinbras was intensified by knowledge of the suffering whereby the Dealer in Happiness had acquired wisdom. East or West, whichever way Fortinbras pointed, he would go.

Thus in some measure he salved his conscience when he left Brantôme. Bigourdin expected him back at the end of his fortnight's holiday. So did Félise. She packed him a little basket of food and wine, and with a smile bade him hasten back. She did not question the purport of his journey. He needed a change, a peep into the great world of Paris and London.

"If you have a quarter the good time I had, I envy you," she said.

And Bigourdin, with a grip of the hand and a knowing smile, as they parted, whispered: "I will give that old dress suit to Anatole, the *plongeur* at the Café de l'Univers. He will be enchanted."

The train steamed out of the station carrying a traitorous, double-dyed villain. It arrived at Paris carrying a sleepless, anxious-eyed young man throbbing with suspense. He drove to the Hôtel du Soleil et de l'Ecosse.

"Ah! Monsieur has returned," said the fat and greasy Bocardon as he entered.

"Evidently," replied Martin, who now had no timidities in the presence of hotel managers and was not impressed by the professional facial memory. Was he not himself on the verge of becoming a French innkeeper? He presented a business card of the Hôtel des Grottes mysteriously inscribed by Bigourdin, and demanded a good room. The beady black eyes of the Provençal regarded him shrewdly.

"Some months ago you were a professor."

"It is always permissible for an honest man to change his vocation," said Martin.

"That is very true," said Bocardon. "I myself made my studies as a veterinary surgeon, but as I am one of those unfortunates whom horses always kick and dogs always bite, I entered the service of my brother, Emile Bocardon, who keeps an hotel at Nîmes."

"The Hôtel de la Curatterie," said Martin.

"You know it?" cried Bocardon, joyously.

"Not personally. But it is familiar to every *commis-voyageur* in France."

His professional knowledge at once gained him the esteem and confidence of Monsieur Bocardon and a magnificent chamber at a minimum tariff. After he had eaten and sent a message to Fortinbras at the new address given him by Bigourdin, he went out into the crisp, exhilarating air, with Paris and all the universe before him.

In the queer profession into which he had drifted, Heaven knows how, of giving intimate counsel not only to the students, but (as his reputation spread) to the small shopkeepers and work-people of the *rive gauche,* at his invariable fee of five francs per consultation, Fortinbras had been able to take a detached view of human problems. In their solution he could forget the ever frightening problem of his own existence, and find a subdued delight. Only in the case of Corinna and Martin had he posed otherwise than as an impersonal intelligence. As an experiment he had brought them into touch with his own personal concerns. And now there was the devil to pay.

For consider. Here he was prepared to deal out

advice to Martin according to the conspiracy into which he had entered with Bigourdin. Martin was to purchase an interest in the Hôtel des Grottes and (although he knew it not) marry Félise. There could not have been a closer family arrangement.

When Fortinbras rose from the frosty *terrasse* of the Café Cardinal, at the corner of the Rue Richelieu and the Boulevard des Italiens, their appointed rendez-vous, and greeted Martin, there was something more than benevolence in his smile, something paternal in his handshake. They entered the Café-Restaurant and sat down at one of the tables not yet laid for *déjeuner,* for it was only eleven o'clock. Fortinbras, attired in his customary black, looked more trim, more prosperous. Collar, cuffs and tie were of an impeccable whiteness. The silk hat which he hung with scrupulous care on the peg against the wall, was startlingly new. He looked like a disguised cardinal in easy circumstances. He made bland enquiries as to the health of the good folks at Brantôme, and ordered an *apéritif* for Martin and black-currant syrup and water for himself. Then Martin said:

"I have come from Brantôme to consult you on a matter of the utmost importance—to myself, of course. It's a question of my whole future."

He laid a five-franc piece on the table. Fortinbras pushed the coin back.

"My dear boy, this is a family affair. I know all about it. For you I'm no longer the *Marchand de Bonheur.*"

"If you're not," said Martin, "I don't know what the devil I shall do." And, with his finger, he flicked the coin midway between them.

"My dear fellow," said Fortinbras, flicking the coin an inch towards Martin, "if you so desire it, I will deal with you in my professional capacity. But as in the case of the solicitor or the doctor it would be unprofessional to accept fees for the settlement of his own family affairs, so, in this matter, I am unable to accept a fee ·from you. Bigourdin, whose character you have had an intimate opportunity of judging, has offered you a share in his business. As a lawyer and a man of the world, I say unhesitatingly, 'Accept it.' As long as Brantôme lasts—and there are no signs of it perishing,—commercial travellers and tourists will visit it and go to the Hôtel des Grottes. And as long as European civilisation lasts, it will demand the gastronomic delicacies of truffles, *pâté de foie gras,* Périgord pie, stuffed quails and compôte of currants which now find their way from the *fabrique* of the hotel to Calcutta, Moscow, San Francisco, Bayswater and Buenos Ayres. As a *marchand de bonheur,* as you are pleased to call me, I also unhesitatingly affirm that in your acceptance you will find true happiness."

He sipped his cassis and water, and leaned back on the plush-covered seat. Martin pushed the five-franc piece three or four inches towards Fortinbras.

"It isn't such a simple, straightforward matter as you seem to imagine," said Martin. "Otherwise I should have closed with Bigourdin's generous offer straight away. I'm not a fool. And I'm devotedly attached to Bigourdin, who, for no reason that I can see, save his own goodness of heart, has treated me like a brother. I haven't come to consult you as a man of business at all. And as for conscientious scruples about Bigourdin being a relative of yours, please put them away." He pushed the coin another inch. "It is solely as *marchand de bonheur,* in the greatest crisis of my life, when I'm torn to pieces by all sorts of conflicting emotions, that I want to consult you. There are complications you know nothing about."

"Complications?" Fortinbras stretched out a benign hand. "Is it possible that there is some little—what shall we say?—sentiment?" He smiled, seeing the young man's love for Félise barring his candid way. "You can be frank with me."

"It's a damned sight more than sentiment," cried Martin with unprecedented explosiveness. "Read this."

He dragged from his pocket a dirty, creased and crumpled letter and threw it across the table. Fortinbras adjusted his glasses and read the imp-inspired message. He took off his glasses and handed back the letter. His face became impassive and he regarded Martin with expressionless, tired, blue eyes.

"Your promise. What was that?"

"To go to Egypt."

"Why should you go to Egypt to meet Lucille Marriton?"

Martin threw up both hands in a wide gesture. "Can't you see? I'm mad to go to Egypt, or Cape Horn, or Hell, to meet her. But I've enough sanity left to come here and consult you."

Fortinbras regarded him fixedly, and nodded his head reflectively many times; and without taking his eyes off him, reached out his hand for the five-franc piece which he slipped into his waistcoat pocket.

"That puts," said he, "an entirely different complexion on the matter."

## CHAPTER XVII

THE astute conspiracy had tumbled to ruins, the keystone, Félise, being knocked out. It was no longer a family affair. Fortinbras listened to the young man's statement of his case with professional detachment. His practised wit questioned. Martin replied until he had laid bare his candid and intoxicated soul. At last Fortinbras, with a wave of his plump hand, and with his benevolent smile, said :—

"Let us now adjourn from labour to refreshment. I will give myself a luxury I have not enjoyed for many a year. I will entertain a guest. You shall lunch with me. When our spirits are fortified and our judgments mellowed by generous food, we shall adjourn from refreshment to labour. Sometimes you can put a five-franc piece into the slot and pull out an opinion. Sometimes you can't. Let us go to another table."

They lunched. Fortinbras talked of men and things and books. He played the perfect host until the first cigarette had been smoked. Then he lay back in the upholstered seat against the wall and looked into vacancy, his face a mask. Martin, sitting by his side, dared not disturb him. He felt like one in the awe-inspiring presence of an oracle. Presently the oracle stirred, shifted his position and resumed human semblance, the smile reappearing in his eyes and at the corners of his pursy mouth.

"My dear Martin," said he, one elbow on the table and the hand caressing his white hair, "I have now fully considered the question, and see distinctly your path to happiness. As my good old friend Montaigne says—an author I once advised you to cultivate——"

"I've done so," said Martin.

Fortinbras beamed. "There is none richer in humanity. In his words, I say 'The wisdom of my instruction consists in liberty and naked truth.' I take the human soul as it is and seek to strip it free from shackles and disguises. I strip yours from the shackles of gross material welfare and the travesty of content. I see it ardent in the pursuit, perhaps of the unattainable, but at any rate in the pursuit of splendour, which is a splendid thing for the soul. Liberty and naked truth are the only watchwords. Sell out some of your capital, equip yourself in lordly raiment, go to Egypt and give your soul a chance."

"I needn't tell you," said Martin, after a pause, "that I was hoping you would give me this advice. It seems all crazy. But still——" he lit a cigarette, which during Fortinbras's discourse he had been holding in his fingers. "Well—there it is. I don't seem to care a hang what happens to me afterwards."

"From my professional point of view," said Fortinbras, "that is an ideal state of mind."

"All the same, I can't help feeling a brute. What the devil can I say to Bigourdin?"

"You can leave that to me," replied Fortinbras. "He is aware that you are a client of mine and not only honour me with your confidence, but are willing to be guided by my counsel. If you will accept my society, I will accompany you to the Land of the Pharaohs——"

"What?" cried Martin, taken aback. "You? Good God! Of course," he added, after recovery, "I should love you to come."

"As I was saying," Fortinbras continued, "I will accompany you, take upon my shoulders your responsibilities with regard to Bigourdin, and, for my own private satisfaction, realise the dream of my life which is to go up to the Sphinx and say, 'Now, my dear creature, confidentially as between Augur and Augur, what the deuce is it all about?' "

Later, when Martin had accustomed himself to the amazing proposal, they discussed ways and means.

"You," said Fortinbras, "in order to drink the deep draughts essential to your evolution, must peacock it with the best. You must dwell in palaces and drive in chariots. I, on the other hand, journeying as a philosopher, need but a palm-tree's shade, a handful of dates and a cup of water. I shall therefore not be of your revellings. But I shall always be near at hand, a sort of private djinn, always at your distinguished service."

"It's most delightful and generous of you to put it that way," laughed Martin, "but for the life of me I can't see why you should do it."

Fortinbras replied simply: "I'm a very weary man, my dear boy, and my heart needs a holiday. That is why I grasp this opportunity of going into the sunshine. As to my offer of counsel, that is a matter which it would be futile to discuss."

His last words were flavoured with mystery. As far as Martin was concerned, Fortinbras was free to go whithersoever he pleased. But why this solicitude as to his welfare, this self-made Slave of the Lamp obligation? Soon he gave up the riddle. Too many exciting thoughts swept his brain.

Until it was written, the letter to Bigourdin weighed on his mind. The problem confronting him was to explain his refusal without reference to Lucilla. To Fortinbras, keeper of his conscience, he could avow his splendid lunacy and be understood. To Bigourdin his English reserve forbade his writing himself down an ass and saying: "The greasy waiter cannot accept partnership with you, as he must follow to the ends of the earth the radiant lady to whom he handed the mutton cutlets." The more he tried the less could he do it. He sat up all night over the letter. It contained all the heart of him that was left for the Hôtel des Grottes and Brantôme and Périgord; but—well— he had arranged to abide by Fortinbras's decision. Fortinbras had advised him to see more of the world before definitely settling his life. With a disingenuousness which stabbed his conscience, he threw the responsibility on Fortinbras. Fortinbras was carrying him to Egypt on an attempt to solve the riddle of the Sphinx. Bigourdin knew the utter faith he had in Fortinbras. He sent his affectionate regards to everybody—and to Félise. It was the most dreadful, heart-tearing letter he had ever had to write.

Meanwhile, Fortinbras, betraying, for the first time in his life, professional secrecy, revealed the whole matter to Bigourdin in an illuminating document. And Bigourdin, reading it, and comparing it with Martin's letter, said *"Bigre!"* and *"Sacrebleu!"* and *"Nom de Dieu de nom de Dieu!"* and all sorts of other things. At first he frowned incredulously. But on every reperusal of the letter the frown grew fainter, until, after the fifth, the placid smile of faith overspread his broad countenance. But Félise, who was only told that Martin was not returning but had gone to Egypt with her father, grew white and thin-lipped, and hated the day she had met Lucilla Merriton and all the days she had spent with Lucilla Merriton, and, in a passion of tears, heaped together everything that Lucilla Merriton had ever given her, gowns and furs and underlinen and trinkets, in a big trunk which she stowed away in an attic. And the *plongeur* from the Café de l'Univers was appointed waiter in Martin's stead and strutted about proudly in Martin's cast-off raiment. He was perhaps the most care-free person in the Hôtel des Grottes.

Martin went on a flying visit to London, and, on the advice of Fortinbras, put up at the Savoy.

"Accustom yourself to lordliness," the latter had counselled. "You can't conquer Egypt with the self-effacing humility of the servitor. By rubbing shoulders with the wealthy, you will acquire that suspicion of arrogance—the whiff of garlic in the salad—in which your present demeanour is so sadly lacking. You will also learn by observation the correct wear in socks and ties, and otherwise steep yourself in the study of indispensable vanities."

Martin studied conscientiously, and when he had satisfactorily arranged his financial affairs, including the opening of a banking account with Messrs. Thomas Cook & Son, visited tailors and haberdashers and hatters and bootmakers, ordering all the things he had seen worn by the opulent youth of the Savoy Hotel. If he had stolen the money to pay for them, or if he had intended to depart with them without paying, he could not have experienced a more terrifying joy. Like a woman clothes-starved for years, who has been given the run of London shops, Martin ran sartorially mad. He saw suitings, hosiery, shoes, with Lucilla's eye. He bought himself a tie-pin, a thing which he had never possessed nor dreamed of possessing in his life before; and, observing that an exquisite young Lothario upon whom he resolved to model himself did not appear with the same tie-pin on two consecutive days, he went out and bought another. Modesty and instinctive breeding saved him from making himself a harlequin.

In the midst of these preoccupations, he called, by arrangement, on Corinna. She was living with another girl on the fifth floor of a liftless block of flats in Wandsworth. The living room held two fairly comfortably. Three sat at somewhat close quarters. So when Martin arrived, the third, Corinna's mate, after a perfunctory introduction, disappeared into a sort of cupboard that served her as a bedroom.

Corinna looked thin and ill and drawn, and her blouse gaped at the back, and her fair hair exhibited the ropiness of neglect. The furniture of the room was of elementary flimsiness. Loose newspapers, pamphlets, handbills, made it as untidy as Corinna's hair. As soon as they were alone, Martin glanced from her to her surroundings and then back again to her.

"My dear Corinna," said he, putting hat, stick and gloves on a bamboo table, "what on earth are you doing with yourself?"

She looked at him defiantly, with a touch of haggardness.

"I am devoting myself to the Cause."

Martin wrinkled a puzzled brow. "What cause?"

"For a woman there is only one," said Corinna.

"Oh!" said Martin. "May I sit down?"

"Please do."

She poked a tiny fire in a diminutive tiled grate, while he selected the most solid of the bamboo chairs. She sat on a stool on the hearthrug.

"I suppose you're anti-suffrage like any other bigoted reactionary," she said.

Martin replied truly: "I haven't worried about it one way or the other."

She turned on him swiftly. "Then you're worse than a downright opponent. It's just the contemptuous apathy of men like you that drive us mad."

She entered upon a long and nervous tirade, trotting out the old arguments, using the stock phrases, parroting a hundred platform speeches. And all the time, though appearing to attack, she was on the defensive, defiant, desperate. Martin regarded her with a shocked expression. Her thin blonde beauty was being pinched into shrewishness.

"But, my dear Corinna," said he. "I've come to

see you, as an old friend. I just want to know how
you're getting on. What's the good of a political argument between us two? You may be wrong or you
may be right. I haven't studied the question. Let us
drop it from a contentious point of view. Let us meet
humanly. Or if you like, let us tell each other the
outside things that have happened to us. You haven't
even asked me why I'm here. You haven't asked after
Félise, or Fortinbras, or Bigourdin." He waxed
warm. "I've just come from Brantôme. Surely you
must have some grateful memories of the folks there.
They treated you splendidly. Surely you must still
take some interest in them."

Corinna supported herself on an outspread hand on
the hearthrug.

"Do you want me to tell you the truth?" She held
him with her pained blue eyes. "I don't take an
interest in any damned thing in God's universe."

"May I smoke?" said Martin. He lit a cigarette,
after having offered her his case which she waved
aside impatiently.

"If that is so," said he, "what in the world is the
meaning of all the stuff you have just been talking?"

"I thought you had the sense to have learned something about me. How otherwise am I to earn my
living? We've gone over the ground a hundred times.
This is a way, anyhow, and it's exciting. It keeps
one from thinking of anything else. I've been to
prison."

Martin gasped, asked her if she had hunger-struck.

"I tried, but I hadn't the pluck or the hysteria.
Isabel Banditch can do it." She lowered her voice
and waved towards her concealed companion. "I
can't. She believes in the whole thing. The vote will
bring along the millennium. Once we have the power,
men are going to be as good as little cherubs terminat-

ing in wings round their necks. Drink will disappear. Wives shall be like the fruitful soda-water siphon on the side-board, and there will be no more struggle for existence and no more wars. Oh! the earth is going to be a devil of a place when we've finished with it."

"Do you talk like this to Miss Banditch?" asked Martin.

She smiled for the first time, and shook her head.

"On the whole you're rather a commonplace person, Martin," she replied, "but you have one remarkable quality. You always seem to compel me to tell you the truth. I don't know why. Perhaps it is just to puzzle you and annoy you and hurt you."

"Why should you want to hurt me?"

She shrugged her shoulders, and sat with her hands clasping her knees. "Well—for one thing, you were my intimate companion for three months and never for a single second did you think of making love to me. For all the impression I made on you I might have been your austere maiden aunt. Sometimes I've wanted to take you between my teeth and shake you as a terrier shakes a rat. Instead, like an ass, I've told you the blatant truth."

"That's interesting," said Martin, calmly. "But you seem to want to hurt everybody—those who don't fall in love with you and those who do. You hurt our poor old Bigourdin and he hasn't got over it."

Corinna looked into the diminutive fire. "I suppose you think I was a fool."

"I can't believe it matters to you what I think," said Martin, his vanity smarting at being lashed for a Joseph Andrews.

"It doesn't. But you think me a fool all the same. I'll go on telling you the truth"—she flashed a glance at him. "Bigourdin's a million times too good for me. I should have led him a beast of a life. He has had a lucky escape. You can tell him that when you go back."

"I'm not going back."

"What?" she said with a start.

He repeated his statement and smiled amiably.

"Fed up with being a waiter? I've wondered how long you could stick it. What are you going to do now? As a polite hostess, I suppose I should have asked that when you first came into the room."

"I did expect something of the sort," Martin confessed, "until you declared you didn't take an interest in any damned thing."

Then they both laughed. Corinna stretched out a hand. "Forgive me," she said. "I've been standing nearly all day in front of the tube station, dressed in a green, mauve and white sandwich-board and selling newspapers, and I'm dog-tired and miserable. I would ask you to have some tea, but that would only bring out Isabel, who would talk our heads off. Why have you left Brantôme?"

He told her of Bigourdin's proposal and of Fortinbras's counsel; but he made no reference to the flashing of the divine Lucilla across his path. Once he had confessed to her the kiss of the onion-eating damsel who had married the plumber. She had jested but understood. His romantic knight-errant passion for Lucilla was stars above her comprehension. When he mentioned the fact of the death of Mrs. Fortinbras, Corinna softened.

"Poor little Félise! It must have been a great sorrow to her. I'll write to her. She's a dear little girl." She paused for a few moments. "Now, look here, Martin," she said, seizing a fragile poker and smiting a black lump of coal the size of a potato, "it strikes me that as fools we're very much in the same box. We've both thrown over a feather-bed existence. I've refused to marry Bigourdin and incidentally to run the Hôtel des Grottes, and you have refused to run the Hôtel des Grottes and incidentally marry Félise."

"There was never any question of my marrying Félise," cried Martin hotly.

She scrambled to her feet and flung an impatient arm.

"You make me tired. Have you a grain of sense in your head or an ounce of blood in your body?"

Martin also rose. "And you?" he countered. "What have you?"

"Neither," said Corinna.

"In that case," said Martin, gathering up hat, stick and gloves, "I don't see why we should continue a futile conversation."

He devoid of sense and blood! He who had probed the soul of Félise and found there virgin indifference! He who had flung aside a gross temptation. He who was consumed with a burning passion for an incomparable goddess! A chasm thousands of miles wide yawned between him and Corinna. In the same box, indeed! He quivered with indignation. She regarded him curiously, through narrowed eyes.

"I do believe," she said slowly, "that I've knocked some sparks out of you at last."

"You would knock sparks out of a putty dog," Martin retorted wrathfully.

She took hat and stick away from him and laid them on the bamboo table. "Don't let us quarrel," she said more graciously. "Sit down again and finish your story. You said something about Egypt and Fortinbras going with you. Why Egypt?"

"Why not?" asked Martin.

"I suppose Fortinbras pointed a prophetic finger. 'There lies the road to happiness.' But what is he doing there himself?"

"He is going to talk to the Sphinx," said Martin.

"And when you've spent all your capital in riotous living, what are you going to do?"

"I don't know and I don't care," said he.

"Well, it's your business, not mine," said Corinna. "You're lucky to be able to get out of this beastly climate. I wish I could."

They talked for a while the generalities of travel. Then he asked her to dine with him and go to a theatre. This brought her back to herself. She couldn't. She had no time. All her evenings were taken up with meetings which she had to attend. And she hadn't an evening gown fit to wear.

"I would rather die than appear in a blouse and skirt in the stalls of a theatre."

"We can go to the pit or upper circle," said Martin, who had never sat in the stalls in his life.

But she declined. The prodigal in the pit was too ludicrous. No. She was conscientious. She had adopted martyrdom as a profession; she was paid for being a martyr; and to martyrdom, so long as it didn't include voluntary starvation, she would stick until she could find a pleasanter and more lucrative means of livelihood.

"It's all very well for you to talk like that," said Martin in his sober way, "but how can you call yourself conscientious when you take these people's money without believing in their cause?"

"Who told you I didn't believe in it?" she cried. "Do you know what it means to be an utterly useless woman? I do. I'm one. It is to prevent replicas of myself in the next generation that I get up at a public meeting and bleat out 'Votes for Women,' and get ignominiously chucked. Can't you see?"

"No," said Martin. "Your attitude is too Laodicean."

"What?" snapped Corinna.

"It's somewhere in the Bible. The Laodiceans were people who blew both hot and cold."

"My father found scriptural terms for me much more picturesque than that," said Corinna, with a laugh.

A door opened and the frozen, blue-nosed head of Miss Banditch appeared.

"I'm sorry to interrupt you, Corinna, but are we never going to have tea?"

Corinna apologised. Tea was prepared. Miss Banditch talked on the One and Only Topic. Martin listened politely. During a pause, while he stood offering a cup for Corinna to fill for the second time, she remarked casually:

"By the way, you met Miss Merriton, didn't you?"

The question was like a knock on the head. He nearly dropped the cup.

"Miss Merriton?"

"She's a friend of mine. I had a note from her at Christmas to say that she had been to Brantôme and made your acquaintance, and had carried off Félise to the south of France. Why haven't you told me about her?"

Under her calm, smiling gaze he felt himself grow hot and red and angry. He fenced.

"You must remember my position in Brantôme."

She poured the milk into his cup. "She said she was going to Egypt. Sugar?"

Miss Banditch resumed her argument. The remainder of the visit was intolerable. As soon as he could swallow his tea, he took his leave. Corinna followed him into the tiny passage by the flat-door.

"My dear old Martin," she said, impulsively throwing an arm round him and gripping his shoulder. "I'm a beast, and a brute, and I hate everybody and everything in this infernal world. But I do wish you the very best of good luck."

She opened the door and with both hands thrust him gently forth; then quickly she closed the door all but a few inches behind him, and through the slit she cried:

"Give my love to Lucilla!"

The door banged, and Martin descended the five flights of stairs, lost in the maze of the Eternal Feminine.

## CHAPTER XVIII

CAIRO station. An illumination of livid blue.
A horde of brown-legged turbaned figures
wearing red jerseys on which flaunted in white
the names of hotels, and reconstructing Babel. An
urbane official, lifting a gold-banded cap in the middle
of a small oasis of silence and inviting Martin in the
name of the Semiramis Hotel, to surrender luggage and
all other cares to his keeping, and to follow the stream
through the exit to the hotel motor. A phantasmagoria
of East and West rendered more fantastic by the
shadows cast by the high arc-lamps. He had lost sight
of Fortinbras, who bag in hand—his impedimenta
being of the scantiest—had disappeared in quest of
the palm-tree against whose trunk he presumably was
to pass the night. Martin emerged from the station,
entered the automobile, one of a long row, and waited
with his fellow passengers until the roof was stacked
with luggage. Then the drive through European
streets suggestive of Paris and the sudden halt at the
hotel. A dazzling vision of a lounge, a swift upward
journey in a lift worked by a Nubian gorgeous in scarlet and gold, a walk down a corridor, a door flung
open, and Martin found himself in his bedroom. An
Arab brought hot water and retired.

Martin opened the shutters of the window and
looked out. It was hard moonlight. Beneath him
shimmered a broad ribbon of water, against which
were silhouetted outlandish masts and spars of craft
moored against the embankment. The dark mass on
the further shore seemed to be pleasant woods. The
water could be nothing else than the Nile; the sacred

river; the first river in which he had taken a romantic
interest, on account of Moses and the Ark and Pha-
raoh's daughter; the mighty river which is the very
life of a vast country; the most famous river in the
world. He regarded it with a curious mixture of awe
and disappointment. On his right it was crossed by
a bridge dotted with the slowly moving lamps of carts
and now and then flashing with the headlights of a
motor-car. It was not unlike any ordinary river—the
Thames, the Seine, the Rhone at Geneva. He had
imagined it broad as the Amazon.

Yet it was wonderful; the historic water, the moonlight, the clear Egyptian air in which floated a vague
perfume of spice, the dimly seen long-robed figures
seated on a bench by the parapet on the other side of
the road, whose guttural talk rose like a proclamation
of the Orient. He leaned out over the iron railing.
On his left stood out dreamily defined against the sky
two shadowy little triangles. He wondered what
they could be. Suddenly came the shock of certainty.
They were the Pyramids. He rubbed his eyes and
looked again. A thrill ran over his skin. He had not
counted on being brought up bang, as it were, against
them. He had imagined that one journeyed for half
a day on a camel through a trackless desert in order
to visit these wonders of the world: but here he was
staring at them from the hotel-window of a luxurious
capital. He stared at them for a long time. Yes:
there was the Nile; there were the Pyramids; and,
after a knock at the door, there was his luggage. He
became conscious of hunger; also of Lucilla more
splendid than moonlit Nile and Pyramids and all the
splendours of Egypt put together. Hunger—it was
half-past nine and he had eaten nothing since lunch
on shipboard—counselled speedy ablutions and a descent in quest of food. Lucilla ordained correctitude
of vesture. His first evening on board ship had taught

him that dinner jacket suit and black tie were the only wear. He changed and went downstairs.

A chasseur informed him that Miss Merriton was staying in the hotel, but that she had gone to the dance at the Savoy. When would she be back? The chasseur, a child rendered old by accumulated knowledge of trivial fact, replied that Cairo was very gay this season, that dances went on till the morning hours, and insinuated that Miss Merriton was as gay as anybody. Martin walked through the lounge into the restaurant and supped. He supped exceedingly well. Bearing in mind Fortinbras's counsel of lordliness and the ways of lordly motorists passing through Brantôme, he ordered a pint of champagne. He was served by an impeccable waiter with lilac revers and brass buttons to his coat. He noted the livery with a professional eye. The restaurant was comparatively empty. Only at one table sat a party of correctly dressed men and women. A few others were occupied by his travelling companions, still in the garb of travel. Martin mellowed by the champagne, adjusted his black tie and preened his white shirt front, in the hope that the tweed-clad newcomers would see him and marvel and learn from him, Martin Overshaw, obscure and ignorant adventurer, what was required by English decorum. After his meal he sat in the lounge and ordered Turkish coffee, liqueur brandy and cigarettes. And so, luxuriously housed, clothed and fed, he entered on the newest phase of his new life.

Six months ago he had considered his sportive ride through France with Corinna a thrilling adventure. He smiled at his simplicity. An adventure, that tame jog-trot tour! As comparable to this as his then companion to the radiant lady of his present quest. Now, indeed, he had burned his boats, thrown his cap over the windmills, cast his frock to the nettles. The reckless folly of it all had kept his veins a-tingle, his head

awhirl. At every moment during the past fortnight
something amazingly new had flashed into his horizon.
The very sleeping-berth in the train de luxe had been
a fresh experience. So too was the awakening to the
warmth and sunshine of Marseilles. Save for a
crowded hour of inglorious life (he was a poor sailor)
now and then on cross-channel boats he had never set
foot on a ship. He wandered about the ocean-going
liner with a child's delight. Fortune favoured him
with a spell of blue weather. He scoffed at sea-sickness. The meals characterised by many passengers as
abominable, he devoured as though they were Lucul-
lian feasts. He made acquaintance with folks going
not only to Egypt, but to Peshawar and Mandalay and
Singapore and other places with haunting names.
Some shocked him by calling them God-forsaken holes
and cursing their luck. Others, mainly women, going
thither for the first time shared his emotions. . . . He
was surprised at the ease with which he fell into casual
talk with strangers. Sometimes a child was a means
of introduction to its mother. Sometimes a woman
in the next deck-chair would open a conversation.
Sometimes Fortinbras chatting with a knot of people
would catch him as he passed and present him blandly.

Among the minor things that gave him cause for
wonder was the swift popularity of his companion.
No longer did his costume stamp Fortinbras as a man
apart from the laity. He wore the easy tweeds and
soft felt hat of a score of other elderly gentlemen on
board: even the gold watch-chain, which he had re-
deemed after a long, long sojourn at the Mount of
Piety. But this very commonplace of his attire brought
into relief the nobility of his appearance. His massive face lined with care, his broad brow, his prominent
light blue kindly eyes, his pursy and benevolent mouth,
his magnificent Abbé Liszt shock of white hair, now
carefully tended, his impressive air of dignity—all

marked him as a personage of distinction. He aroused
the idle curiosity of the idle voyagers. Husbands were
bidden by wives to talk to him and see what he was
like. Husbands obeyed, as is the human though mar-
riage-vow-subversive way of husbands, and meekly
returned with information. A capital fellow; most
interesting chap; English of course; very courtly old
bird; like so-and-so who was Ambassador; old school;
knows everything; talks like a book. Quoth any one
of the wives, her woman's mind intent on the particular. "But who *is* he?" The careless husband, his
masculine mind merely concerned with the general, did
not know. He had not thought of asking. How could
he ask? And what did it matter? The wife sighed.
"Bring him along and I will soon find out." Fortinbras at fit opportunity was brought along. The lady
unconsciously surrendered to his spell—one has not
practised as a *marchand de bonheur* for nothing.
"Now I know all about him," said any one of the
wives to any one of the husbands. "Why are men so
stupid? He is an old Winchester boy. He is a retired
philosopher and he lives in France." That was all
she learned about Fortinbras; but Fortinbras in that
trial interview learned everything about the lady serenely unconscious of intimate avowal.

"My young friend," said he to Martin, "the secret
of social influence is to present yourself to each individual rather as a sympathetic intelligence, than as a
forceful personality. The patient takes no interest in
the morbid symptoms of his physician: but every patient is eager to discuss his symptoms with the kindly
physician who will listen to them free, gratis and for
nothing. By adopting this attitude I can evoke from
one the dramatic ambitions of her secret heart, from
another the history of her children's ailments and the
recipe for the family cough-cure, from a third the moving story of strained relations with his parents because

he desired to marry his uncle's typist, the elderly crown and glory of her sex, and from a fourth an intricate account of a peculiarly shady deal in lard."

"That sounds all right," said Martin; "but in order to get people to talk to you—say in the four cases you have mentioned, you must know something about the theatre, bronchitis, love and the lard-trade."

Said Fortinbras, touching the young man's shoulder:

"The experienced altruist with an eye to his own advantage knows something about everything."

Martin, following the precepts of his Mentor, practised the arts of fence, parrying the thrusts of personal questions on the part of his opponent and riposting with such questions on his own.

"It is necessary," said the sage. "What are you among these respectable Britons of substance, but an adventurer? Put yourself at the mercy of one of these old warriors with grey motor-veils and steel knitting needles and she will pluck out the heart of your mystery in a jiffy and throw it on the deck for all to feed on."

Thus the voyage—incidentally was it not to Cythæra?—transcended all his dreams of social amenity. It was a long protracted party in which he lost his shyness, finding frank welcome on all sides. To the man of thirty who had been deprived, all his man's life, of the commonplace general intercourse with his kind, this daily talk with a girl here, a young married woman there, an old lady somewhere else, and all sorts and conditions of men in the smoking room and on deck, was nothing less than a kind of social debauch, intoxicating him, keeping him blissfully awake of nights in his upper berth, while Fortinbras snored below. Then soon after daybreak, to mount to the wet, sunlit deck after his cold, sea-water bath; perhaps to meet a hardy and healthy English girl, fresh as the Ægean morning; to tramp up and down with her for development of appetite, talking of nothing but the glitter of the sea, the stuffiness of cabins, the dishes they each would choose for breakfast; to descend into the warm, comforting smell of the dining-saloon; to fall voraciously on porridge and eggs and kidneys and marmalade; to go on deck again knowing that in a couple of hours' time stewards would come to him fainting from hunger with bowls of chicken broth, that in an hour or two afterwards there would be lunch to be selected from a menu a foot long in close print, and so on during the golden and esurient day; to meet Fortinbras, late and luxurious riser; to bask for an hour, like a plum, in the sunshine of his wisdom; to continue the debauch of the day before; to sight great sailing vessels with bellying canvas, resplendent majesty of past centuries, or, on the other hand, the grey grim blocks of battleships; to pass the sloping shores of historic islands—Crete, home of the Minotaur, whose inhabitants—(Cretans are liars. Cretans are men. Therefore all men are liars)—had furnished the stock example of fallacy in the Syllogism; to watch the green wake cleaving the dark-blue sea; to make his way up and down decks, through the steerage, and stand in the bows, swept by the exhilarating air, with the pulse racking sense that he was speeding to the lodestar of his one desire—to find wildness of delight in these commonplaces of travel; to live as he lived, to vibrate as he vibrated with every nerve from dawn to dawn, to be drunk with the sheer ecstasy of existence, so that the past becomes a black abyss, and the future an amethystine haze glorified by the Sons of the Morning singing for joy, is given but to few, is given to none but poor, starved souls, is given to none of the poor, starved souls but those whom the high Gods in obedience to their throw of the dice happen to select.

Martin sitting in a deep armchair in the Semiramis

Hotel dreamed of all these things, unconscious of the flight of time.  Suddenly he became aware that he was the only occupant of the lounge, all the other folk having returned soberly to their rooms.  Already a few early arrivals from the Savoy dance passed across the outer hall on their way to the lift.  Drowsy with happiness he went to bed.  To-morrow, Lucilla.

He became aware of her standing by the bureau licking a stamp to put on a letter.  She wore a white coat and skirt and a straw hat with cherries on it.  He could not see her face, but he guessed the blue veins on the uplifted, ungloved hand that held the stamp.  On his approach, she turned and uttered a little laughing gasp of recognition, stuck the stamp on hastily and stretched out her hand.

"Why," she cried, "it's you!  You really have come!"

"Did you think I would break my promise?" he asked, his eyes drinking in her beauty.

"I didn't know how seriously you regarded it."

"I've thought of nothing but Egypt, since I said you had pointed out the way," he replied.  "You commanded.  I obeyed."

She caught up her long parasol and gloves that lay on the ledge of the bureau.  "If everybody did everything I told them," she laughed, "I should have my hands full.  They don't, as a general rule, but when they do I take it as a compliment.  It makes me feel good to see you.  When did you come?"

She put him through a short catechism.  What boat?  What kind of voyage?  Where was he staying? . . . Finally:

"Do you know many people in Cairo?"

"Not a soul," said Martin.

With both arms behind her back, she rested lightly on the parasol, and beamed graciously.

"I know millions," she said, not without a touch of exaggeration which pleased him. "Would you like to trust yourself to me, put yourself entirely in my hands?"

"I could dream of nothing more enchanting," replied Martin. "But——"

"But——?"

"I don't want to make myself an infliction."

"You're going to be a delight. You know in the cinematograph how an invisible pencil writes things on the sheet—or how a message is stamped out on the tape, and you look and wonder what's coming next. Well, I want to see how this country is going to be stamped letter by letter on your virgin mind. It's a thing I've been longing for—to show somebody with sense like yourself, Egypt of the Pharaohs and Egypt of the English. How long can you stay?"

"Indefinitely," said Martin. "I have no plans."

"From here you might go to Honolulu or Rangoon?"

"Or Greenland or Cape Horn," said Martin.

She nodded smiling approval. "That is what I call a free and enlightened Citizen of the World. Let us sit down. I'm waiting for my friend, Mrs. Dangerfield of Philadelphia. Her husband's here too. You will like them. I generally travel round with somebody, just for the sake of a table-companion. I'm silly enough to feel a fool eating alone every day in a restaurant."

He drew a wicker chair for her and sat beside her. She deposited parasol and gloves on the little round table, and swept him with a quizzical glance from his well-fitting brown shoes to his trim black hair.

"May I without impertinence compliment you on your colour-scheme?"

His olive cheek flushed like a girl's. He had devoted an hour's concentrated thought to it before he rose. How should he appear in the presence of the divinity? He had decided on grey flannels, grey shirt, purple socks and tie. He wondered whether she guessed the part she had played in his anxious selection. Remembering the splotch of grease, he said:

"I hadn't much choice of clothes when you last saw me."

She laughed. "Tell me all about Brantôme. How is my dear little friend Félise?"

He gave her discreet news. "And the incomparable Fortinbras?"

"You'll doubtless soon be able to judge for yourself. He's here."

"In Cairo? You don't say!"

Mingled with her expression of surprise was a little perplexity of the brow, as though, seeing the Fortinbras of the Petit Cornichon, she wondered what on earth she could do with him.

"He came with me," said Martin.

"Is he staying in this hotel?"

"No," said Martin.

Her brow grew smooth again. "How did he manage to get all this way? Has he retired from business?"

"I don't think so. He needed a holiday. You see he came into a little money on the death of his wife."

"His wife dead?" Lucilla queried. "Félise's mother? I didn't know. Perhaps that's why she hasn't written to me for such a long time. I think there must be some queer story connected with that mother," she added shrewdly. "Anyway, Fortinbras can't be broken-hearted, or he wouldn't come on a jaunt to Egypt."

Too well-bred to examine Martin on his friend's private affairs, she changed the talk in her quick, imperious way. Martin sat like a man bewitched, fascinated by her remembered beauties—the lazy music of

her voice, her mobile lips, her brown eyelashes. . . .
His heart beat at the realisation of so many dreams.
He listened, his brain scarcely following what she
said; that she spoke with the tongue of an angel was
enough.

Presently a stout, pleasant-faced woman of thirty
came towards them with many apologies for lateness.
This was Mrs. Dangerfield. Lucilla presented Martin.

"Behold in me the complete dragoman. Mr. Overshaw has engaged me for the season. It's his first
visit to Egypt and I'm going to show him round.
I'll draw up a programme for a personally conducted
tour, every hour accounted for and replete with dis-
traction."

"It sounds dreadful," laughed Mrs. Dangerfield.
"Do you think you'll survive, Mr. Overshaw?"

"Not only that," said Martin, "but I hope for a new
lease of life."

"We start," said Lucilla, "with a drive through the
town, during which I shall point out the Kasr-el-Nil
Barracks, the Bank of Egypt and the Opera House.
Then we shall enter on the shopping expedition in
the Mousky, where I shall prevent Mrs. Dangerfield
from being robbed while bargaining for Persian lacq.
I'm ready, Laura, if you are."

She led the way out. Martin exchanging words of
commonplace with Mrs. Dangerfield, followed in an
ecstasy. Did ever woman, outside Botticelli's *Primavera,* walk with such lissomeness? A chasseur turned
the four-flanged doors and they emerged into the
clear morning sunshine. The old bearded Arab carriage porter called an hotel *arabeah* from the stand.
But while the driver, correct in metal-buttoned livery
coat and tarbush, was dashing up with his pair, Martin
caught sight of Fortinbras walking towards them.

"There he is," said Martin.

"Who?"

"Fortinbras."

"Nonsense," said Lucilla. "That's an English Cabinet Minister, or an American millionaire, or the keeper of a gambling saloon."

But when he came nearer, she admitted it was Fortinbras. She waved her hand in recognition. Nothing could have been more charming than her greeting; nothing more urbane than his acknowledgment, or his bow, on introduction to Mrs. Dangerfield. He had come, said he, to lay his respectful homage at her feet; also to see how his young friend was faring in a strange land. Lucilla asked him where he was staying.

"When last I saw you," he answered, "I said something about the perch of the old vulture."

She eyed him, smiling: "You look more like the wanton lapwing."

"In that case I need even a smaller perch, the merest twig."

"But 'Merest Twig, Cairo,' isn't an address," cried Lucilla. "How am I to get hold of you when I want you?"

Fortinbras regarded her with humorous benevolence. The question was characteristic. He knew her to be generous, warm-hearted and impatient of trivial convention: therefore he had not hesitated to go to her in his anxious hour; but he also knew how those long delicate fingers had an irresistible habit of drawing unwary humans into her harmless web. He had not come to Cairo just to walk into Lucilla's parlour. He wanted to buzz about Egypt in philosophic and economical independence.

"That, my dear Lucilla," said he, "is one more enigma to be put to the credit of the Land of Riddles."

Ibrahim stood impassively holding open the door of the *arabeah*. A couple of dragomen in resplendent

robes and turbans, seeing a new and prosperous English tourist, had risen from their bench on the other
side of the road and lounged gracefully forward.

"You're the most exasperating person I ever met,"
exclaimed Lucilla. "But while I have you, I'm going
to keep you. Come to lunch at one-fifteen. If you
don't I'll never speak to you again."

"I'll come to lunch at one-fifteen, with very great
pleasure," said Fortinbras.

The ladies entered the carriage. Martin said
hastily:

"You gave me the slip last night."

"I did," said Fortinbras. He drew the young man
a pace aside, and whispered: "You think those are
doves harnessed to the chariot. They're not. They're
horses."

Martin broke away with a laugh, and sprang to
the back seat of the carriage. It drove off. The
dragoman came up to the lonely Fortinbras. Did he
want a guide? The Citadel, the Pyramids, Sakkara?
Fortinbras turned to the impassive Ibrahim and in his
grand manner and with impressive gesture said:

"Will you tell them they are too beautiful. They
would eclipse the splendour of all the monuments I
am here to visit."

He walked away and Ibrahim, translating roughly
to the dragomen, conveyed uncomplimentary refer-
ences to the virtue of their grandmothers.

Meanwhile Martin, in beatitude, sat on the little
seat, facing his goddess. She was an integral part of
the exotic setting of Cairo. It was less real life than
an Arabian Night's tale. She was interfused with all
the sunshine and colour and wonder. Only the camels
padding along in single file, their bodies half hidden
beneath packs of coarse grass, seemed alien to her.
They held up their heads, as the carriage passed them,
with a damnably supercilious air. One of them

seemed to catch his eye and express contempt unfathomable. He shook a fist at him.

"I hate those brutes," said he.

"Good gracious! Why?" asked Lucilla. "They're so picturesque! A camel is the one thing I really can draw properly."

"Well, I dislike them intensely," said he. "They're inhuman."

He could not translate his unformulated thought into conventional words. But he knew that at the summons of the high gods all the world of animate beings would fall down and worship her: every breathing thing but the camel. He hated the camel.

# CHAPTER XIX

LUCILLA kept her word. She was not a woman of half measures. Just as she had set out, impelled by altruistic fancy, to carry provincial little Félise through part of a Riviera season, and had thoroughly accomplished her object, so now she devoted herself whole-heartedly to the guidance of Martin through the Land of Egypt. In doing so she was conscious of helping the world along. Hitherto it was impeded in its progress by a mild, scholarly gentleman wasting his potentialities in handing soup to commercial travellers. These potentialities she had decided to develop, so that in due season a new force might be evolved which could give the old world a shove. To express her motives in less universal terms, she set herself the holiday task of making a man of him. To herself she avowed her entire disinterestedness. She had often thought of adopting and training a child; but that would take a prodigiously long time, and the child might complicate her future life. On the other hand, with grown men and women, things went more quickly. You could see the grass grow. The swifter process appealed to her temperament.

First she incorporated him, without chance of escape, in her own little coterie, the Dangerfields, and the Watney-Holcombes, father, mother and daughter, Americans who lived in Paris. They received him guaranteed by Lucilla as an Englishman without guile, with democratic American frankness. Of Mr. Dangerfield, a grim-featured banker, possessing a dry, subrident humour, Martin was somewhat afraid. But with the Watney-Holcombes, cheery, pleasure-loving folk, he was soon at his ease.

"The only thing you mustn't do," said Lucilla, "is
to fall in love with Maisie"—Maisie was a slip of
a girl of nineteen, whom he regarded as an amusing
and precocious child—"There is already a young man
floating about in the smoke of St. Louis."

It was an opportunity to make romantic repudiation,
to proclaim the faith by which he lived. But he had
not yet the courage. He laughed, and declared that
the smoky young man might sleep peacefully of nights.
The damsel herself took him as a new toy and played
with him harmlessly and, subtly inspired by Lucilla,
commanded her father, a chubby, innocent man, with
a face like a red, gold-spectacled apple, to bring Martin from remote meal solitude and establish him permanently at their table. Thus, Martin being an accepted
member of a joyous company, could go here, there and
everywhere with any one of them without furnishing
cause for gossip. Lucilla had a deft way of not putting herself in the wrong with a censorious though
charming world. Under the nominal auspices of the
Dangerfields and the Watney-Holcombes, Martin
mingled with the best of Cairo society. He attended
race-meetings, golf-club teas, hotel balls and merry
little suppers. He went to a reception at the Agency
and shook hands with the great English ruler of
Egypt. He was swept away in automobiles to Helouan
and Heliopolis, to the Mena House to see the Pyramids
and the Sphinx both by daylight and by moonlight. A
young soldier discovering a bond in knowledge of
love of France invited him to Mess on a guest night.
Lucilla, ever watchful and tactful, saw that he went
in full dress, white tie and white waistcoat, and not
in dinner jacket. She pervaded his atmosphere, teaching him, training him, opening up new vistas for his
mind and soul. Every encomium passed on him she
accepted as a tribute to herself. It was infinitely more
interesting than training a dog or a horse.

Martin, blissfully unaware of experiment, or even of guidance, lived in a dream of delight. His goddess seemed ever ready to hand. Together they visited mosques and spent enchanted hours in the Bazaar. She knew her way about the labyrinth, could even speak a few words of Arabic. Supreme fair product of the West she stood divinely pure amid the swarthy vividness of the unalterable East. She was a flawless jewel in the barbaric setting of those narrow streets, filled with guttural noise, outlandish bustle of camels and donkeys and white-clad men, smells of hoary spiciness, colour from the tattered child's purple and scarlet to the yellow of the cinnamon pounded at doorways in the three-foot mortars; those streets winding in short joints, each given up to its particular industry—copper beaters, brass-workers, leather-sellers, workers in cedar and mother-of-pearl, sellers of cakes and kabobs, all plying their trades in the frontless caves that served as shops; streets so narrow and sunless that one could see but a slit of blue above the latticed fronts of the crazy houses. He loved to see her deal with the supple Orientals. In bargaining she did not haggle; with smiling majesty she paid into the long slender palm a third, or a half or two-thirds of the price demanded, according to her infallible sense of values, and walked away serene possessor of the merchandise. Lucilla, having a facile memory, had not boasted in vain that she could play dragoman. He found from the books that her archæological information was correct; he drank in her wisdom.

For his benefit she ordained a general expedition to Sakkara. One golden day the party took train to Badrashen, whence, on donkeys, they plunged into the desert. Riding in front with him, she was his for most of that golden day; she discoursed on the colossal statue, stretched by the wayside, of Rameses II, on the step pyramid, on the beauties of the little tombs of

Thi and Ptah-hetep, whose sculptures and paintings of the Vth Dynasty were alive, proceeding direct from the soul of the artist and thus crying shame on the conventional imitations of a thousand or two years later with which most of the great monuments of Egypt are adorned.  And all she said was Holy Writ. And at Mariette's House where they lunched—the bungalow pitched in the middle of the baking desert and overlooking the crumbling brown masses of tombs—he glanced around at their picnicking companions and marvelled at her grace in eating a hard-boiled egg.  It was a noisy, excited party and it was "Lucilla this," and "Lucilla that," all the time, for there was hot argument.

"I don't take any stock in bulls, so I'm not going to see the Serapeum," declared Miss Watney-Holcombe.

"But Lucilla says you've got to," exclaimed Martin. Then he realised that unconsciously he had used her Christian name.  He flushed and under cover of the talk turned to her with an apology.  He met laughing eyes.

"Scrubby little artists in Paris call me Lucilla without the quiver of an eyelash."

"What may be permissible to a scrubby little artist in Paris," said Martin, "mayn't be permitted to one who ought to know better."

She passed him a plate containing the last banana. He declined with a courteous gesture.

"Martin," she said, deliberately dumping the fruit in front of him, "if you don't look out, you will die of conscientiousness."

During part of the blazing ride back to Badrashen when the accidents of route and the vagrom whimsies of donkeys brought him to the side of the dry Mr. Dangerfield, he reflected on the attitude of men admitted to the intimacy of goddesses and great queens.

What did Leicester call the august Elizabeth when she deigned to lay aside her majesty?  And what were the sensations of Anchises, father of pious Æneas, when he first addressed Venus by her *petit nom?*

"Well," said Fortinbras, the next day, "and how is my speculator in happiness getting on?"

They were sitting on the terrace of Shepheard's Hotel, their usual mid-day meeting-place.  Save on these occasions the philosopher seemed to live dimly, in a sort of Oriental twilight.  Yet all that Martin had seen (with the exception of the social moving-picture) he had also seen and therefrom sucked vastly more juice than the younger man.  How and in what company he had visited the various monuments he did not say.  It amused him to maintain his mysterious independence.  Very rarely, and only when compelled by the imperious ruthlessness of Lucilla, did he otherwise emerge from his obscurity than on these daily visits to the famous terrace.  There surrounded by chatter in all tongues and by respresentatives of all cities from Seattle round the earth's girth to Tokio, he loved to sit and watch the ever-shifting scene— the traffic of all the centuries in the narrow street, from the laden ass driven by a replica of one of Joseph's brethren to the modern Rolls-Royce sweeping along with a fat and tarbushed dignitary of the court; the ox-cart omnibus carrying its dingy load of veiled women; the poor funeral procession, the coffin borne on shoulders amid the perfunctory ululations of hired mourners; on the footpaths the contrast of slave attended, black-robed, trim-shod Egyptian ladies in yashmaks and the frank summer-clad Western women; Soudanese and Turks and Greeks and Jews and straight, clear-eyed English officers, and German tourists attired for the wilds of the Zambesi; and here and there a Gordon Highlander swinging along in kilts and white tunic; and lounging against the terrace balustrade, the dragomen, flaunting villains gay in rainbow robes, and the vendors of beads and fly-whisks and post-cards holding up their wares at arm's height and regarding prospective purchasers with the eyes of a crumb-expectant though self-respecting dog who sits on his tail by his master's side; and, across the way, the curio shops rich with the spoils of Samarcand. From all this when alone he garnered the harvest of a quiet eye. When Martin was with him, he shared with his pupil the golden grain of the panorama.

"How," said he, "is my speculator in happiness getting on?"

"The stock is booming," replied Martin with a laugh.

"What an education," said Fortinbras, "is the society of American men of substance!"

"It pleases you to be ironical," said Martin, "but you speak literal truth. An American doesn't set a man down as a damned fool because he is ignorant of his own particular line of business. Dangerfield, for instance, who keeps a working balance of his soul locked up in a safe in Wall Street, has explained to me the New York Stock Exchange with the most courteous simplicity."

"And in return," said Fortinbras, waving away a seller of rhinoceros-horn amber, with the gesture of a monarch dismissing his chamberlain, "you have given him an exhaustive criticism, not untempered with jaundice, of lower middle-class education in England."

"Now, how the deuce," said Martin, recklessly throwing his half-finished cigarette over the balustrade—"How the deuce did you know that?"

"*C'est mon secret,*" replied Fortinbras. "It is also the secret of a dry and successful man like Mr. Dangerfield, with whom I am sorry to have had no more than ten minutes' conversation. In those ten

minutes I discovered in him a lamentable ignorance
of the works of Chaucer, Cervantes and Tourguenieff,
but for my benefit he sized up in a few clattering epi-
grams the essence of the Anglo-Saxon, Spanish and
Sclavonic races, and, for his own, was extracting
from me all I know about Tolstoi, when Lucilla called
me away to expound to his wife the French family
system. From which you will observe that the American believes in a free exchange of knowledge as a
system of education. To revert to my original question, however, you imagine that your present path is
strewn with roses?"

"I do," said Martin.

"That's all I desire to know, my dear fellow," said
Fortinbras benevolently.

"And what about yourself?" asked Martin. "What
about your pursuit of happiness?"

"I am studying Arabic," replied Fortinbras, "and
discussing philosophy with one Abu Mohammed, a
very learned Doctor of Theology, with a very long
white beard, from whose sedative companionship I
derive much spiritual anodyne."

Soon after this the whole Semiramis party packed
up their traps and went by night train to Luxor.
There they settled down for a while and did the
things that the floating population of Luxor do. They
rode on donkeys and on camels and they drove in
carriages and sand-carts. They visited the Tombs of
the Kings and the Tombs of the Queens, and the
Tombs of the Ministers and Karnak and their own
private and particular Temple of Luxor. And Martin amassed a vast amount of erudition and learned
to know gods and goddesses by their attitudes and
talked about them with casual intimacy. His nature
drank in all that there was of wonder and charm
in these relics of a colossal past like an insatiable

sponge; and in Upper Egypt the humble present is
but a relic of the past.  The twentieth-century fella-
heen guiding the ox-drawn wooden plough might
have served for models of any bas-relief or painting
in any tomb of thousands of years ago.  So too might
the half-naked men in the series of terraced trenches
draining water from the Nile by means of rude
wooden lever and bucket to irrigate the land.  The
low mud houses of the villages were the same as
those which covering vast expanses on either side of
the river made up the mighty and populous city of
Thebes.  And the peasantry purer in type than the
population of Cairo, which till then was all the Egypt
that Martin knew, were of the same race as those
warriors who gained vain victories for unsympathetic
Kings.

The ridgy, rocky, sandy desert, startlingly yellow
against the near-blue dome of sky.  A group of donkeys, donkey-boys, violently clad dragomen, one or
two black-robed, white-turbaned official guides, Eu-
ropeans as exotic to the scene as Esquimaux in Hyde
Park.  An excavated descent to a hole surmounted by
a signboard as though it were the entrance to some
underground boozing-ken, an Egyptian soldier in
khaki and red tarbush.  An inclined plane, then flight
after flight of wooden steps through painted chamber after painted chamber, and at last, deep down in
the earth, lit by electric light, the heart of the tomb's
poor mystery: the mummified body of a great King,
Amen-Hetep II, in an uncovered sandstone sarcopha-
gus.  It is the world's greatest monument to the
awful and futile vanity of man.

"Thank God," said Martin, as he came out with Lucilla into the open air.  "Thank God for the great
world and sunshine and life.  The whole thing is fascinating, is soul-racking, but I hate these people who

lived for nothing but death. I wanted to bash that King's face in. There was that poor devil of an artist who spent his soul over those sculptures, going at them hammer and chisel in the black bowels of the earth with nothing but an oil-lamp on the scaffold beside him, for years and years—and when he had finished, calmly put to death by that brute lying there, so that he should not glorify any other swollen-headed worm of a tyrant."

They sat down on the sand in a triangular patch of shade. Lucilla regarded him with approbation.

"I love to hear you talk vehemently," she remarked.

"It's because I have learned to feel vehemently," said Martin.

"Since when?"

"Since I first met you," said Martin, with sudden daring.

"It's not my example you've been profiting by," she laughed. "You've never heard me raving at a poor old mummy."

Cool and casual, she warded off the shaft of his implied declaration. He had not another weapon to hand. He said:

"You've said things equally violent when you have felt deeply. That is your great power. You live intensely. Everything you do you put your whole self into. You have the faculty of making everybody around you do the same."

At that moment Mr. Watney-Holcombe appeared at the mouth of the tomb, mopping his rubicund face. At Lucilla he shook a playful fist.

"Not another darned monument for me this day."

"I don't seem to have succeeded with him, anyway," she said in a low and ironical voice.

Martin, gentlest of creatures, felt towards Mr. Watney-Holcombe for the moment as he had felt towards Amen-Hetep. The rosy-faced gentleman sat

beside them and talked flippantly of gods and goddesses; and soon the rest of the party joined them.
The opportunity for which Martin had waited so long,
of which he had dreamed the extravagant dreams of
an imaginative child, was gone.  He would have to
wait yet further.  But he had spoken as he had never
before dared to speak.  He had told her unmistak-
ably that she had taught him to feel and to live.  As
the other ladies approached he sprang to his feet and
held out a hand to aid the divinity to rise.  She accepted it frankly, nodded him pleasant thanks.  The
pressure of her little moist palm kept him a-tingle for
long afterwards.

They had a gay and intimate ride home.  The donkey boys thwacked the donkeys so that they galloped
to the shattering of sustained conversation between
the riders.  But in one breathing space, while they
jogged along side by side, she said:

"If I have done anything to help you on your
way, I regard it as a privilege."

"You've done everything for me," said Martin.
"To whom else but you do I owe all this?"  His gesture embraced earth and sky.

"I only made a suggestion," said Lucilla.

"You've done infinitely more.  Anybody giving advice could say: 'Go to Egypt.'  You said, 'Come to
Egypt,' and therein lies all the difference.  You have
given me of yourself, so bountifully, so generously——"  He paused.

"Go on," she said.  "I love to hear you talk."

But the donkey-boys perceiving Mr. Dangerfield
mounted on a fleet quadruped about to break through
the advance guard, thwacked the donkeys again, and
Martin, unless he shouted breathlessly, could not go
on talking.

That evening there was a dance at the Winter Palace Hotel, where they were staying.  Martin, on his

arrival at Cairo, had been as ignorant of dancing as a giraffe; but Lucilla, Mrs. Dangerfield and Maisie having commandeered the Watney-Holcombe's private sitting room at the Semiramis whenever it suited them, had put him through a severe and summary course. He threw himself devotedly into the new delight. A lithe figure and a quick ear aided him. Before he left Cairo he could dance one-steps and two-steps with the best; and so a new joy was added to his existence. And to him it was a joy infinitely more sensuous and magnetic than to those who from childhood have regarded dancing as a commonplace social pleasure. To understand, you must put yourself in the place of this undeveloped, finely tempered man of thirty.

His arm was around the beloved body, his hand clasped hers, the fragrance of her hair was in his nostrils, their limbs moved in perfect unison with the gay tune. His heart sang to the music, his feet were winged with laughter. In young enjoyment, she said with literal truthfulness:

"You are a born dancer."

He glowed and murmured glad incoherencies of acknowledgment.

"You're a born all sorts of other things, I believe," she said, "that only need bringing out. You have a rhythmical soul."

What she meant precisely she did not know, but it sounded mighty fine in Martin's ears. Ever since his first interview with Fortinbras he had been curiously interested in that vague organ and its evolution. Now it was rythmical. To explain herself she added: "It is in harmony with the great laws of existence."

A new light shone in his eyes and he held himself proudly. He looked quite a gallant fellow, straight, English, masterful. Her skirts swished the feet of a couple of elderly English ladies sitting by the wall.

Her quick woman's ears caught the remark: "What a handsome couple." She flushed and her eyes sparkled into his. He replied to her psychological dictum:

"At any rate it's in harmony with the deepest of them all."

"What is that?"

"The fundamental law," said he.

They danced the gay dance to the end. They stopped breathless, and laughed into each other's eyes. She took his arm and they left the ball-room.

"Unless you will dance with me again," he said, "this is my last dance to-night."

"Why?"

"I leave you to guess," said he.

"It was as near perfection as could be," she admitted. "I feel rather like that myself. Perhaps more so; for I don't want to spoil things even by dancing with you again."

"Do you really mean it?"

She nodded frankly, intimately, deliciously.

"Let us go outside, away from everybody," he suggested.

They crossed the lounge and reached the Western door. Both were living a little above themselves.

"When last we talked sense," she said, "you spoke about a fundamental law. Come and expound it to me."

They stood on the terrace amid other flushed and happy dancers.

"Let us get away from these people."

"Who know nothing of the fundamental law," said Lucilla.

So they went along a spur of the terrace, a sort of rococo bastion guarding the entrance to the hotel, and there they found solitude. They sat beneath the velvet, star-hung sky. Fifty yards away flowed the Nile, with now and then a flashing ripple. From a ghyassa with ghostly white sail creeping down the river came an Arab chant. The flowers of the bougainvillea on the hotel porch gleamed dim and pale. A touch of khamsin gave languor to the air. Lucilla drew off her gloves, bade him put them down for her. He preferred to keep them warm and fragrant, a part of herself.

"Now about this fundamental law," she said in her lazy contralto.

Her hand hung carelessly, temptingly over the arm of her chair. Graciously she allowed him to take and hold it.

"Surely you know."

"I want you to tell me, Mr. Philosopher."

He dallied with the adorable situation.

"Since when have I become Master and you Pupil, Lucilla?"

"Since you began, presumably to plunge deep into profundities of wisdom where I can't follow you. Behold me at your feet."

He moved his chair close to hers and she allowed him to play with her slender fingers.

"The fundamental law of life," said he, bending towards her, "is love."

"I wonder!" said Lucilla.

She lay in the long chair, her head against the back. He drew her fingers to his lips.

"I'm sure of it. I'm sure of it as I'm sure that there's a God in Heaven, as that," he whispered, in what the sophisticated may term an anti-climax, "there's a goddess on earth."

"Who is the goddess?" she murmured.

"You," said he.

"I like being called a goddess," she said, "especially after dancing the two-step. Hymns Ancient and Modern."

"Do you know what is the most ancient hymn in the world?"

"No."

"Shall I tell you?"

"Am I not here to be instructed?"

"You are beautiful and I love you. You are wonderful and I love you. You are adorable and I love you."

"How did you learn to become so lyrical?"

Martin knew not. He was embarked on the highest adventure of his life. A super-Martin seemed to speak. Her tone was playful, not ironical. It encouraged him to flights more lyrical still. In the daylight of reason what he said was amazing nonsense. Beneath the Egyptian stars, in the atmosphere drowsy with the scents of the East and the touch of khamsin it sounded to receptive ears beautifully romantic. Through the open door came the strains of an old-fashioned waltz, perhaps meretricious, but in the exotic surroundings sensuous and throbbing with passion. He bent over her and now possessed both hands.

"All that I feel for you, all that you are to me," he said, concluding his rhapsody. Then, as she made no reply, he asked: "You aren't angry with me?"

"I'm not a granite sphinx," she said, in her low voice. "No one has ever said things like that to me before. I don't say men haven't tried. They have; but they've always made themselves ridiculous. I've always wanted to laugh at them."

Said Martin: "You are not laughing at me?"

"No," she whispered. And after a long pause: "No, I am not laughing at you."

She turned her face to him. Her lips were very near. Mortal man could have done neither more nor less than that which Martin did. He kissed her. Then he drew back shaken to the roots of his being. She lay with closed eyes; he saw the rise and fall of her bosom. The universe, earth and stars and the living bit of the cosmos that was he, hung in breathless suspense. Time stopped. There was no space.

He was holding her beloved hands so delicately and adorably veined: before his eyes, in the dim light, were her lips, slightly parted, which he had just kissed.

Presently she stirred, withdrew her hands, passed them across her eyes and with dainty touches about her hair, as she sat up. Time went on and there was space again and the stars followed their courses. Martin threw an arm round her.

"Lucilla," he cried quiveringly.

But with a quick movement she eluded his embrace and rose to her feet. She kept him off with a little gesture.

"No, no, Martin. There has been enough foolishness for one night."

But Martin, man at last, caught her and crushed her to him with all his young strength and kissed her, not as worshipper kisses goddess, but as a man kisses a woman.

At last she said, like millions of her sisters in similar circumstances: "You're hurting me."

Like millions of his brethren, he released her. She panted for a moment. Then she said: "We must go in. Let me go first. Give me a few minutes' grace. Good-night."

Mortal gentleman and triumphant lover could do no more or no less. She sped down the terrace and disappeared. He waited, his soul aflame. When he entered the lounge, she was not there. He saw the Dangerfields and the Watney-Holcombes and one or two others sitting in a group over straw-equipped glasses. He knew that Lucilla was not in the dancing-room. He knew that she had fled to solitude. Cheery Watney-Holcombe catching sight of him, waved an inviting hand. Martin, longing for the sweet loneliness of the velvet night, did not dare refuse. His wits were sharpened. Refusal would give cause for intolerable gossip. He came forward.

"What have you done with Lucilla?" cried Mrs. Dangerfield.

"She has gone to bed. We've had a heavy day. She's dead beat," said Martin.

And thus he entered into the Kingdom of the Men of the World.

## CHAPTER XX

THE next morning, Martin enquiring for Miss Merriton learned that she had already started on a sketching excursion with Hassan, the old, one-eyed dragoman. Her destination was unknown; but the fact that Hassan had taken charge of a basket containing luncheon augured a late return. Martin spent a sorry forenoon at Karnak which, deprived of the vivifying influence of the only goddess that had ever graced its precincts, seemed dead, forlorn and vain. It was a day, too, of khamsin, when hot stones and sand are an abomination to the gasping and perspiring sense. And yet Lucilla had gone off into the desert. She would faint at her easel. She would get sunstroke. She would be brought back dead. And anxious Martin joined a languid luncheon table. There was talk of the absent one. If she had not been Lucilla they would have accounted her mad.

He sat through the sweltering afternoon on the eastern terrace over a novel which he could not read. Last night he had held her passionately in his arms. Her surrender had been absolute and eloquent avowal. Already the masculine instinct of possession spoke. Why did she now elude him? He had counted on a morning of joy that would have eclipsed the night. Why had she gone? Deep thought brought comforting solution. To-morrow they were to migrate to Assouan. This was their last day in Luxor where, up to now, Lucilla had not made one single sketch. Now, had she not told him in Brantôme that her object in going to Egypt was to paint it? Generously she had put aside her art for his sake—until the last moment. Of this last moment she was taking advantage. Still—why not a little word to him? He turned to his book. But the thrill of the great kiss pulsated through his veins. He gave himself up to dreams.

Later in the afternoon, Watney-Holcombe, fly-whisk in one hand and handkerchief in the other, took him into the cool, darkened bar, and supplied him with icy drink and told him tales of his early days in San Francisco. A few other men lounged in and joined them. Desultory talk furnished an excuse for systematic imbibing of cold liquid. When Martin reached the upper air he found that Lucilla had already arrived and had gone to her room for rest. He only saw her when she came down late for dinner. She was dressed in a close-fitting charmeuse gown of a strange blue shade like an Egyptian evening. Her pleasant greeting differed no whit from that of twenty-four hours ago. Not by the flicker of a brown eyelash did she betray recollection of last night's impassioned happenings.

She talked of her excursion to the eager and reproachful group. A sandstorm had ruined a masterpiece, her best brushes, her hair and old Hassan's temper. She had swallowed half Sahara with her food. Her very donkey, cocking round an angry eye, had called her the most opprobrious term in his vocabulary—an ass. Altogether she had enjoyed herself immensely.

"You ought to have come, Martin," she said coolly.

He made the obvious retort. "You did not give me the chance."

"If only you had been up at dawn," she laughed.

"I was," he replied. "I lay awake most of the night and I saw the sunrise from my bedroom window."

"Oh, dear!" she sighed. "You were looking the wrong way. You were adoring the East while I was going out to the West."

"All that is very pretty, but I'm dying of hunger," said Watney-Holcombe, carrying her off to the dining room.

The rest followed. At table, she sat between her captor and Dangerfield, so that Martin had no private speech with her. After dinner Watney-Holcombe and Dangerfield wandered off to the bar to play billiards. Martin declining an invitation to join them remained with the four ladies in the lounge. Lucilla had manœuvred herself into an unassailable position between the two married women. Martin and Maisie sat sketchily on the outskirts behind the coffee table. The band discoursed unexhilarating music. Talk languished. At last Maisie sprang to her feet and took Martin unceremoniously by the arm.

"If I sit here much longer I shall sob. Come on out and do something."

Martin rose. "What can we do?"

"Anything. We can gaze at the stars and you can swear that you love me. Or we can go and look at Cook's steamboat."

"Will you come with us, Lucilla?" asked Martin.

She shook her head and smiled. "I'm far too tired and lazy."

The girl, still holding his arm, swung him round. He had no choice but to obey. They walked along the quay as far as the northern end of the temple. By the time of their return Lucilla had gone to bed. She had become as elusive as a dream.

He did not capture her till the next morning on the railway station platform, before their train started. By a chance of which he took swift advantage, she stood some paces apart from the little group of friends. He carried her further away. Moments were precious; he went at once to the root of the matter.

"Lucilla, why are you avoiding me?"

She opened wide eyes. "Avoiding you, my dear Martin?"

"Yesterday you gave me no opportunity of speaking to you, and this morning it has been the same. And I've been in a fever of longing for a word with you."

"I'm sorry," she said. "And now you have me, what is the word?"

"I love you," said Martin.

"Hush," she whispered, with an involuntary glance round at the red-jerseyed porters and the stray passengers. "This is scarcely the place for a declaration."

"The declaration was the night before last."

"Hush!" she said again, and laid her gloved hand on his arm. But he insisted.

"You haven't forgotten?"

"Not yet. How could I? You must give me time."

"For what?" he asked.

"To forget."

A horrible pain shot through him. "Do you want to forget all that has passed between us?"

She raised her eyes, frankly, and laughed. "My dear boy, how can we go into such intimate matters among this rabble?"

"Oh, my dear," said Martin, "I am only asking a very simple question. Do you want to forget?"

"Perhaps not quite," she replied softly, and the pain through his heart ceased and he held up his head and laughed, and then bent it towards her and asked forgiveness.

"If I didn't forgive you, I suppose you'd be miserable?"

"Abjectly wretched," he declared.

"That wouldn't be a fit frame of mind for a six-hour stifling and dusty railway journey. So let us be happy while we can."

At Assouan they went to the hotel on the little green island in the middle of the Nile. In the hope of her redeeming a half promise of early descent before dinner, he dressed betimes and waited in the long lounge, his eyes on the lift. She appeared at last, fresh, radiant, as though she had stepped out of the dawn. She sat beside him with an adorable suggestion of intimacy.

"Martin," she said, "I want you to make me a promise, will you?"

His eyes on hers, he promised blindly.

"Promise me to be good while we're here."

"Good?" he queried.

"Yes. Don't you know what 'good' means? It means not to be tempestuous or foolish or inquisitive."

"I see," said Martin, with a frown between his brows. "I mustn't"—he hesitated—"I mustn't do what I did the other night, and I mustn't say that all my universe, earth and sun and moon and stars are packed in this"—his fingers met the drapery of her bodice in a fugitive, delicate touch—"and I mustn't ask you any questions about what you may be thinking."

There was a new tone in his voice, a new expression in his eyes and about the corners of his lips, all of which she was quick to note. She cast him a swift glance of apprehension, and her smile faded.

"You set out the position with startling concreteness."

"I do," said he. "Up to a couple of days ago I worshipped you as a divine abstraction. The night before last, things, to use your words, became startlingly concrete. You are none the less wonderful and adorable, but you have become the concrete woman of flesh and blood I want and would sell my soul for."

She glanced at him again, anxiously, furtively, half afraid. In such terms do none but masterful men speak to women; men who from experience of a deceitful sex know how to tear away ridiculous veils; or else men who, having no knowledge of woman whatever, suddenly awaken with primitive brutality to the sex instinct. Her subtle brain worked out the rapid solution. Her charming idea of making a man of Martin had succeeded beyond her most romantic expectations. She realised that facing him dry and cold, as she was doing now, would only develop a dramatic situation which would be cut uncomfortably short by the first careless friend who stepped out of the lift. She temporised, summoning the smile to her eyes.

"Anyway, you've promised."

"I have," said Martin.

"You see, you can't stand with a pistol at my head whenever we meet alone. You must give me time."

"To forget?"

"To make up my mind whether to forget or remember," she declared radiantly. "Now what more do you want an embarrassed woman to say?"

Swiftly she had reassumed command. Martin yielded happily. "If it isn't all I want," said he, "it's much more than I dared claim."

She rose and he rose too. She passed her hand through his arm. "Come and see whether anybody has had the common sense to reserve a table for dinner."

Thus during her royal pleasure, their semi-loverlike relations were established; rather perhaps were they nicely balanced on a knife-edge, the equilibrium dependent on her skill. As at Luxor, so at Assouan did they the things that those who go to Assouan do. They lounged about the hotel garden. They took the motor ferry to the little town on the mainland and wandered about the tiny bazaar. They sailed on the Nile. They went to the merriest race meetings in heathendom, where you can back your fancy in camel, donkey or buffalo for a shilling upwards at the state *pari-mutuel.* They made an expedition to the Dam. The main occupation, as it is that of most who go to Assouan, was not to pass the time, but to sit in the sun and let the time pass. A golden fortnight or so slipped by. Martin lived as freely in his goddess's company as he had done at Cairo or Luxor. She had ordained a period of probation. All his delicacy of sentiment proclaimed her justified. She comported herself as the most gracious of divinities, and the most warmly sympathetic of human women, leading him by all the delicate devices known to Olympus and Clapham Common, to lay bare to her his inmost soul. He told her all that he had to tell: much that he had told already: his childhood in Switzerland, his broken Cambridge career, his life at Margett's Universal College, his adventures with Corinna, his waiterdom at Brantôme, his relations with Fortinbras, Bigourdin, Félise. The only thing in his simple past that he hid was his knowledge of the tragedy in the life of Fortinbras. "And then you came," said he, "and touched my dull earth, and turned it into a New Jerusalem of 'pure gold like unto clear glass.'" And he told her of his consultation with the Dealer in Happiness, and his journey to London and his meeting with Corinna in the flimsy flat. It seemed to him that she had the divine power of taking his heart in her blue-veined hands and making it speak like that of a child. For everything in the world for which that heart had longed she had the genius to create expression.

In spite of all the delicious intimacy of such revelation he observed his compact loyally. For the quivering moment it was enough that she knew and accepted his love; it was enough to realise that when she smiled on him, she must remember unresentfully the few holy seconds of his embrace. And yet, when alone with her, in the moonlit garden, so near that accidental

touch of arm or swinging touch of skirt or other delicate physical sense of her, was an essential part of
their intercourse, he wondered whether she had a notion of the madness that surged in his blood, of the
tensity of the grip in which he held himself.

And so, lotus-eating, reckless of the future, happy
only in the throbbing present, he remained with Lucilla and her friends at Assouan until the heat of spring
drove them back to Cairo.

There, on the terrace of Shepheard's, on the noon of
his arrival, he found Fortinbras. The Dealer in Happiness, economically personally (though philosophically) conducted, had also visited Luxor and had
brought away a rich harvest of observation. He bestowed it liberally on Martin, who, listening with perplexed brow, wondered whether he himself had
brought away but chaff. After a while Fortinbras
enquired:

"And the stock we wot of—is it still booming?"

Martin said: "I've been inconceivably happy. Don't
let us talk about it."

Presently Lucilla and Mrs. Dangerfield joined them
and Fortinbras was carried off to the Semiramis to
lunch. It was a gay meal. The Watney-Holcombes
had gathered in a few young soldiers, and youth asserted itself joyously. Fortinbras, urbane and de-
bonair, laughed with the youngest. The subalterns
thinking him a personage of high importance who was
unbending for their benefit, paid him touching deference. He exerted himself to please, dealing out
happiness lavishly; yet his bland eyes kept keen watch
on Martin and Lucilla sitting together on the opposite side of the great round table. Once he caught and
held her glance for a few seconds; then she flushed,
as it seemed, angrily, and flung him an irrelevant question about Félise. When the meal was over and he
had taken leave of his hosts, he said to Martin, who

accompanied him to the West door by which he elected
to emerge:

"Either you will never want me again, or you will
want a friendly hand more than you have wanted a
friendly hand in your life before—and I am leaving
this land of enchantment the day after to-morrow.
*Dulce est dissipere etc.* But dissipation is the thief
of professional advancement. If a dealer in cheaper
and shoddier happiness arises in the quartier I am lost.
There was already before I left, a conscientious and
conscienceless Teuton who was trying to steal my
thunder and retail it at the ignominous rate of a franc
a reverberation. I cannot afford to let things drift.
Neither, my son," he tapped the young man impres-
sively on the shoulder. "Neither can you."

Martin straightened himself, half resentful, and
twirled his trim moustache.

"It's all very well, my son," said Fortinbras with his
benevolent smile, "but all the let-Hell-come airs in the
world can't do anything else but intensify the fact that
you're a Soldier of Fortune. Faint heart—you know
the jingle—and faintness of heart is not the attribute
of a soldier. Good-bye, my dear Martin." He held
out his hand. "You will see me to-morrow at our
usual haunt."

Fortinbras waved adieu. Martin lit a cigarette and
sat in a far corner of the verandah. The westering
sun beat heavily on the striped awning. Further along,
by the door, a small group of visitors were gathered
round an Indian juggler. For the first time, almost,
since his landing in Egypt, he permitted himself to
think. A Soldier of Fortune. The words conveyed
sinister significance: a predatory swash-buckler in
search of any fortune to his hand: Lucilla's fortune.
Hitherto he had blinded himself to sordid considerations. He had dived, figuratively speaking, into his
bag of sovereigns, as into a purse of Fortunatus. The

magic of destiny would provide for his material wants. What to him, soul-centred on the ineffable woman, were such unimportant and mean preoccupations? He had lived in his dream. He had lived in his intoxication. He had lived of late in the splendour of a seismic moment. And now, crash! he came to earth. A Soldier of Fortune. An adventurer. A swindler. The brutal common-sense aspect grinned in his face. On ship-board Fortinbras had warned him that he was an adventurer. He had not heeded. . . . He was a Soldier of Fortune. He must strike the iron while it was hot. That was what Fortinbras meant. He must secure the heiress. He hated Fortinbras. The sudden realisation of his position devastated his soul. And yet he loved her. He desired her as he had not dreamed it to be in a man's power to desire.

At last his glance rested on the little crowd around the Indian juggler; and then suddenly he became aware of her flashing like a dove among crows. Her lips and eyes were filled with a child's laughter at the foolish conjuring. When the trick was over she turned and, seeing him, smiled. He beckoned. She complied, with the afterglow of amusement on her face; but when she came near him her expression changed.

"Why, what's the matter?" she asked.

He pushed a chair for her. They sat.

"I must speak to you, once and for all," he said.

"Don't you think it's rather public?"

"The Indian is going," he replied, with an indicating gesture, "and the people too. It's too hot for them to sit out here."

"Then what about me?" she asked.

He sprang to his feet with an apology. She laughed.

"Never mind. We are as well here as anywhere. Sit down. Now, why this sudden tragic resolution?"

"An accidental word from Fortinbras. He called me a Soldier of Fortune. The term isn't pretty. You are a woman of great wealth. I am a man practically penniless. I have no position, no profession. I am what the world calls an adventurer."

She protested. "That's nonsense. You have been absolutely honest with me from first to last."

"Honest in so far as I've not concealed my material situation. But honourable? . . . If you had known in Brantôme that I had already dared to love you, would you have suggested my coming to Egypt?"

"Possibly not," replied Lucilla, the shadow of an ironical smile playing about her lips. "But—we can be quite frank—I don't see how you could have told me."

"Of course I couldn't," he admitted. "But loving you as I did, I ought not to have come. It was not the part of an honourable man."

His elbow on the arm of the cane chair and his chin on his hand he looked with haggard questioning into her eyes. She held his glance for a brief moment, then looked down at her blue-veined hands.

"You see," he said, "you don't deny it. That's why I call myself an adventurer."

Her eyes still downcast, she said: "You have no reason in the world to reproach yourself. As soon as you could, with decency, tell me that you loved me, you did. And you made it clear to me long before you told me. And I don't think," she added in a low voice, "that I showed much indignation."

"Why didn't you?" he asked.

She intertwined her fingers nervously. "Sometimes a woman feels it good to be loved. And I've felt it good—and wonderful—all the time. Once—there was a man, years ago; but he's dead. Since then other men have come along and I've turned them down as gently as I could. But no one has done the mad thing that you have done for my sake. And no one has been so simple and loyal—and strong. You are different. I have had the sense of being loved by a man pure and unstained. God knows you are without blame."

"Then, my dear," said he, bending his head vainly so as to catch her face otherwise than in profile and to meet the eyes hidden beneath the adorable brown lashes, "what is to happen between us two?"

For answer, she made a little despairing gesture.

"If I had the right of an honest man seeking a woman in marriage," he said, "I would take matters into my own hand. I would follow you all over the world until I won you somehow or the other."

She turned on him in a flash of passion.

"If you say such things, you will make me marry you out of humiliation and remorse."

"God forbid I should do that," said Martin.

She averted her head again. There was a span of silence. At the extreme end of the long deserted verandah, beneath the sun-baked awning, with only the occasional clatter of a carriage or the whirr of a motor breaking the stillness of this drowsy embankment of the Nile, they might have been miles away in the desert solitude under the palm-tree of Fortinbras's dream.

Lucilla was the first to speak. "It is I who am to blame.for everything. No; let me talk. I've got the courage to talk straight and you've got the courage to listen. You interested me at Brantôme. Your position there was so un-English. Of course I liked you. I thought you ought to be roused from stagnation. It was just idle fancy that made me talk about Egypt. I thought it would do you good to cut everything and see the world. When I took Félise away with me and saw how she expanded and developed, I thought of you. I've done the same often before with girls, like Félise, who have never been given a chance, and it has been a fascinating amusement. I had never made the experiment with a man. I wanted to see how you would shape, what kind of impression all the new kind of life

would make on you. I realise it now, but till now I
haven't, that all my so-called kindnesses to girls have
been heartless experimenting. I could keep twenty
girls in luxury for twenty years without considering
the expense. That's the curse of unlimited money!
one abuses its power. . . . With you, of course,
money didn't come in. I hadn't the insanity to ask
you to be my guest, as I could ask young women. But
money aside, I knew I could give you what I gave
them; and from what Félise let drop I gathered you
had some little private means. So I wrote to you—on
the off-chance. I thought you would come. People
have a way of doing what I ask them. You were going to be the most fascinating amusement of all. You
see, that's how it was."

She paused. His face hardened. "Well," said he,
"go on."

"Can't you guess the rest?"

"No," said he, "I can't."

There was a note in his voice that seemed to tear
her heart. She pressed both hands to her eyes.

"If you knew how I despise and hate myself!"

"No, no, my dear," said Martin. He touched her
shoulder, warm and soft. Only the convention of a
diaphanous flimsy sleeve gave sanction. She let his
hand remain there for a moment or two; then gripped
it and flung it away. But the nervous clasp of her fingers denied resentment. She turned a white face.

"I knew you loved me. It was good, as I've told
you, to feel it. I meant to escape as I've escaped before. I don't excuse myself. Then came the night at
Luxor. I let myself go. It was a thing of the senses.
Something snapped, as it has done in the case of millions of women under similar conditions. You could
have done what you liked with me. I shall never forget if I live to be ninety. Do you think I've been sleeping peacefully all these nights ever since? I haven't."

She looked at him defiantly.  Said Martin:

"You must care for me—a little.  The veriest little is all I dare ask for."

"No, it isn't," she answered, meeting his eyes. "Don't delude yourself.  You are asking for everything.  And if I had everything to give I would give it to you.  You may think I have played with you heartlessly for the last three or four weeks.  Any outsider knowing the bare facts would accuse me.  Perhaps I ought to have sent you away; but I hadn't the strength.  There.  That's a confession.  Make what you will of it."

"All I can make of it," said Martin tremulously, "is that you're the woman for me, and that you know it."

"I do," she said.  "I'm up against facts and I face them squarely.  On the other hand you're not the man for me.  If ever a woman has tried to love a man, I've tried to love you.  That's why I've made you stay. I've plucked my heart out—all, all but the roots. There's a dead man there, at the roots"—she flung out both hands and her shoulders heaved—"and he is always up between us, and I can't, I can't.  It's no use. I must give myself altogether, or not at all.  I'm not built for the half-and-half things."

He sat grim, feeling more a stone than a man.  She clutched his arm.

"Suppose I did marry you.  By all the rules of the game I ought to.  But it would only be misery for both of us.  There would be twenty thousand causes for misery.  Don't you see?"

"I see everything," said Martin.  He rose and leaned both elbows on the verandah and faced her with bent brows.  "I see everything.  You have put your case very clearly.  But suppose I say that you haven't played the game.  Suppose I say that you should have known that no man who wasn't in love with you—except an imbecile—would have followed you to Egypt as I've done. Suppose I say that you've played havoc with my life. Suppose I instance everything that has passed between us, and I assert the rules of the game, and I ask you as a man, shaken to his centre with love of you, to marry me, what would you say?"

She rose and stood beside him, holding her head very proudly.

"Put upon my honour like that," she replied, "I should have to say 'Yes.' "

He took both her hands in his and raised them to his lips.

"That's all I want to know. But as I don't reproach you, I'm not going to ask you, my dear. If I were Lord of the Earth or a millionth part of the earth I would laugh and take the risk. But as things are, I can't accept your generosity. You are the woman I love and shall always love. Good-bye and God bless you."

He wrung her hand and marched down the verandah, his head in the air, looking a very gallant fellow. After a few seconds' perplexity she ran swiftly in pursuit.

"Martin!" she cried.

He turned and awaited her approach.

"I feel I've behaved to you like the lowest of women. I'll make my amends if you like. I'll marry you. There!"

Martin stood racked with the great temptation. All his senses absorbed her beauty and her wonder. At length he asked:

"Do you love me?"

"I've told you all about that."

"Then you don't. . . . Yes or No? It's a matter of two lives."

"I've tried and I will try again."

"But Yes or No?" he persisted.

"No," she said.

Again he took her hands and kissed them.

"That ends it. If I married you, my dear, I should indeed be a Soldier of Fortune, and you would have every reason to despise me. Now it is really good-bye."

Her gaze followed him until he disappeared into the hotel. Then she moved slowly to the balustrade baking in the sunshine, and leaning both elbows on it stared through a blur of tears at the detested beauty of the world.

# CHAPTER XXI

FORTINBRAS paced the deck of the homeward bound steamer deep in thought. He still wore the costume of the elderly cabinet minister; but his air was that of the cabinet minister returning to a wrecked ministry. His broad shoulders were rounded and bent; his face had fallen from its benevolent folds into fleshy haggardness. He felt old; he felt inexpressibly lonely. He had not repeated the social experiment of the voyage out. Save to his Dutch and Russian table neighbours he had not the heart to speak to any one. A deep melancholy enwrapped him. After his philosophical communion with the sage Abu Mohammed he shrank from platitudinous commerce with the profane. It was for the heart and not for the mind that he craved companionship. He was travelling (second-class, for economy's sake) back to the old half-charlatan life. For all one's learning and wisdom, one cannot easily embark on a new career in the middle-fifties. He must be *Marchand de Bonheur* to the end.

He wondered whether he would miss Cécile. Such things had happened. No matter how degraded, she had been a human thing to greet him on his return from his preposterous toil. Also, her needs had been an incentive; they had sharpened the hawk's vision during the daily round of cafés and restaurants, and quickened his pounce upon the divined five-franc piece. Would he have the nerve, the unwearied patience, the bitter sense of martyrdom, wherewith to carry on his trade? Again, in days past his heavy heart had been uplifted by the love of a child like the wild flowers

314

from which Alpine honey is made, away in the depths
of old-world France. But now he had forfeited her
love. She had written to him, all these weeks in Egypt,
dutifully, irreproachably; had given him the news, such
as it was, of Brantôme. She had told him of the state
of her uncle's health—invariably robust; of the arrivals
and departures of elegant motorists; of the march
through the town decorated for the occasion of a host
of *petits soldats,* amid the enthusiasm and Marseillaise
singing of the inhabitants; of the sudden death by
apoplexy of the good Madame Chauvet, and the sudden development of business on the part of her daughters, who almost immediately had taken the next shop
and launched out into iron wreaths and crosses, and
artificial flowers and funeral inscriptions, touching and
pious; of the purchases of geese; of the infatuation
of the elderly Euphémie for the youthful waiter, erst-
while *plongeur* of the Café de l'Univers; of all sorts
and conditions of unimportant happenings; finally of
the betrothal of Monsieur Lucien Viriot and Estelle
Mazabois, the daughter of the famous Mazabois who
kept a great drapery establishment of Périgueux—
"she has the dowry of a princess and the head of a
rocking-horse, so they are sure to be happy," wrote
Félise. The manner of this last announcement shocked
him. Félise had changed. She had given him all the
news, but her letters had grown self-conscious and
artificial. To avoid the old, artless expressions of en-
dearment, she rushed into sprightly narrative, and
signed herself "his affectionate daughter." He had
lost Félise.

Yes, he felt old and lonely, unnerved for the struggle. Even Martin had forsaken him.

He had encountered a stony-faced, wrong-headed
young man on the terrace of Shepheard's Hotel the
noon before he sailed, and found all his nostrums for
happiness high-handedly rejected. Martin had been

an idle woman's toy, a fiery toy as it turned out; and when she burned her fingers, she had dropped him. So much was obvious; most of it he had foreseen. He had counted on eventual declaration and summary dismissal; but he had not reckoned on a prelude of reciprocated sentiment. Contrary to habit, Martin gave him but a confused view of his state of mind. The unhappy lover would hear not a word against his peerless lady. On the other hand, his love for her had blasted his existence. This appalling fact, though he did not proclaim it so heroically, he allowed Fortinbras to apprehend. He neither reproached him for past advice nor asked for new. To the suggestion that he should return to Brantôme and accept Bigourdin's offer, he turned a deaf ear. He had cut himself adrift; he must go whithersoever winds and tides should carry him, and they were carrying him far from Périgord.

"In what direction?" Fortinbras had enquired.

"Thank Heaven, I don't know myself," he had answered. "Anyhow, I am going to seek my fortune. I must have money and power so that I can snap my fingers at the world. That's what I'm going to live for."

And soon after that declaration he had wrung Fortinbras by the hand, and hailing an *arabeah* had driven off into the unknown. Fortinbras had felt like the hen who sees her duckling brood sail away down the brook. He had lost control of his disciple; he mattered nothing to the young man setting forth on his wild-goose chase after fortune. His charming little scheme had failed. He anticipated the reproaches of Bigourdin, the accusation in the eyes of Félise. "Why did you side with the enemy? Why did you drive Martin away?" . . .

He felt old and lonely, a pathetic failure; so he walked the second-class deck with listless shoulders and bowed head, his hands in his pockets.

"*Tiens!* Monsieur Fortinbras! who would have thought it?" cried a fresh voice.

He looked up and saw a dark-eyed girl, her head enveloped in a motor-veil, who extended a friendly hand.

"*Mademoiselle* . . ." he began uncertainly.

"*Mais oui!* Eugénie Dubois. You must remember me. There was also *le grand Jules*—Jules Massart."

"Yes, I remember," he said courteously, with a wan smile.

"You saved us both from a pretty mess."

"I remember the saving; but I forget the mess. It is my rule always to forget such things."

She laughed gaily, burst into an account of herself. She was a modiste in the great Paris firm of Odille et Compagnie, which had a branch at Cairo. Now she was recalled for the Paris and London season.

"*Et justement*"—she plucked at his sleeve and led him to a seat—"I am in a tangle of an affair which keeps me awake of nights. You fall upon me from the skies like an angel. Be good and give me a consultation."

She fished out her purse and extracted a twenty-five piastre piece. He motioned her hand away.

"*Mon enfant,*" said he. "You are an honourable little soul. But I don't do business on a holiday. *Raconte-moi ton affaire.*"

But she protested. She would not abuse his kindness. Either a consultation at the regulation price or no consultation at all. At last he said:

"*Eh bien!* give me your five francs."

She obeyed. He rose. "Come," said he, and led the way to the stairhead by the saloon where was fixed the collecting box in aid of the Fund for Shipwrecked Mariners. He slipped the coin down the slot.

"Now," said he, "honour is satisfied."

But listening to her artless and complicated tale,

he wondered, while a shiver ran over his frame, whether he would ever be able again to slip a five-franc piece into his waistcoat pocket. He felt yet older than before, incapable of piercing to the root of youth's perplexities. He counselled with oracular vagueness, conscious of not having earned his fee. He paced the deck again.

"Were it not for Abu Mohammed," he said, "I should call it a disastrous journey."

Meanwhile Martin, lonelier even than he, sat in the bows of a great Eastward bound steamer, his eyes opened to the staring facts of life. No longer must he masquerade as the man of fashion—never again until he had bought the right. The remains of his small capital he must keep intact for the day of need. No more the luxury of first-class travel. This voyage in the steerage was but a means of transit to the new lands where he would win his way to fortune. He needed no advice. He had spiritually and morally outgrown his tutelage. No longer, so he told himself, would he nourish his soul on dreams. It could feed if it liked on memories. The madness had passed. He drew the breath of an honest man. If he had taken Lucilla at her word and married her, what would have been his existence? Trailing about the idle world in the wake of a rich wife, dependent on her bounty even for a pair of shoe-laces; eating out his heart for the love she could not give; at last, perhaps, quarrelling desperately, or else with sapped will-power sunk in sloth, accepting from her an allowance on condition that they should live apart. He had heard of such marriages since he had mingled with the wealthy. Even had she met him with a love as passionate as his own, would the happiness have lasted? In his grim mood he thought not. He reasoned himself into the conviction that his loss had been his gain. Far better

that he should be among these few poor folk who sat
down to table in their shirt-sleeves, than that he should
be eating the flesh-pots of dishonour in the land of
Egypt. He himself dined in his shirt-sleeves, as he
had done many a time before in the kitchen of the
Hôtel des Grottes.

Yet he hungered for her. It seemed impossible that
he should never see her again, never again watch the
sweep of the adorable brown eyelashes, the subtle play
of laughter around her mobile lips; never again greet
with delicious heart-pang the sight of her slim figure
willowy like those in the *Primavera*. In vain he
schooled himself to regard her as one dead. The
witchery of her obsessed him night and day. He
learned what it was to suffer.

He had taken his deck passage to Hong-Kong—
why he could scarcely tell. It sounded very far away
—as far away from her as practicable. As the sultry
days went on, he realised that he had not reckoned
on the tremendous distance of Hong-Kong. It was
past Bombay, Colombo, Penang and Singapore. At
such ports as he could, he landed, but the glamour of
the East had gone. He was a man who had expended
his power of wonder and delight. He looked on them
coldly as places he might possibly exploit, should Hong-
Kong prove barren. Also the period of great heat
had begun, and he found danger in strolling about the
deadly streets. On ship-board he slept on deck. As
they neared Hong-Kong his heart sank. For the first
time he wished that Fortinbras were with him. Perhaps he had repaid affection with scant courtesy. He
occupied himself with a long letter to his friend, setting out his case. He then imagined the reply. "My
son," said the mellow, persuasive voice, "have you not
been carrying on from thrill to thrill the Great Adventure begun last August, when you threw off the
chains of Margett's? Have you not filled your brain

and your soul with new and breathless sensations? Have you not tasted joys hitherto unimagined? Have you not been admitted to the heart of a great and loyal nation? Have you not flaunted it in the dazzling splendour of the great world? Have you not steeped your being in the gorgeous colour of the East? Have not your pulses throbbed with an immortal passion for a woman of surpassing beauty? Have you not known, what is only accorded to the select of the sons of men, a supreme moment of delirious joy when Time stood still and Space was not? Have you not lived intensely all this wonderful year? Are you the same blank-minded, starving-souled, mild negation of a man who sat as a butt for Corinna's pleasantries at the Petit Cornichon? Have you not progressed immeasurably? Have you not gained spiritual stature, wisdom both human and godlike? And are you not now, having passed through the fiery furnace not only unscathed but tempered, setting out on the still greater adventure —the conquest of the Ends of the Earth? Less than a year ago what were you but a slave? What are you now? A free man."

So through the ears of fancy ran the sonorous rhetoric of Fortinbras. Martin tore up his letter and scattered the fragments on the sea. A day or two afterwards, with a stout heart, he landed at Victoria, the capital of Hong-Kong.

A half-caste clerk to whom he had entrusted his card returned from the inner office.

"Mr. Tudsley will see you, sir."

Martin followed him into a darkened office, cooled by an electric fan, where a white-clad, gaunt, yellow-faced Englishman sat at a desk. The clerk closed the door and retired. The yellow-faced Englishman rose and smiled, after glancing at Martin's card on the desk before him.

"Mr. Overshaw? What can I do for you?"

"You can give me some work," said Martin.

"I'm afraid I can't."

"I'm sorry," said Martin. "I must apologise for troubling you."

He was about to withdraw. Mr. Tudsley glanced at him shrewdly.

"Wait a minute. Sit down. I don't seem to place you. Who are you and where do you come from?"

"That's my name," said Martin, pointing to his card, "and I have just arrived from Europe, or to be more exact, from Egypt."

"By the *Sesostris?*"

"Yes."

Mr. Tudsley took up and scanned a type-written sheet of paper.

"I don't see your name on the passenger list."

"Possibly not," said Martin. "I came steerage."

"Indeed?" Martin, spruce in his well-cut grey flannels, looked anything but a deck passenger. "What made you do that?"

"Economy," said Martin.

"And why have you come to me?"

"I made a list last night, at the hotel, of the leading firms in Hong-Kong and yours was among them."

"Haven't you any introductions?"

"No."

"Then what induced you to come to this particular little Hell upon Earth?"

"Chance," said Martin. "One place is pretty much the same to me as another."

"What kind of work are you looking for?"

"Anything. From sweeping the floor to running a business."

"Only coolies sweep floors here," said Mr. Tudsley, tilting back his chair and clasping his hands behind his back. "And only experienced men of business run businesses. What business have you run?"

"None," said Martin.

"Well, what business qualifications have you?"

"None. But I'm an educated man—Cambridge——"

"Yes, yes, one sees that," the other interrupted. "There are millions of them."

"I'm bilingual, English and French, and my German is good enough for ordinary purposes."

"Do you know anything of accounts?"

"No," said Martin.

"Can you add up figures correctly?"

"I daresay," said Martin.

"Have you ever tried?"

"No," said Martin.

Mr. Tudsley handed him a mass of type-written papers pinned together. "Do you know what that is?"

Martin glanced through the document. "It seems to be a list of commodities."

"It's a Bill of Lading. First time you've ever seen one?"

"Yes," said Martin.

"Have you any capital?"

"A little. A few hundred pounds."

"Then stick to it like grim death. Don't part with it here."

"I haven't the slightest intention of doing so," said Martin.

The lean, yellow-faced man brought his chair back to normal perpendicularity and swung it round—it worked on a swivel.

"Mr. Overshaw," said he, "pardon a perfect stranger giving you advice—but you seem to be a frank, straight man. You've made a mistake in coming to Hong-Kong. It's a beast of a climate. In a few days' time the rains will begin. Then it will rain steadily, drearily, hopelessly, damply, swelteringly, deadlily day after day, hour after hour, for four months. That's one way of looking at things. There's another. I am perfectly sure there's not a vacancy for an amateur clerk in the whole of Hong-Kong. If we want a linguist—your specialty—we can get Germans by the dozen who not only know six languages but who have been trained as business experts from childhood—and we can get them for twopence halfpenny a month."

Martin, remembering the discussions at the Café de l'Univers, replied:

"And when the war comes?"

"What war?"

"Between England and Germany."

"My dear fellow, what in the world are you talking of? There's not going to be any war. Besides," he smiled indulgently, "suppose there was—what then?"

"First," said Martin, "you would have given the enemy an intimate knowledge of your trade, which by the way he is even now reporting by every mail to his government"—he was quoting the dictum of a highly placed Egyptian official whom he met at a dinner party in Cairo—"and then you would have to fall back upon Englishmen."

Mr. Tudsley laughed and rose, so as to end the interview.

"I'll take the risk of that," he said easily. "But the immediate question is: 'What are you to do?' Have you visited any other firms?"

"Several," said Martin.

"And what have they said?"

"Much the same as you, Mr. Tudsley, only not so kindly and courteously."

"That's all right," said Mr. Tudsley, shy at the compliment. "I don't see why Englishmen meeting at the other end of nowhere shouldn't be civil to each other. But my advice is: Clear out of Hong-Kong. There's nothing doing."

"What about Shanghai?"

"That's further still from Europe."

"Singapore?"

"That's better—on the way back."

"I must thank you," said Martin, "for giving me so much of your time."

"Not a bit. I am only sorry I can't give you a job or put you on to one. But you see the position, don't you?"

Martin smiled wryly. "I'm beginning to see it with painful clearness."

"Good-bye and good luck," said Mr. Tudsley.

"Good-bye," said Martin.

Between then and the date of sailing of the next homeward bound steamer, Martin knocked at every door in Hong-Kong. Nobody wanted him. There was nothing he could do. There was no place for him on the very lowest rung of any ladder to fortune.

He sailed to Singapore.

## CHAPTER XXII

WHEN Martin landed at Marseilles he found the world on the brink of war.

He had spent the early summer roaming about the East looking, as he had looked at Hong-Kong, for work that might lead to fortune and finding none. A touch of fever had caused a friendly doctor at Penang to pack him off to Europe by the first boat. It had been a Will o' the Wisp chase mainly in the rains, when the Straits Settlements are not abodes of delight. It is bad enough that your boots should be mildewed every morning; but when the mildew begins to attack your bones it is best to depart. Martin embarked philosophically. He had tried the East because it was nearer to his original point of departure. Now he would try the West—America or Canada. In a temperate climate he could undertake physical labour. His muscles were solid, and save for the touch of fever of which the sea-air had soon cured him, his health was robust. He could hew wood, draw water, dig the earth. In a new country he could not starve. At the last pinch he could fall back on the profession he had learned at the Hôtel des Grottes. Furthermore, by eating the bread and choosing the couch of hardship he had spent comparatively little of his capital. His vagabondage had hardened him physically and morally. He knew the world. He had mixed with all kinds and conditions of men. Egypt seemed a sensuous dream of long ago. He deafened his heart to its memories. It would take ten years to make anything of a fortune. If he succeeded, then, in ten years' time, he would seek Lucilla. In the meanwhile he would not waste away in despair. He faced the future with confidence. While standing with his humble fellow passengers in the bows of the vessel, he felt his pulses thrill at the first sight of the blue islands of Marseilles. It was France, country almost of his adoption. He rejoiced that he had decided not to book his ticket to Southampton, but to pass through the beloved land once again before he sailed to another Hemisphere. Besides, his money and most of his personal effects (despatched from Egypt) were lying at Cook's office in Paris. The practical therefore turned sentiment into an easy channel. He landed, carrying his bag in his hand, bought a paper on the quay from a screaming urchin, and to his stupefaction found the world on the brink of war.

At Gibraltar he had not seen a newspaper. None had penetrated to the steerage and he had not landed. He had taken it for granted that the good, comfortable old earth was rolling its usual course. Now, at Marseilles, he became aware of every one in the blazing sunshine of the quays staring at newspapers held open before them. At the modest hotel hard by, where he deposited his bag, he questioned the manager. Yes, did not he know? Austria had declared war on Servia. Germany had rejected all proposals from England for a conference. The President of the Republic had hurried from Russia. Russia would not allow Servia to be attacked by Austria. France must join Russia. It was a *coup* prepared by Germany. *"Ça y est, c'est la guerre,"* said he.

Martin went out into the streets and found a place on the crowded terrace of one of the cafés on the Cannebière. All around him was the talk of war. The rich-voiced Provençaux do not speak in whispers. There was but one hope for peace, the successful intervention of England between Russia and Austria. But Germany would not have it. War was inevitable.

Martin bribed a chasseur to find him some English papers, no matter of what date. With fervent anxiety he scanned the history of the momentous week. What he read confirmed the talk. Whatever action England might take, France would be at war in a few days. He paid for his drink and walked up the Cannebière. He saw no smiling faces. The shadow of war already overspread the joyous town. A battalion of infantry passed by, and people stood still involuntarily and watched the soldiers with looks curiously stern. And Martin stood also, and remained standing long after the clanging tram-cars temporarily held up had blocked them from his sight. And he knew that he could not go to America.

In a little spot in the heart of France lived all the friends he had in the world; all the brave souls he had learned to love. Brantôme appeared before him as in a revelation, and a consciousness of ingratitude smote him so that he drew a gasping breath. Not that he had forgotten them. He had kept up a fitful correspondence with Bigourdin who had never hinted a reproach. But until an hour or two ago he had been prepared to wipe Brantôme out of his life, to pass through France without giving it an hour of greeting —even an *ave atque vale*.

In the past seven months of mad folly and studied poverty, where had he met characters so strong, ideals so lofty, hearts so loyal? What had he learned among the careless superficial Anglo-American society in Egypt comparable with that which he had learned in this world-forgotten little bourgeoisie in France? Which of them had touched his nature below the layer of his vanity? What ideals had he met with in the East? Could he so term the complacent and pessimistic opportunism of the Tudsleys; the querulous grumbling of officials; the honest dulness of sea-captains and sea-men? He judged superficially, it is true; for one has

to strike deep before one can get at the shy soul of a
Briton. But a man is but the creature of his impressions. From his own particular journeyings of seven
months he had returned almost bewilderingly alone.
East of Marseilles there dwelt not a human being
whose call no matter how faint sounded in his ears.
England, in so far as intimate personal England was
concerned, had no call for him either. Nor had
America, unknown, remote, unfriendly as Greenland.

Jostled, he walked along the busy thoroughfare, a
man far away, treading the paths of the spirit. In
this mighty convulsion that threatened the earth, there
was one spot which summoned him, with a call clear
and insistent. His place was there, in Périgord, to
share in its hopes and its fears, its mourning and its
joy.

He returned to the hotel for his bag and took the
first train in the direction of Brantôme. What he
would do when arrived, he had no definite notion. It
was something beyond reason that drove him thither.
Something irresistible; more irresistible than the force
which had impelled him to Egypt. Then he had hesitated, weighed things for and against. Now, one moment had decided him. It never occurred to him to
question. Through the burning south of France he
sped. As yet only the shadow of war hung over the
land; the awful Word had not yet gone forth. Swarthy
men and women worked in the baking vineyards and
gathered in the yellow harvest. But here and there on
flashing glimpses of white road troops marched dustily
and military waggons lumbered along. And in the
narrow, wooden-seated third-class carriage on the slow
and ever stopping train, the talk even of the humblest
was of war. At every station some of the passengers
left, some entered. There seemed to be a sudden con-
centration homewards. At every station were soldiers
recalled from leave to their garrisons. These, during

the journey, were questioned as authoritative functionaries. Yes, for sure, there would be war. Why they did not know, except that the *sales bêtes* of Germans were, at last, going to invade France.

Said one, "I saw an officer yesterday in our village —the son of Monsieur le Comte de Boirelles who has the big *château là-bas*—we have known each other from childhood—and he said, *'Hein, mon brave, ca y est!'* And I said: 'What, *mon lieutenant?'* And he said, *'V'là le son, le son du canon.'* Fight like a good son of Boirelles, or I'll cut off your ears.' And I replied, *quasiment comme ça:* 'You will not have the opportunity, *mon lieutenant,* you being in the artillery and I in the infantry.' And he laughed with good heart. 'Anyhow,' said he, 'if you return to the village, when the war is over, without the military medal, and I am alive, I'll make my mother do it, in the courtyard of the château, with her own scissors.' I tell you this to prove to you that I know there is going to be war."

And the women, holding their blue bundles on their knees in the crowded compartment—for in democratic France demos is not allowed the luxury of luggage-racks—looked at the future with anxious eyes. What would become of them? The government would take their men. Their men would be killed or maimed. Even if the men returned safe and sound, in the meantime, how would they live? *Ah, mon Dieu! Cette rosse de guerre!* They cursed the war as though it were a foul and conscious entity.

The interminable journey, by day, by night, with tedious waits at great ghostly junctions, at last was over. Martin emerged from the station of Brantôme and immediately before him stood the familiar ramshackle omnibus of the Hôtel des Grottes. Old Grégoire, the driver, on beholding him staggered back and almost fell over the step of the vehicle.

*"Monsieur Martin! C'est vous?"*

Recovering, he advanced with great, sun-glazed hand.

"Yes. It is indeed I," laughed Martin.

"It is everybody that will be content," cried Grégoire. "How one has talked of you, and wished you were back. And now, that this *sacrée guerre* is coming——"

"That's why I've come," said Martin. "How are monsieur and mademoiselle?"

Both were well. It was they who would be glad to see Monsieur Martin. The old fellow, red-faced, white-haired, clean shaven, with a comfortable gash of a mouth, clapped him on the shoulder.

*"Mais v'là un solide gaillard?"*

*"Tu trouves?"*

Why, of course Grégoire found him transformed into a stout fellow. When he had arrived a year ago he was like a bit of wet string. What a thing it was to travel. And yet he had been in China where people ate rats and dogs, which could not be nourishing food. In a fortnight, on the good meat and *foie gras* of Périgord, he would develop into a veritable giant. If Monsieur Martin would enter. . . . He held the door open. No one else had arrived by the train.

The omnibus jolted and swayed along the familiar road, through the familiar cobble-paved streets, along the familiar quays, past many a familiar face. They all seemed to chant the welcome of which the old driver had struck the key. Martin felt strangely happy and the tears were very near his eyes. Monsieur Richard, the butcher, catching sight of him, darted a pace or two down the pavement so as to make sure, and threw up both hands in greeting. And as they turned the corner of the hill surmounted by the dear grey tower of the old Abbey, Monsieur le Curé saw him and smiled and swept a salute with his old dusty hat, which Martin acknowledged through the end window of the omnibus.

They drew up before the familiar door of the old white inn. Baptiste was there, elderly, battered, in his green baize apron.

"*Mais, mon Dieu, c'est vous?—mais——*" He wrung Martin's hand. And, as once before, on the return of Félise, not being able to cope with his emotions, he shouted on the threshold of the vestibule: "*Monsieur, monsieur, c'est Monsieur Martin qui arrive!*"

"*Qu'est-ce que tu dis là?*" cried a familiar voice from the bureau.

"*C'est Monsieur Martin.*"

Martin entered, and in the vestibule encountered Bigourdin.

"*Mais mon vieux,*" cried the vast man. "*C'est toi? C'est vraiment toi, enfin?*"

It was the instinctive, surprised and joyous greeting of the two servants. Martin stood unstrung. What had he done to deserve it? Before he could utter a word, he felt two colossal arms swung round him and a kiss implanted on each cheek. Then Bigourdin held him out and looked at him, and, like Grégoire, told him how solid he looked.

"*Enfin!* You've come back. Tell me how and when and why. Tell me all."

Martin's eyes were moist. "My God!" said he, with a catch in his voice, "you are a good fellow."

"Not a bit, *mon cher*. We are friends, and in friendship there is something just a little bit sacred. But tell me, *nom d'une pipe!* all about yourself."     . . . . . .

"I was on my way," said Martin, with his conscientious honesty, "from Penang to New York. At Marseilles I heard for the first time of the war in which France will be involved and of which we have so often talked. And something, I don't know what, called me here—*et me voici!*"

"*C'est beau. C'est bien beau de ta part,*" said Bigourdin seriously. "Let us go and find Félise."

Now, when a Frenchman characterises a deed as *beau,* it is in his opinion very fine indeed.

But before they could move, Euphémie rushed from her kitchen and all but embraced the wanderer and Joseph, late *plongeur* at the Café de l'Univers and now waiter at the hôtel, came shyly from the *salle-à-manger,* and the brightness of his eyes was only equalled by the lustre of the habiliments that formerly had belonged to Martin. Bigourdin despatched him in quest of Félise. Soon she came, from the *fabrique,* looking rather white. Joseph had shot his news at her. But she came up looking Martin straight in the eyes, her hand extended.

"*Bonjour,* Martin. I am glad to see you again."

"So am I," said he. "More than glad. It's like coming back to one's own people."

She drew up her little head and asked with a certain bravura: "How is Lucilla?"

He winced; but he did not show it. He smiled. "I don't know. I haven't heard of her since March."

"Neither have I," she said. "Not since January. She seems to be a bird of passage through other people's lives."

Bigourdin laughed, shaking a great forefinger. "I bet that is not original. I bet you are quoting your old philosopher of a father!"

She coloured and said defiantly: "Yes. I confess it. It is none the less true."

"And how is the good Fortinbras?" asked Martin, to turn a distressful conversation.

"*A merveille!* We are expecting him by any train. It is I who am making him come. To-morrow I may be called out. France will want more than the Troupes

Metropolitaines and the Réserves to fight the Germans. They will want the Territorials, *et c'est moi, l'armée territoriale.*" He thumped his chest. "It was written that I should strike a blow for France like my fathers. But while I am striking the blow who is to look after my little Félise and the Hôtel des Grottes? It is well to be prepared. When the mobilisation is ordered, there will be no more trains for civilians."

"And what do you feel about the war, Félise?" asked Martin.

She clenched her hands: "I would give my immortal soul to be a man!" she cried.

Bigourdin hugged her. "That is a daughter of France! I am proud of our little girl. *On dirait une Jeanne d'Arc.* But where is the Frenchwoman now who is not animated by the spirit of La Pucelle d'Orléans?"

"In the meanwhile, *mon oncle,*" said Félise, disengaging herself demurely from his embrace, "Martin looks exceedingly dusty and hungry, and no one has even suggested that he should wash or eat or have his bag carried up to his room."

Bigourdin regarded her with admiration. "She is wonderful. She thinks of everything. Baptiste. Take up Monsieur Martin's things to the *chambre d'honneur.*"

"But, my dear fellow," Martin protested, "I only want my old room in which I have slept so soundly."

But Bigourdin would have none of it. He was the Prodigal Son. *"Et justement!"* he cried, slapping his thigh, "we have a good calf's head for *déjeuner.* Yes, it's true," he laughed delightedly. "The fatted calf. It was fatted by our neighbour Richard. *C'est extraordinaire!"*

So Martin shaved and washed in the famous bath room, and changed, and descended to the *salle-à-manger.* The only guests were a few anxious-faced com-

mercial travellers at the centre table. All but one were
old acquaintances. He went the round, shaking hands,
amid cordial greetings. It was the last time, they said.
To-morrow they would be mobilised. The day after
they would exchange the sample box for the pack of
the soldier; in a week they would have the skin torn
off the soles of their feet; and in a month they would
be blown to bits by shells. They proclaimed a lack of
the warrior spirit. They had a horror of blood, even
a cat's. It stirred up one's stomach. *Mais enfin* one
did not think of such unimportant things when France
was in peril. If your house was in danger of being
swept away by flood, there was no sense in being afraid
to catch cold through having your feet wet. Each
in his way expressed the same calm fatalistic patriotism. They had no yearning to be killed. But if they
were killed—they shrugged their shoulders. They
were France and France was they. No force could
dismember them from France without France or themselves bleeding to death. It was very simple.

Martin left them and sat down with Bigourdin and
Félise, at their table in the corner by the door. It was
the first time he had ever done so. Félise ate little
and spoke less. Now and again, as he told of his mild
adventures in the Far East, he caught her great dark
eyes fixed on him, and he smiled, unaccountably glad.
But always she shifted her glance and made a pretence
of eating or drinking. Once, when Bigourdin, called
by innkeeper's business to one of the commercial travellers, had left the table, she said:

"You have changed. One would say it was not the
same man."

"What makes you think so?" he laughed.

"You talk differently. There is a different expression on your face."

"I'm sorry," said he.

"I don't see why you should be sorry," said Félise.

"If you no longer recognise me," said he—they talked in French—"I must come to you as a stranger."

She bit her lip and flushed. "I did not know what I was saying. Perhaps it was impertinent."

"How could it be, Félise?" he asked, bending across the table. "But if I have changed, is it for the better or the worse?"

"Would you be a waiter here again?"

Martin looked for a second into his soul.

"No," said he.

"*Voilà!*" said Félise.

"But I couldn't tell you why."

"It's not necessary," said Félise.

Bigourdin joined them. The meal ended. Félise went off to her duties. Bigourdin said:

"Let us go and drink our coffee at the Café de l'Univers. Everybody is there, at this hour, the last day or two. We may learn some news."

They descended the hill and walked along the blazing quays. Martin knew every house, every stone, every old woman who pausing from beating her linen on the side of the Dronne waved him a welcome. And men stopped him and slapped his shoulder and shook him by the hand.

"You recognise the good heart of Périgord," said Bigourdin.

Martin replied, with excusable Gallic hyperbole: "*C'est mon pays.* I find it again, after having wandered over the earth."

They turned into the narrow, cool Rue de Périgueux. On the opposite side of the street, they saw Monsieur Foure, *adjoint du maire,* walking furiously, mopping a red forehead, soft straw hat in hand. He sped across to them, too excited to realise that Martin had gone and returned.

"Have you heard the news? The Mayor has re-

ceived a telegram from Paris.  The order of mobilisation goes out to-day."

"*Bon,*" said Bigourdin.

The terrace of the Café de l'Univers was crowded
with the notables of the town, who, in their sober
way, only frequented the café after dinner.  The special côterie had their section apart, as at night.  They
were all assembled—Fénille of the Compagnie du Gaz;
Beuzot, Professor of the Ecole Normale; the Viriots,
father and son; Thiébauld, managing director of the
quarries; Bénoît of the railway; Rutillard, the great
chandler of corn and hay; and they did not need the
*adjoint du Maire* to tell them the news.  The fresh
arrivals, provided speedily with chairs by the waiters,
were swallowed up in the group.  And Martin was
assailed.

"*Et maintenant, l'Angleterre.   Qu'est-ce qu'elle va
faire?*"

It was the question on all French lips that day until
England declared war.

And Martin proclaimed, as though inspired from
Whitehall, that England would fight.  For the moment
his declaration satisfied them.  The talk swayed from
him excitedly.  France at war, at last, after forty
years, held their souls.  They talked in the air, as men
will, of numbers, of preparations, of chances, of the
solidarity of the nation.  When there was a little pause,
the square-headed, white-haired Monsieur Viriot rose
and with a gesture, imposed silence.

"This is a moment," said he, " for every misunder-
standing between loyal French hearts to be cleared up.
We are now brothers in the defence of our beloved
country. *Mon brave ami Bigourdin, donne-moi ta
main.*"

Bigourdin sprang up,—in the public street—but
what did that matter?—and cried: "*Mon vieux Viriot,*"
and the two men embraced and kissed each other, and

every one, much affected, cried "Bravo! Bravo!" And
then Bigourdin, reaching over the marble tables, took
young Lucien Viriot's hands and embraced him and
shook him by the shoulders, and cried: "Here is a
cuirassier who is going to cut through the Germans
like bladders of lard!"

It was a memorable reconciliation.

Fortinbras arrived late at night, probably by the
last regular train-services; for on the next day and
for many days afterwards there were wild hurry and
crowds and confusion on roads and railways all
through France.

Into the town poured all the men of the surround-
ing villages, and the streets were filled with them and
their wives and mothers and children, and strange officers in motor-cars whirled through the Rue de Périgueux.   Bands of young men falling into the well-
remembered step marched along the quays to the station singing the Marseillaise, and women stood at their
doorsteps blowing them kisses as they passed.   And
at the station the great military trains adorned with
branches of trees and flowers, steamed away, a massed
line of white faces and waving arms; and old men
and women young and old waved handkerchiefs until
the train disappeared, and then turned away weeping
bitterly.   Martin, Fortinbras and Bigourdin went to
many a train to see off the flower of the youth of the
little town.   Lucien Viriot went gallantly.   "A good
war horse suits me better than an office-stool," he
laughed.   And Joseph, sloughing for ever Martin's
shiny black raiment, went off too; and the younger
waiters of the Café de l'Univers, and Beuzot, the
young professor at the Ecole Normale, and the son of
the *adjoint,* and *le petit Maurin,* who helped his
mother at her *Débit de Tabac.*   Many a familiar face
was carried away from Brantôme towards some unknown battle-line and the thunder and the slaughter—

a familiar face which Brantôme was never to see again. And after a day or two the town seemed futile, like a ball room from which the last dancers had gone.

Grave was the evening côterie at the Café de l'Univers. The rumour had gone through France that England more than hesitated. Fortinbras magnificently defended England's honour. He had been very quiet at home, tenderly shy and wistful with Félise, unsuggestive of paths to happiness with Martin; his attitude towards intimate life one of gentle melancholy. He had told Martin that he had retired from business as *Marchand de Bonheur*. He had lost the trick of it. At Bigourdin's urgency he had purchased an annuity which sufficed his modest and philosophic needs. No longer having the fierce incentive to gain the hard-earned five-franc piece, no longer involved in a scheme of things harmonious with an irregular profession, he was like the singer deprived of the gift of song, the telepathist stricken with inhibitory impotence. For all his odd learning, for all his garnered knowledge of the human heart, and for all his queer heroic struggle, he stood before his own soul an irremediable failure. So an older and almost a broken Fortinbras had taken up his quarters at the Hôtel des Grottes. But stimulated by the talk of war, he became once more the orator and the seer. He held a brief for England and his passionate sincerity imposed itself on his hearers.

"Thank God!" said he afterwards, "I was right."

But in the meanwhile, Martin, strung in every fibre to high pitch by what he had heard, by what he had seen and by what he had felt, knew that just as it was ordained that he should come to Brantôme, so it was ordained that he should not stay.

"You talk eloquently and with conviction, Monsieur," said the Mayor to Fortinbras—there were a dozen in the familiar café corner, tense and eager-eyed, and Monsieur Cazensac, the Gascon proprietor, stood by—"but what proofs have you given us of England's co-operation?"

Martin, with a thrill through his body, said in a loud voice:

"Monsieur le Maire, there is not a living English-man with red blood in his veins who has any doubt. I the most obscure of Englishmen, speak for my coun-try. Get me accepted as a volunteer, the humblest foot-soldier, and I will fight for France. Take up my pledge, Monsieur le Maire. It is the pledge of the only Englishman in Brantôme on behalf of the British Empire. There are millions better than I from all ends of the earth who will be inspired by the same sentiments of loyalty. Get me accepted!"

In English Martin could never have said it. Words would have come shyly. But he was among French-men, attuned to French modes of expression. A mur-mur of approbation arose.

"Yes," cried Martin. "I offer France my life as a pledge for my country. Get me accepted, Monsieur le Maire."

The Mayor, a lean, grey-eyed, bald-headed man, with a straggly, iron-grey beard, looked at him in-tently for a few moments.

"*C'est bien,*" said he. "I take up your pledge. I have to go to-morrow to Périgueux to see *Monsieur le Préfet,* who has a certain friendliness for me. He has influence with the *Ministère de la Guerre.* Accom-pany me to Périgueux. I undertake to see that it is arranged."

"I thank you, Monsieur le Maire," said Martin.

Then everybody talked at once, and lifted their glasses to Martin, and Monsieur Viriot despatched Cazensac for the sweet champagne in which nearly a year ago they had drunk Lucien's health; and Bigour-din embraced him; and when the wine was poured out, there were cries of *"Vive l'Angleterre!"* *"Vive la*

*France!" "Vive Martin!"* And the square-headed old Monsieur Viriot set the climax of this ovation by lifting his glass at arm's length and proclaiming *"Vive notre bon Périgordin!"*

Said Fortinbras, who sat next to him, "I would give the rest of my life to be as young as you, just for the next few months. My God, you must feel proud!"

Martin's steady English blood asserted itself: "I don't," said he, "I feel a damned premature hero."

It is only in the Légion Etrangère, that fantastic, romantic regiment of dare-devil desperadoes capable of all iniquities and of all heroisms, that a foreigner can enlist straight away, no questions asked. To be incorporated in the regular army of France is another matter. Wires have to be pulled. They were pulled in Martin's case. It was to his credit that he had served two years—gaining the stripes of a corporal—in the Rifle Corps of the University of Cambridge. At the psychological moment of pulling, England declared war on Germany. The resources of the British Empire, men and money and ships and blood were on the side of France. England and France were one. A second's consideration of the request of the Préfet de la Dordogne and a hurriedly scrawled signature constituted Martin a potential member of the French Army.

It happened that, when the notice of authorisation came, the first person he ran across was Félise, by the door of the *fabrique*. He waved the paper.

"I am accepted."

She turned pale and put her hand to her heart, but she met his eyes bravely.

"When do you go?"

"At once—straight to Périgueux to enlist."

"And when will you come back?"

"God knows," said he.

Then he became aware of her standing scared, with parted lips and heaving bosom.

"Of course I hope to come back; some time or other, when the War's over. Naturally—but——"

She said quaveringly—"You may be killed."

"So may millions. I take my chance."

She turned aside, clapped both hands to her face and broke into a passion of weeping. Instinctively he put an arm around her. She sobbed on his shoulder. He whispered:

"Do you care so much about what happens to me?"

She tore herself away and faced him with eyes flashing through her tears.

"Do you think I'm a stick or a stone? I am half English, half French. You are going to fight for England and France. Don't you think women feel these things? You are a part of the Englishwoman and the Frenchwoman that is going out to fight, and I would hate you if you didn't fight, but I don't want you to be killed."

She fled. And not till he left the Hôtel des Grottes did he see her again alone. When with Bigourdin and Fortinbras he was about to enter the old omnibus to take him to the station, she pinned a tricolour ribbon on his coat, and then saying "Good-bye and God bless you," looked him squarely in the eyes. It was in his heart to say, "You're worth all the Lucillas in the universe." But there were Bigourdin and Fortinbras and Euphémie and Baptiste and Grégoire and the chambermaid and a few straggling girls from the *fabrique* all standing by. He said:

"God bless you, Félise. I shall never part with your ribbon as long as I live."

Grégoire climbed to his seat. Bigourdin closed the door. The omnibus jolted and swayed down the road. The elfin figure of Félise was suddenly cut off at the turn.  And that was the last of the Hôtel des Grottes.

A week or so later, Martin drilling in the hot bar-
rack square realised that just a year had passed since
he first set eyes on Brantôme.  A year ago he had been
a spineless, aimless drudge at Margett's Universal
College.  Now, wearing a French uniform, he was
about to fight for France and England in the greatest
of all wars that the world had seen.  And during
those twelve months through what soul-shaking experiences had he not passed!  Truly a wonderful year.

*"Mais vous, num'ro sept!  Sacré nom de Dieu!
Qu'est-ce que vous faites-là!"* screamed the drill sergeant.

Whereupon Martin abruptly realised the intense
importance of the present moment.

# CHAPTER XXIII

THE weary weeks passed by with their alternations of hopes and fears. Martin, insignificant speck of blue and red, was in the Argonne. Sergeant Bigourdin of the *Armée Territoriale* was up in the north. The history of their days is the history of the war which has yet to be written; the story of their personal lives is identical with that of the personal lives of the millions of men who have looked and are looking Death always in the face, cut off as it were from their own souls by the curtain of war.

Things went drearily at the Hôtel des Grottes. But little manhood remained at Brantôme. Women worked in the fields and drove the carts and kept the shops where so few things were sold. Félise busied herself in the *fabrique,* her staff entirely composed of women. Fortinbras made a pretence of managing the hotel to which for days together no travellers came. No cars of pleasant motorists were unloaded at its door. Now and then an elderly bagman in vain quest of orders sat in the solitary *salle-à-manger,* and Fortinbras waited on him with urbane melancholy. Thrown intimately together father and daughter grew nearer to each other. They became companions, walking together on idle afternoons and sitting on mild nights on the terrace, with the town twinkling peacefully below them. They talked of many things. Fortinbras drew from the rich store of his wisdom, Félise from her fund of practical knowledge. There were times when she forgot the harrowing mystery of her mother, and, only conscious of a great and yearning sympathy, unlocked her heart and cried a little in

close and comforting propinquity. Together they read
the letters from the trenches, all too short, all too elusive in their brave cheeriness. The epistles of Martin and Bigourdin were singularly alike. Each said
much the same. They had not the comforts of the
Hôtel des Grottes. But what would you have? War
was war. They were in splendid health. They had
enough to eat. They had had a sharp tussle with the
*Boches* and many of their men were killed. But vic-
tory in the end was certain. In the meanwhile they
needed some warm underclothes as the nights were
growing cold; and would Félise enclose some choco-
late and packets of Bastos. Love to everybody and
*Vive la France!*

These letters Fortinbras would take to the Café de
l'Univers and read to the grey-headed remnant of the
coterie, each of whom had a precisely similar letter to
read. The *Adjoint du Maire* was the first to come
without a letter. He produced a telegram which was
passed from hand to hand in silence. He had come
dry-eyed and brave, but when the telegram reached
him, after completing its round, he broke down.

"*C'est stupide!* Forgive me, my friends. I am
proud to have given my son to my country. *Mais
enfin*, he was my son—my only son. For the first
time I am glad that his mother is no longer living."
Then he raised his head valiantly. "*Et toi*, Viriot—
Lucien, how is he doing?"

Then some one heard of the death of Beuzot, the
young professor at the Ecole Normale.

At last, after a long interval of silence came disastrous news of Bigourdin, lying seriously, perhaps
mortally wounded in a hospital in a little northern
town. There followed days of anguish. Telegrams
elicited the information that he had been shot through
the lung. Félise went about her work with a pinched
face.

In course of time a letter came from Madame Clothilde Robineau at Chartres:

MY DEAR NIECE:
Although your conduct towards me was ungrateful, I am actuated by the teachings of Christianity in extending to you my forgiveness, now that you are alone and unprotected. I hear from a friend of the Abbé Duloup, a venerable priest who is administering to the wounded the consolations of religion, that your Uncle Gaspard is condemned to death. Christian duty and family sentiment therefore make it essential that I should offer you a home beneath my roof. You left it in a fit of anger because I spoke of your father in terms of reprobation. But if you had watched by the death-bed of your mother, my poor sister, as I did, in the terrible garret in the Rue Maugrabine, you would not judge me so harshly. Believe me, dear child, I have at heart your welfare both material and spiritual. If you desire guidance as to the conduct of the hotel I shall be pleased to aid you with my experience.
Your affectionate Aunt,<br>CLOTHILDE ROBINEAU.

The frigid offer well meant according to the woman's pale lights, Félise scarcely heeded. Father or no father, uncle or no uncle, protector or no protector, she was capable of conducting a score of hotels. The last thing in the world she needed was the guidance of her Aunt Clothilde. Save for one phrase in the letter she would have written an immediate though respectful refusal and thought nothing further of the matter. But that one phrase flashed through her brain. Her mother had died in the Rue Maugrabine. They had told her she had died in hospital. Things hitherto bafflingly dark to her became clear—on one awful, tragic hypothesis. She shook with the terror of it.

It was the only communication the postman had brought that late afternoon. She stood in the vestibule to read it. Fortinbras engaged in the bureau over some simple accounts looked up by chance and saw her staring at the letter with great open eyes, her lips apart, her bosom heaving. He rose swiftly, and hurrying through the side door came to her side.

"My God! Not bad news?"

She handed him the letter. He read, his mind not grasping at once that which to her was essential.

"The priests are exaggerating. And as for the proposal——"

"The Rue Maugrabine," said Félise.

He drew the quick breath of sudden realisation, and for a long time they stood silent, looking into each other's eyes. At last she spoke, deadly white:

"That woman I saw—who opened the door for me —was my mother."

She had pierced to the truth. No subterfuge he could invent had power to veil it. He made a sad gesture of admission.

"Why did you hide it from me?" she asked.

"You had a beautiful ideal, my child, and it would have been a crime to tear it away."

She held herself very erect—there was steel in the small body—and advanced a step or so towards him, her dark eyes fearless.

"You know what you gave me to understand when I saw her?"

"Yes, my child," said Fortinbras.

"You also were an ideal."

He smiled. "You loved me tenderly, but I was not in your calendar of saints, my dear."

She mastered herself, swallowing a sob, but the tears rolled down her cheeks.

"You are now," she said.

He laughed uncertainly. "A poor old sinner of a saint," he said, and gathered her to him.

And later, in the salon, before the fire, for the autumn was damp and cold, he told her the cheerless story of his life, concealing nothing, putting the facts before her so that she could judge. She sat on the rug, her arm about his knee. She felt very tired, as though some part of her had bled to death. But a new wonder filled her heart. In a way she had been prepared for the discovery. In her talks with her uncle and with Martin she had been keen to mark a strange disingenuousness. She had accused them of conspiracy. They were concealing something; what, she knew not; but a cloud had rested on her mother's memory. If, on that disastrous evening, the frowsy woman of the Rue Maugrabine had revealed herself as her mother, her soul would have received a shock from which recovery might have been difficult. Now the shock had not only been mitigated by months of torturing doubt, but was compensated by the thrill of her father's sacrifice.

When he had ended, she turned and wept and knelt before him, crying for forgiveness, calling him all manner of foolish names.

He said, stroking her dark hair: "I am only a poor old bankrupt *Marchand de Bonheur!*"

"You will be *Marchand de Bonheur* to the end," she said, and with total want of logical relevance she added: "See what happiness you have brought me to-night."

"At any rate, my dear," said he, "we have found each other at last."

She went to bed and lay awake till dawn looking at a new world of wrong doing, suffering and heroism. Who was she, humble little girl, living her sequestered life, to judge men by the superficialities of their known

actions? She had judged her father almost to the
catastrophe of love. She had judged Martin bitterly.
What did she know of the riot in his soul? Now he
was offering his life for a splendid ideal. She felt
humble beside her conception of him. And her Uncle
Gaspard, great, tender, adored, was lying far, far
away in the north, with a bullet through his body.
She prayed her valiant little soul out for the two of
them. And the next morning she arose and went to
her work brave and clear-eyed, with a new hope in
God based upon a new faith in man.

A day or two later she received a wild letter from
Corinna Hastings. Corinna's letters were as frequent
as blackberries in March. Félise knitted her brows
over it for a long time. Then she took it to her father.

"The sense," she said, "must lie in the scrabble I
can't make out."

Fortinbras put on his spectacles and when, not
without difficulty, he had deciphered it, he took off the
spectacles and smiled the benevolent smile of the
*Marchand de Bonheur*.

"Leave it to me, my dear," said he. "I will answer
Corinna."

In the tiny town of Wendlebury, in the noisy bosom
of her family, Corinna was eating her heart out. During the latter days of June she had returned to the
fold, an impecunious failure. As a matter of theory
she had upheld the principles of woman suffrage. As
a matter of practice, in the effort to obtain it, she
loathed it with bitter hatred. She lacked the inspiration of its overwhelming importance in sublunary affairs. She was willing enough to do ordinary work
in its interests, at a living wage, even to the odious
extent of wearing an anæmic tricolor and selling newspapers in the streets. But when her duties involved in-
cendiarism, imprisonment and hunger, striking, Co-

rinna revolted. She had neither the conviction nor the courage. Miss Banditch reviled her for a recreant, a snake in the grass and a spineless doll and left the flat, forswearing her acquaintance for ever. Headquarters signified disapproval of her pusillanimity. Driven to desperation she signified her disapproval of Headquarters in unmeasured terms. The end came and prospective starvation drove her home to Wendlebury. When the war broke out, in common with the rest of the young maidenhood of the town, she yearned to do something to help the British Empire. Her sister Clara, to satisfy this laudable craving, promptly married a subaltern, and, when he was ordered to the front, went to live with his people. The next youngest sister, Evelyn, anxious for Red Cross work, found herself subsidised by an aunt notoriously inimical to Corinna. Corinna therefore had to throw in her lot with Margaret and Winnie, chits of fifteen and thirteen—the intervening boys having flown from the nest. What was a penniless and, in practical matters, a feckless young woman to do? She knitted socks and mufflers and went round the town collecting money for Belgian refugees. So did a score of tabbies, objects of Corinna's scornful raillery who district-visited the poor to exasperation. She demanded work more glorious, more heroic; but lack of funds tied her to detested knitting-needles. As the Vicar's daughter she was compelled to go to church and listen to her father's sermons on the war; compared with which infliction, she tartly informed her mother, forcible feeding was a gay amusement.

Once or twice she had a postcard from Martin in the Argonne. She cursed herself, her destiny and her sex. If only she was a man she would at least have gone forth with a gun on her shoulder. But she was a woman; the most helpless thing in women God ever made. Even her mother, whom she had rated low on account of intellectual short-comings, she began to envy. At any rate she had generously performed her woman's duty. She had brought forth ten children, five men children, two of whom had rushed to take up arms in defence of their country. Martin's last postcard had told Corinna of Bigourdin being called away to fight. In her enforced isolation from the great events of the great world she became acutely conscious that in all the great world only one individual had ever found a use for her. A flash of such knowledge either scorches or illuminates the soul.

Then early in November she received a misspelt letter laboriously written in hard pencil on thin, glazed paper. It was addressed from a hospital in the North of France.

MADEMOISELLE CORINNA:

I have done my best to strike a blow for my beloved country. It was written that I should do so, and it was written perhaps that I should give my life for her. I am dictating these words to my bedside neighbour who is wounded in the knee. For my part, a German bullet has penetrated my lung, and the doctors say I may not live. But while I still can speak, I am anxious to tell you that on the battlefield your image has always been before my eyes and that I always have in my heart a love for you tender and devoted. Should I live, Mademoiselle, I pray you to forget this letter, as I do not wish to cause you pain. But should I die, let me now have the consolation of believing that I shall have a place in your thoughts as one who has died, not unworthily or unwillingly, in a noble cause.

GASPARD-MARIE BIGOURDIN.

Corinna sat for a long time, frozen to her soul, looking out of her bedroom window at the hopeless autumn drizzle, and the sodden leaves on the paths of the vicarage garden. Then, with quivering lips, she sat down at the rickety little desk that had been hers since childhood and wrote to Bigourdin. She sealed it and went out in the rain and dropped it in the nearest pillar box. When she reached her room again, the realisation of the inadequacy of her words smote her. She threw herself on her bed and sobbed. After which she wrote her wild letter to Félise.

For the next few days a chastened Corinna went about the Vicarage. An unusual gentleness manifested itself in her demeanour, and at last emboldened Mrs. Hastings, good, kind soul, to take the unprecedented step of enquiring into her wayward and sharp-tongued daughter's private affairs.

"I'm afraid, dearie, that letter you had from France contained bad news."

"Yes, mother," said Corinna, with a sigh.

They were alone in the drawing room. Mrs. Hastings laid aside her knitting, rose slowly—she was a portly woman—and went across to Corinna and put her arm about her shoulders.

"Can't you tell me what it was, dearie?" she whispered.

Corinna melted to the voice. It awakened memories of unutterable comfort of childish years. She surrendered to the embrace.

"Yes, mother. The truest man I have ever known —a Frenchman—is dying over there. He asked me to marry him a year ago. And I was a fool, mother. Oh! an awful fool!"

And half an hour later, she said tearfully: "I've been a fool in so many ways. I've misjudged you so, mother. It never occurred to me that you would understand."

"My dear," said Mrs. Hastings, stroking her hair, "to bring ten children into the world and keep them going on small means, to say nothing of looking after a husband, isn't a bad education."

The next day came a telegram.

"Re letter Félise. If you want to find yourself at last go straight to Bigourdin. Fortinbras."

The message was a lash. She had not contemplated the possibility of going to France. In the sleepless nights she had ached to be with him. But how? In Tierra del Fuego he would be equally inaccessible.

"Go straight to him." The words were very simple. Of course she would go. Why had she waited for Fortinbras to point out her duty?

Then came the humiliating knowledge of impotence. She looked in her purse and counted out her fortune of thirteen shillings and sevenpence halfpenny. A very humble Corinna showed letter and telegram to her mother.

"The war seems to have turned everything upside down," said the latter. "You ought to go, dear. It's a sacred duty."

"But how can I? I have no money. I can't ask father."

"Come upstairs," said Mrs. Hastings.

She led the way to her bedroom and from a locked drawer took an old-fashioned japanned despatch-box, which she opened.

"All my married life," she said, "I have managed to keep something against a rainy day. Take what you want, dear."

Thus came the overthrowal of all Corinna's scheme of values. She went to France, a woman with a warm and throbbing heart.

# CHAPTER XXIV

IT was with difficulty that she reached the little French town, and it was with infinitely more difficulty that she overcame military obstacles and penetrated into the poor little whitewashed school that did duty as a hospital. It was a great bare room with a double row of iron bedsteads, a gangway between them. Here and there an ominous screen shut off a bed. A few bandaged men half dressed were sitting up smoking and playing cards. An odour of disinfectant caught her by the throat. A human form lying by the door with but little face visible, was moaning piteously. She shrank on the threshold, aghast at this abode of mangled men. The young *aide-major* escorting her, pointed up the ward.

"You will find him there, Mademoiselle, Number Seventeen."

"How is he?" she asked.

"The day before yesterday he nearly went," he snapped his finger and thumb. "A hemorrhage which we stopped. But the old French stock is solid as oak, Mademoiselle. A hole or two doesn't matter. He is going along pretty well."

"Thank God!" said Corinna.

A nurse with red-cross badge met them. "Ah, it is the lady for Sergeant Bigourdin. He has been expecting you ever since your letter."

His eyes were all of him that she recognised at first. His great, hearty face had grown hollow and the lower part was concealed by a thick, black beard. She remembered having heard of *les poilus,* the hairy-ones, as the Territorial Troops were affectionately termed

353

in France. But his kind, dark eyes were full of gladness. The nurse set a stool for Corinna by the bedside. On her left lay another black-bearded man who looked at her wistfully. He had been Bigourdin's amanuensis.

"This angel of tyranny forbids me to move my arms," whispered Bigourdin apologetically. The little whimsical phrase struck the note of the man's unconquerable spirit. Corinna smiled through tears. The nurse said: "Talk to him and don't let him talk to you. You can only have ten minutes." She retired.

*"Cela vous fait beaucoup souffrir, mon pauvre ami?"* said Corinna.

He shook his head. "Not now that you are here. It is wonderful of you to come. You have a heart of gold. And it is that little talisman, *ce petit cœur d'or,* that is going to make me well. You cannot imagine— it is like a fairy tale to see you here."

Instinctively Corinna put out her hand and touched his lips. She had never done so feminine and tender a thing to a man. She let her fingers remain, while he kissed them. She flushed and smiled.

"You mustn't talk. It is for me who have sound lungs. I have come because I have been a little imbecile, and only at the eleventh hour I have repented of my folly. If I had been sensible a year ago, this would not have happened."

He turned happy eyes on her; but he said with his Frenchman's clear logic:

"All my love and all the happiness that might have been would not have altered the destinies of Europe. I should have been brought here, all the same, with a ridiculous little hole through my great body."

Corinna admitted the truth of his statement. "But," said she, "I might have been of some comfort to you."

His eyebrows expressed the shrug of which his

maimed frame was incapable. "It is all for the best. If I had left you at Brantôme, my heart would have been torn in two. I might have been cautious to the detriment of France. As it was, I didn't care much what happened to me. And now they have awarded me the *médaille militaire;* and you are here, to make, as Baudelaire says, *'ma joie et ma santé.'* What more can a man desire?"

Now all this bravery was spoken in a voice so weak that the woman in Corinna was stirred to its depths. She bent over him and whispered—for she knew that the man with the wistful gaze in the next bed was listening:

*"C'est vrai que tu m'aimes toujours?"*

She saw her question answered by the quick illumination of his eyes, and she went on quickly: "And I, I love you too, and I will give you all my poor life for what it is worth. Oh!" she cried, "I can't imagine what you can see in me. Beside you I feel so small, of so little account. I can do nothing—nothing but love you."

"That's everything in the world," said Bigourdin.

They were silent for a moment. Then he said: "I should like to meet the *Boche* who fired that rifle."

"So should I," she cried fiercely. "I should like to tear him limb from limb."

"I shouldn't," said Bigourdin. "I should like to decorate him with a pair of wings and a little bow and arrow. . . ."

The nurse came up. "You must go now, mademoiselle. The patient is becoming too excited. It is not your fault. Nothing but a bolster across their mouths will prevent these Périgordins from talking."

A tiny bedroom in a house over a grocer's shop was all the accommodation that she had been able to secure, as the town was full of troops billeted on the inhabitants. As it was, that bedroom had been given up to her by a young officer who took pity on her distress. She felt her presence impertinent in this stern atmosphere of war. After seeing Bigourdin, she wandered for a while about the rainy streets and then retired to her chilly and comfortless room, where she ate her meal of sardines and sausage. The next day she presented herself at the hospital and saw the *aide-major*.

"Can you give me some work to do?" she asked. "I don't pretend to be able to nurse. But I could fetch and carry and do odd jobs."

But it was a French hospital, and the *reglement* made no provision for affording prepossessing young Englishwomen romantic employment.

Of course, said the *aide-major,* if Mademoiselle was bent upon it, she could write an application which would be forwarded to the proper quarter. But it would have to pass through the *bureaux*—and she, who knew France so well, was aware what the passing through the *bureaux* meant. Unless she had the ear of high personages, it would take weeks and perhaps months.

"And in the meantime," said Corinna, "my *grand ami,* Number 17 down there, will have got well and departed from the hospital."

"Mademoiselle," said he, "you have already saved the life of one gallant Frenchman. Don't you think that should give you a sentiment of duty accomplished?"

She blushed. He was kind. For he was young and she was pretty.

"I can let you see your *gros heureux* to-day," said he. "It is a favour. It is against the *règlement*. If the *major* hears of it, there will be trouble. By the grace of God he has a bilious attack which confines him to his quarters. But, *bien entendu,* it is for this time only."

She thanked him and again found herself by Bigourdin's bedside. The moment of her first sight of him was the happiest in her life. She had wrought a miracle. He was a different man inspired with the supreme will to live. The young doctor had spoken truly. A spasm of joy shook her. At last she had been of some use in the world. . . . She saw too the Bigourdin whom she had known. His great, black beard had vanished. One of the *camarades,* with two disposable arms, had hunted through the kits of the patients for a razor and had shaved him.

"They tell me I am getting on magnificently," said he. "This morning there is no longer any danger. In a few months I shall be as solid as ever I was. It is happiness that has cured me."

They talked. She told him of her conversation with the *aide-major.* He reflected for a moment. Then he said:

"Do you wish to please me?"

"What am I here for?" asked Corinna.

"You are here to spoil me. Anyhow—if you wish to please me, go to Brantôme, and await me. To know that you are there, *chez-moi,* will give me the courage of a thousand lions, and you will be able to console my poor Félise who every night is praying for Martin by the side of her little white bed."

And so it was arranged. After two days extraordinary travel, advancing from point to point by any train that happened to run, shunted on sidings for interminable periods, in order to allow the unimpeded progress of military trains, waiting weary hours at night in cold, desolate stations, hungry and broken, but her heart aglow with a new and wonderful happiness, she reached Brantôme.

She threw her arms round the neck of an astonished, but ever urbane elderly gentleman in the vestibule of the Hôtel des Grottes and kissed him.

"He's getting well," she cried a little hysterically. "He sent me here to wait for him. I'm so happy and I'm just about dead."

"But yet there's that spark of life in you, my dear Corinna," said Fortinbras, "which, according to the saying, distinctly justifies hope. Félise and I will see to it that you live."

It was winter before Bigourdin was well enough to return. By that time Corinna had settled down to her new life wherein she found the making of *foie gras* an enticing mystery. Also, in a town where every woman had her man—husband, brother, son or lover—either in hourly peril of death, or dead or wounded, there was infinite scope for help and consolation. And when a woman said: *"Hélas! Mon pauvre homme. Il est blessé là-bas,"* she could reply with a new, thrilling sympathy and a poignant throb of the heart: "And my man too." For like all the other women there, she had *"son homme."* Her man! Corinna tasted the fierce joy of being elemental.

There was much distress in the little town. The municipality did its best. In many cases the wives valiantly carried on the husband's business. But in the row of cave dwellings where the quarrymen lived no muscular arms hewed the week's wages from the rocks. Boucabeille, Martin's Bacchanalian friend, had purged all his offences in heroic battle, and was lying in an unknown grave. Corinna, learning how Martin had carried the child home on his shoulders, brought her to the hotel and cared for her, and obtained work for the mother in the *fabrique*.

Never before had Corinna had days so full; never before had she awakened in the morning with love in her heart. Félise, grown gentler and happier since the canonisation of her father, gave her unstinted affection.

And then Bigourdin arrived, nominally on sick-leave, but with private intimation that his active services would be required no longer. This gave a touch of sadness to his otherwise joyous home-coming.

"I have not killed half enough Boches," said he.

A few days after his return came a letter from Martin. And it was written from a hospital.

My Dearest Félise:

I am well and sound and in perfect health. But a bullet got me in the left arm while we were attacking a German trench, and a spent bit of shrapnel caught me on the head and stunned me. When I recovered I was midway between the trenches in the zone of fire and I had to lie still between the dead bodies of two of our brave soldiers. I thought much, my dear, while I was lying there expecting every minute a bullet to finish me. And some of what I thought I will tell you, when I see you, for I shall see you very soon. After some thirty-six hours I was collected and brought to the field hospital, where I was patched up, and in the course of a day or so sent on to the base. I lay on straw during the journey in a row of other wounded. France has the defects of her qualities. Her soil is so fertile that her stalks of straw are like young oak saplings. When I arrived I had such a temperature and was so silly with pain that I don't very well remember what happened. When I got sensible they told me that gangrene had set in and that they had chopped off my arm above the elbow. I always thought I was an incomplete human being, dear, but I have never been so idiotically incomplete as I am now. Although I am getting along splendidly I want to do all sorts of things with the fingers that aren't there. I turn to pick up something and there's nothing to pick it up with. A week before I was wounded, I had a finger nail torn off, and it still hurts me, somewhere in space, about a foot away from what is *me*. You would laugh if you knew what a nuisance it is. . . . I make no excuses for asking you to receive me at Brantôme; all that is dear to me in the world is there—and what other spot in the wide universe have I to fly to?

"But *sacré nom d'une pipe!*" cried Bigourdin—for Félise, after private and tearful perusal of the letter, was reading such parts of it aloud as were essential for family information—"What is the imbecile talking of? Where else, indeed, should he go?"

Félise continued. Martin as yet unaware of Bigourdin's return, sent him messages.

"When you write, will you tell him I have given to France as much of myself as I've been allowed to? Half an arm isn't much. *Mais c'est déjà quelque chose.*"

"*Quelque chose!*" cried Bigourdin. "But it is a sacred sacrifice. If I could get hold of that little bit of courageous arm I would give it to Monsieur le Curé and bid him nail it up as an object venerable and heroic in his parish church. *Ah! le pauvre garçon, le pauvre garçon,*" said he. "*Mais voyez-vous,* it is the English character that comes out in his letter. I have seen many English up there in the North. No longer can we Frenchmen talk of *le phlègme britannique*. The astounding revelation is the unconquerable English gaiety. *Jamais de longs visages.* If a decapitated English head could speak, it would launch you a whimsical smile and say: "What annoys me is that I can't inhale a cigarette." And here our good Martin makes a joke about the straw in the ambulance-train. *Mon Dieu!* I know what it is, but it has never occurred to me to jest about it."

In the course of time Martin returned to Bran-

tôme. The railway system of the country had been
fairly adjusted in the parts of France that were distant
from scenes of military operations. Bigourdin bor-
rowed Monsieur le Maire's big limousine which had
not been commandeered—for the Mayor was on many
committees in the Department and had to fly about
from place to place and with Corinna and Félise and
Fortinbras he met Martin's train at Périgueux. As
it steamed in a hand waved from a window below a
familiar face. They rushed to the carriage steps and
in a moment he was among them—in a woollen Kepi
and incredibly torn blue-grey greatcoat and ragged red
trousers, the unfilled arm of the coat dangling down
idly. But it was a bronzed, clear-eyed man who met
them, for all his war battering.

Bigourdin welcomed him first, in his exuberant way,
called him *mon brave, mon petit héros,* and hugged
him. Fortinbras gripped his hand, after the English
manner. Corinna, happy and smiling through glistening eyes, he kissed without more ado. And then he
was free to greet Félise, who had remained a pace
or two in the background. Her great, dark eyes were
fixed upon him questioningly. She put out a hand
and touched the empty sleeve. She read in his face
what she had never read before. His one poor arm,
stretched in an instinctive curve—with a little sobbing
cry she threw herself blindly into his embrace.

The tremendous issues of existence with which for
five months he had been grappling had wiped out from
his consciousness, almost from his memory, the first
enthralling kiss of another woman. Caked with mud,
deafened by the roar of shells, sleeping in the earth of
his trench, an intimate of blood and death day after
day, he had learned that Lucilla had been but an *ignis
fatuus* leading him astray from the essential meaning
of his life. He knew, as he lay wounded beneath the
hell of machine-gun fire between the trenches that

there was only one sweet, steadfast soul in the world who called him to the accomplishment of his being.

When, in the abandonment of her joy and grief his lips met the soft, quivering mouth of Félise, care, like a garment, fell from him. He whispered: "You have a great heart. I've not deserved this. But you're the only thing that matters to me in the world."

Félise was content. She knew that the war had swept his soul clean of false gods. Out of that furnace nothing but Truth could come.

And so Martin returned for ever to the land of his adoption, which on the morrow was to take him after its generous and expansive way as a hero to its bosom. The Englishman who had given a limb for Périgord was to be held in high honour for the rest of his days.

He was a man now who had passed through most human experiences. A man of fine honour, of courage tested in a thousand ways, of stiffened will, of high ideals. The life that lay before him was far dearer than any other he could have chosen. For it matters not so much the life one leads as the knowledge of the perfect way to live it. And that knowledge, based on wisdom, had Martin achieved. He knew that if the glittering prizes of the earth are locked away behind golden bars opening but to golden keys, there are others far more precious lying to the hand of him who will but seek them in the folds of the familiar hills.

The five sat down to dinner that evening in the empty *salle-à-manger;* for not a guest, even the most decrepit commercial traveller, was staying at the hotel. Yet never had they met at a happier meal. Félise cut up Martin's food as though it had been blessed bread. In the middle of it Fortinbras poured out half a glass of wine.

"My children," said he, "I am going to break

through the habit of years. This old wine of Burgundy is too generous to betray me on an occasion so beautiful and so solemn. I drink to your happiness."

"But to whom do Martin and I owe our happiness?" cried Corinna, with a flush on her cheek, and a glistening in her blue eyes. "It is to you—from the first to last to you, *Marchand de Bonheur!*"

"My God! Yes," said Martin, extending his one arm to Fortinbras.

The ex-Dealer in Happiness regarded them both benevolently. "For the first time in my life," said he, "I think I have reason to be proud of my late profession. Like the artist who has toiled and struggled, I can, without immodesty, recognise my masterpiece. It was my original conception that Martin and Corinna, crude but honest souls, should find an incentive to the working out of their destiny by falling in love. Therefore I sent them out together. That they should have an honourable asylum, I sent them to my own kin. When I found they wouldn't fall in love at all, I imagined the present felicitous combination. I have been aided by the little accident of a European war. But what matter? The Gods willed it, the Gods were on my side. Out of evil there inscrutably and divinely cometh good. My children, my heart is very full of the consolation that, at the end of many years that the locust hath eaten, I have perhaps justified my existence."

"*Mon père,*" cried Félise, "all my life long your existence has had the justification of heroic sacrifice."

"My dear," said he, "if I hadn't met adversity with a brave face, I should not have been a man—still less a philosopher. And now that my duty here is over, if I don't go back to Paris and find some means of helping in the great conflict, I shall be unworthy of the name of Englishman. So as soon as I see you safely and exquisitely married, I shall leave you. I shall, however, come and visit you from time to time. But when I die"—he paused and fishing out a stump of pencil scribbled on the back of the menu card— "when I die, bury me in Paris on the south side of the Seine and put this inscription on my tombstone. One little vanity is accorded by the gods to every human being."

He threw the card on the table. On it was written:

*"Ci-gît*
*Fortinbras*
*Marchand de Bonheur."*

When the meal was over they went up to the prim and plushily furnished salon, where a wood fire was burning gaily. Bigourdin brought up a cobwebbed bottle of the Old Brandy of the Brigadier and uncorked it reverently.

"We are going to drink to France," said he.

He produced from the cupboard whose doors were veiled with green-pleated silk, half a dozen of the great glass goblets and into each he poured a little of the golden liquid, which, as he had once said, contained the soul of the *Grande Armée*.

"Stop a bit," said Martin. "You're making a mistake. There are only five of us."

"I am making no mistake at all," said Bigourdin. "The sixth glass is for the shade of the brave old Brigadier. If he is not here now among us to honour the toast, I am no Christian man."

THE END